Keiko Suenobu

LIMIT

D1443973

VERTICAL.

contents

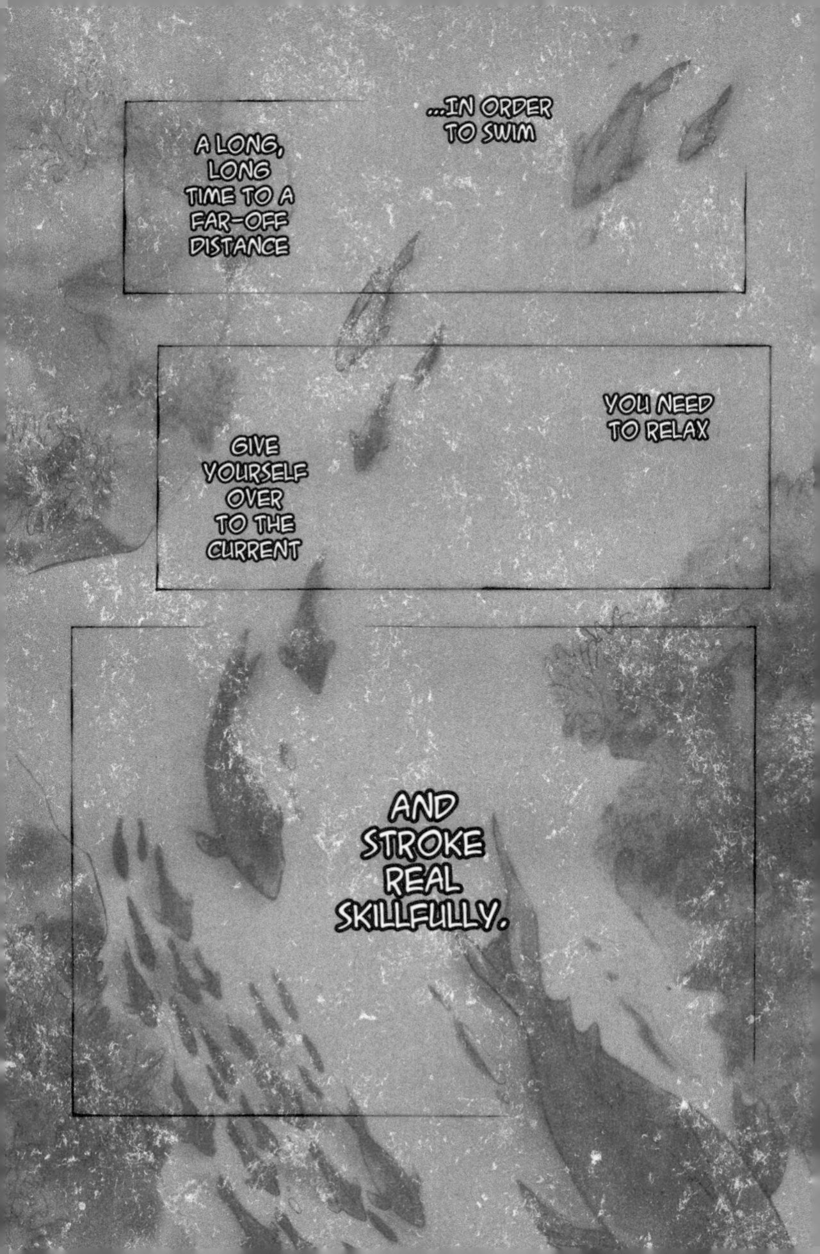
...IN ORDER TO SWIM
A LONG, LONG TIME TO A FAR-OFF DISTANCE
YOU NEED TO RELAX
GIVE YOURSELF OVER TO THE CURRENT
AND STROKE REAL SKILLFULLY.

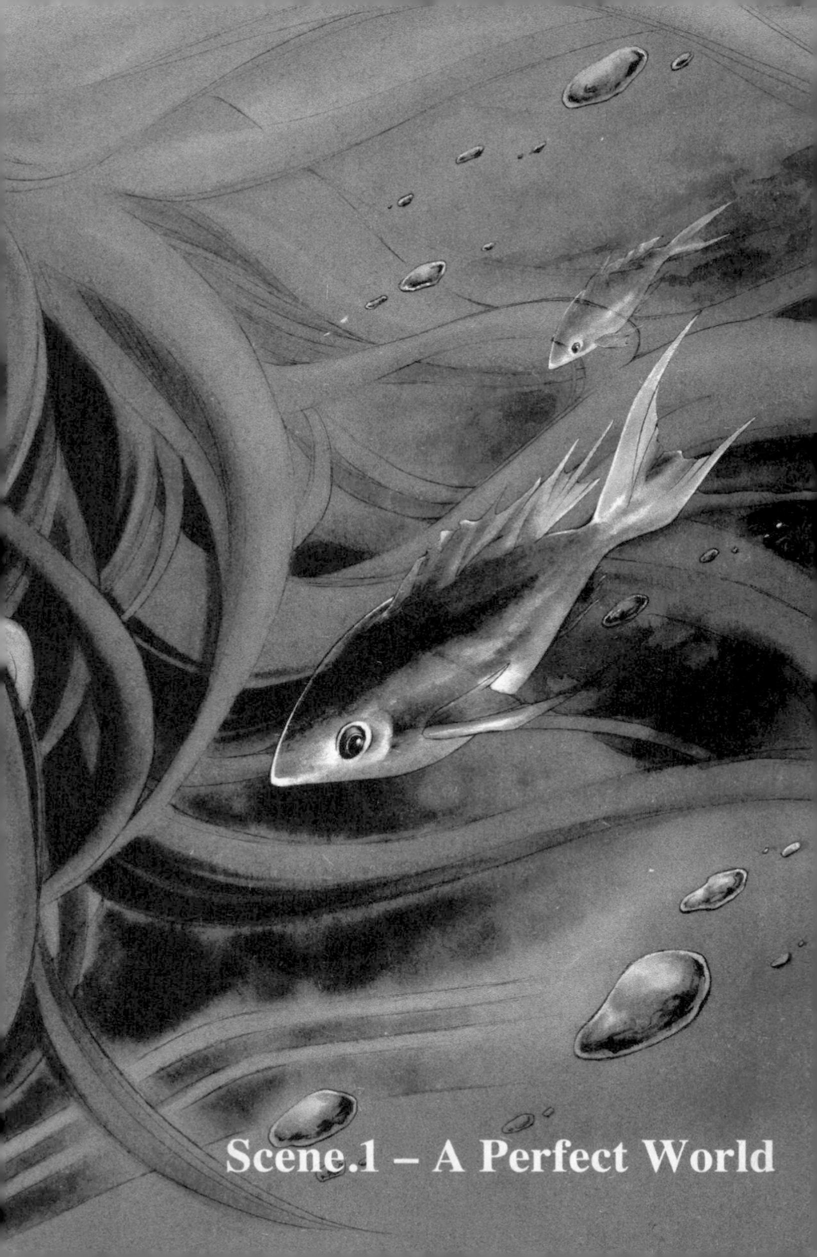

Scene.1 – A Perfect World

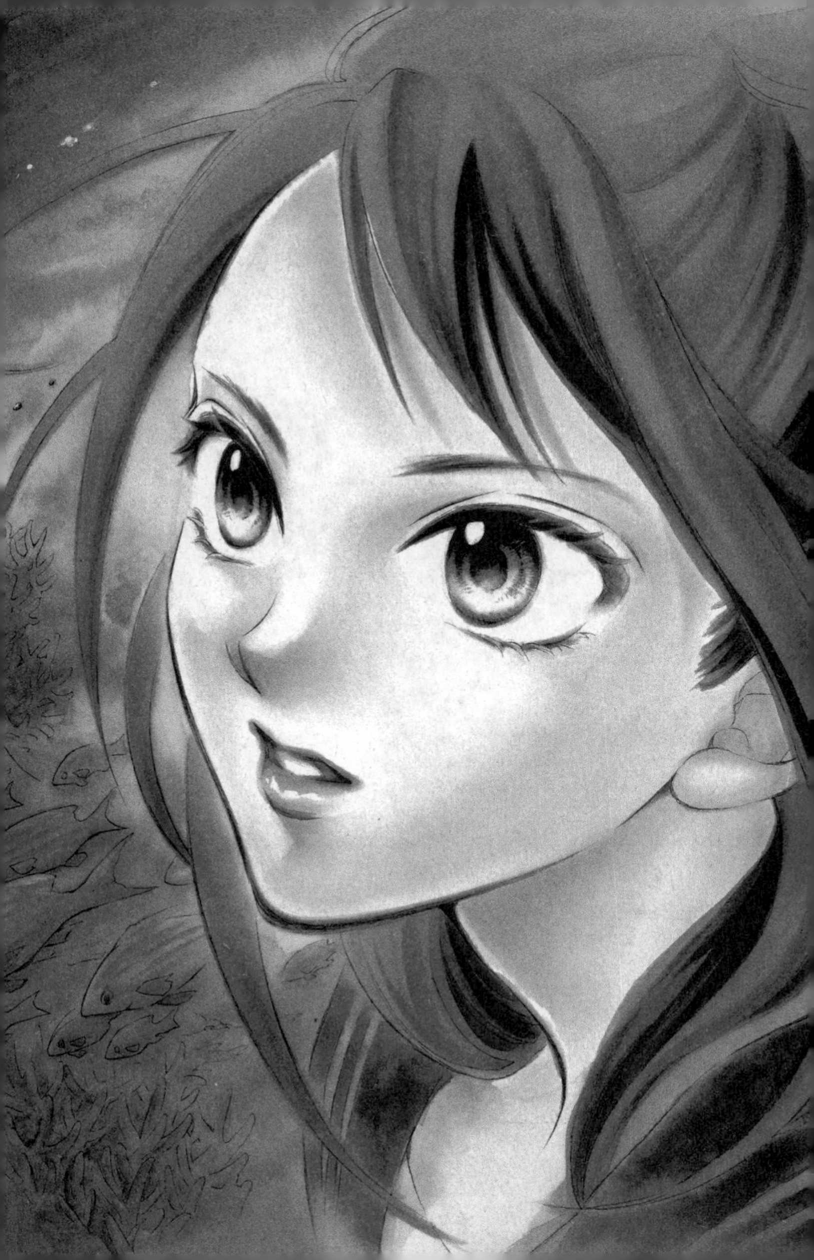

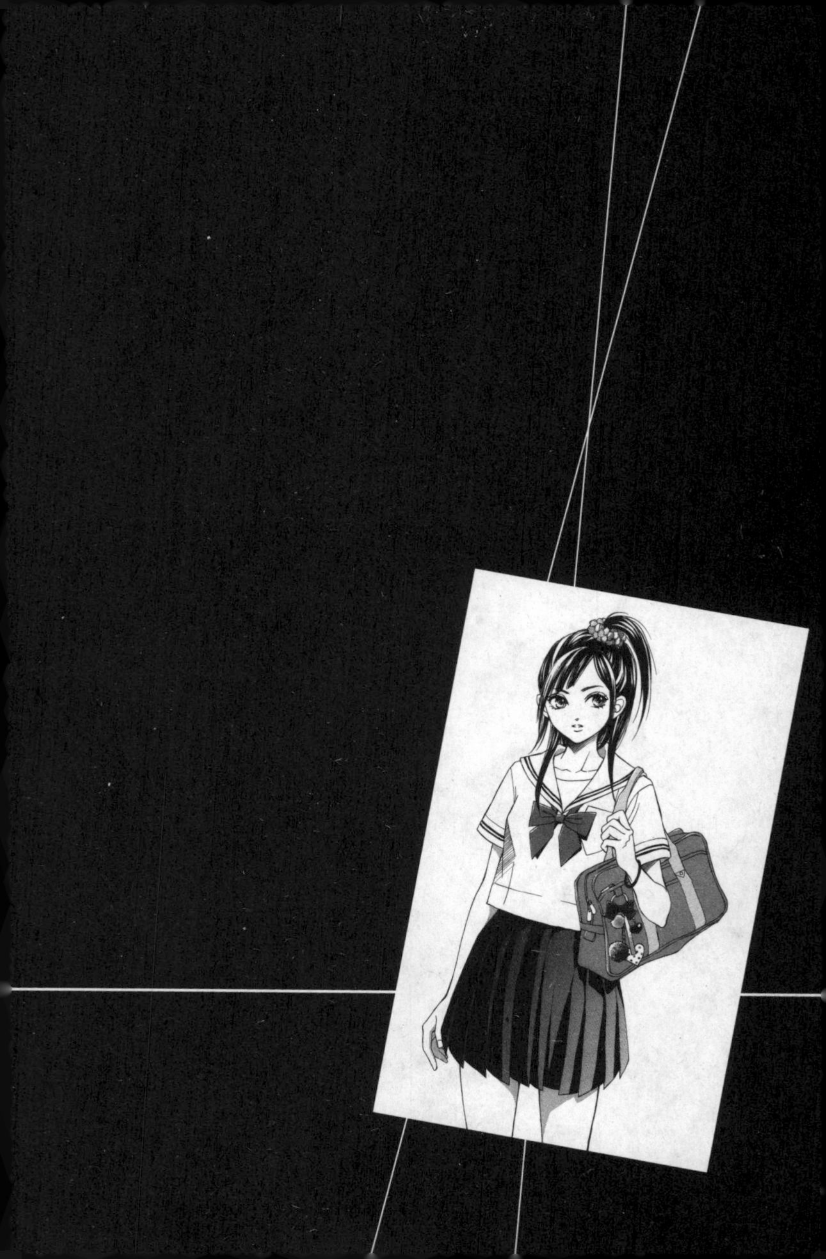

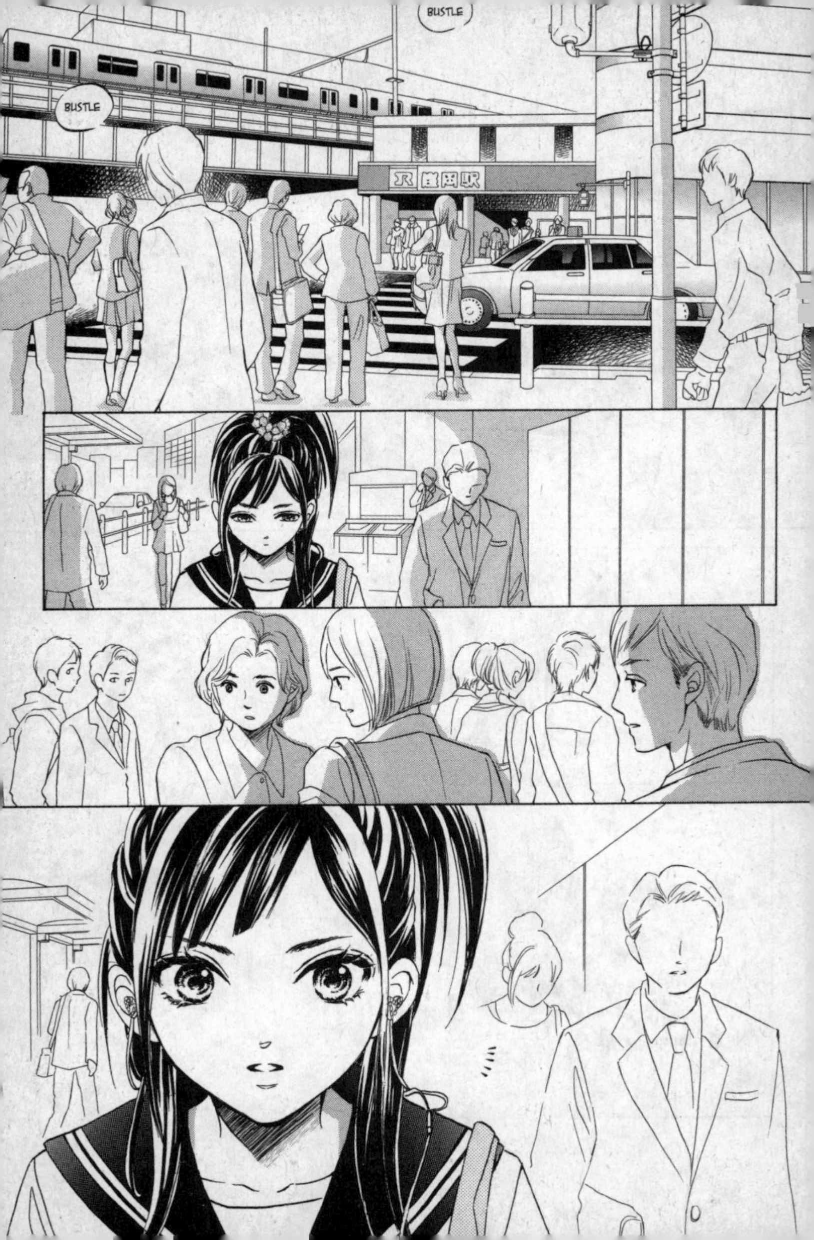
BUSTLE
BUSTLE

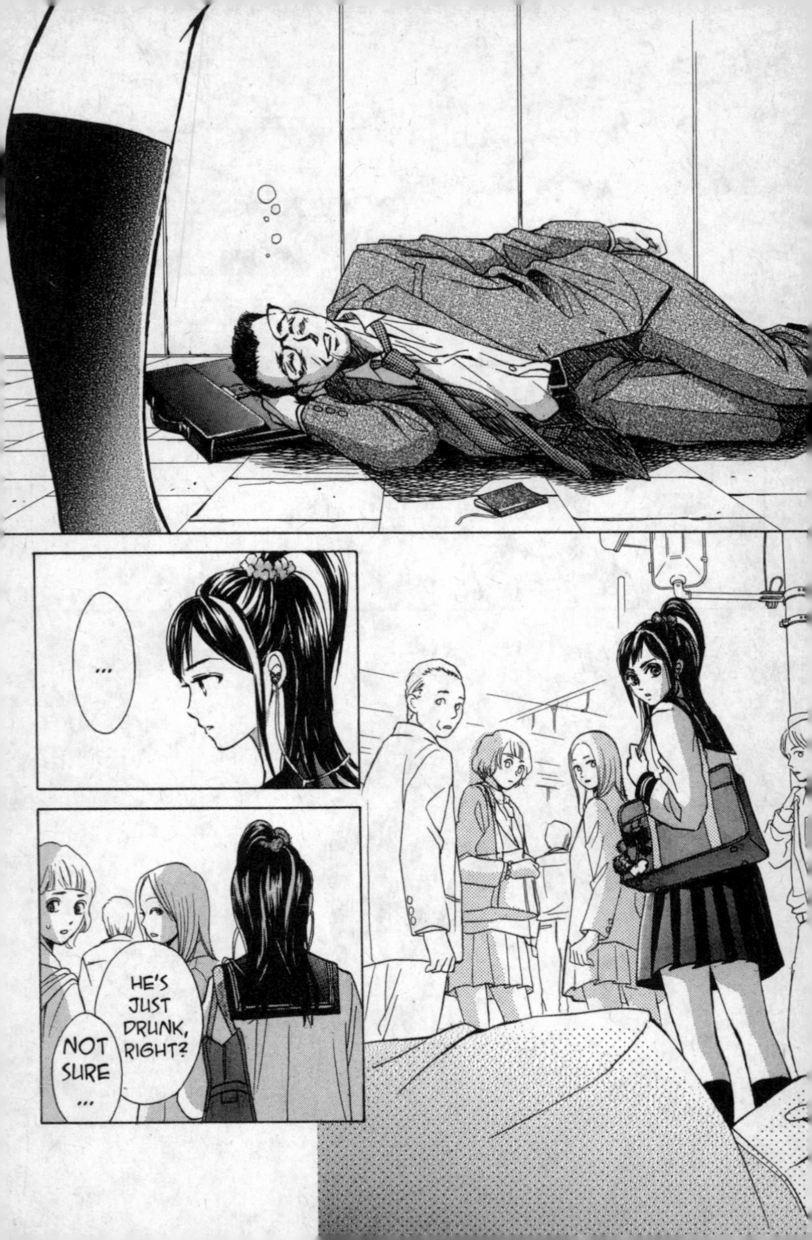
...
HE'S JUST DRUNK, RIGHT?
NOT SURE ...

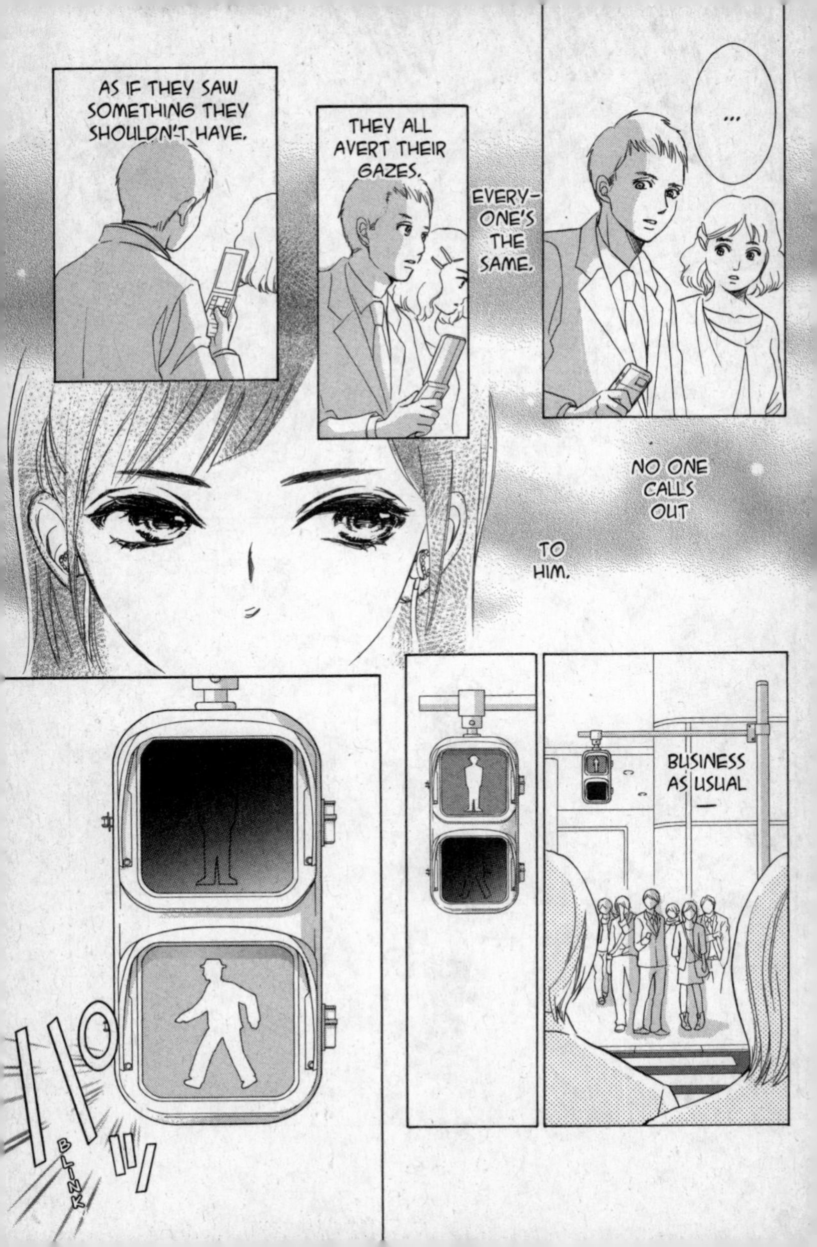
...
EVERY-ONE'S THE SAME.
THEY ALL AVERT THEIR GAZES.
AS IF THEY SAW SOMETHING THEY SHOULDN'T HAVE.
NO ONE CALLS OUT
TO HIM.
BUSINESS AS USUAL —
BLINK

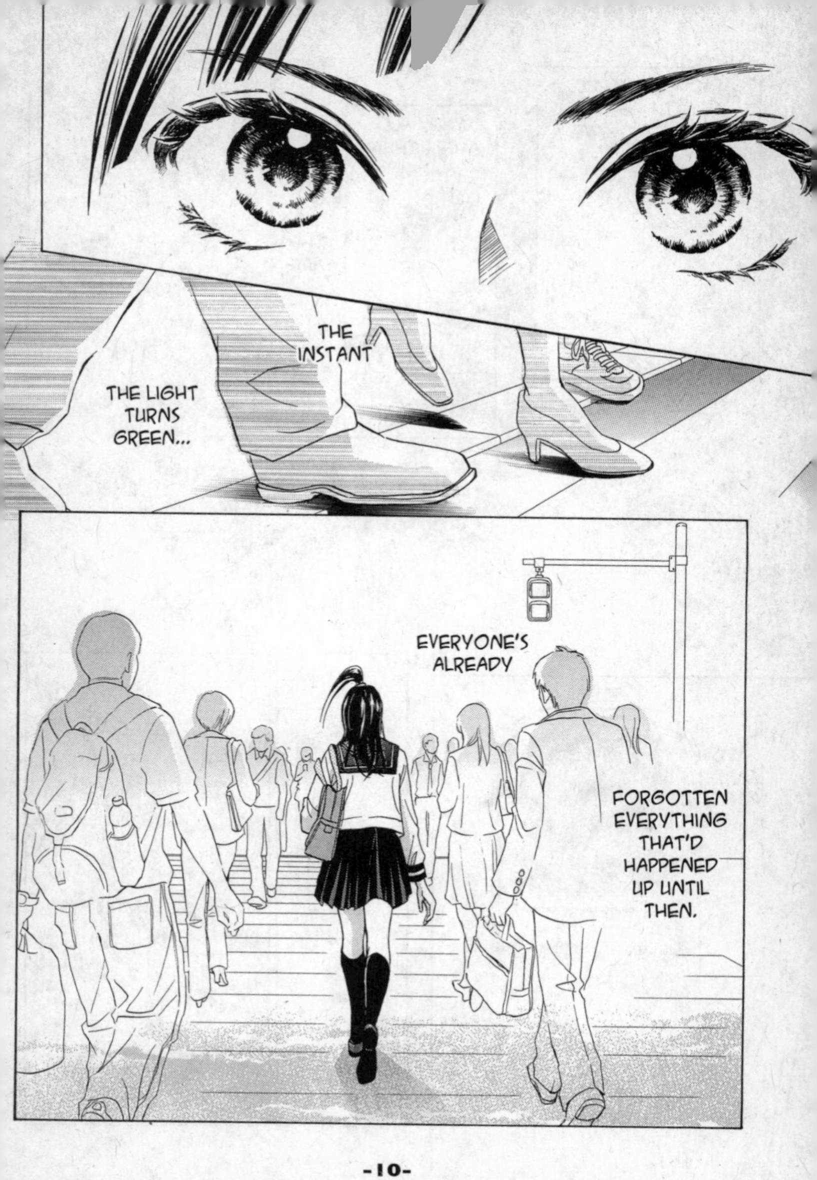
THE INSTANT
THE LIGHT TURNS GREEN...
EVERYONE'S ALREADY
FORGOTTEN EVERYTHING THAT'D HAPPENED UP UNTIL THEN.

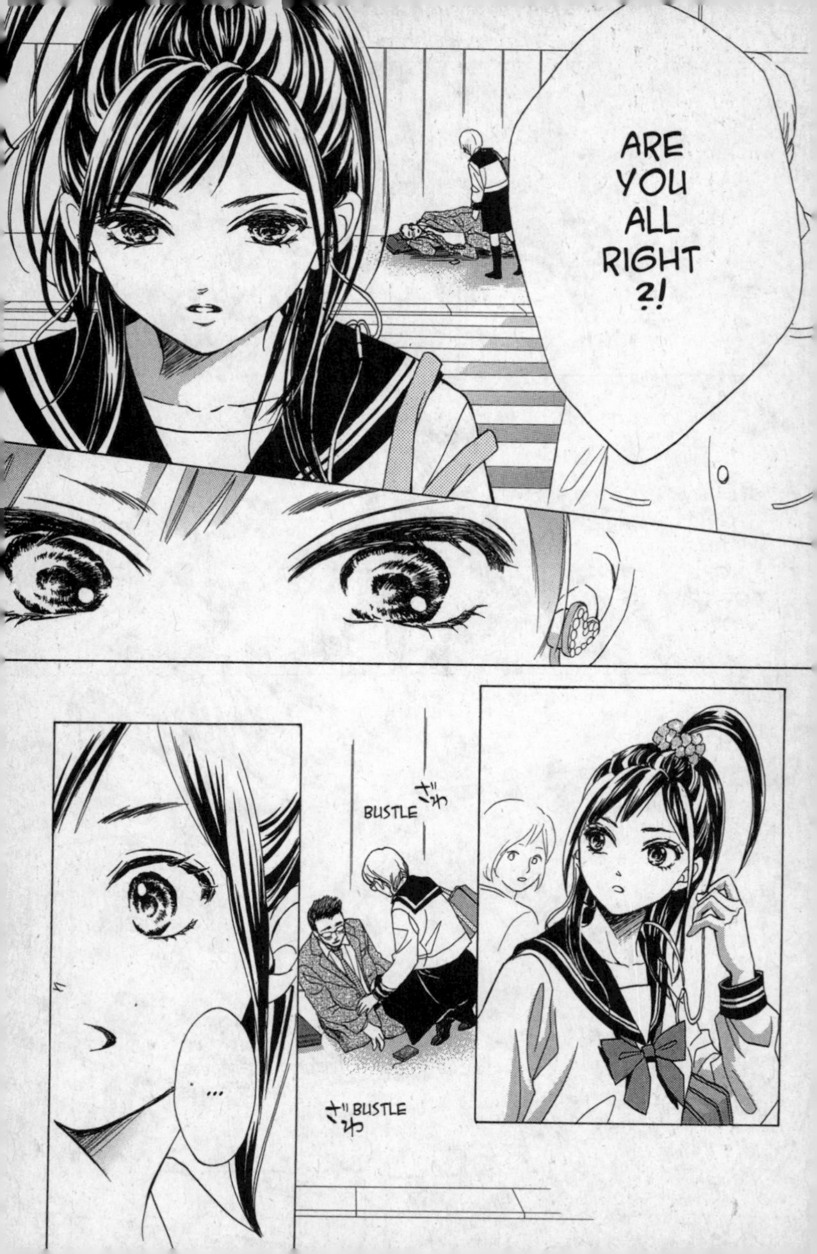
ARE YOU ALL RIGHT ?!
ざわ BUSTLE
ざわ BUSTLE
...

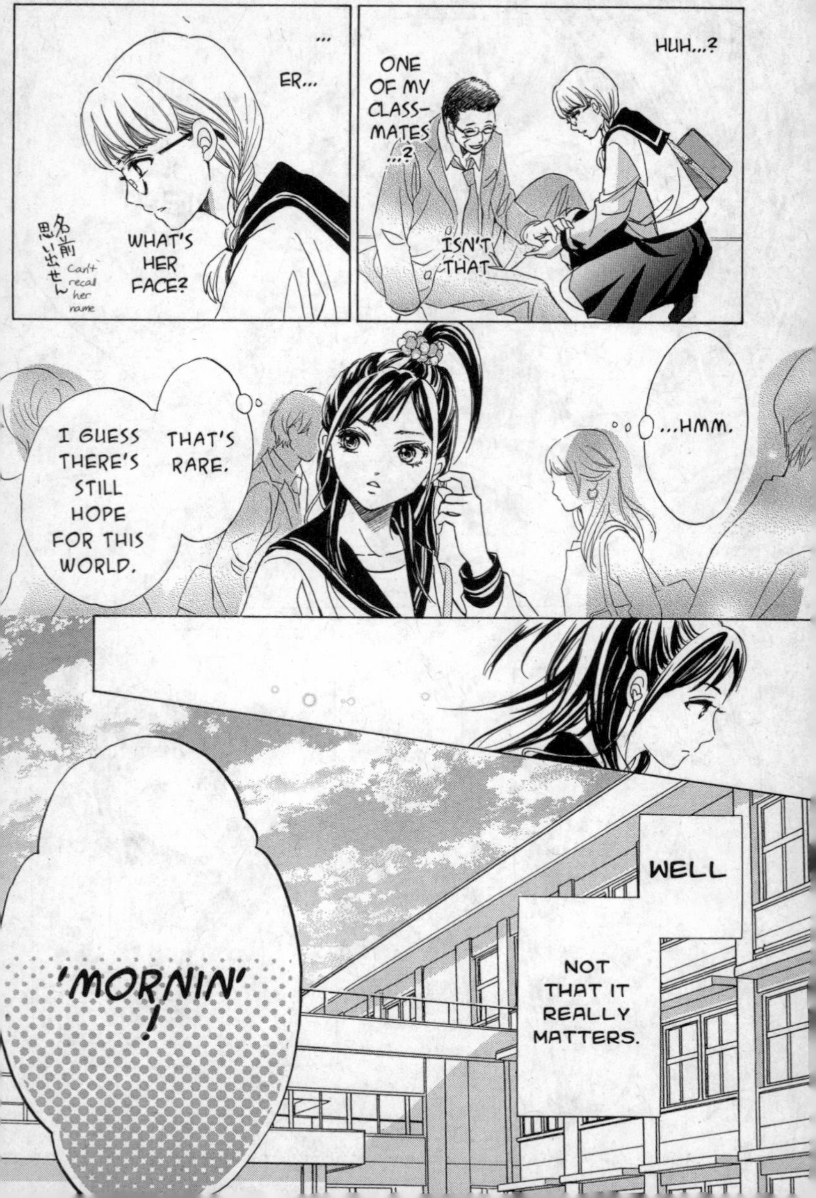
HUH...?
ONE OF MY CLASS-MATES ...?
ISN'T THAT
...
ER...
WHAT'S HER FACE?
名前思い出せん
Can't recall her name
...HMM.
THAT'S RARE.
I GUESS THERE'S STILL HOPE FOR THIS WORLD.
WELL
NOT THAT IT REALLY MATTERS.
'MORNIN'!

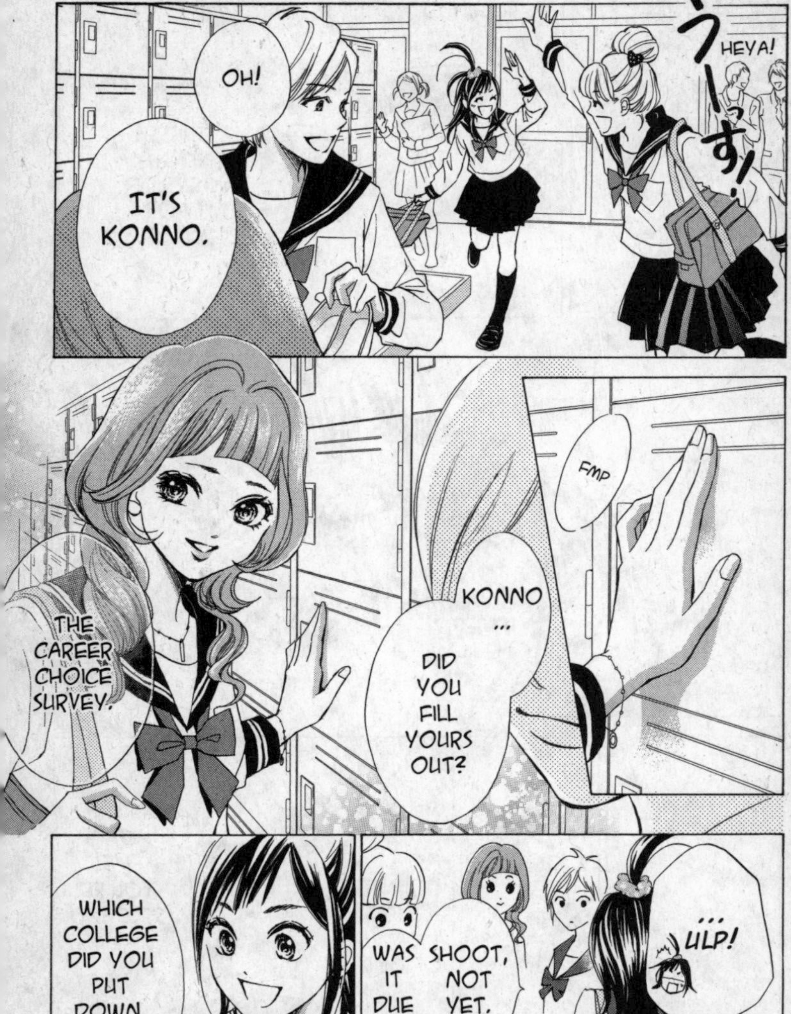
うーっす!
HEYA!
OH!
IT'S KONNO.
FMP
KONNO ... DID YOU FILL YOURS OUT?
THE CAREER CHOICE SURVEY.
... ULP!
SHOOT, NOT YET.
WAS IT DUE TO-DAY?
WHICH COLLEGE DID YOU PUT DOWN, SAKURA?

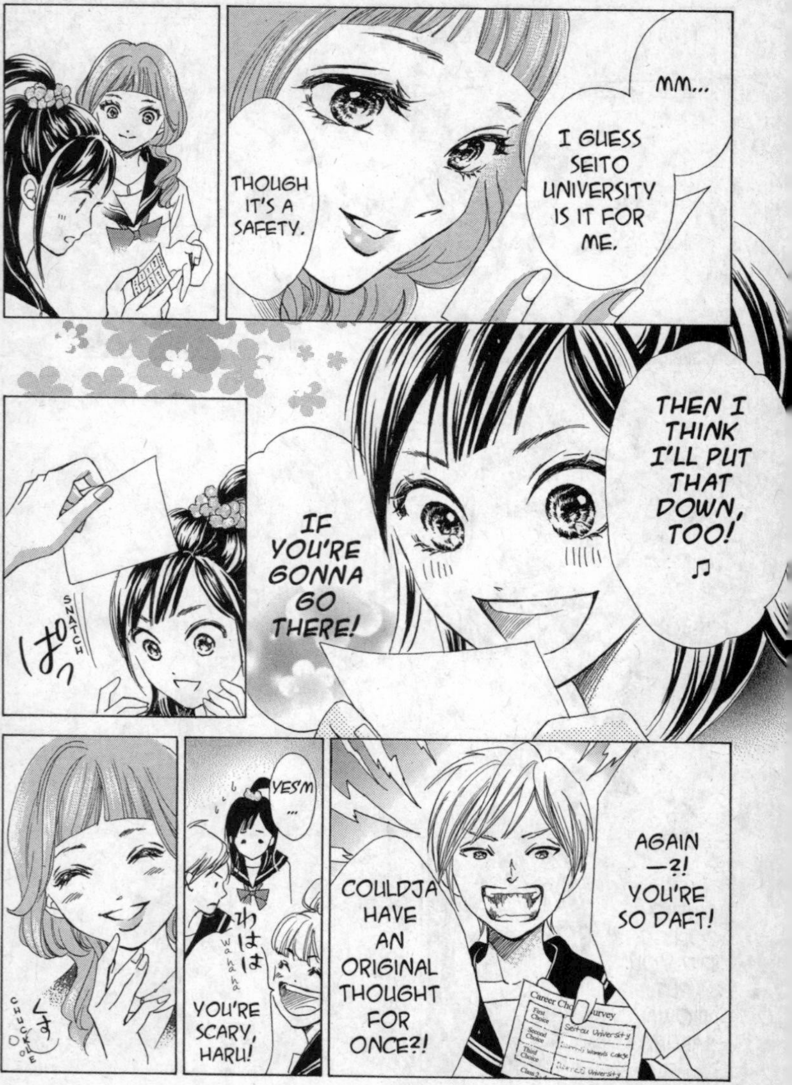
MM...
I GUESS SEITO UNIVERSITY IS IT FOR ME.
THOUGH IT'S A SAFETY.
THEN I THINK I'LL PUT THAT DOWN, TOO! ♫
IF YOU'RE GONNA GO THERE!
ぱっ
SNATCH
AGAIN —?! YOU'RE SO DAFT!
COULDJA HAVE AN ORIGINAL THOUGHT FOR ONCE?!
First Choice
Seitou University
Second Choice
Third Choice
YES'M ...
わはは
wahaha
YOU'RE SCARY, HARU!
くすっ
CHUCKLE

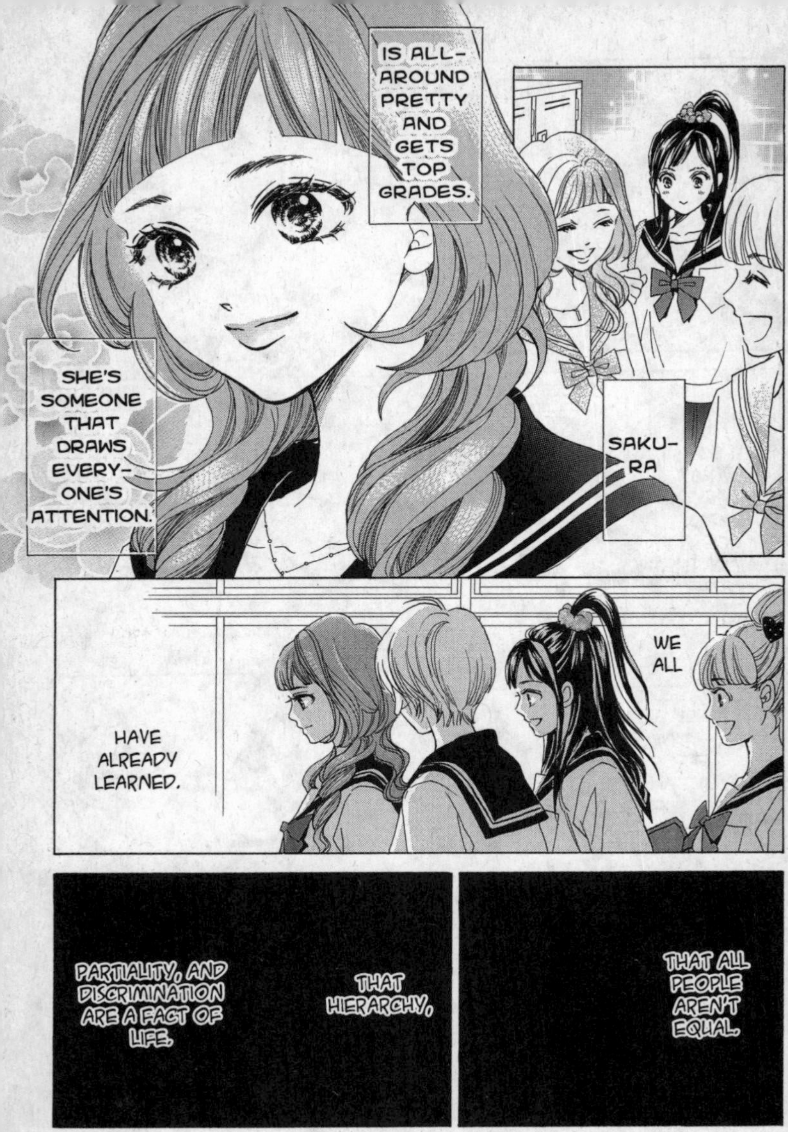
SAKU-RA
IS ALL-AROUND PRETTY AND GETS TOP GRADES.
SHE'S SOMEONE THAT DRAWS EVERY-ONE'S ATTENTION.
WE ALL
HAVE ALREADY LEARNED.
THAT ALL PEOPLE AREN'T EQUAL.
THAT HIERARCHY,
PARTIALITY, AND DISCRIMINATION ARE A FACT OF LIFE.

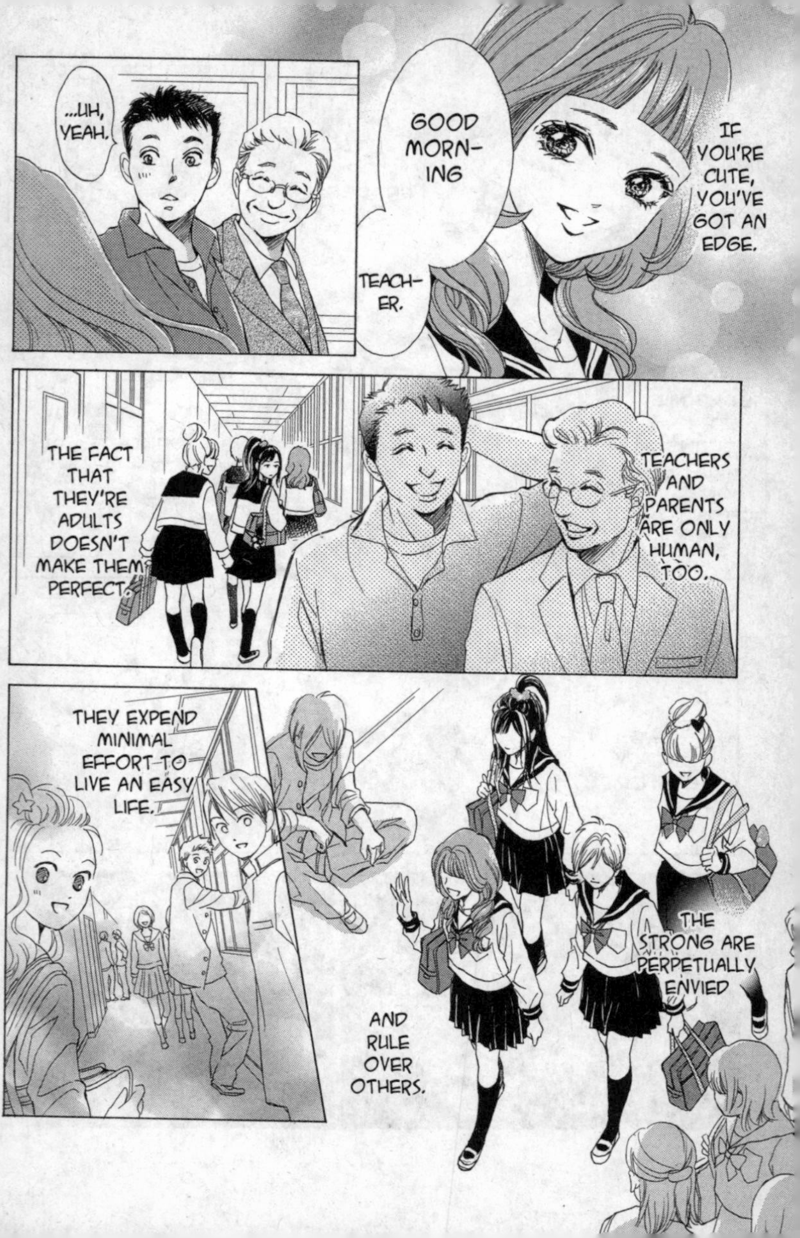
IF YOU'RE CUTE, YOU'VE GOT AN EDGE.
GOOD MORNING
TEACHER.
...UH, YEAH.
TEACHERS AND PARENTS ARE ONLY HUMAN, TOO.
THE FACT THAT THEY'RE ADULTS DOESN'T MAKE THEM PERFECT.
THE STRONG ARE PERPETUALLY ENVIED
AND RULE OVER OTHERS.
THEY EXPEND MINIMAL EFFORT TO LIVE AN EASY LIFE.

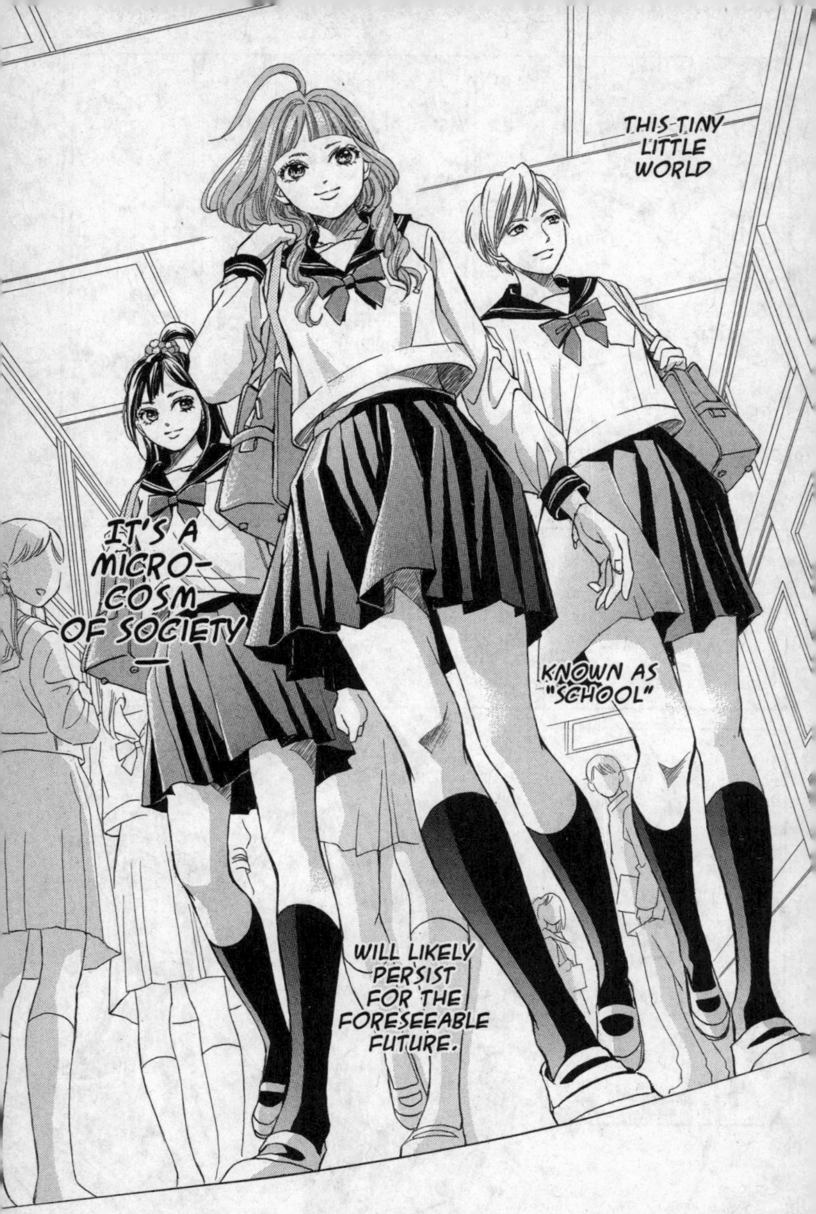
THIS TINY LITTLE WORLD
IT'S A MICRO-COSM OF SOCIETY —
KNOWN AS "SCHOOL"
WILL LIKELY PERSIST FOR THE FORESEEABLE FUTURE.

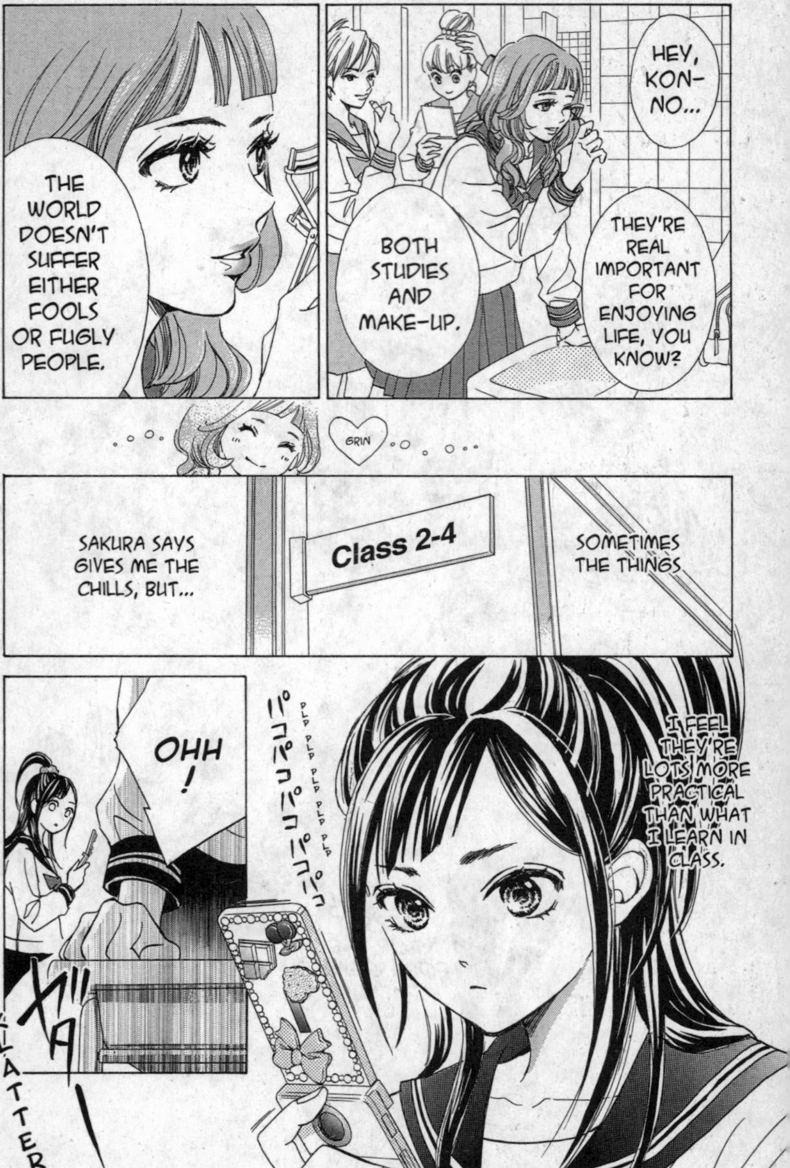
HEY, KON-NO...
THEY'RE REAL IMPORTANT FOR ENJOYING LIFE, YOU KNOW?
BOTH STUDIES AND MAKE-UP.
THE WORLD DOESN'T SUFFER EITHER FOOLS OR FUGLY PEOPLE.
GRIN
SOMETIMES THE THINGS
Class 2-4
SAKURA SAYS GIVES ME THE CHILLS, BUT...
I FEEL THEY'RE LOTS MORE PRACTICAL THAN WHAT I LEARN IN CLASS.
パコパコパコパコ
PLP PLP PLP PLP PLP
OHH!
ガタ
KLATTER

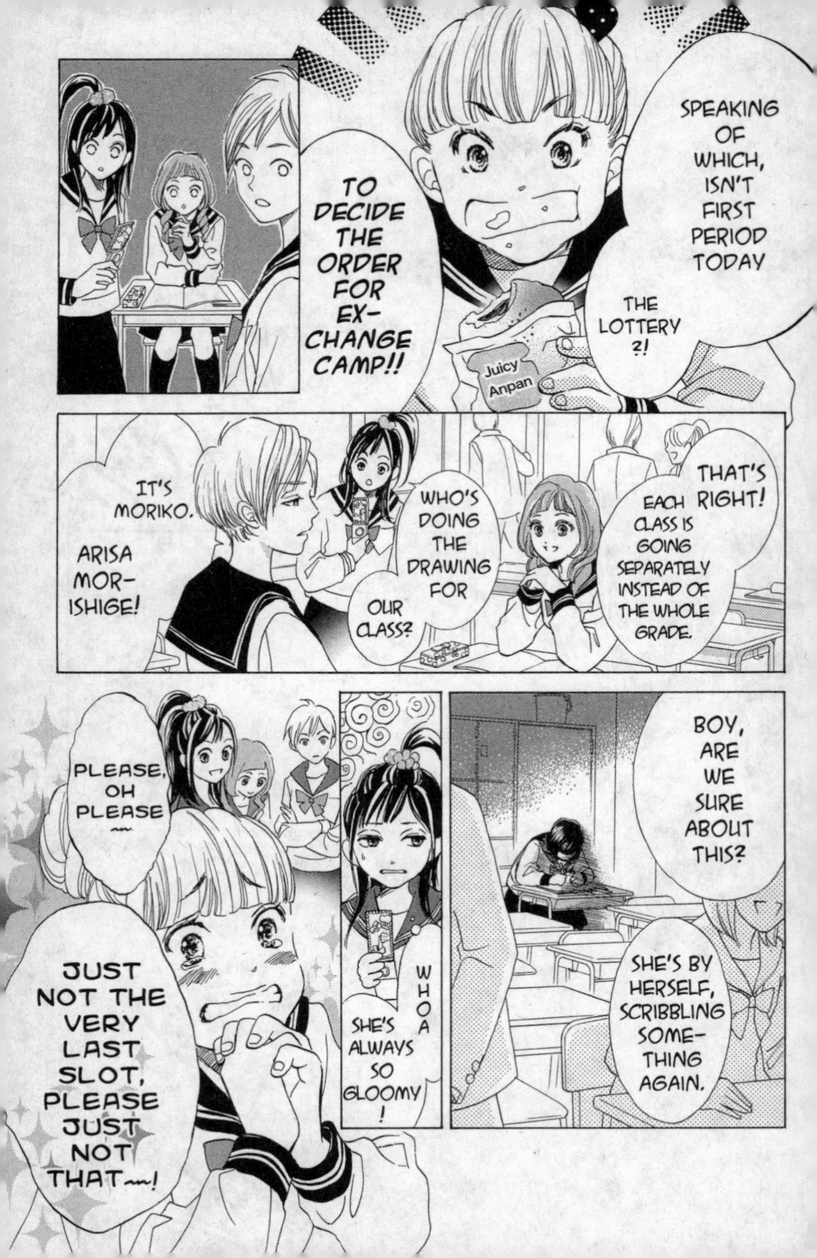
SPEAKING OF WHICH, ISN'T FIRST PERIOD TODAY
THE LOTTERY ?!
Juicy Anpan
TO DECIDE THE ORDER FOR EX-CHANGE CAMP!!
THAT'S RIGHT!
EACH CLASS IS GOING SEPARATELY INSTEAD OF THE WHOLE GRADE.
WHO'S DOING THE DRAWING FOR
OUR CLASS?
IT'S MORIKO.
ARISA MOR-ISHIGE!
BOY, ARE WE SURE ABOUT THIS?
SHE'S BY HERSELF, SCRIBBLING SOME-THING AGAIN.
WHOA
SHE'S ALWAYS SO GLOOMY!
PLEASE, OH PLEASE ~
JUST NOT THE VERY LAST SLOT, PLEASE JUST NOT THAT~!

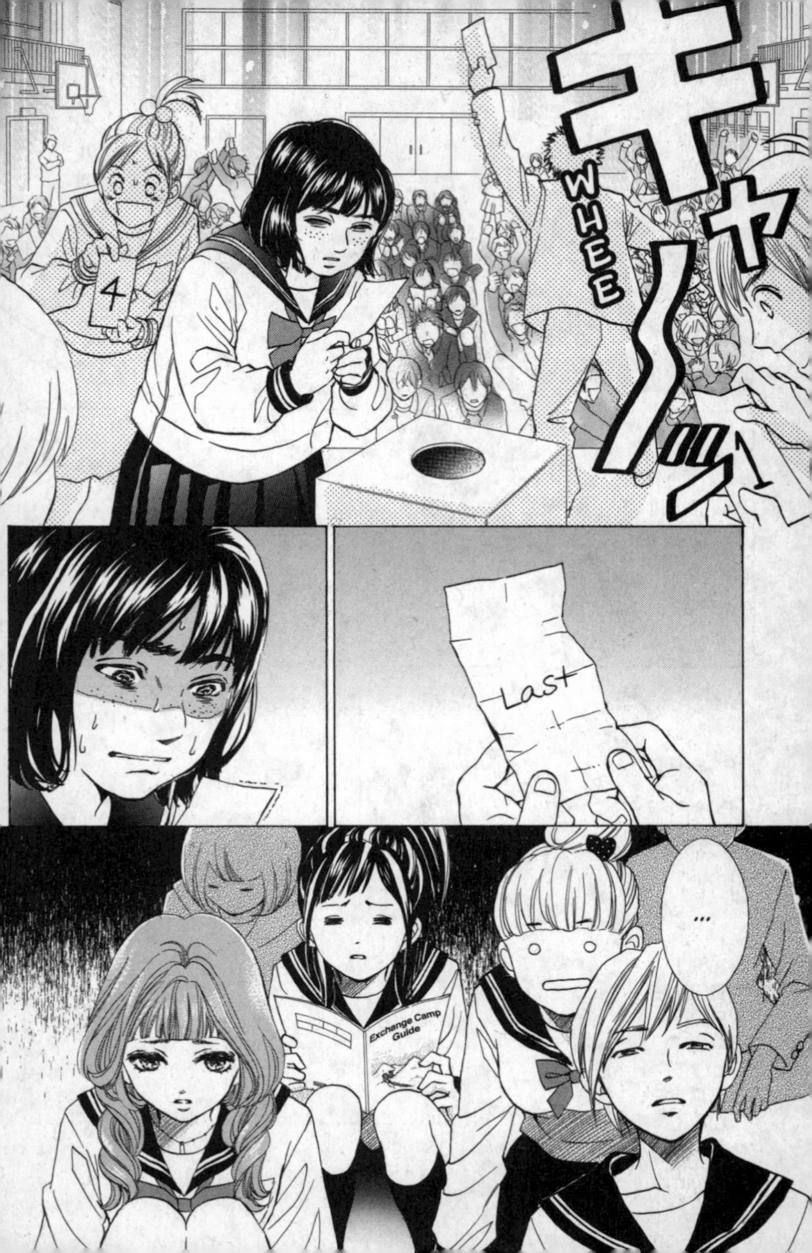
WHEE
4
Last
...
Exchange Camp Guide

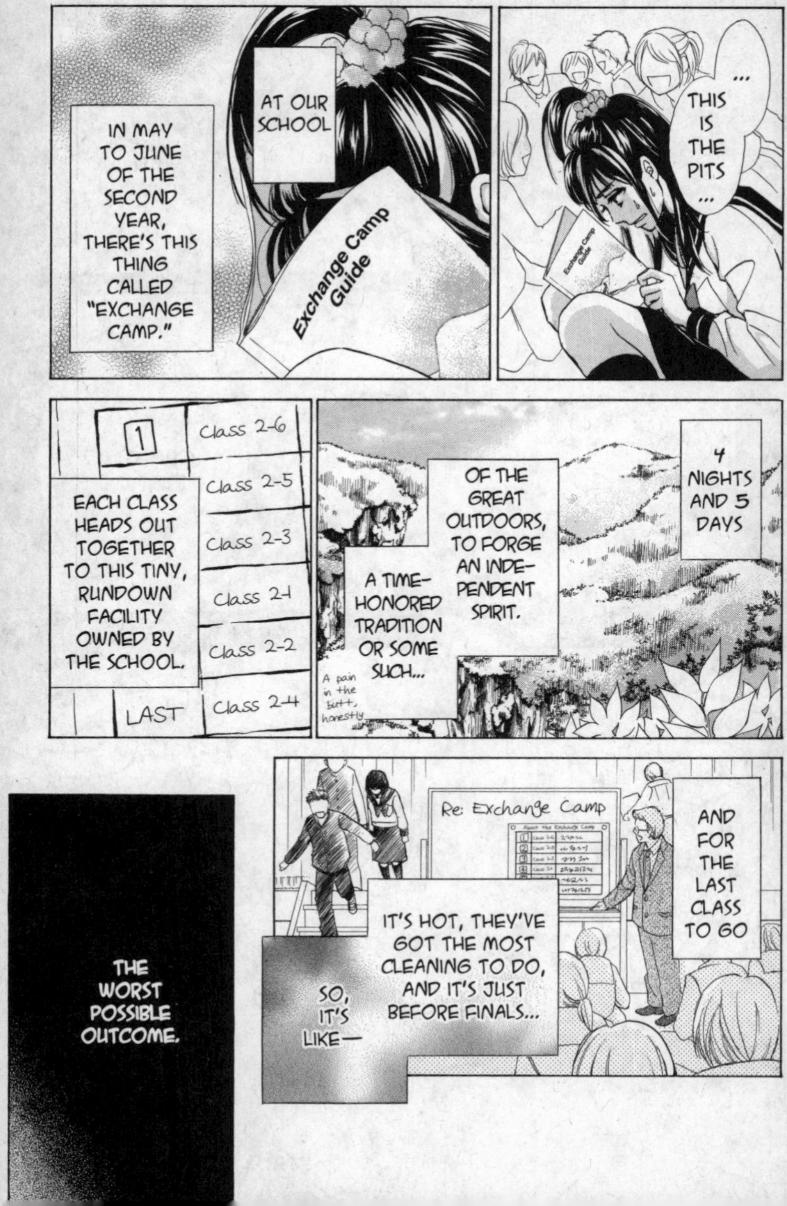
... THIS IS THE PITS ...
Exchange Camp Guide
AT OUR SCHOOL
IN MAY TO JUNE OF THE SECOND YEAR, THERE'S THIS THING CALLED "EXCHANGE CAMP."
Exchange Camp Guide
4 NIGHTS AND 5 DAYS
OF THE GREAT OUTDOORS, TO FORGE AN INDE-PENDENT SPIRIT.
A TIME-HONORED TRADITION OR SOME SUCH...
A pain in the butt, honestly
1 Class 2-6
Class 2-5
Class 2-3
Class 2-1
Class 2-2
LAST Class 2-4
EACH CLASS HEADS OUT TOGETHER TO THIS TINY, RUNDOWN FACILITY OWNED BY THE SCHOOL.
AND FOR THE LAST CLASS TO GO
Re: Exchange Camp
IT'S HOT, THEY'VE GOT THE MOST CLEANING TO DO, AND IT'S JUST BEFORE FINALS...
SO, IT'S LIKE—
THE WORST POSSIBLE OUTCOME.

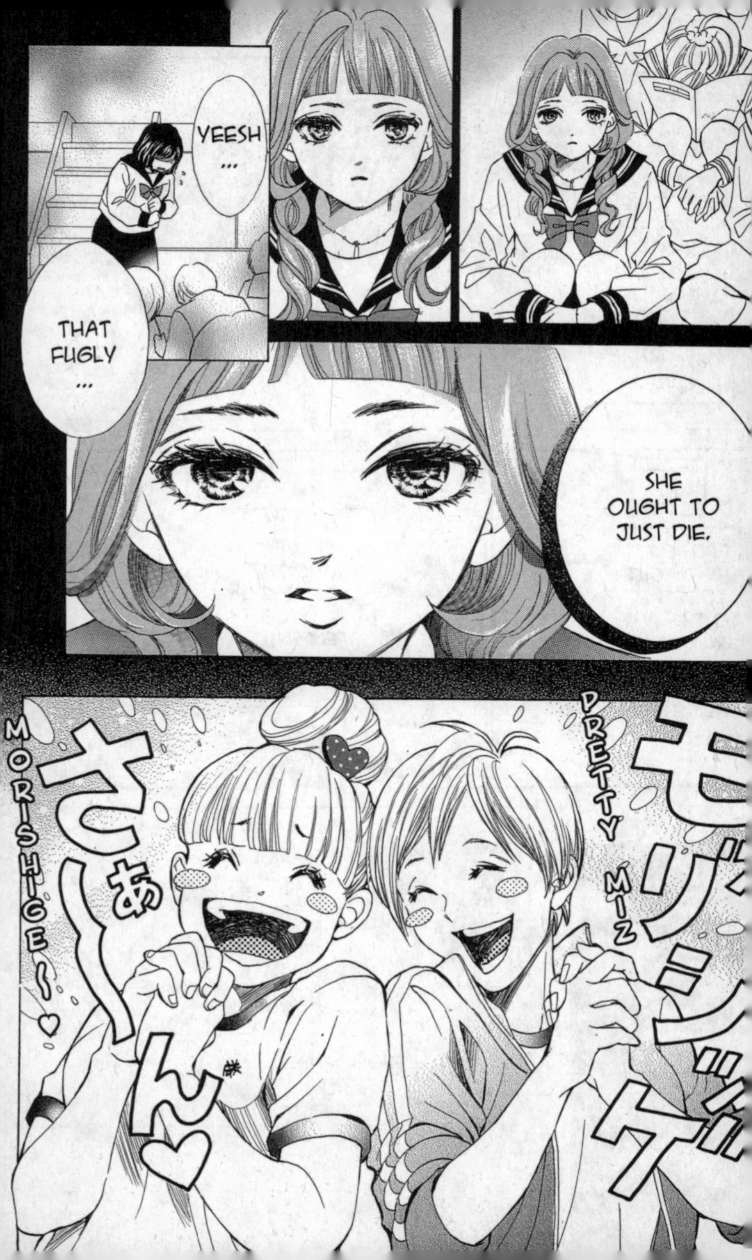
YEESH ...
THAT FUGLY ...
SHE OUGHT TO JUST DIE.
モリシゲ
PRETTY MIZ
さあ～ん♥
MORISHIGE~♥

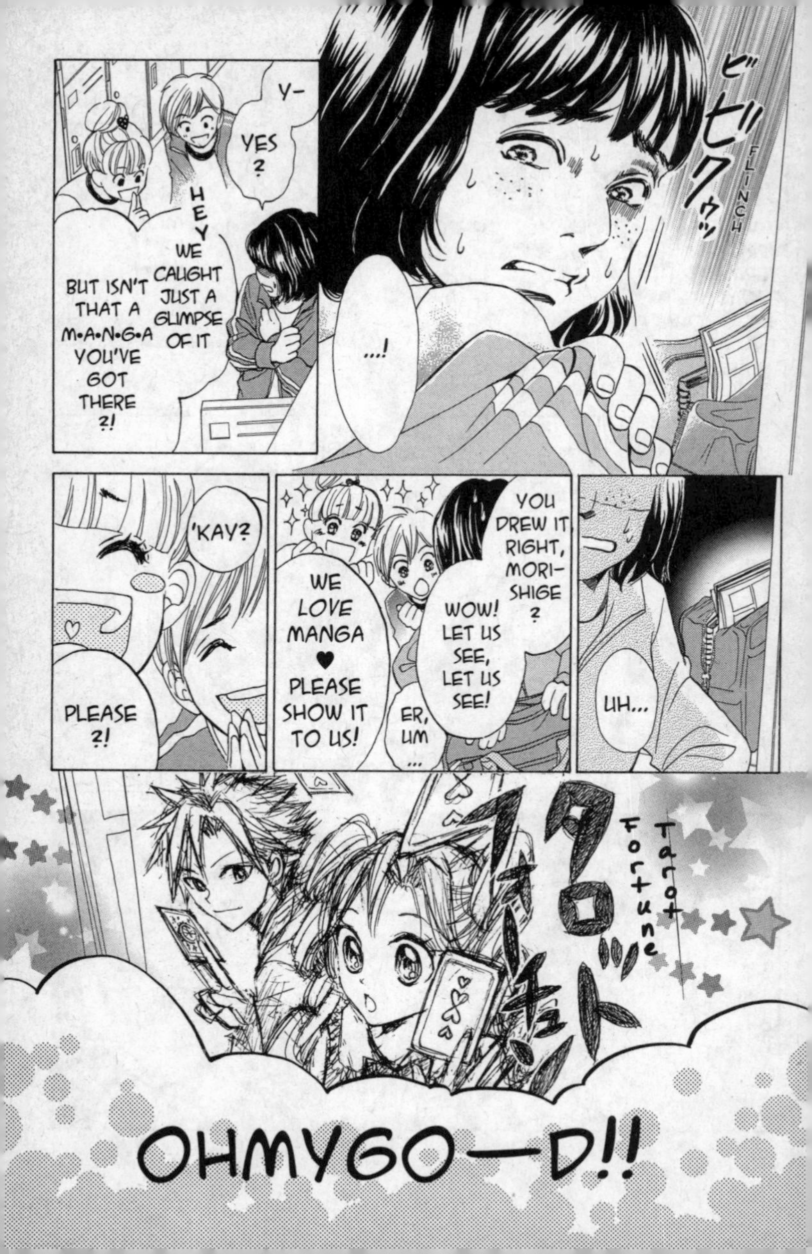
FLINCH
...!
Y- YES?
HEY WE CAUGHT JUST A GLIMPSE OF IT
BUT ISN'T THAT A M•A•N•G•A YOU'VE GOT THERE ?!
UH...
YOU DREW IT RIGHT, MORI-SHIGE ?
WOW! LET US SEE, LET US SEE!
ER, UM ...
WE LOVE MANGA ♥ PLEASE SHOW IT TO US!
'KAY?
PLEASE ?!
Tarot Fortune
OHMYGO—D!!

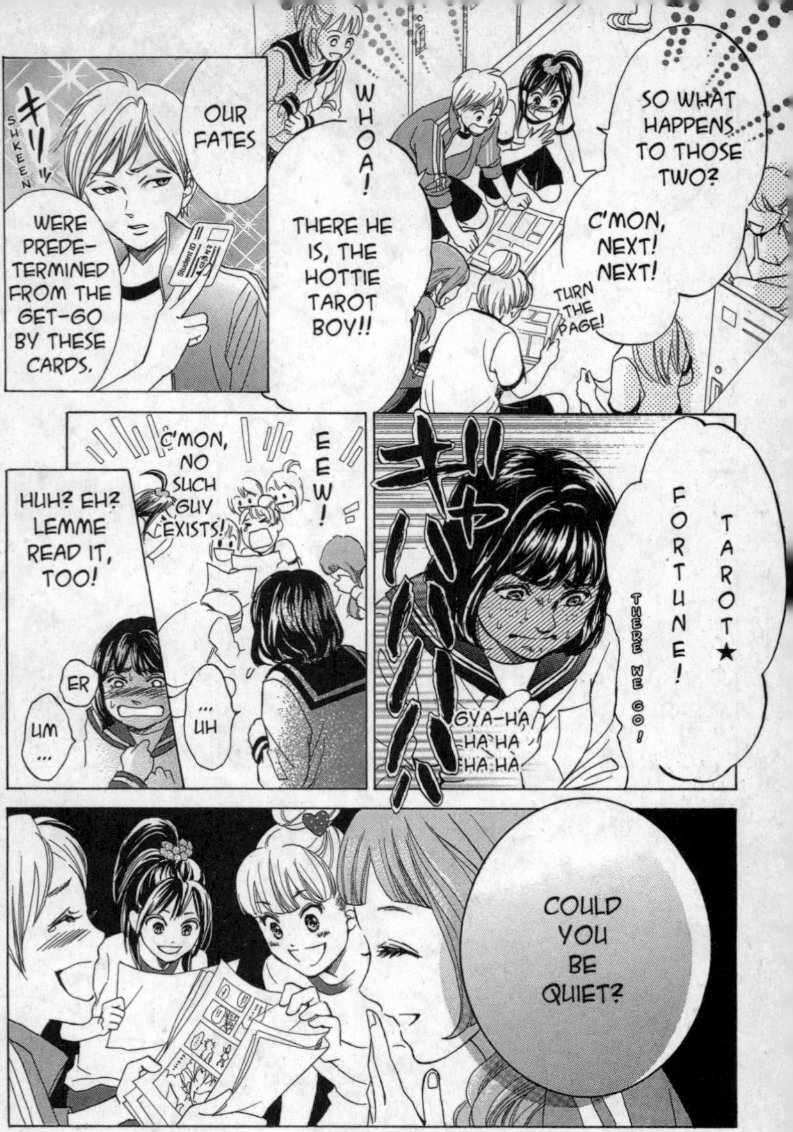
SO WHAT HAPPENS TO THOSE TWO?
C'MON, NEXT! NEXT!
TURN THE PAGE!
WHOA!
THERE HE IS, THE HOTTIE TAROT BOY!!
SHKEEN
OUR FATES
WERE PREDETERMINED FROM THE GET-GO BY THESE CARDS.
Student ID
TAROT★ FORTUNE!
THERE WE GO!
GYA-HA HA HA HA HA
EEEW!
C'MON, NO SUCH GUY EXISTS!
HUH? EH? LEMME READ IT, TOO!
...UH
ER
UM...
COULD YOU BE QUIET?

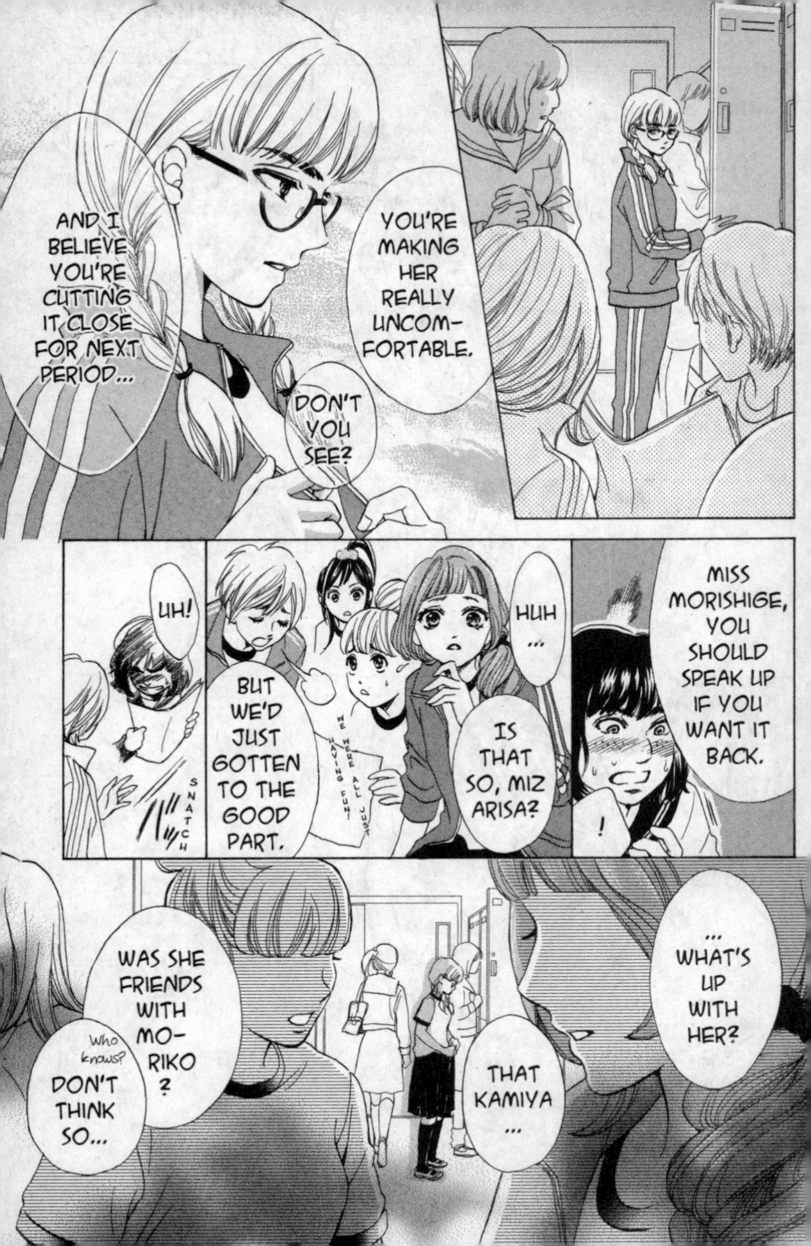
YOU'RE MAKING HER REALLY UNCOMFORTABLE.
DON'T YOU SEE?
AND I BELIEVE YOU'RE CUTTING IT CLOSE FOR NEXT PERIOD...
MISS MORISHIGE, YOU SHOULD SPEAK UP IF YOU WANT IT BACK.
!
HUH ...
IS THAT SO, MIZ ARISA?
WE WERE ALL JUST HAVING FUN!
BUT WE'D JUST GOTTEN TO THE GOOD PART.
UH!
SNATCH
... WHAT'S UP WITH HER?
THAT KAMIYA ...
WAS SHE FRIENDS WITH MO-RIKO?
Who knows?
DON'T THINK SO...

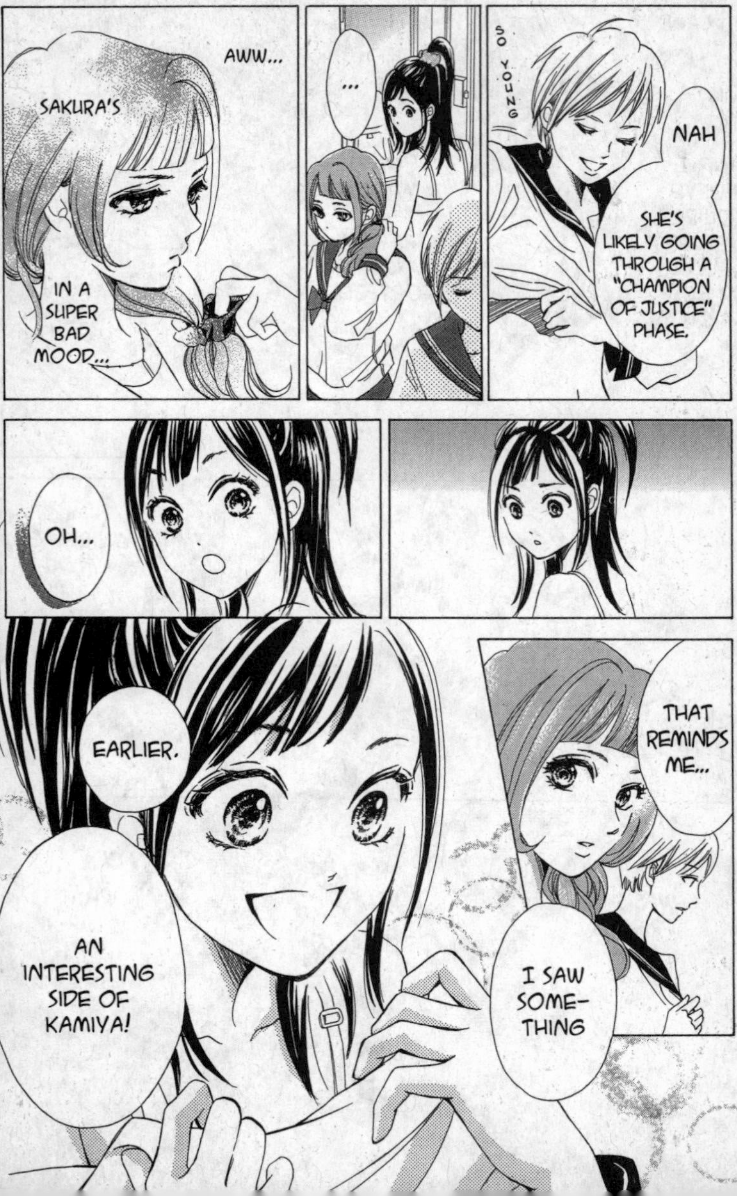
NAH
SHE'S LIKELY GOING THROUGH A "CHAMPION OF JUSTICE" PHASE.
SO YOUNG
...
AWW...
SAKURA'S
IN A SUPER BAD MOOD...
OH...
THAT REMINDS ME...
I SAW SOME-THING
EARLIER.
AN INTERESTING SIDE OF KAMIYA!

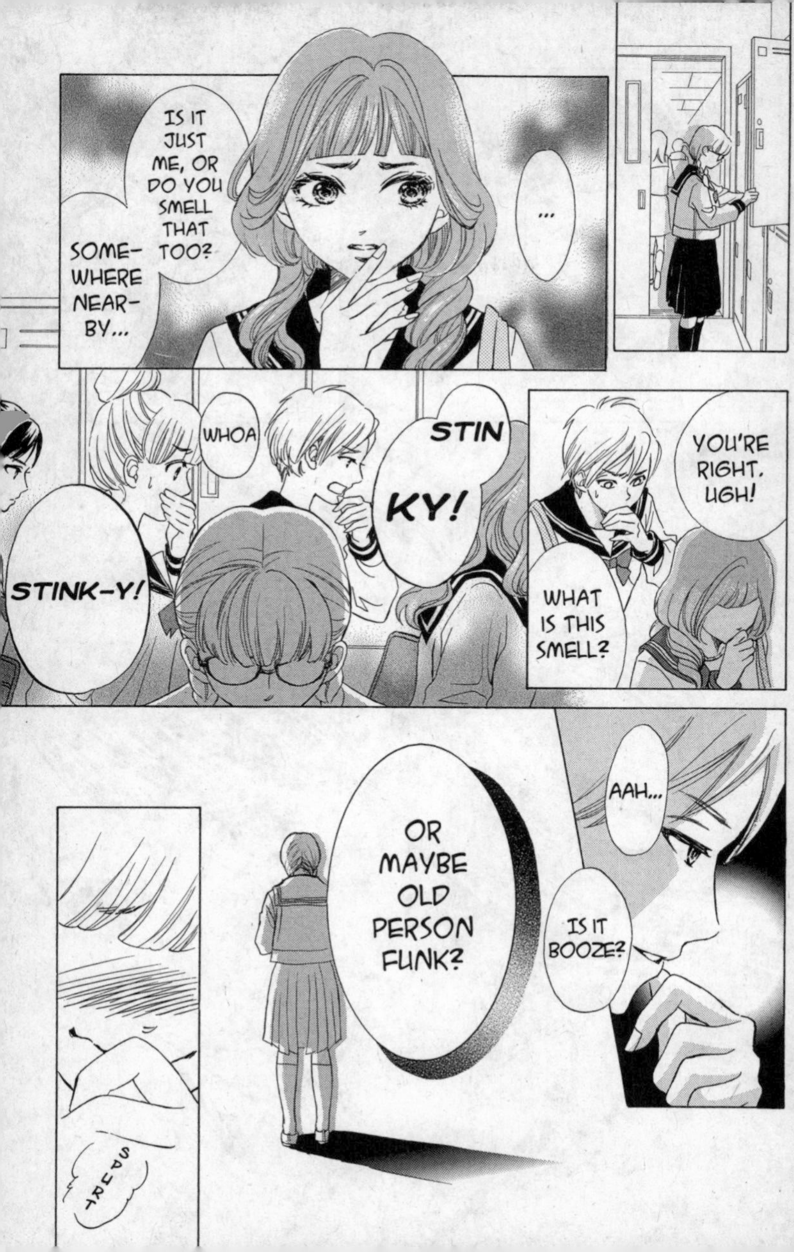
...
IS IT JUST ME, OR DO YOU SMELL THAT TOO?
SOME-WHERE NEAR-BY...
YOU'RE RIGHT. UGH!
WHAT IS THIS SMELL?
STIN KY!
WHOA
STINK-Y!
AAH...
IS IT BOOZE?
OR MAYBE OLD PERSON FUNK?
SPURT

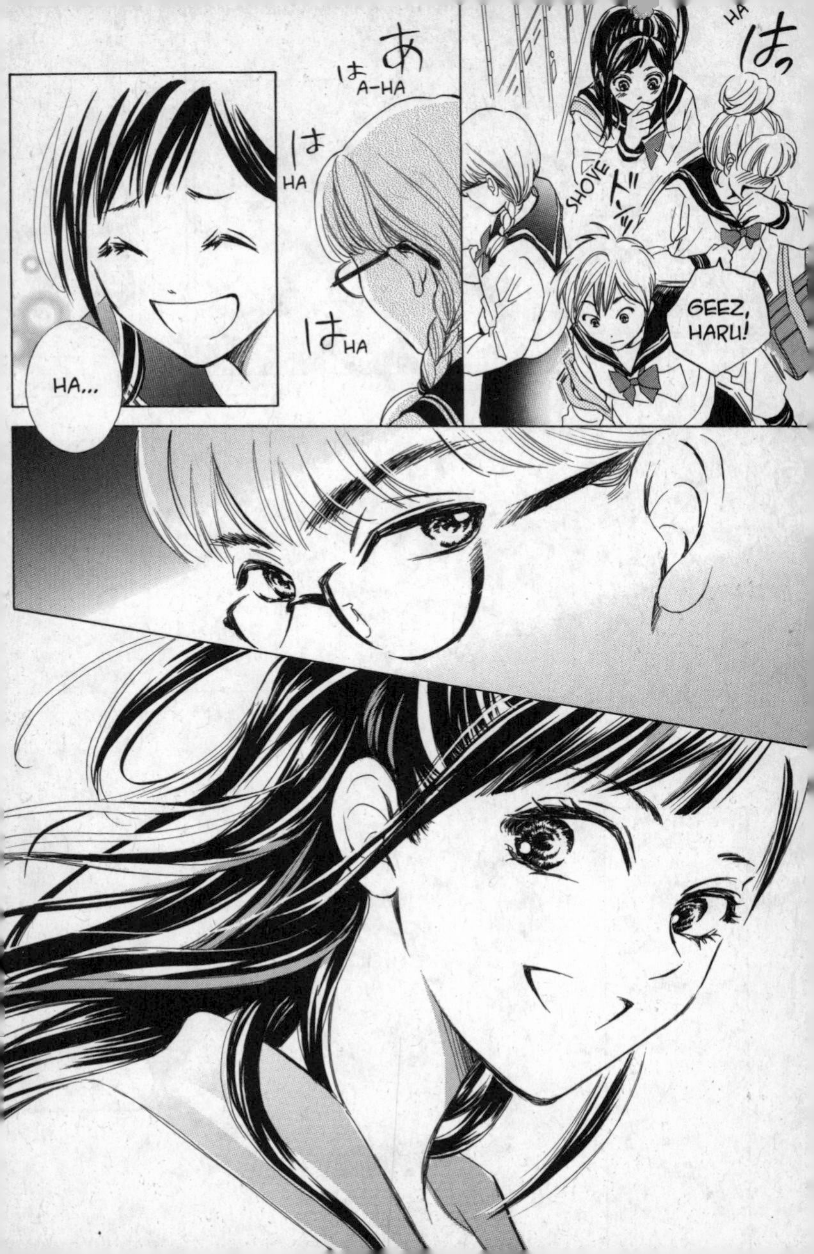
はっ HA
SHOVE
GEEZ, HARU!
あ はA-HA
は HA
は HA
HA...

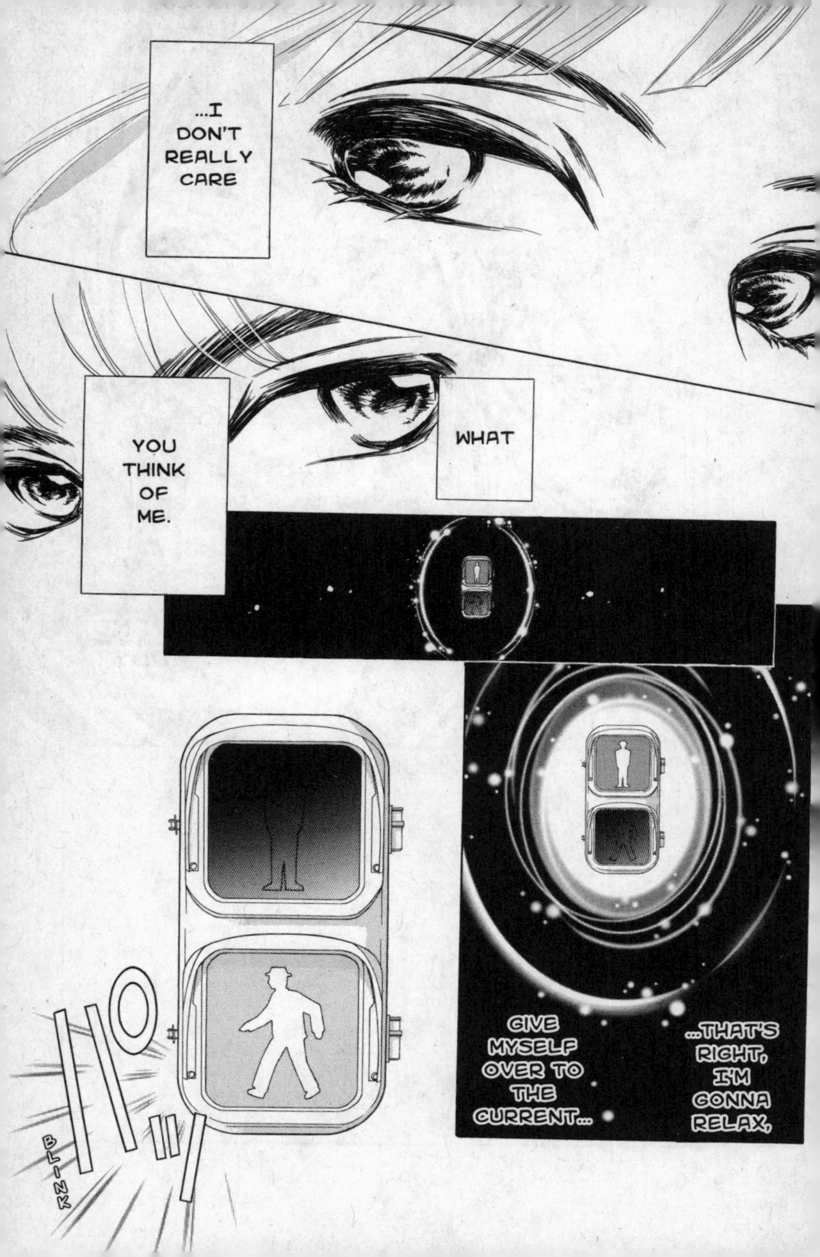
...I DON'T REALLY CARE
WHAT
YOU THINK OF ME.
...THAT'S RIGHT, I'M GONNA RELAX,
GIVE MYSELF OVER TO THE CURRENT...
BLINK

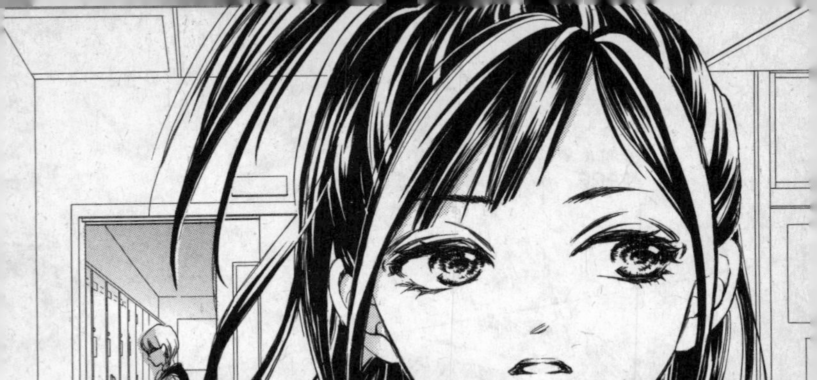
...AND JUST
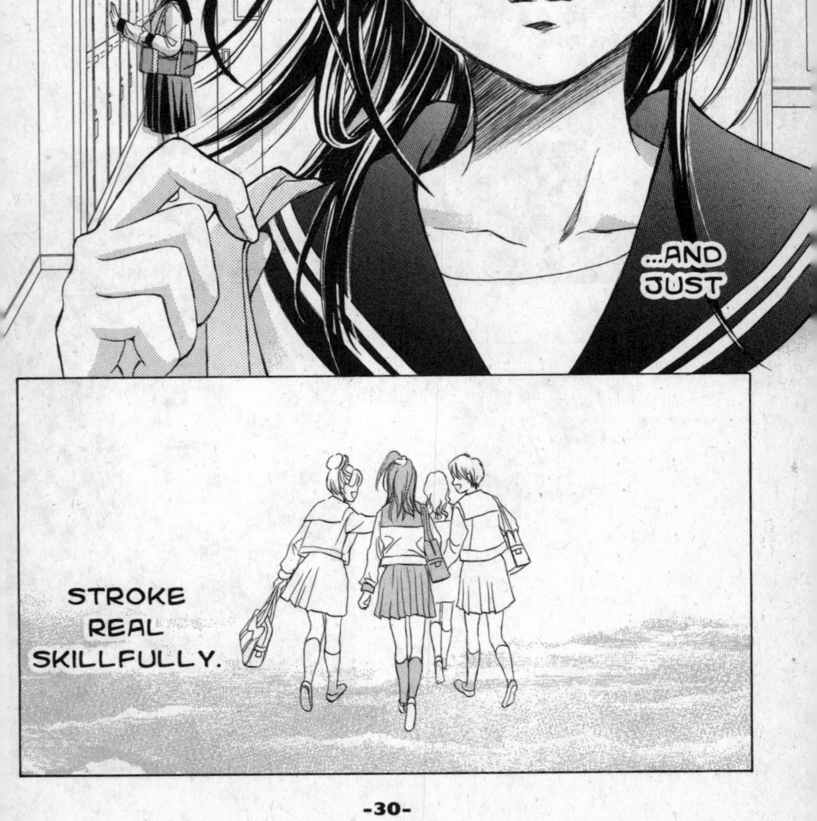
STROKE REAL SKILLFULLY.

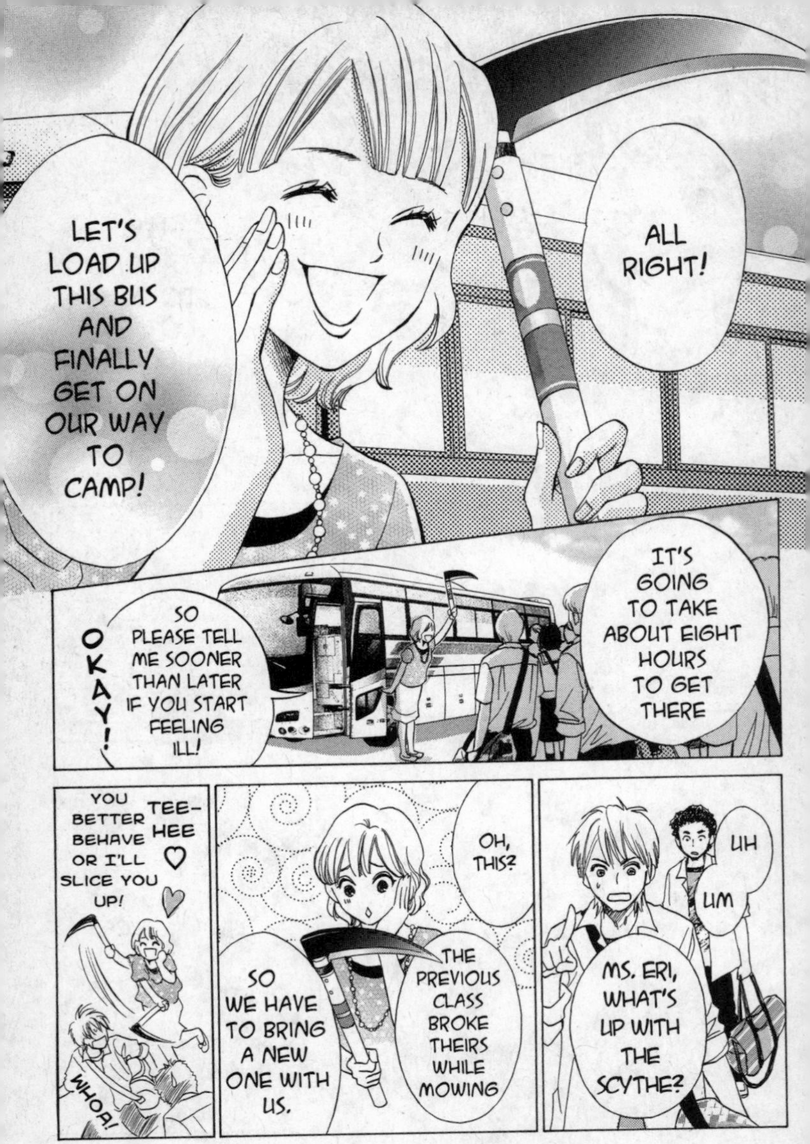
ALL RIGHT!
LET'S LOAD UP THIS BUS AND FINALLY GET ON OUR WAY TO CAMP!
IT'S GOING TO TAKE ABOUT EIGHT HOURS TO GET THERE
SO PLEASE TELL ME SOONER THAN LATER IF YOU START FEELING ILL!
OKAY!
UH
UM
MS. ERI, WHAT'S UP WITH THE SCYTHE?
OH, THIS?
THE PREVIOUS CLASS BROKE THEIRS WHILE MOWING
SO WE HAVE TO BRING A NEW ONE WITH US.
TEE-HEE ♡
YOU BETTER BEHAVE OR I'LL SLICE YOU UP!
WHOA!

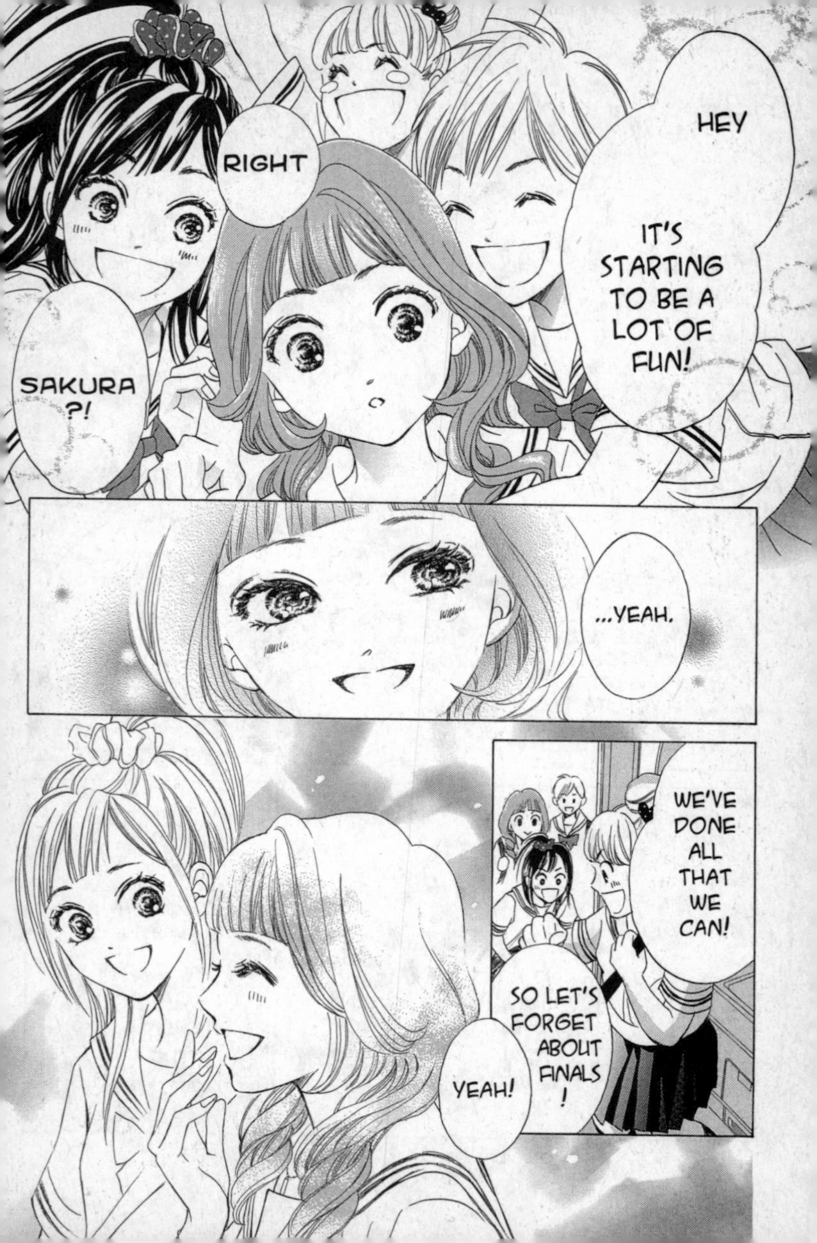
HEY IT'S STARTING TO BE A LOT OF FUN!
RIGHT
SAKURA ?!
...YEAH.
WE'VE DONE ALL THAT WE CAN!
SO LET'S FORGET ABOUT FINALS !
YEAH!

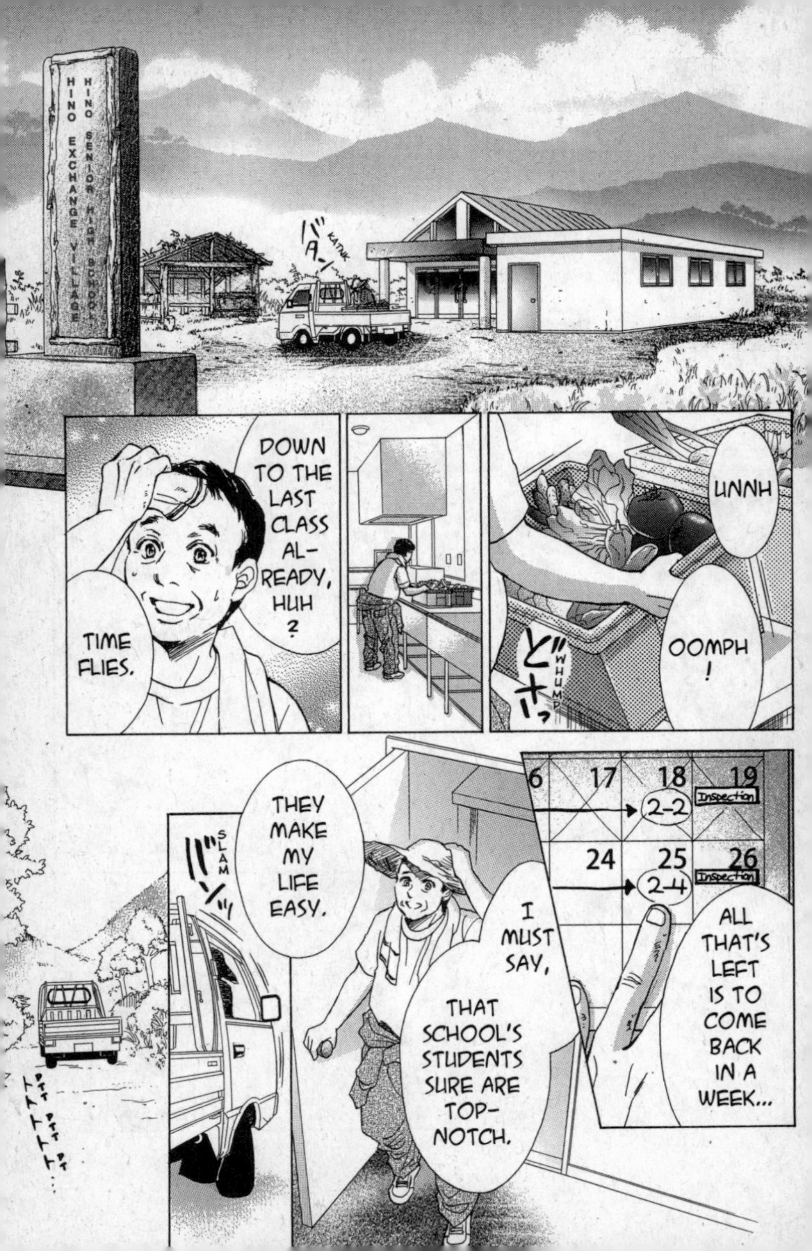
HINO SENIOR HIGH SCHOOL
HINO EXCHANGE VILLAGE
KATNK
UNNH
OOMPH!
WHUMP
DOWN TO THE LAST CLASS ALREADY, HUH?
TIME FLIES.
6 17 18 19
2-2
Inspection
24 25 26
2-4
Inspection
ALL THAT'S LEFT IS TO COME BACK IN A WEEK...
I MUST SAY,
THAT SCHOOL'S STUDENTS SURE ARE TOP-NOTCH.
THEY MAKE MY LIFE EASY.
SLAM
PTT PTT PT...

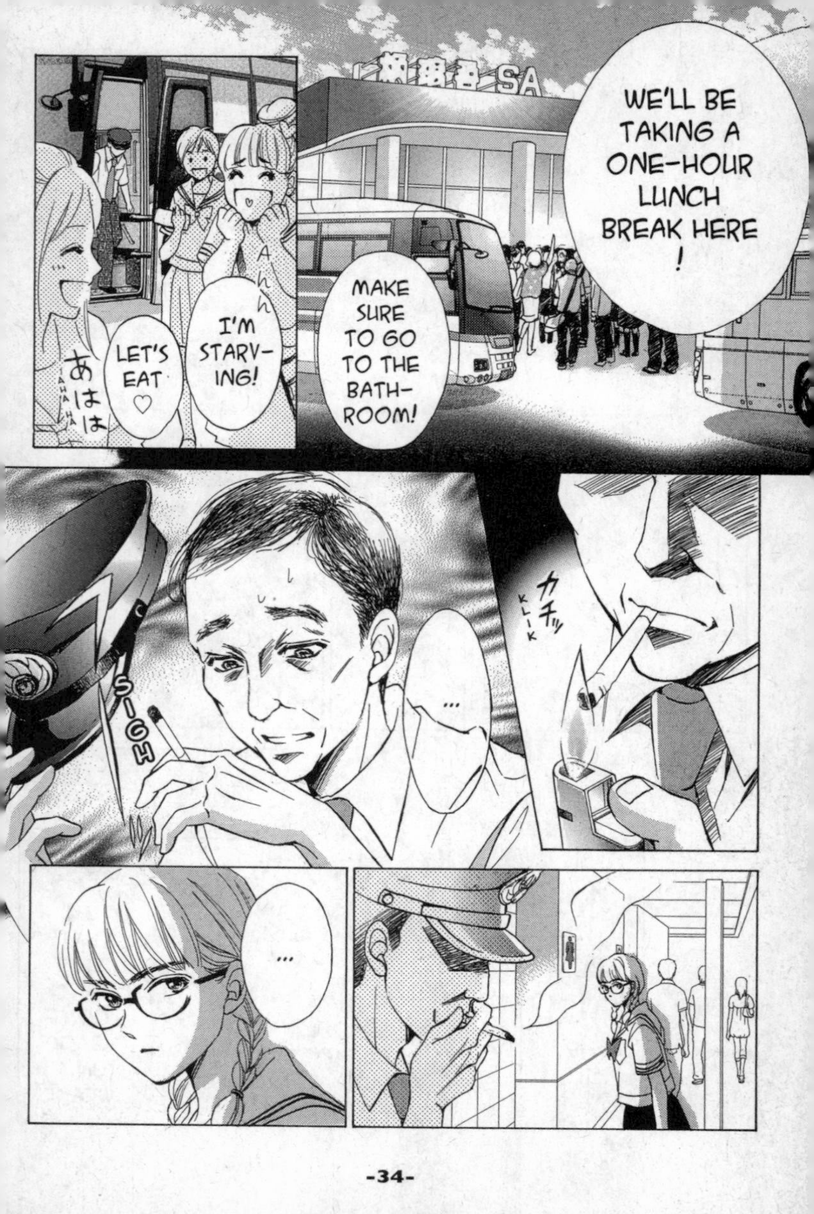
SA
WE'LL BE TAKING A ONE-HOUR LUNCH BREAK HERE!
MAKE SURE TO GO TO THE BATH-ROOM!
Ahhh
I'M STARV-ING!
LET'S EAT ♡
あはは AHAHA
カチッ KLIK
...
SIGH
...

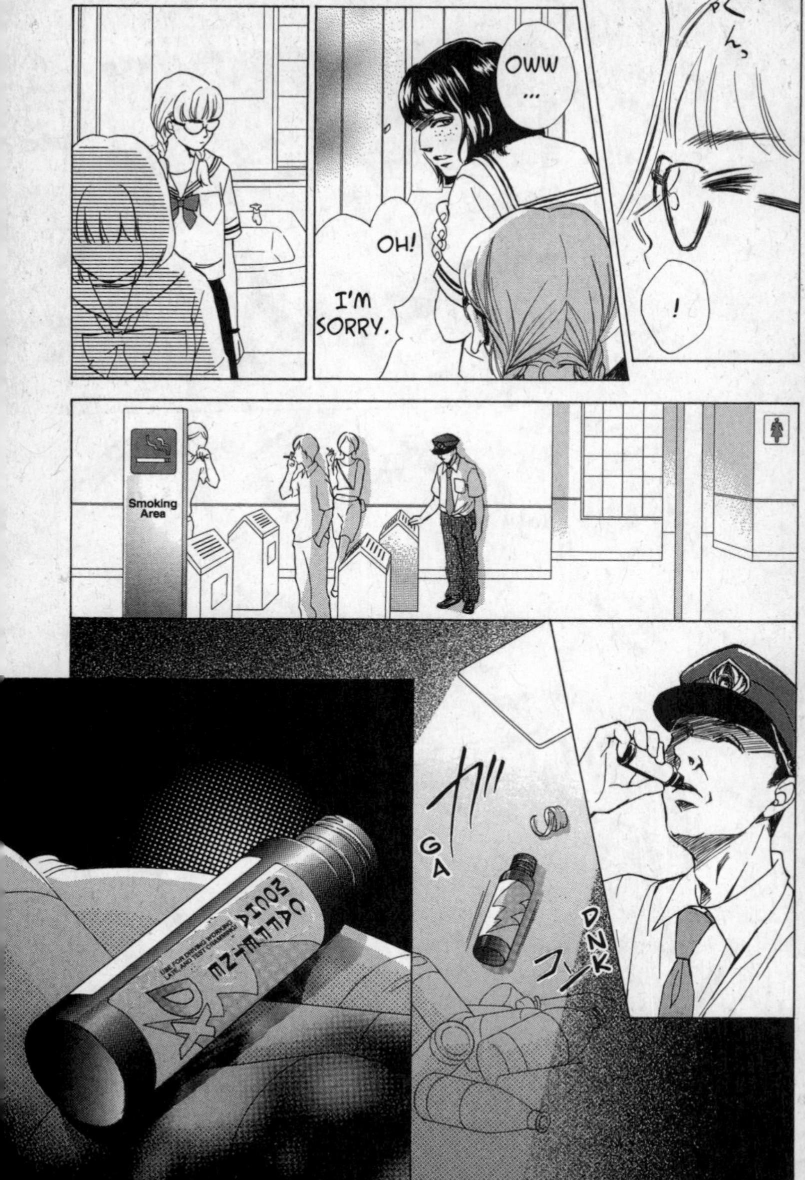
DMP
どんっ
!
OWW ...
OH!
I'M SORRY.
Smoking Area
ガ
GA
DNK
USE FOR DRIVING, WORKING LATE, AND TEST CRAMMING!
DX

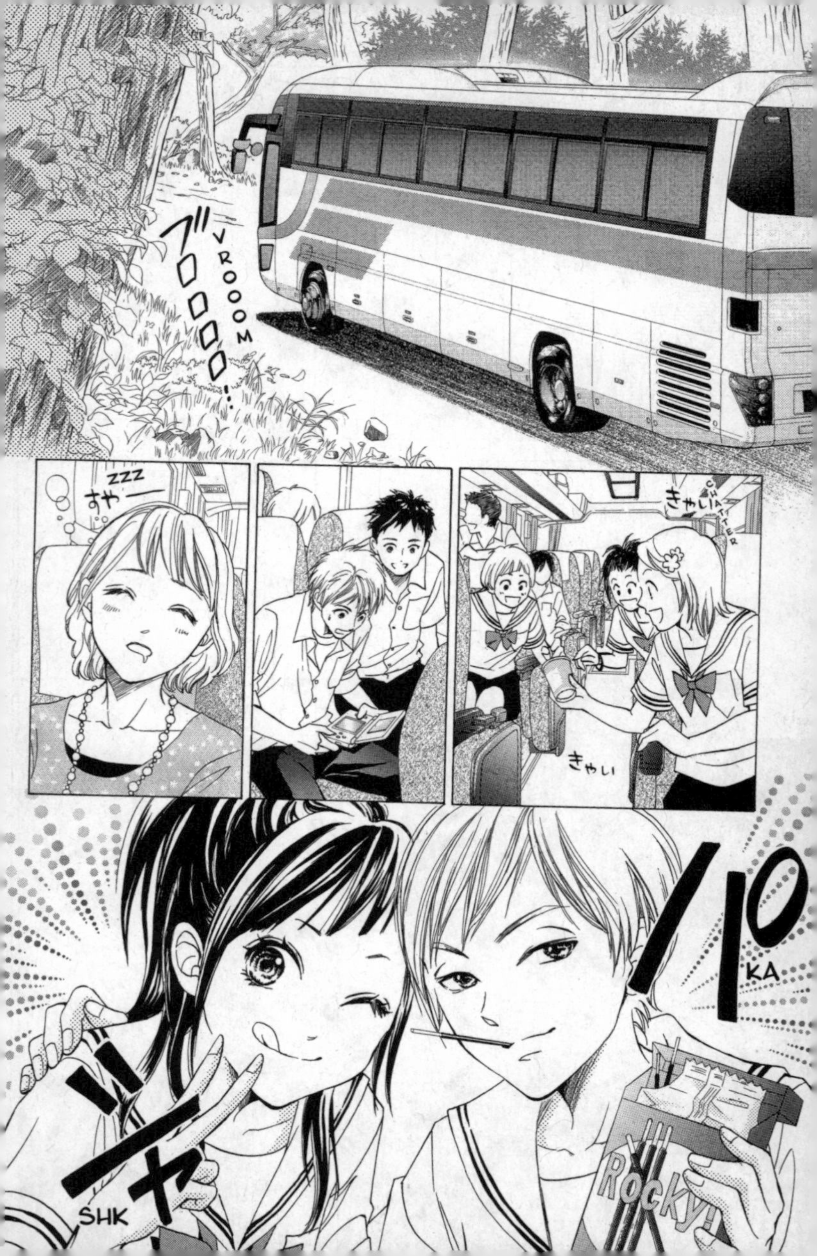
ブロロロロロ!!
VROOOOM
きゃい
CHATTER
きゃい
すやー
ZZZ
パ
KA
シャ
SHK
Rocky!

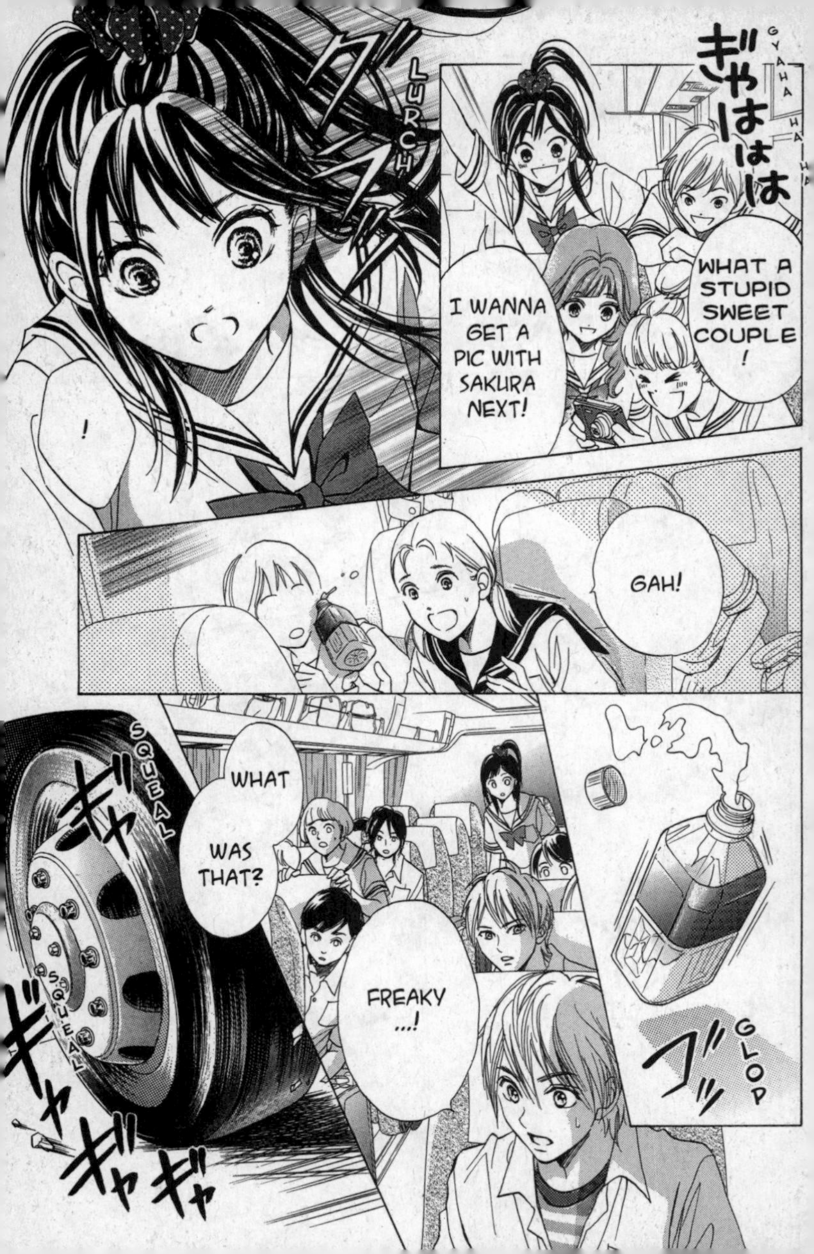
ぎゃははは
GYAHAHAHA
WHAT A STUPID SWEET COUPLE!
I WANNA GET A PIC WITH SAKURA NEXT!
グ
LURCH
!
GAH!
ゴッ
GLOP
WHAT WAS THAT?
FREAKY ...!
ギャ
SQUEAL
SQUEAL
ギャギャギャ

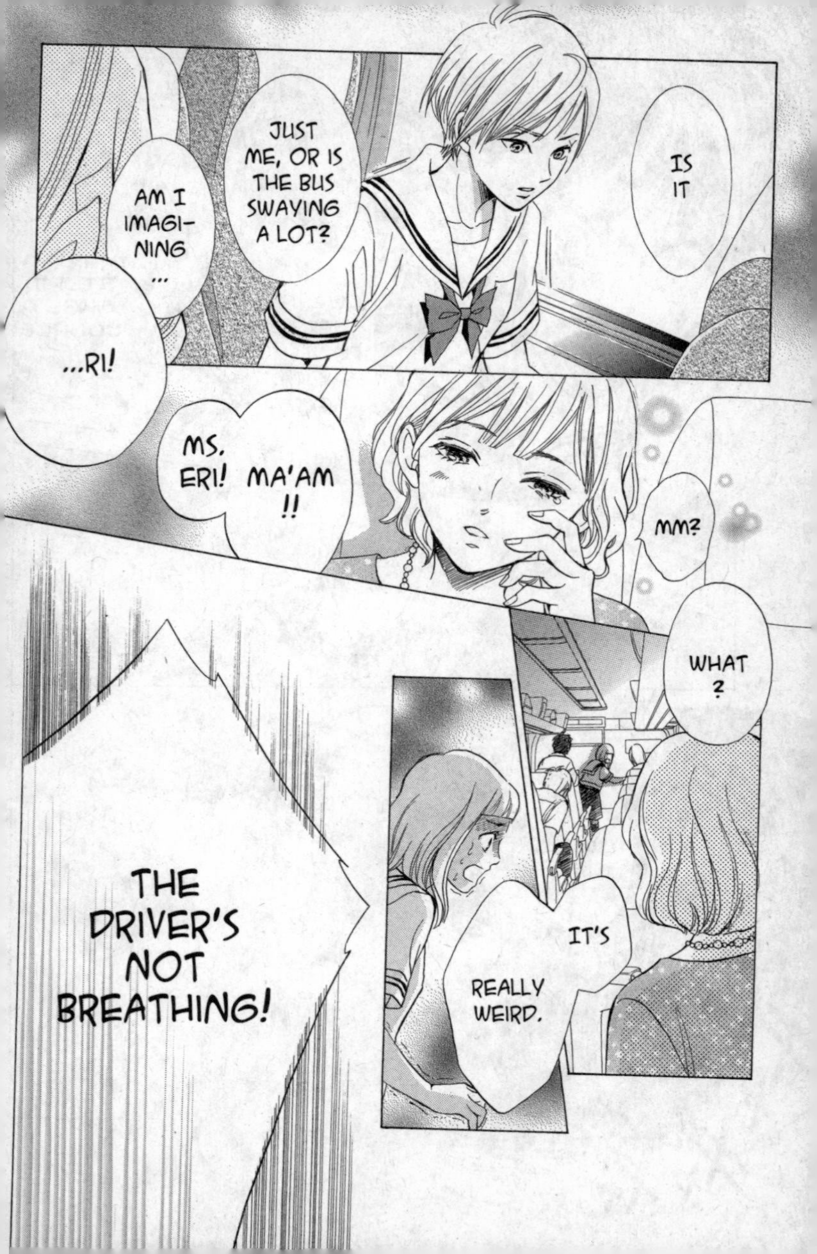
IS IT
JUST ME, OR IS THE BUS SWAYING A LOT?
AM I IMAGINING...
...RI!
MM?
MA'AM!!
MS. ERI!
WHAT?
IT'S
REALLY WEIRD.
THE DRIVER'S NOT BREATHING!

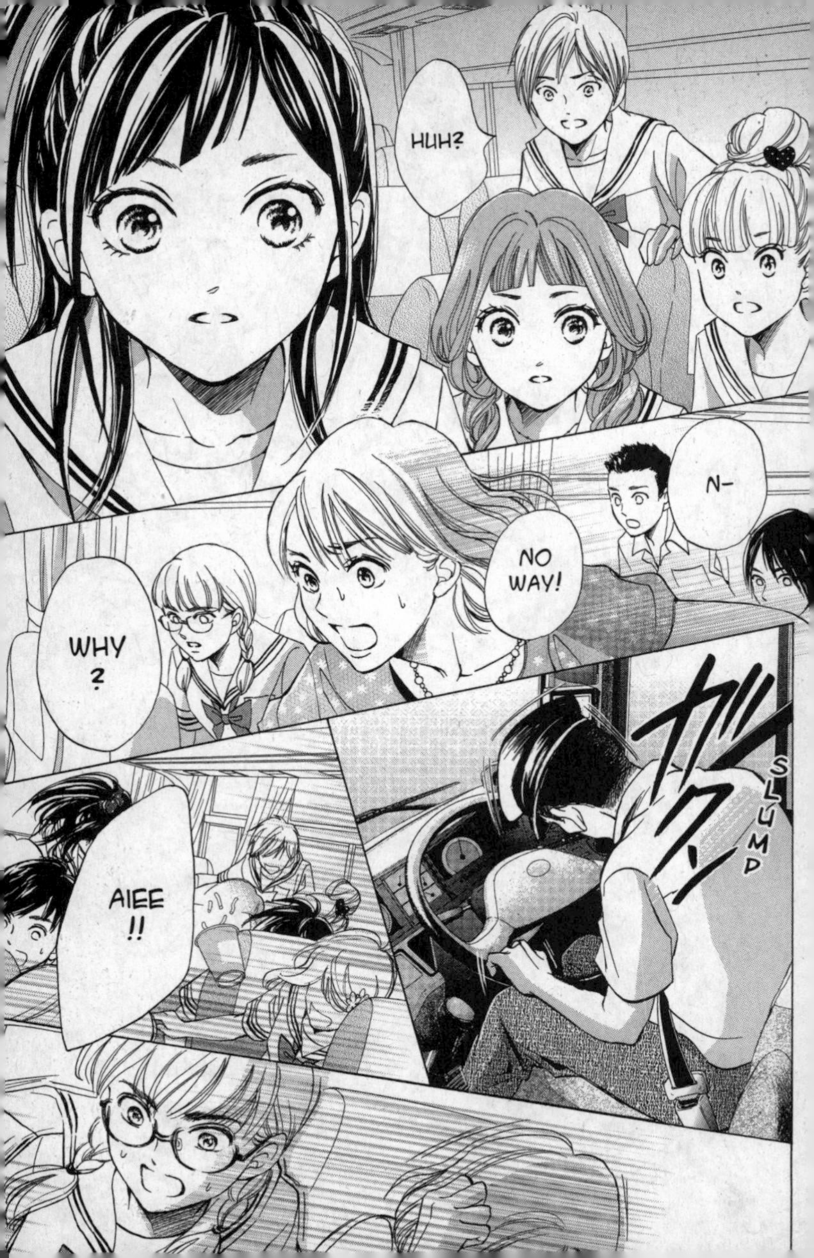
HUH?
N-
NO WAY!
WHY ?
SLUMP
AIEE !!

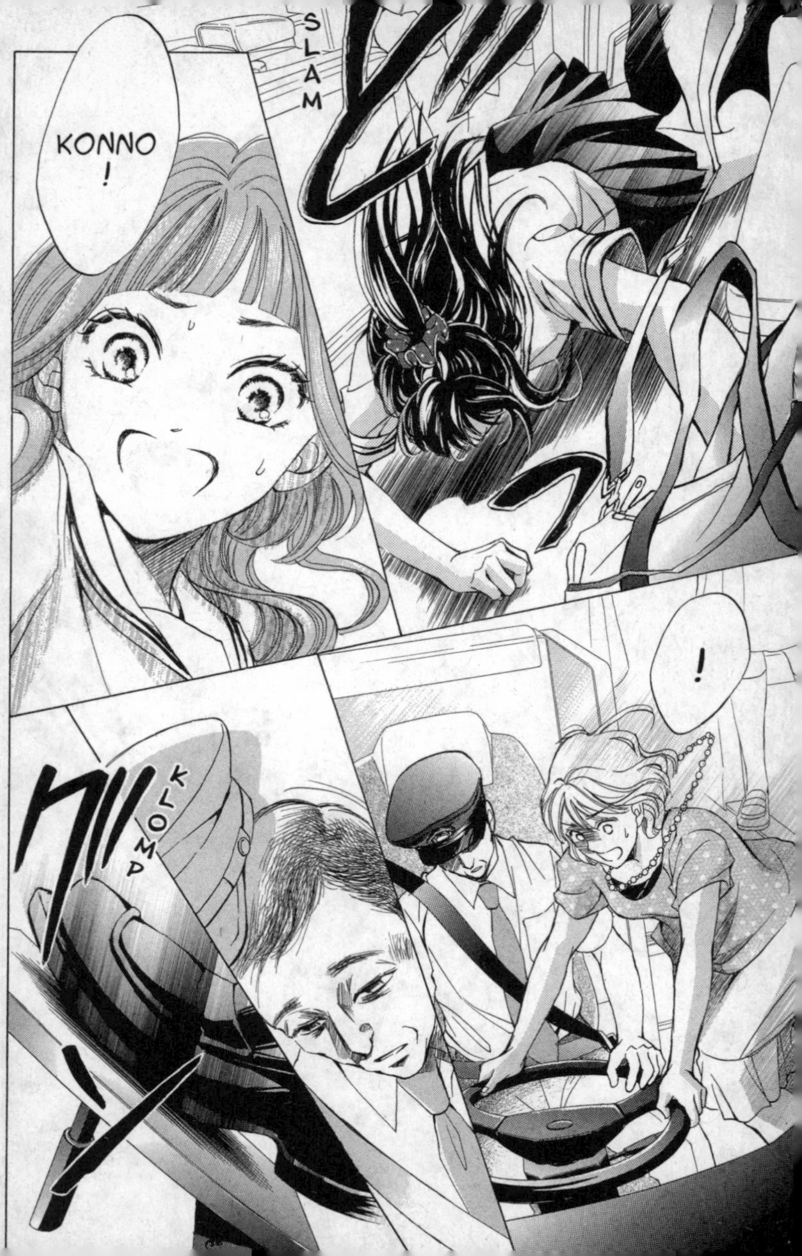
SLAM
KONNO !
!
KLOMP

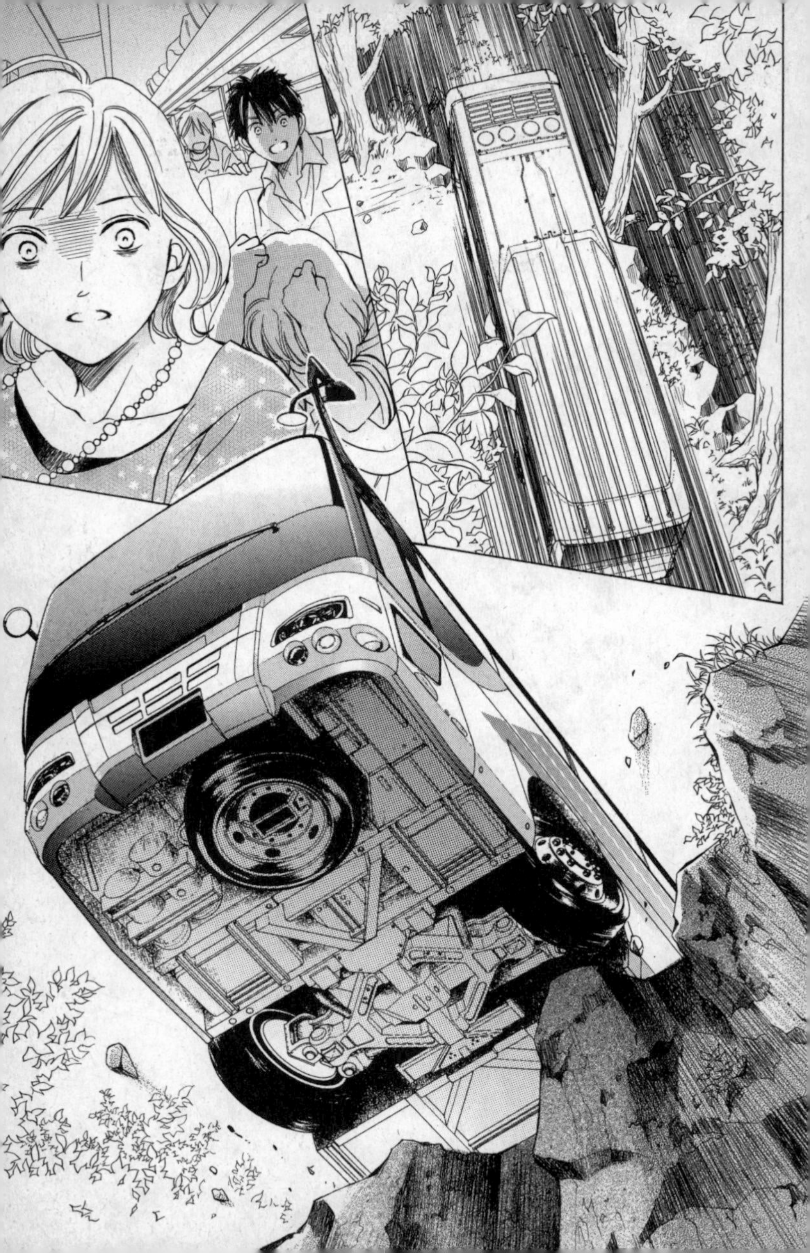

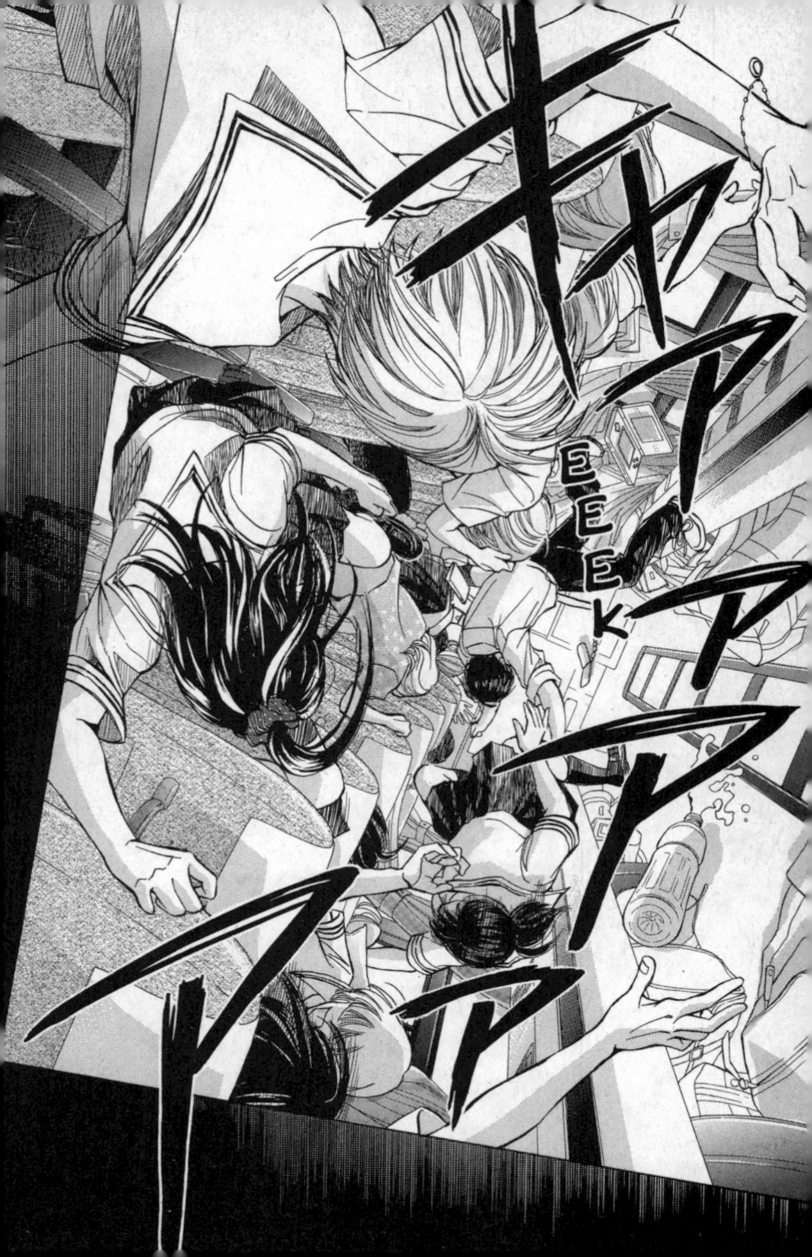
キャアアアア
EEEEK

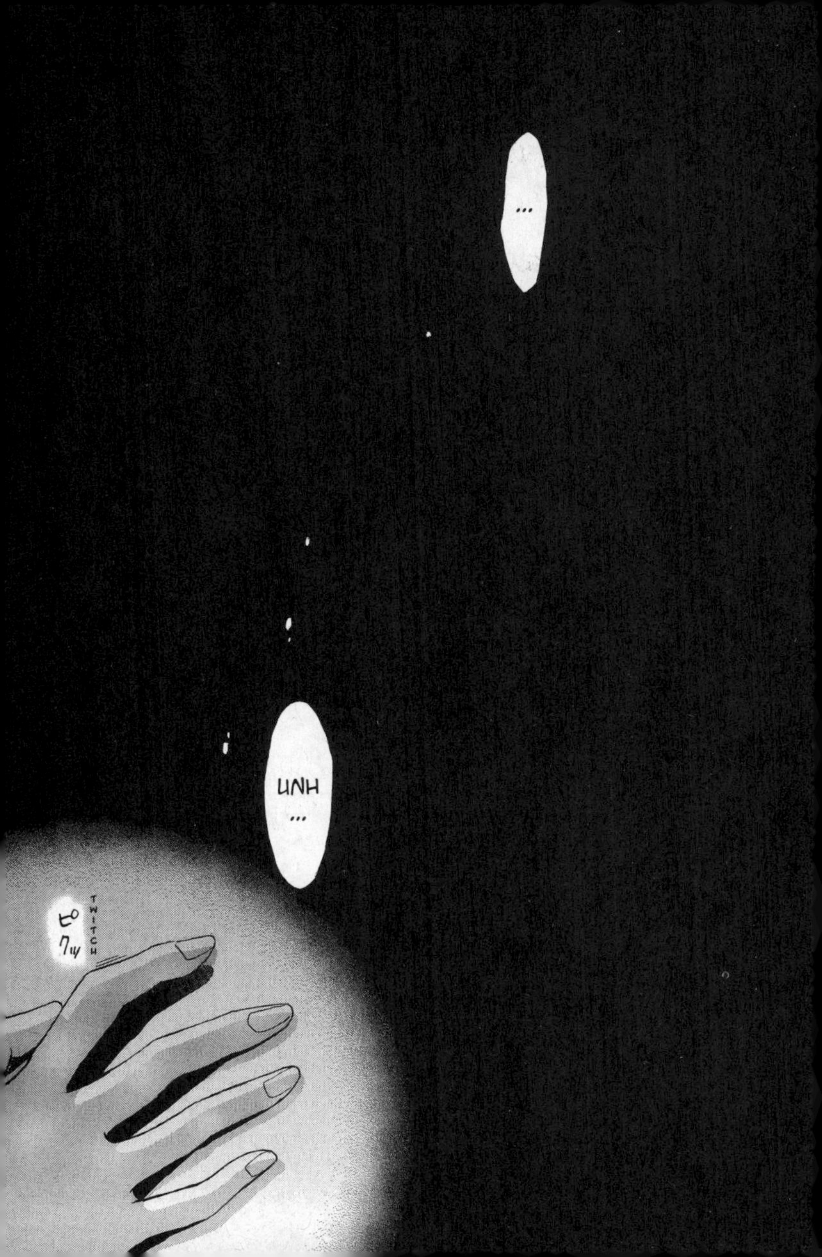
...
UNH
...
ピクッ
TWITCH

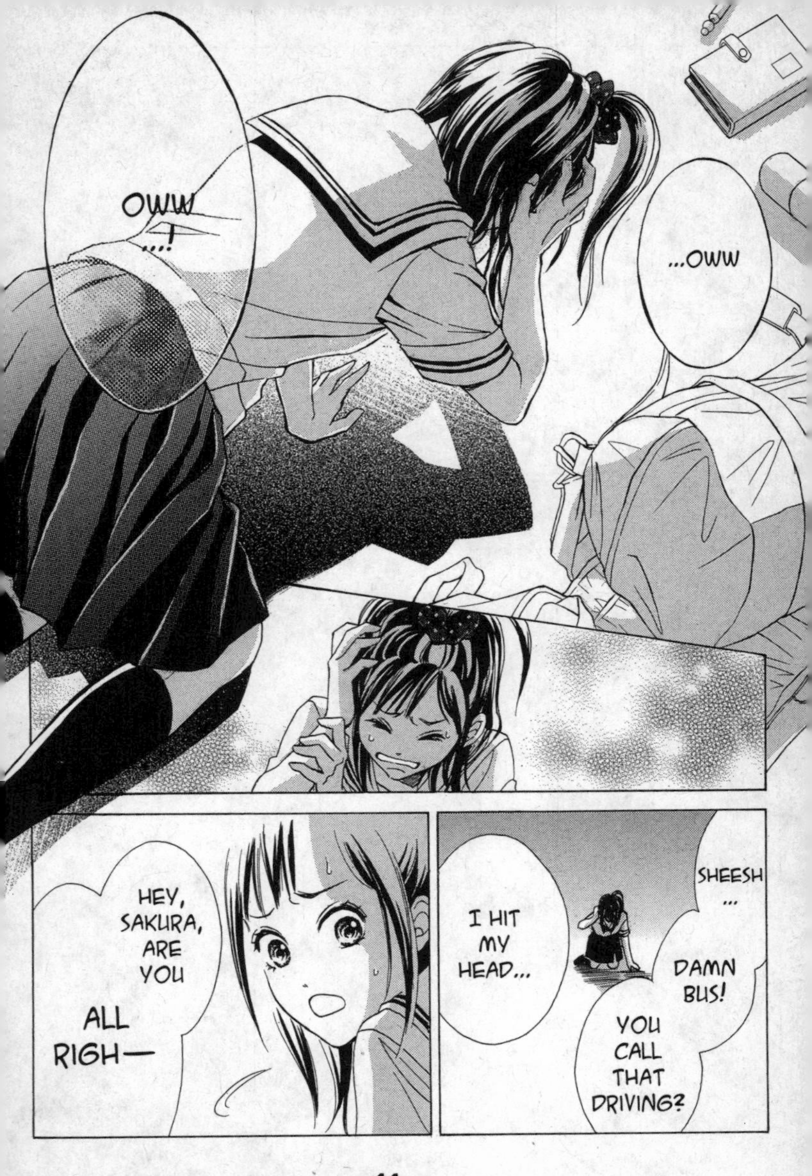
...OWW
OWW ...!
SHEESH ... DAMN BUS!
I HIT MY HEAD...
YOU CALL THAT DRIVING?
HEY, SAKURA, ARE YOU ALL RIGH—

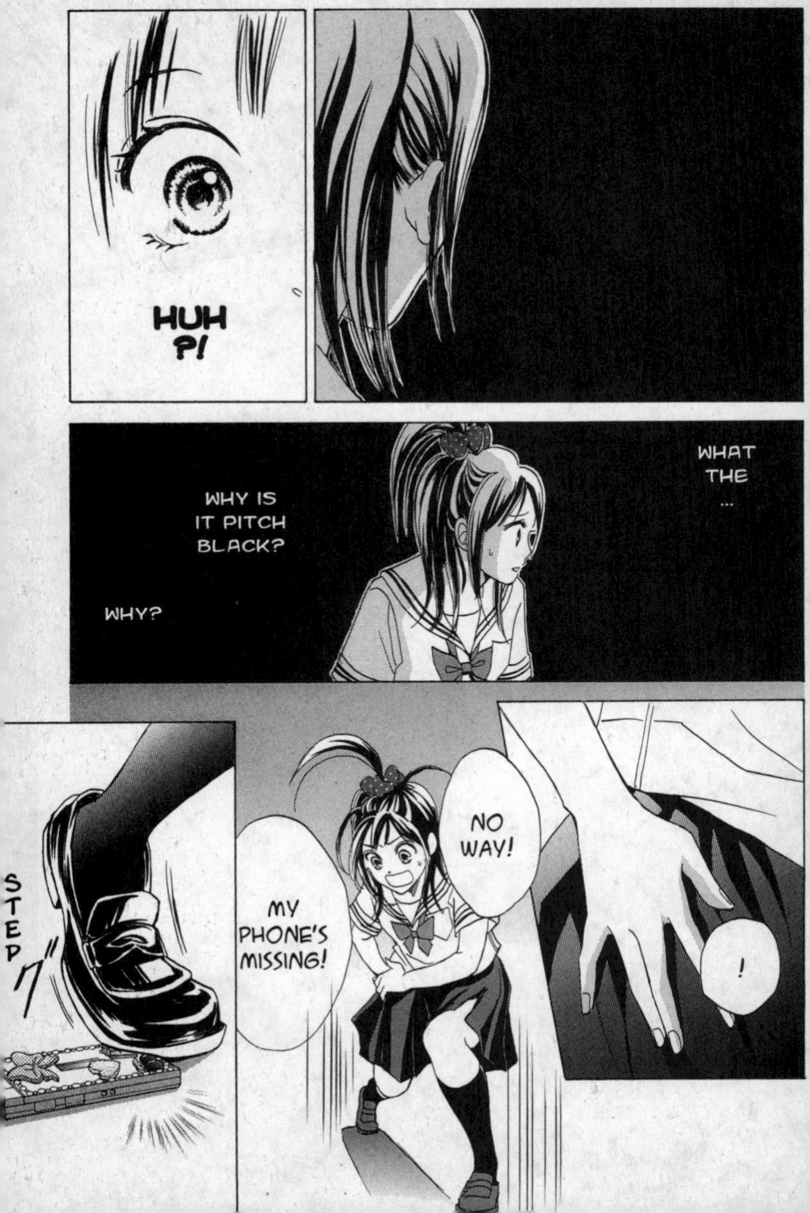
HUH ?!
WHAT THE ...
WHY IS IT PITCH BLACK?
WHY?
!
NO WAY!
MY PHONE'S MISSING!
STEP

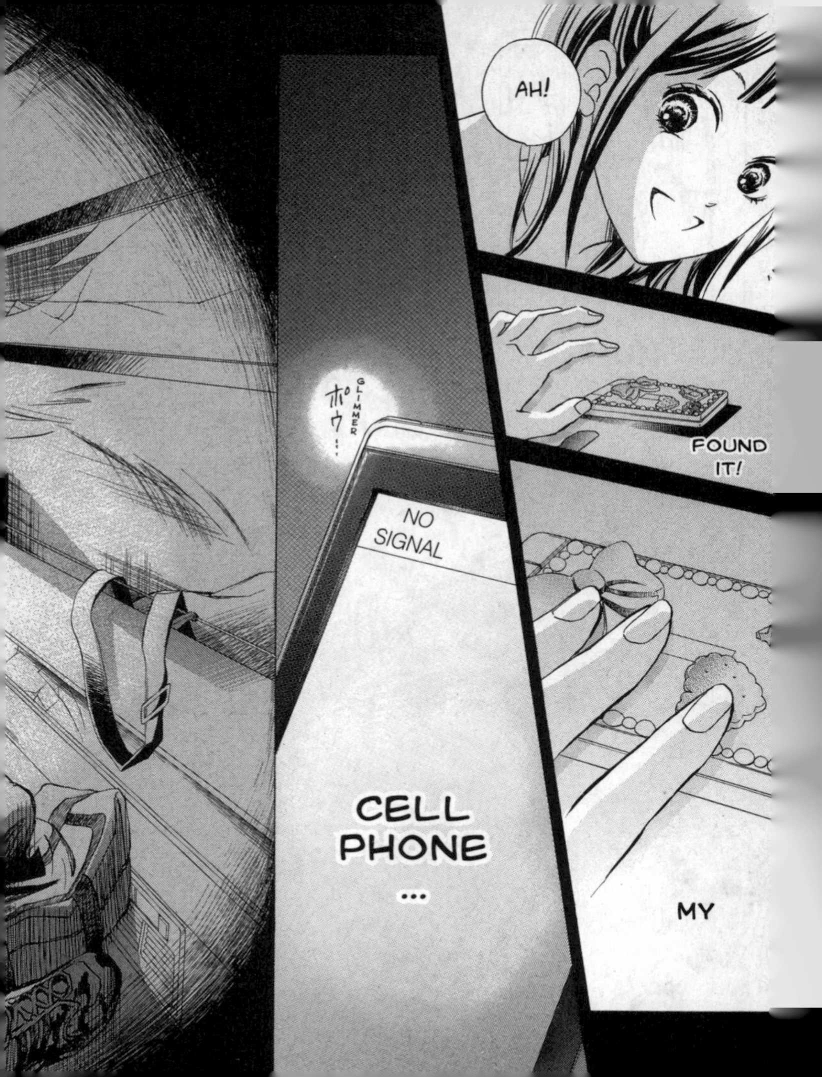
AH!
FOUND IT!
MY
ポウ…
GLIMMER
NO SIGNAL
CELL PHONE ...

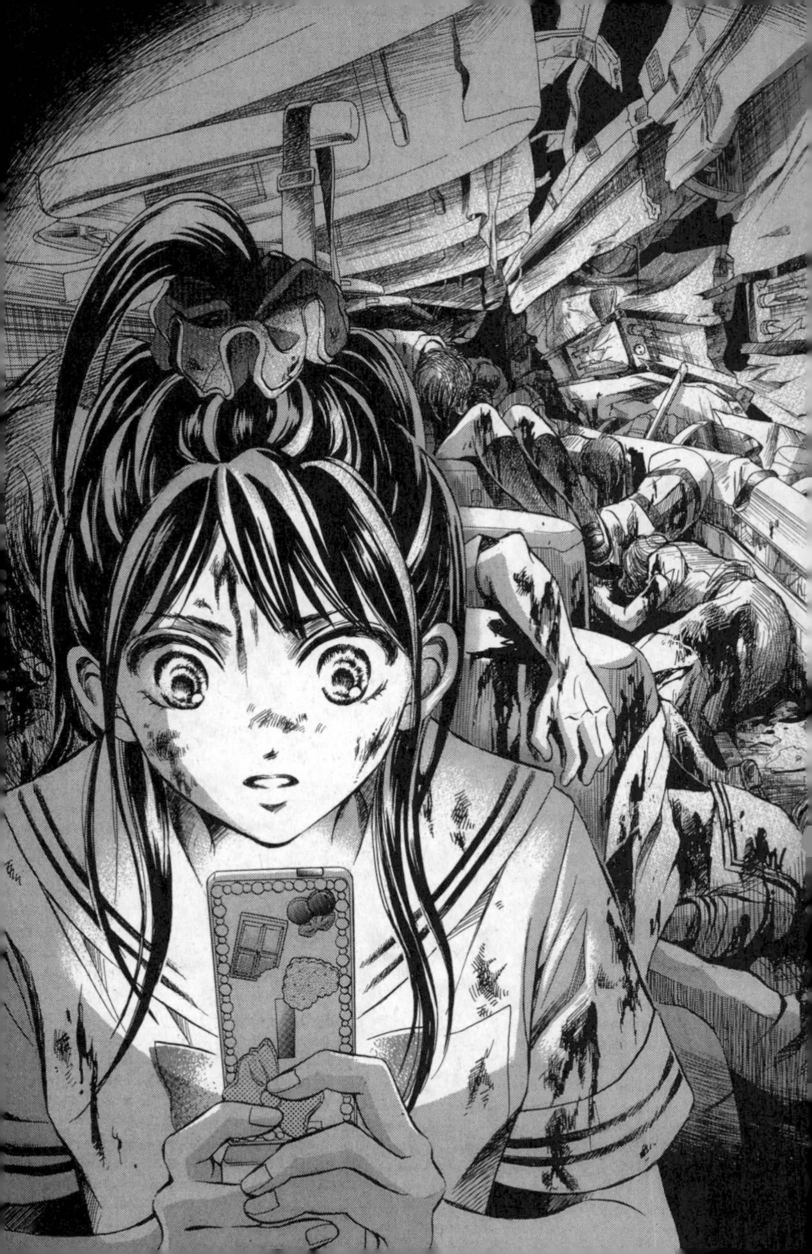

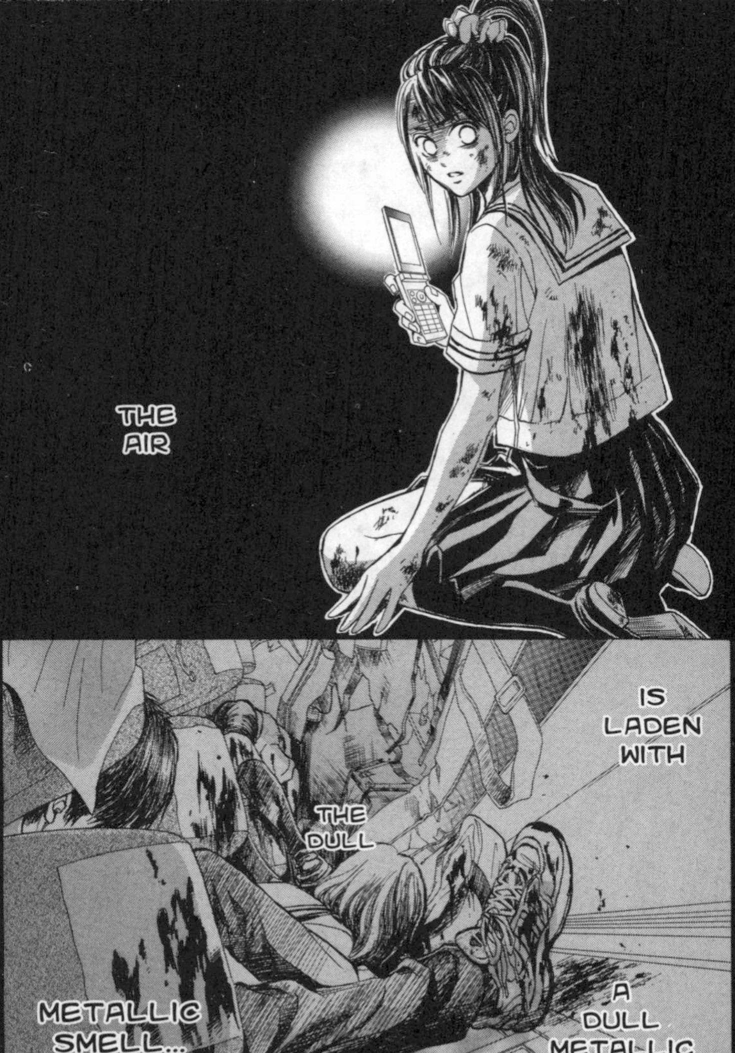
THE AIR
IS LADEN WITH
A DULL METALLIC SMELL
THE DULL
METALLIC SMELL...

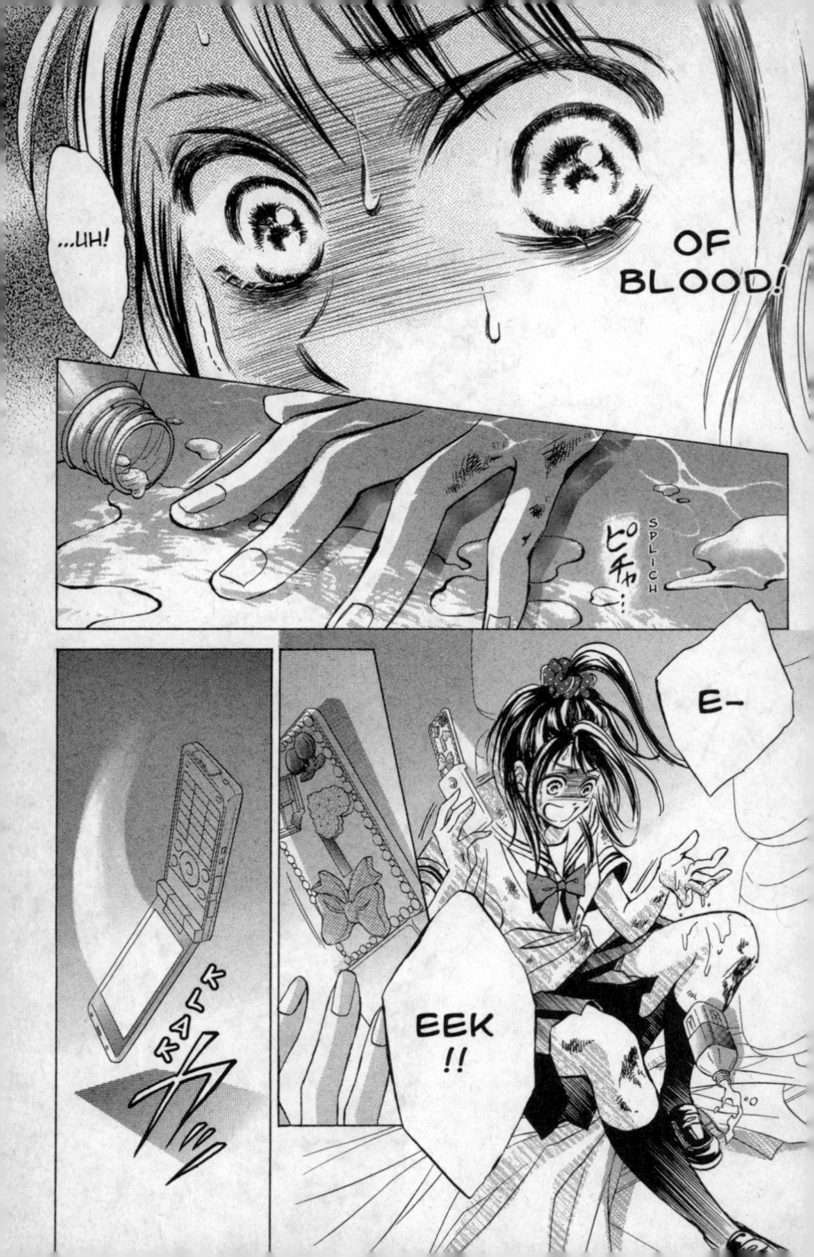
OF BLOOD!
...UH!
SPLICH
ピチャ…
E-
EEK !!
KRALK

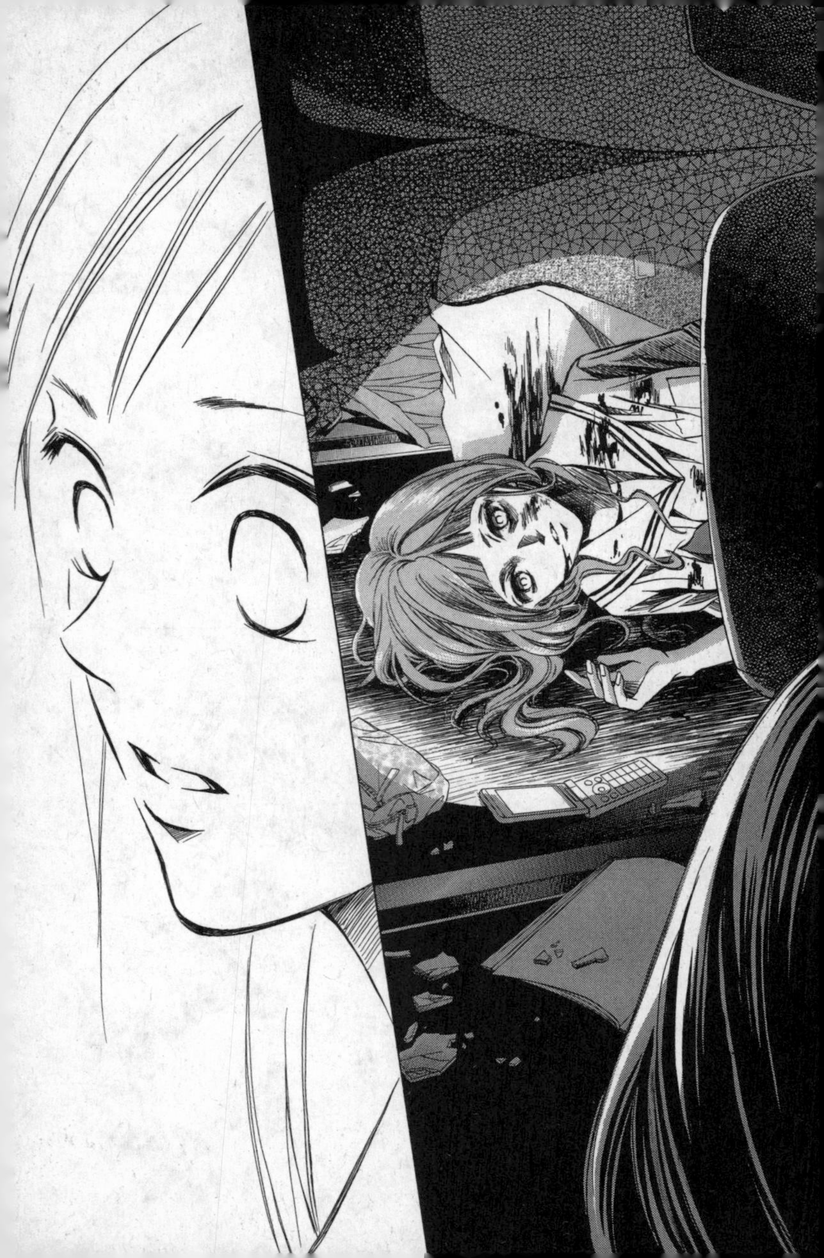

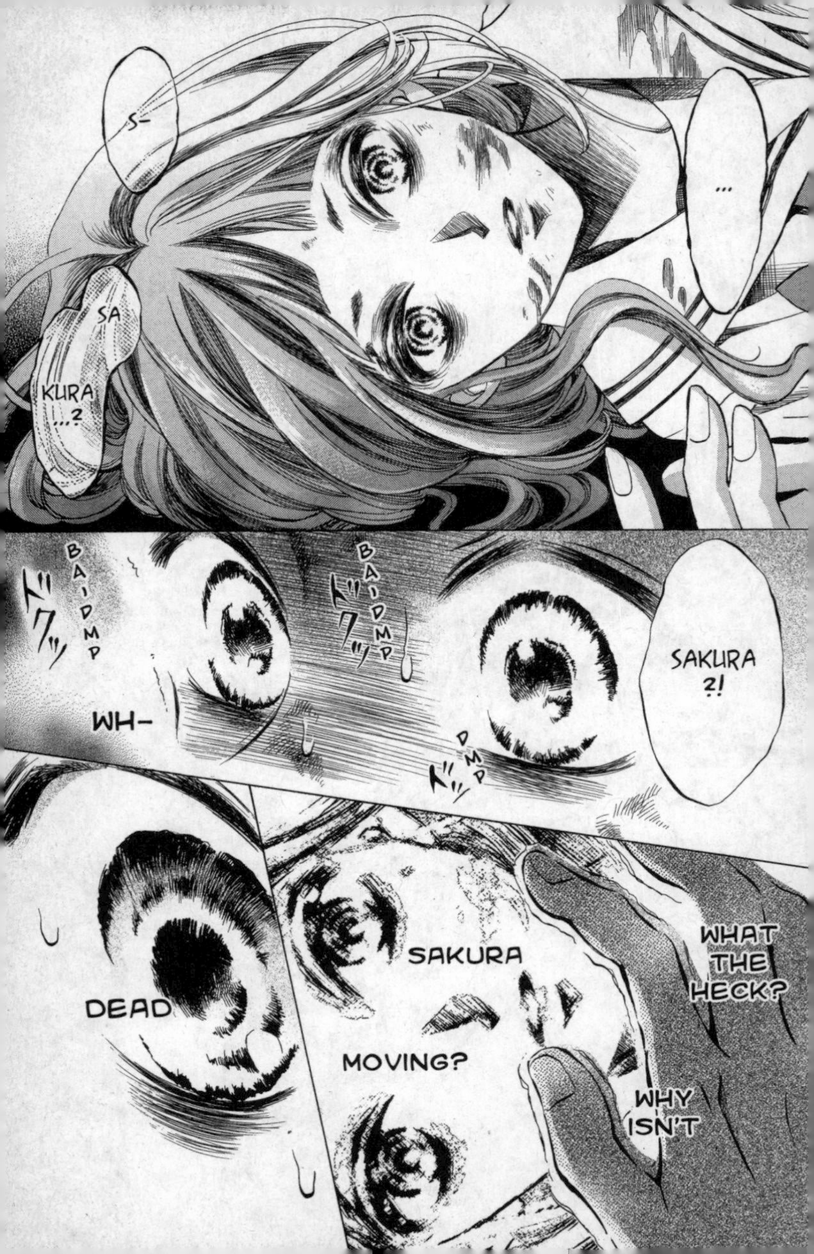
...
S-
SA
KURA
...?
SAKURA
?!
BA-DMP
BA-DMP
DMP
WH-
WHAT
THE
HECK?
WHY
ISN'T
SAKURA
MOVING?
DEAD

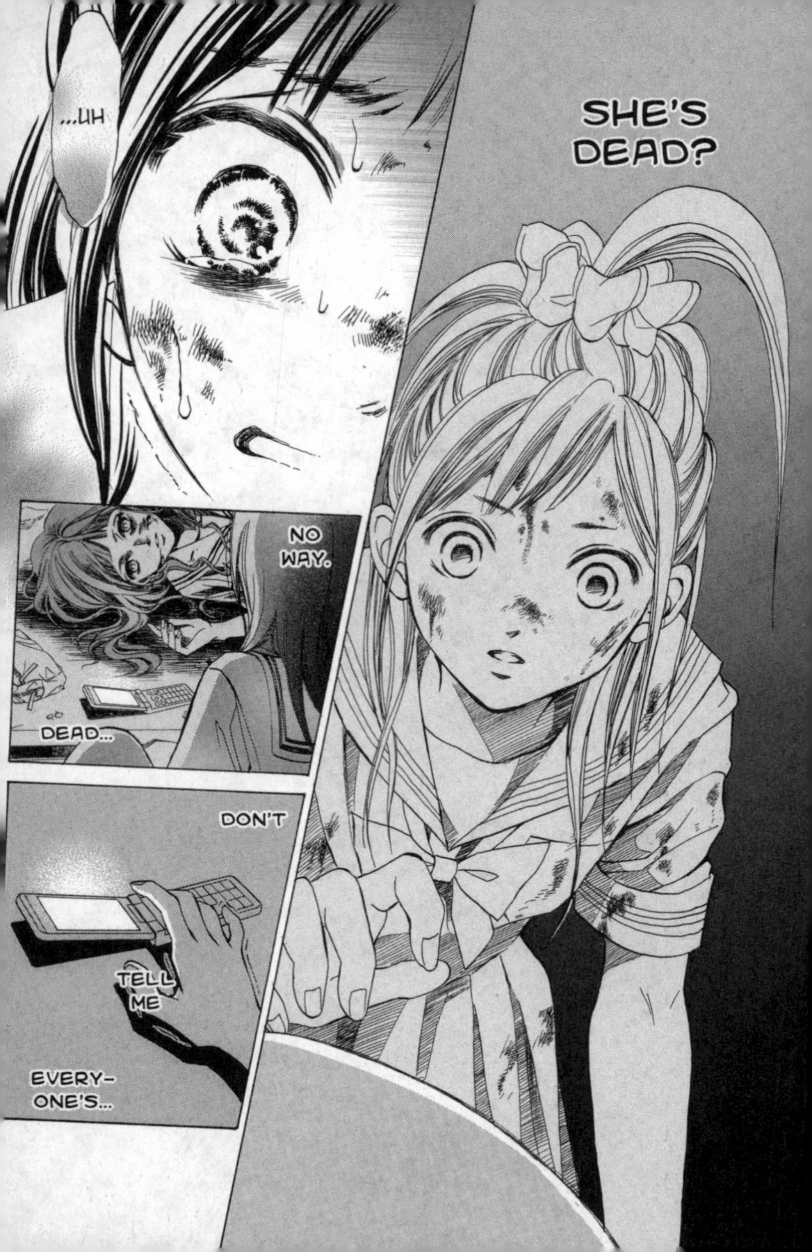
SHE'S DEAD?
...UH
NO WAY.
DEAD...
DON'T
TELL ME
EVERY-ONE'S...

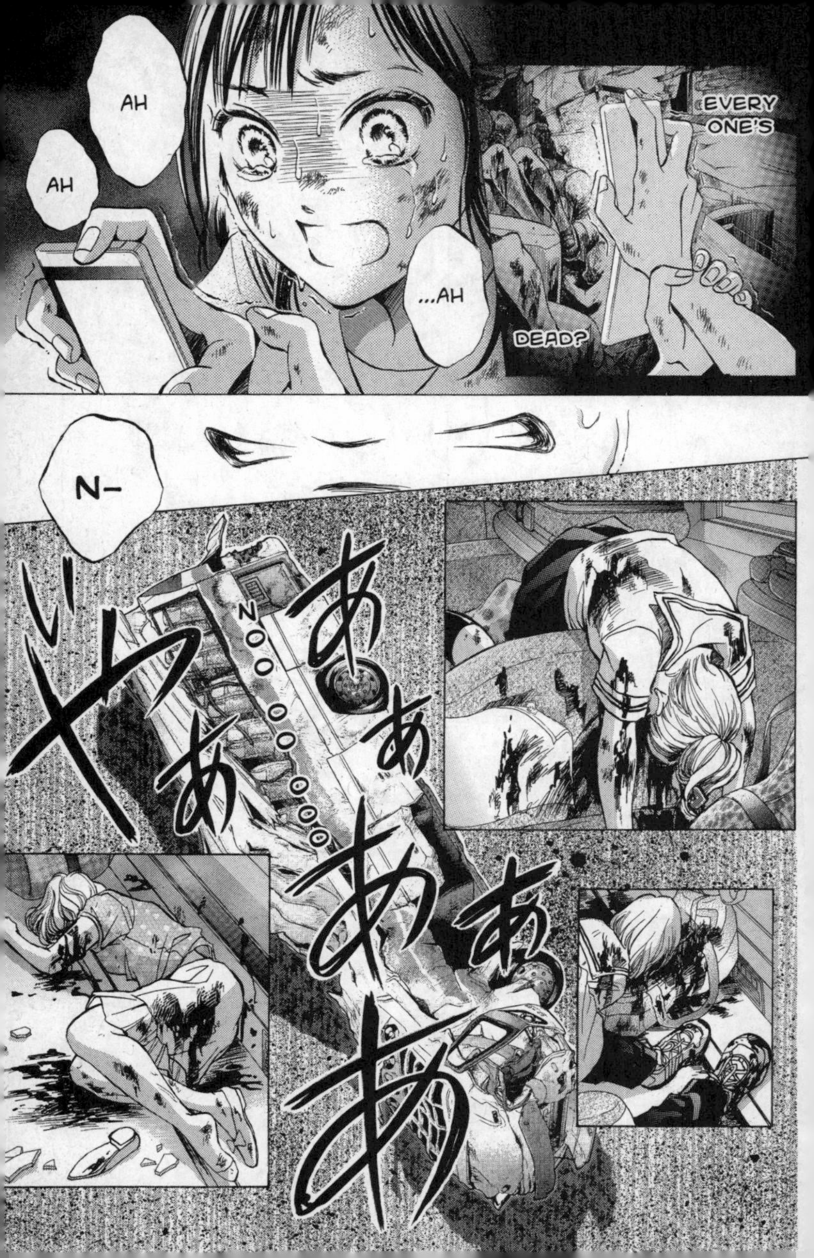
EVERY ONE'S
DEAD?
...AH
AH
AH
N-
NOOOOOOOOO
あああああ
いやあ

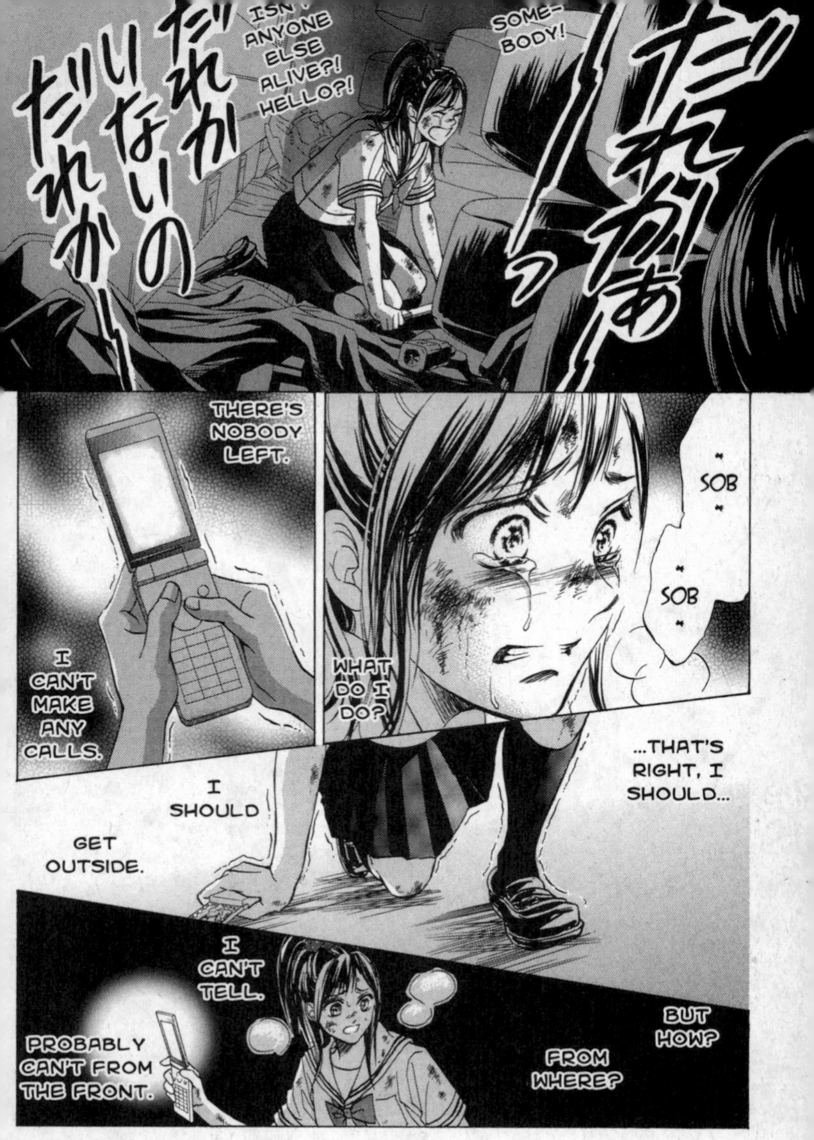

だれかぁーっ
SOME-BODY!
ISN
ANYONE ELSE ALIVE?! HELLO?!
だれかいないの
だれか
SOB SOB
WHAT DO I DO?
THERE'S NOBODY LEFT.
I CAN'T MAKE ANY CALLS.
...THAT'S RIGHT, I SHOULD...
I SHOULD
GET OUTSIDE.
BUT HOW?
FROM WHERE?
I CAN'T TELL.
PROBABLY CAN'T FROM THE FRONT.

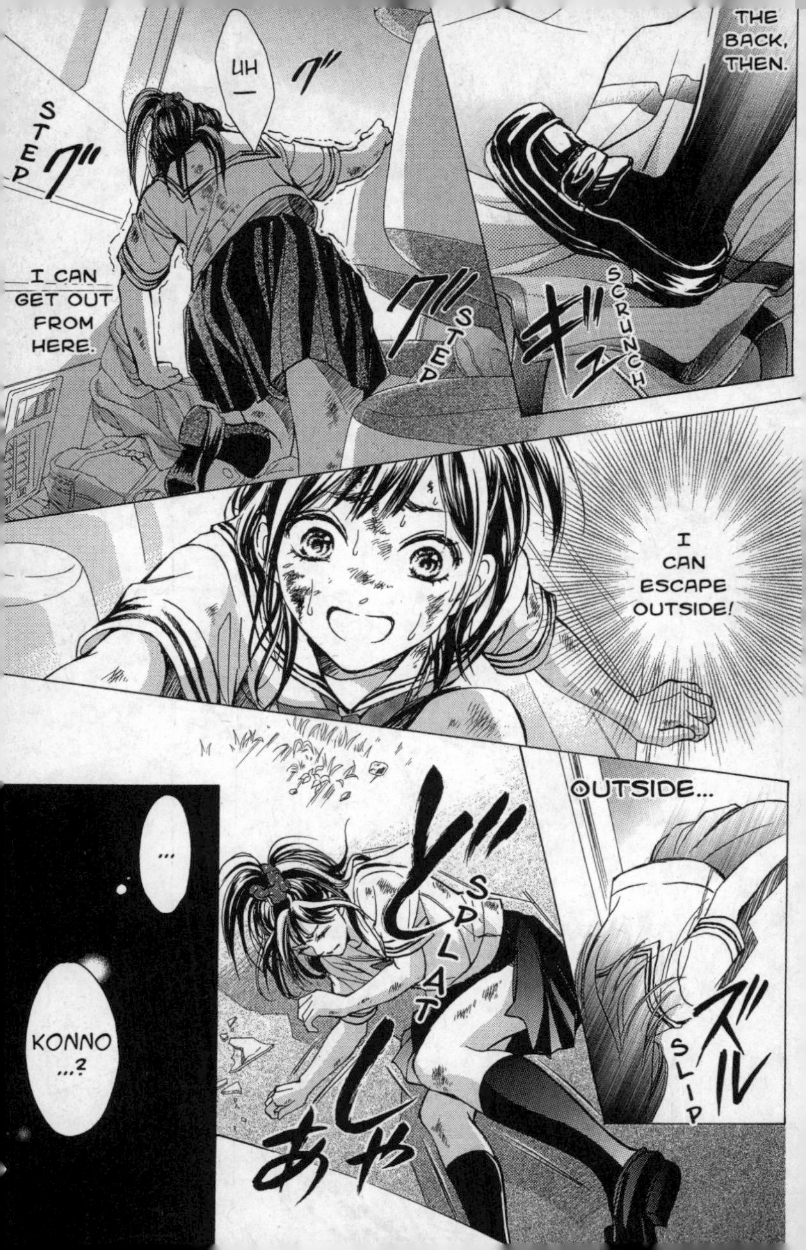
THE BACK, THEN.
SCRUNCH
UH —
STEP
I CAN GET OUT FROM HERE.
STEP
I CAN ESCAPE OUTSIDE!
OUTSIDE...
SLIP
SPLAT
...
KONNO ...?

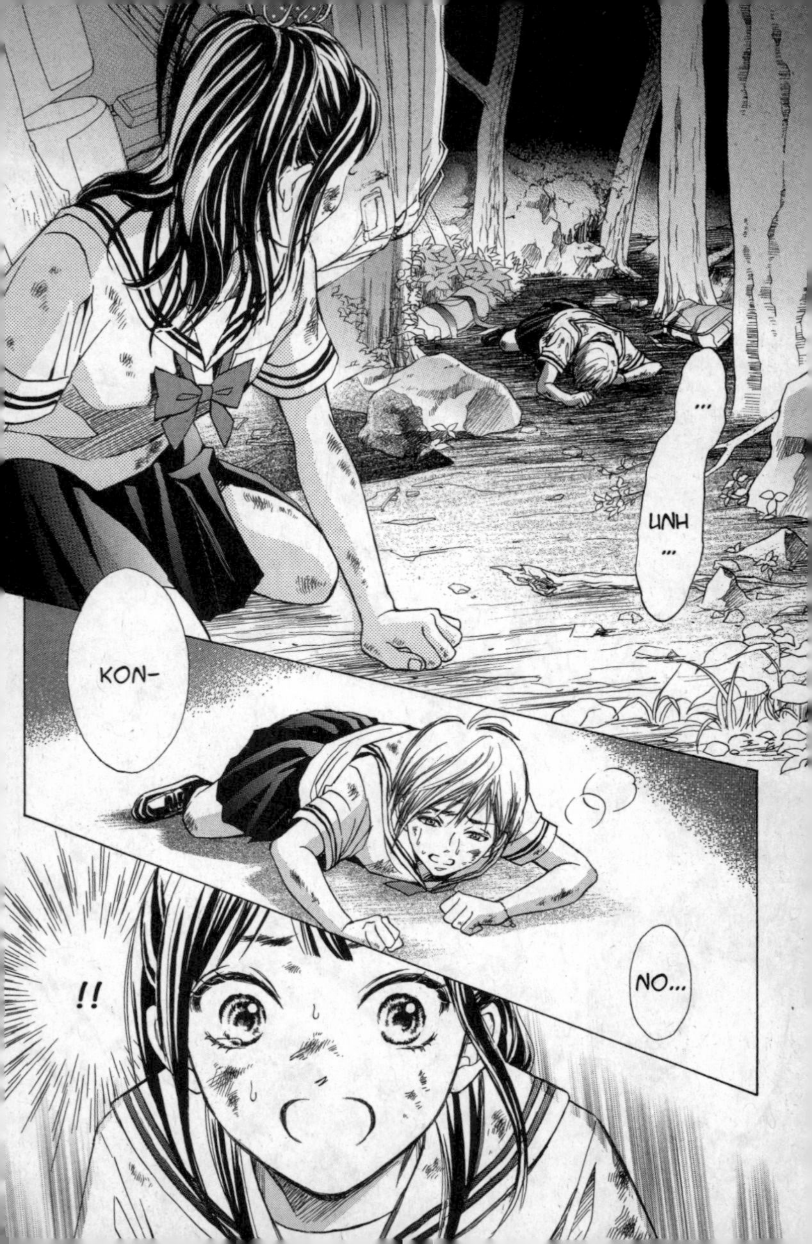

... UNH ...
KON-
NO...
!!

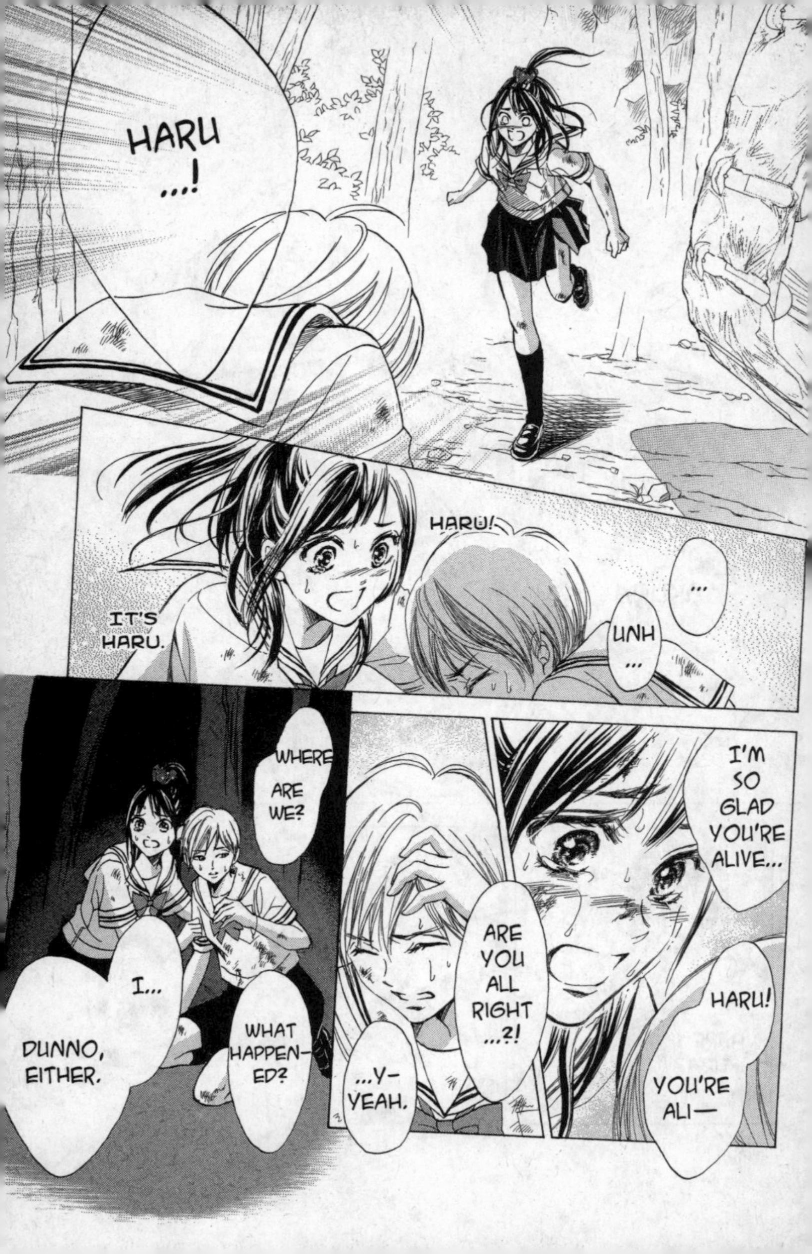
HARU ...!
...
UNH ...
HARU!
IT'S HARU.
I'M SO GLAD YOU'RE ALIVE...
HARU!
YOU'RE ALI—
ARE YOU ALL RIGHT ...?!
...Y-YEAH.
WHERE ARE WE?
WHAT HAPPEN-ED?
I... DUNNO, EITHER.

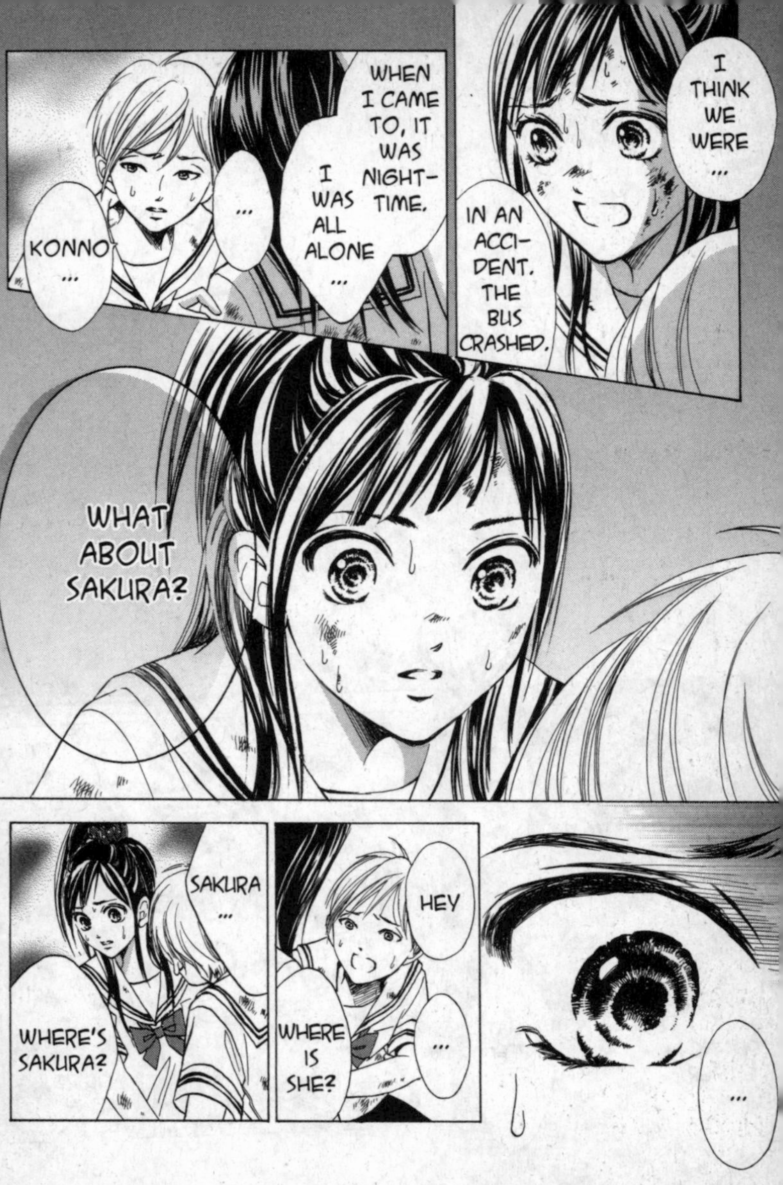
I THINK WE WERE ...
IN AN ACCIDENT. THE BUS CRASHED.
WHEN I CAME TO, IT WAS NIGHTTIME.
I WAS ALL ALONE ...
...
KONNO ...
WHAT ABOUT SAKURA?
...
HEY
...
WHERE IS SHE?
SAKURA ...
WHERE'S SAKURA?

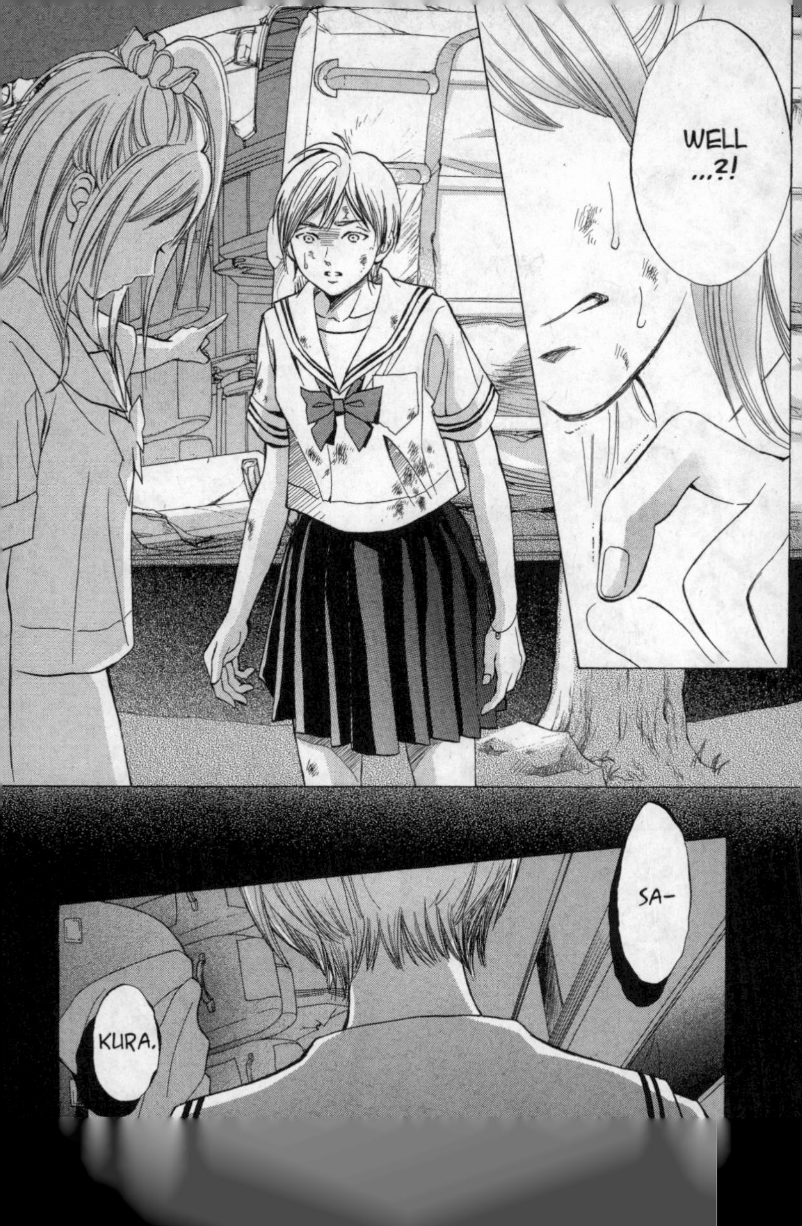
WELL ...?!
SA-
KURA.

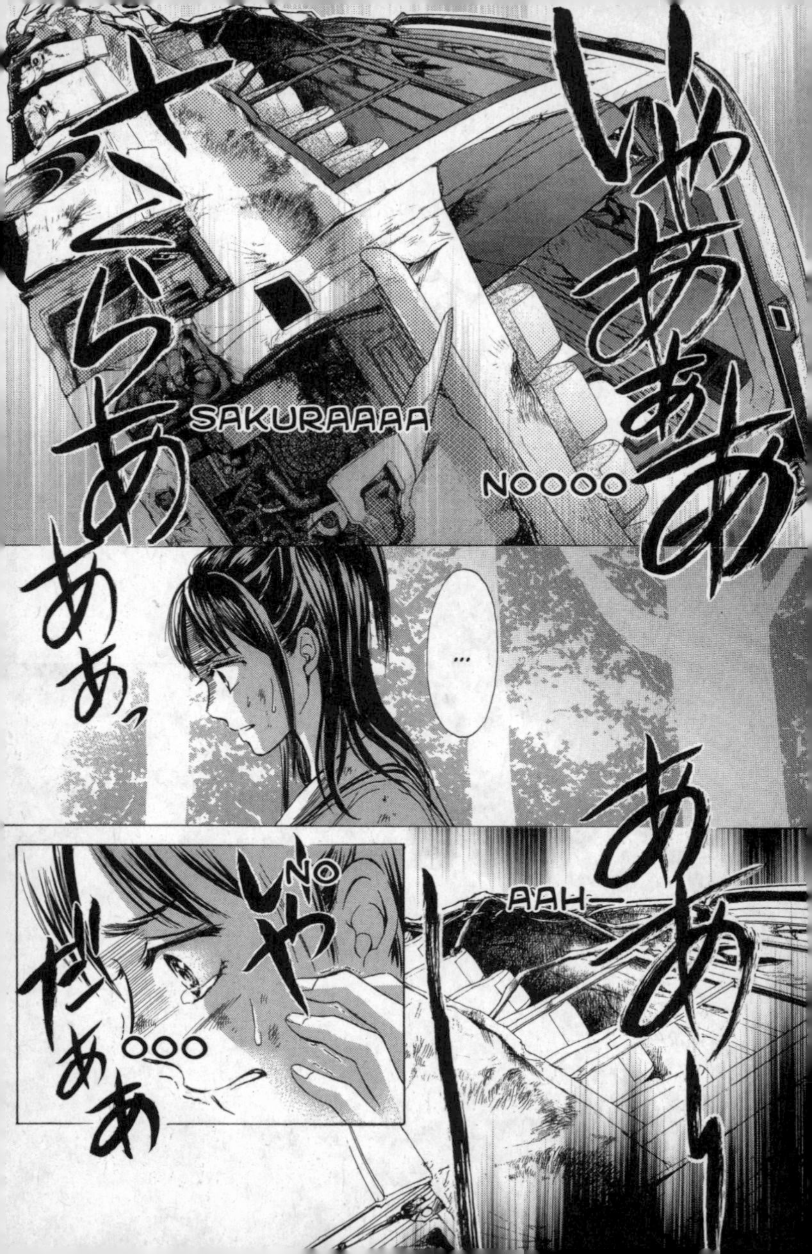

いやあああ
NOOOO
さくらあ
SAKURAAAA
ああっ
...
あああ
AAH—
いや
NO
だあああ
OOO

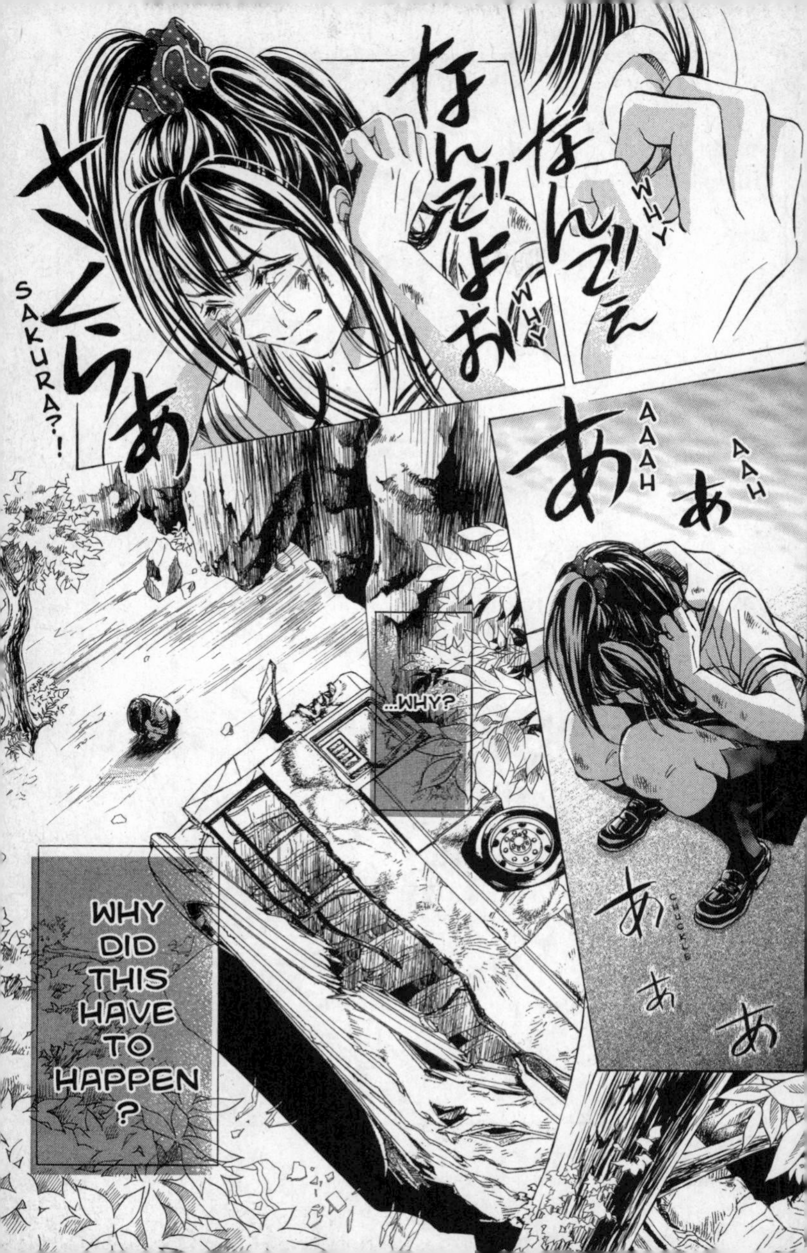
なんでぇ
WHY
なんでよお
WHY
さくらあ
SAKURA?!
あ
AAAH
あ
AAH
あ
CHUCKLE
あ
あ
...WHY?
WHY DID THIS HAVE TO HAPPEN?

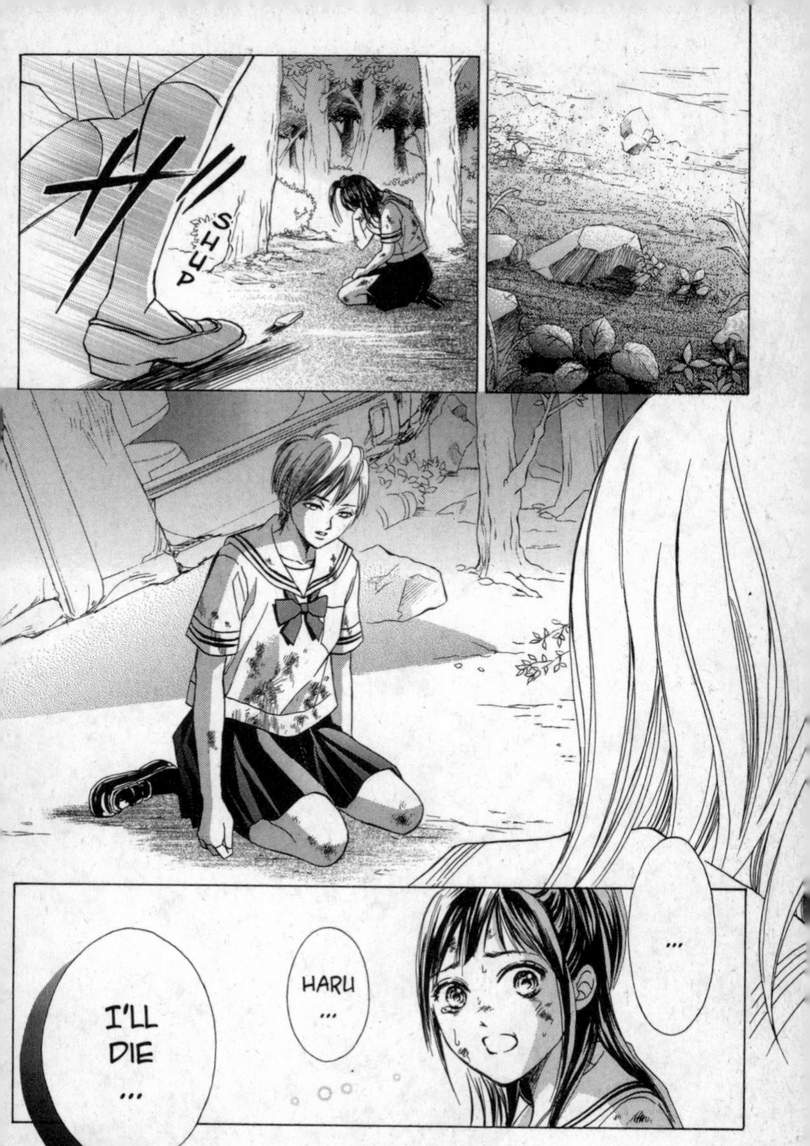
SHUP
...
HARU ...
I'LL DIE ...

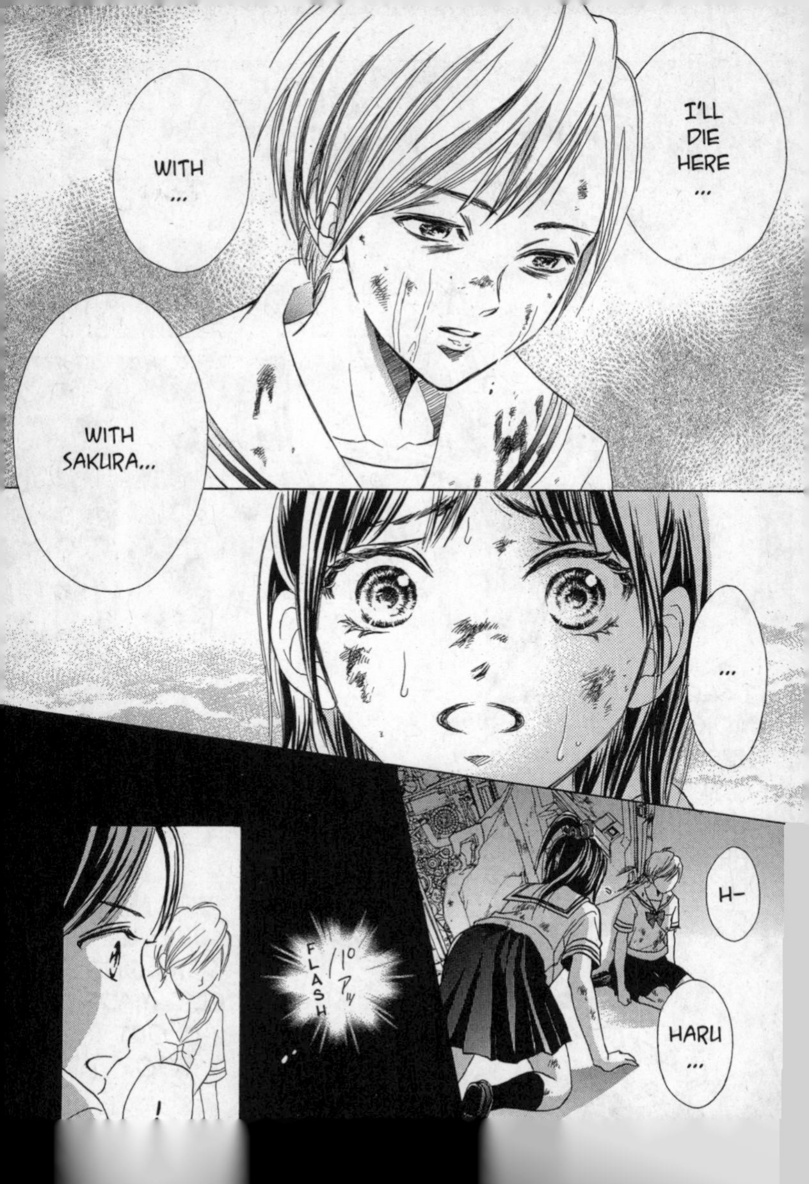

I'LL DIE HERE ...
WITH ...
WITH SAKURA...
...
H-
HARU ...
FLASH
!

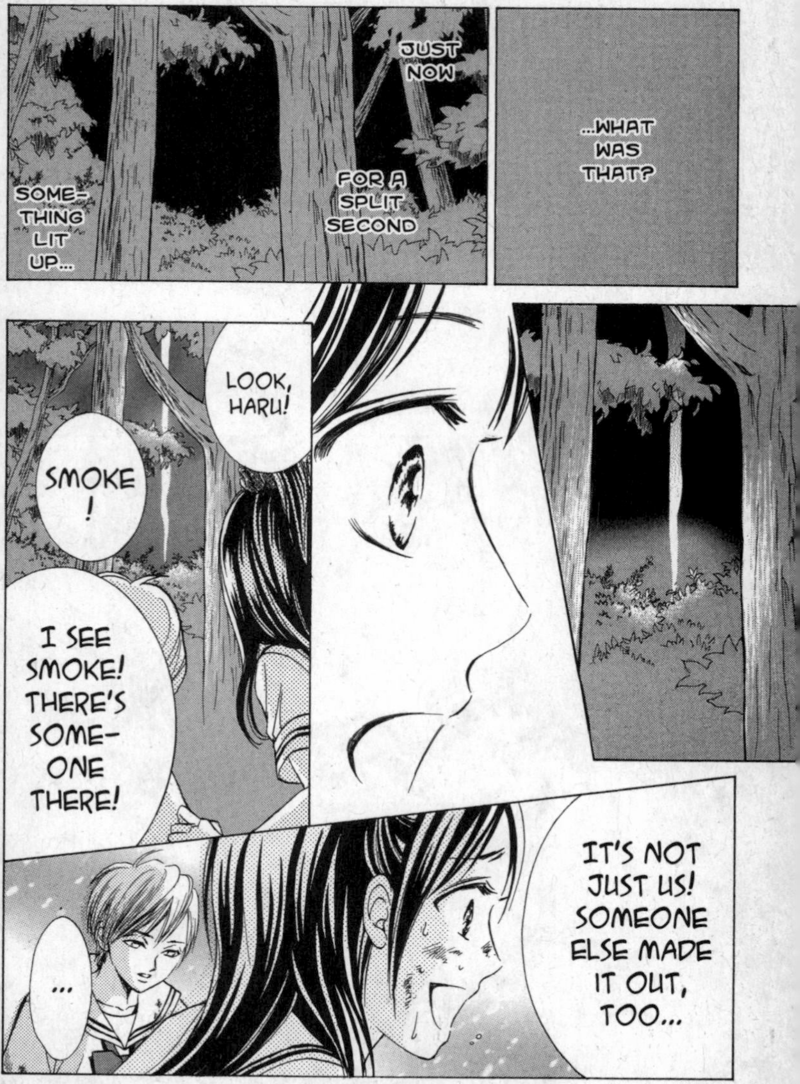
...WHAT WAS THAT?
JUST NOW
FOR A SPLIT SECOND
SOME-THING LIT UP...
LOOK, HARU!
SMOKE!
I SEE SMOKE! THERE'S SOME-ONE THERE!
IT'S NOT JUST US! SOMEONE ELSE MADE IT OUT, TOO...
...

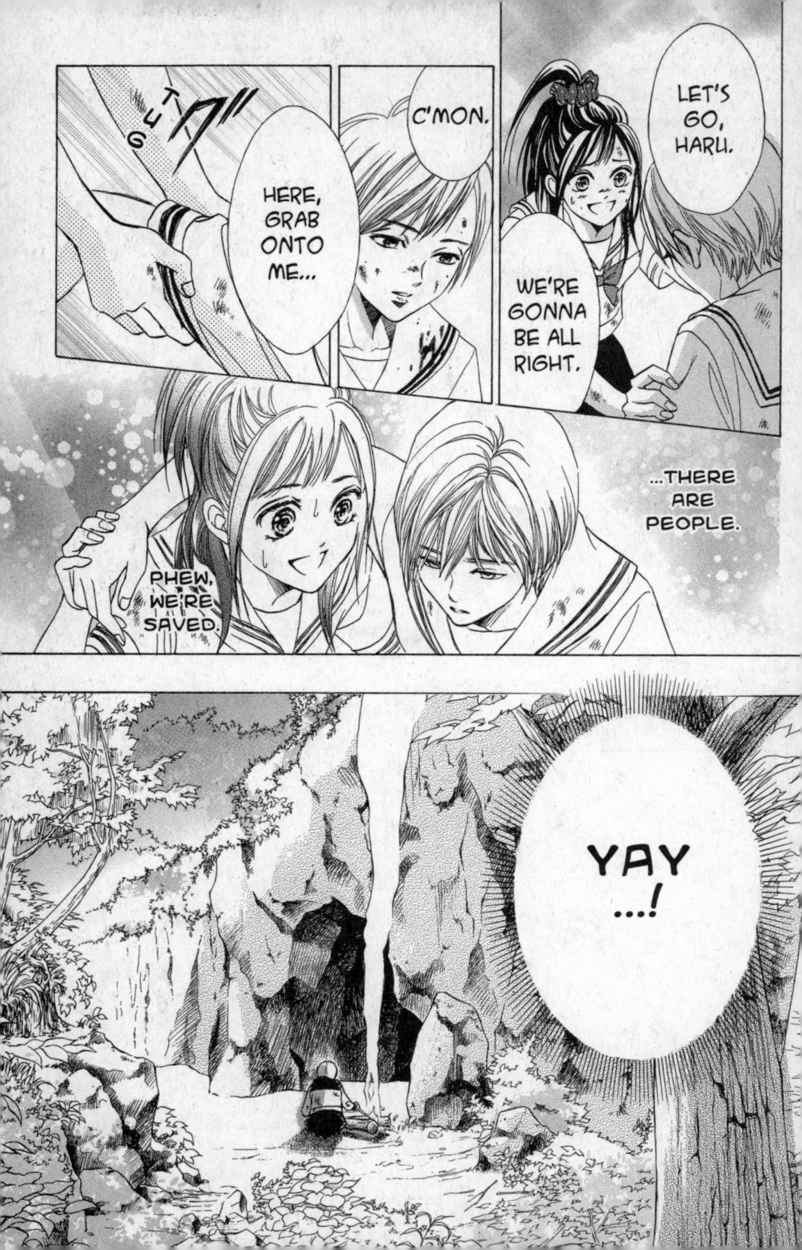
LET'S GO, HARU.
WE'RE GONNA BE ALL RIGHT.
C'MON.
HERE, GRAB ONTO ME...
TUG
...THERE ARE PEOPLE.
PHEW, WE'RE SAVED.
YAY ...!

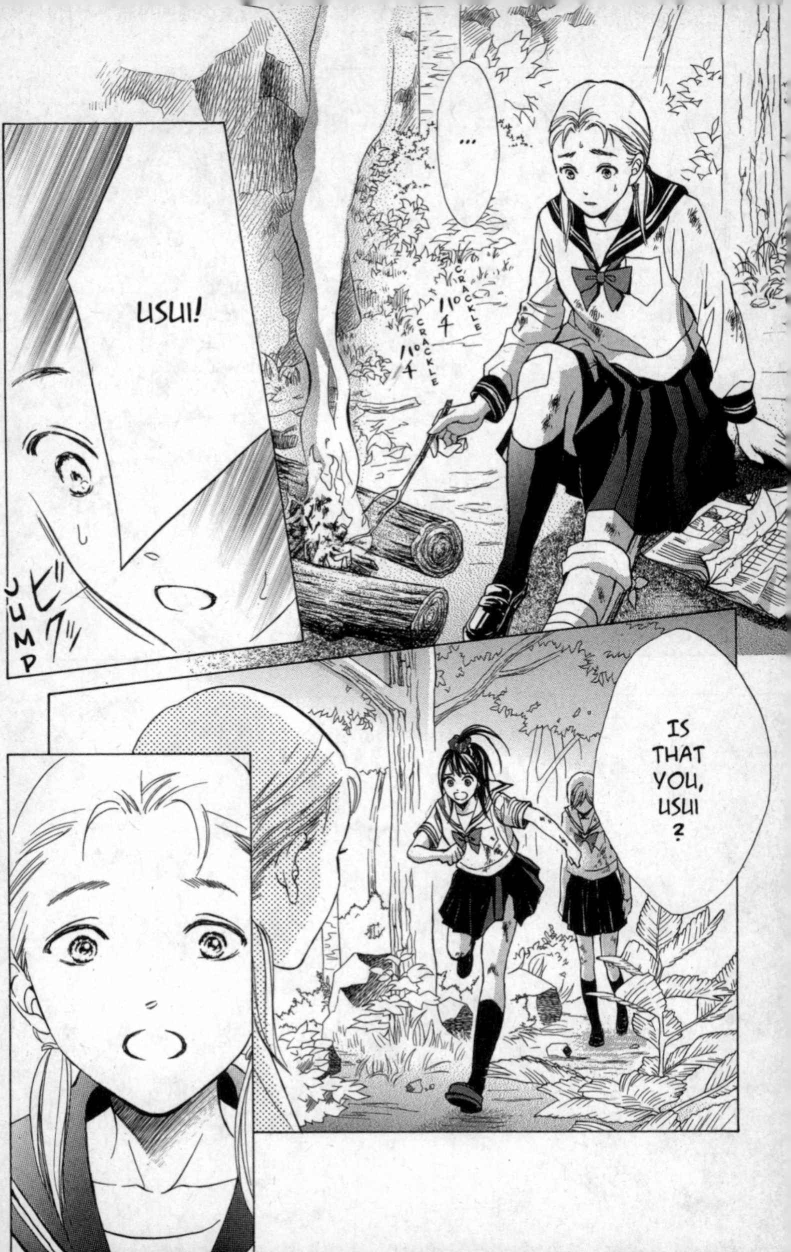
...
パチ CRACKLE
パチ CRACKLE
USUI!
ビクッ JUMP
IS THAT YOU, USUI?

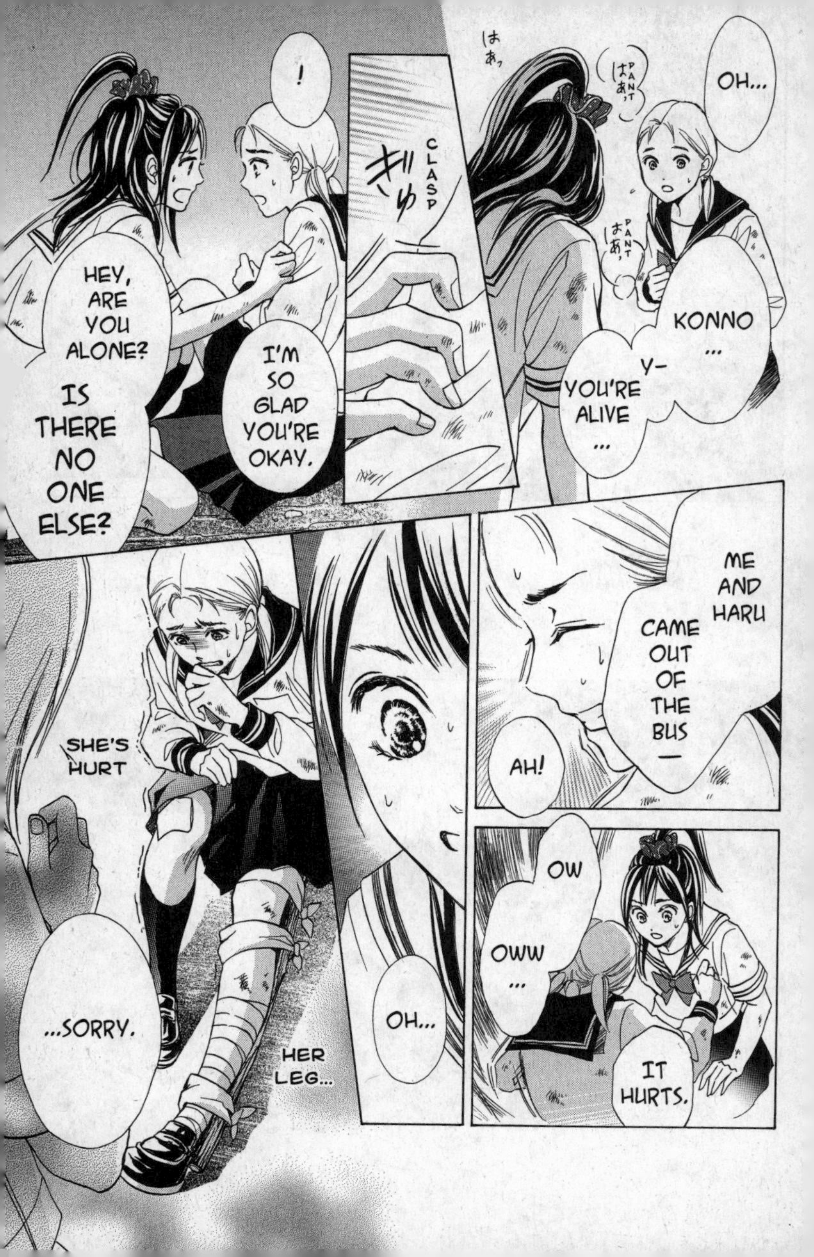

OH...
はあっ PANT
はあ PANT
はあっ
KONNO ...
Y-YOU'RE ALIVE ...
ぎゅ CLASP
!
I'M SO GLAD YOU'RE OKAY.
HEY, ARE YOU ALONE?
IS THERE NO ONE ELSE?
ME AND HARU CAME OUT OF THE BUS —
AH!
OW
OWW ...
IT HURTS.
OH...
HER LEG...
SHE'S HURT
...SORRY.

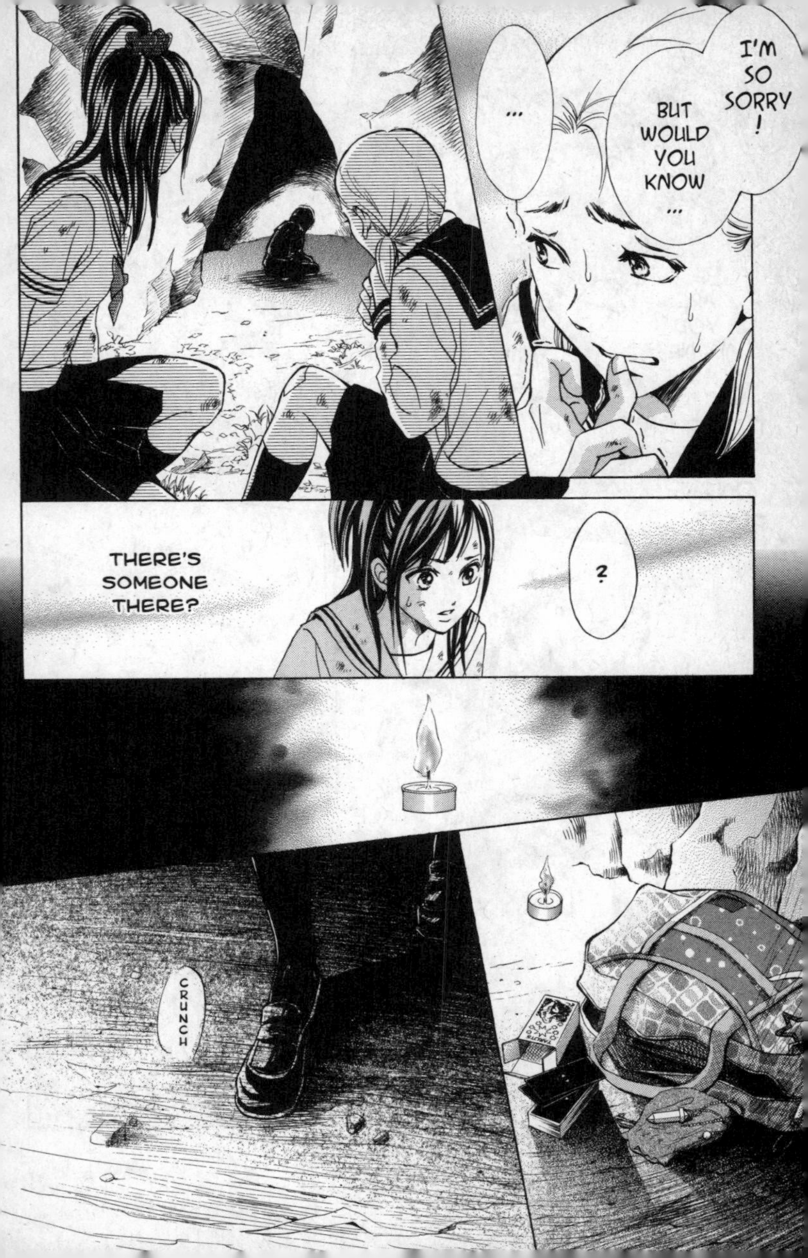
I'M SO SORRY!
BUT WOULD YOU KNOW ...
...
?
THERE'S SOMEONE THERE?
CRUNCH

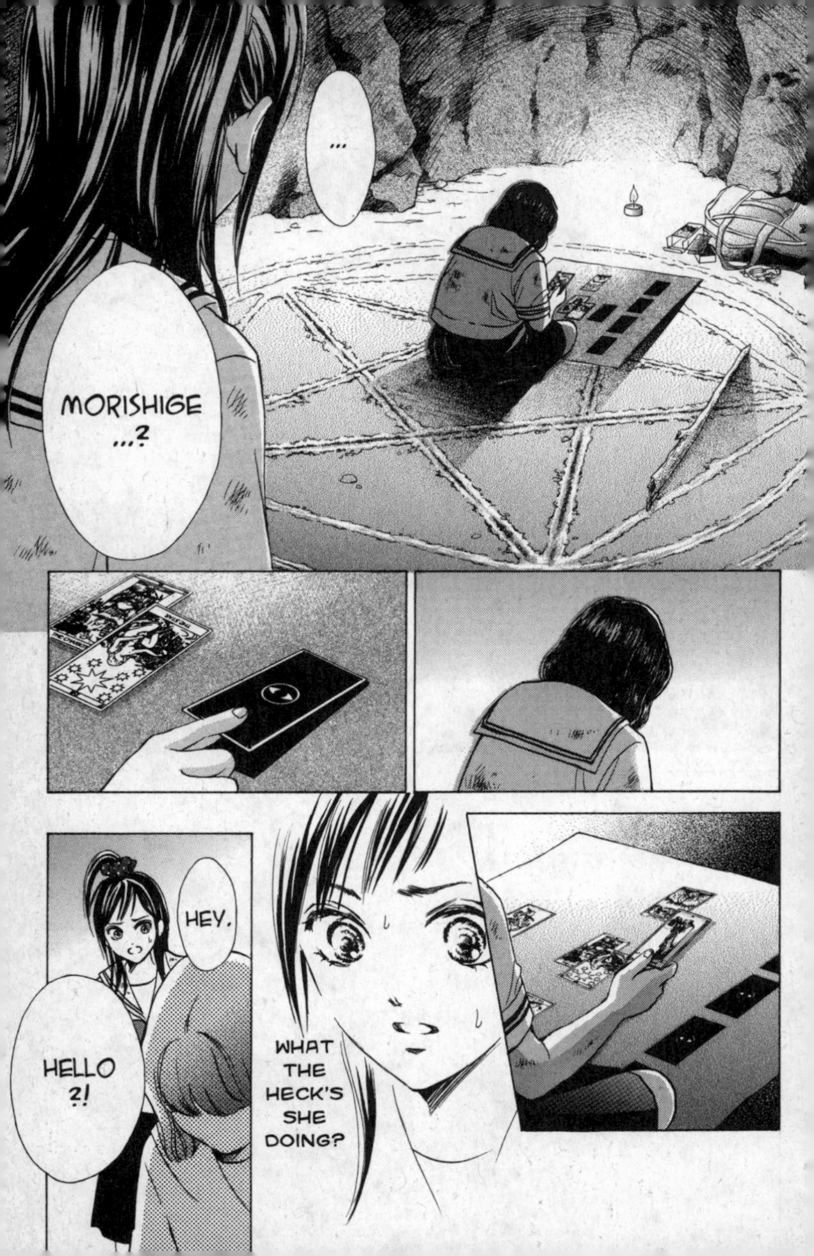
...
MORISHIGE ...?
WHAT THE HECK'S SHE DOING?
HEY.
HELLO ?!

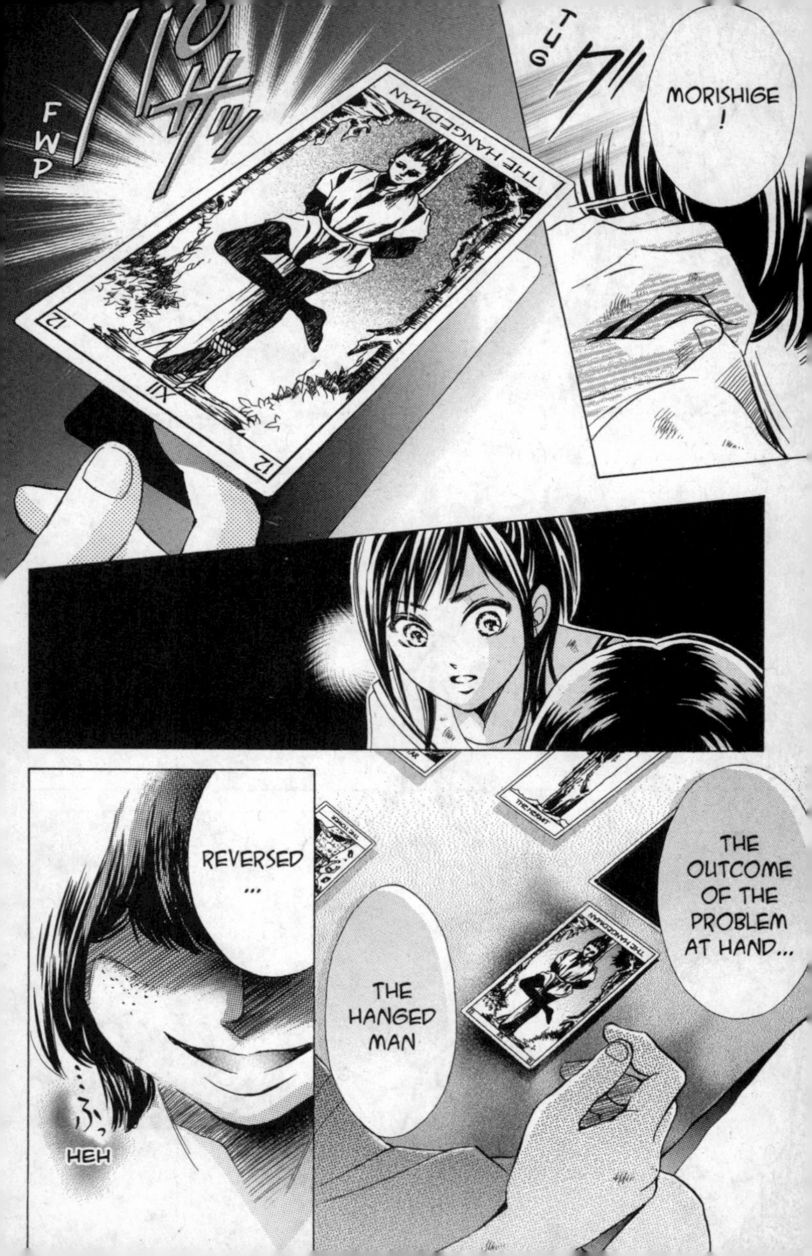
TUG
MORISHIGE
!
FWP
THE HANGEDMAN
XII
12
12
THE OUTCOME OF THE PROBLEM AT HAND...
THE HANGED MAN
REVERSED
...
…ふっ
HEH

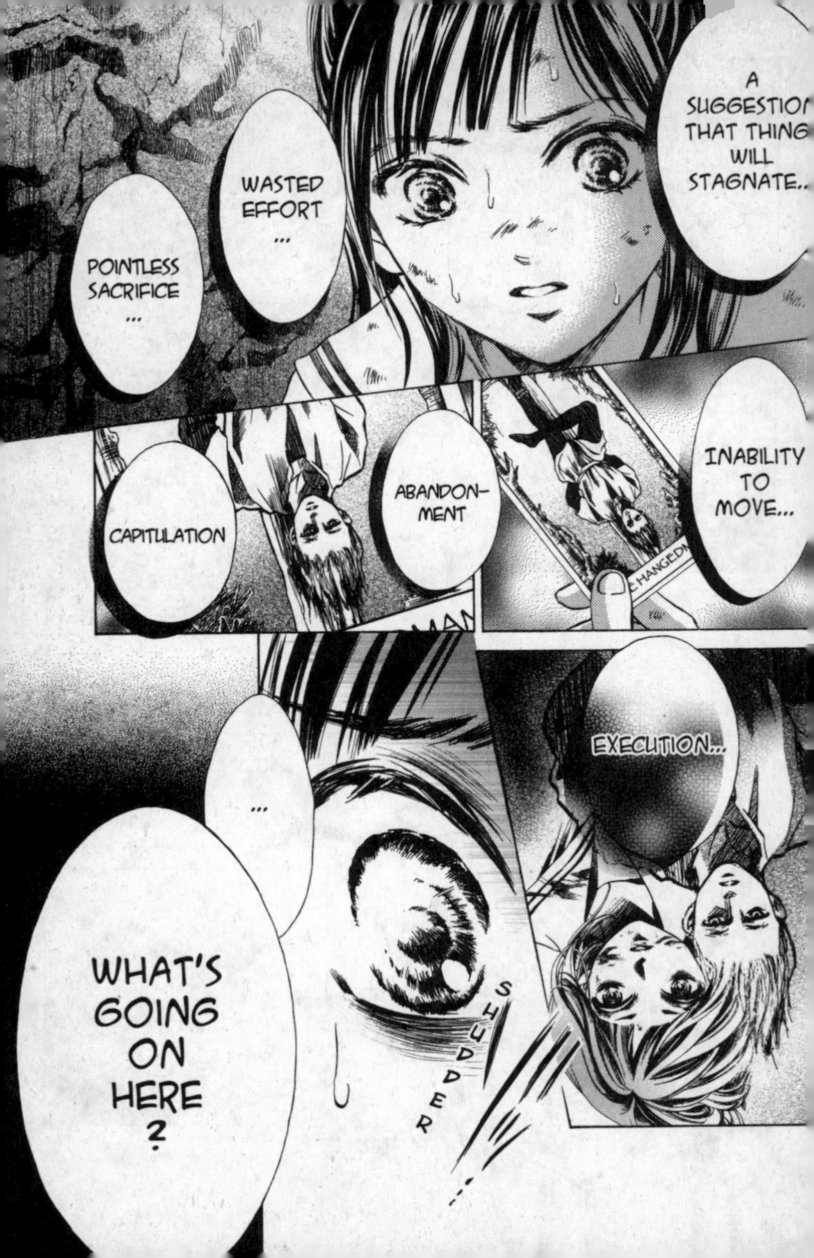
A SUGGESTIO THAT THING WILL STAGNATE..
WASTED EFFORT ...
POINTLESS SACRIFICE ...
INABILITY TO MOVE...
ABANDONMENT
CAPITULATION
EXECUTION...
...
SHUDDER...
WHAT'S GOING ON HERE?

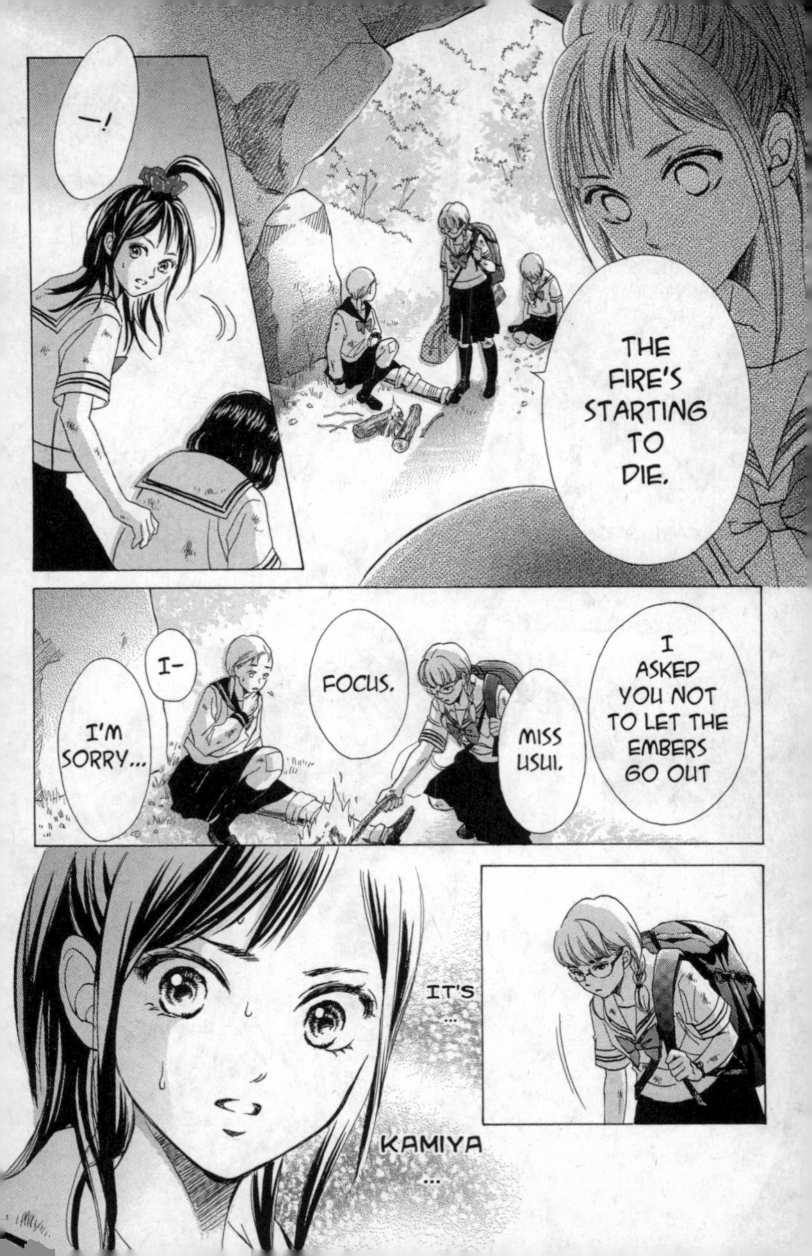
THE FIRE'S STARTING TO DIE.
—!
I ASKED YOU NOT TO LET THE EMBERS GO OUT
MISS USUI.
FOCUS.
I–
I'M SORRY...
IT'S ...
KAMIYA ...

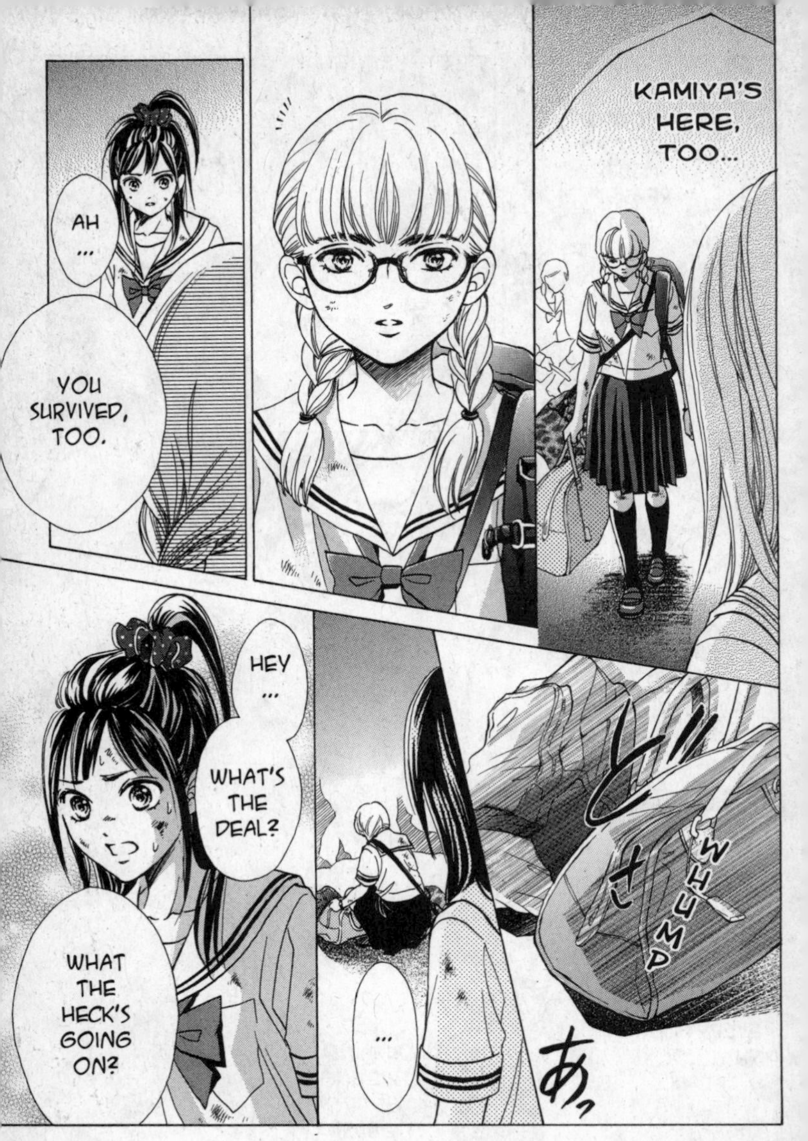
KAMIYA'S HERE, TOO...
AH ...
YOU SURVIVED, TOO.
どさ
WHUMP
あっ
...
HEY ...
WHAT'S THE DEAL?
WHAT THE HECK'S GOING ON?

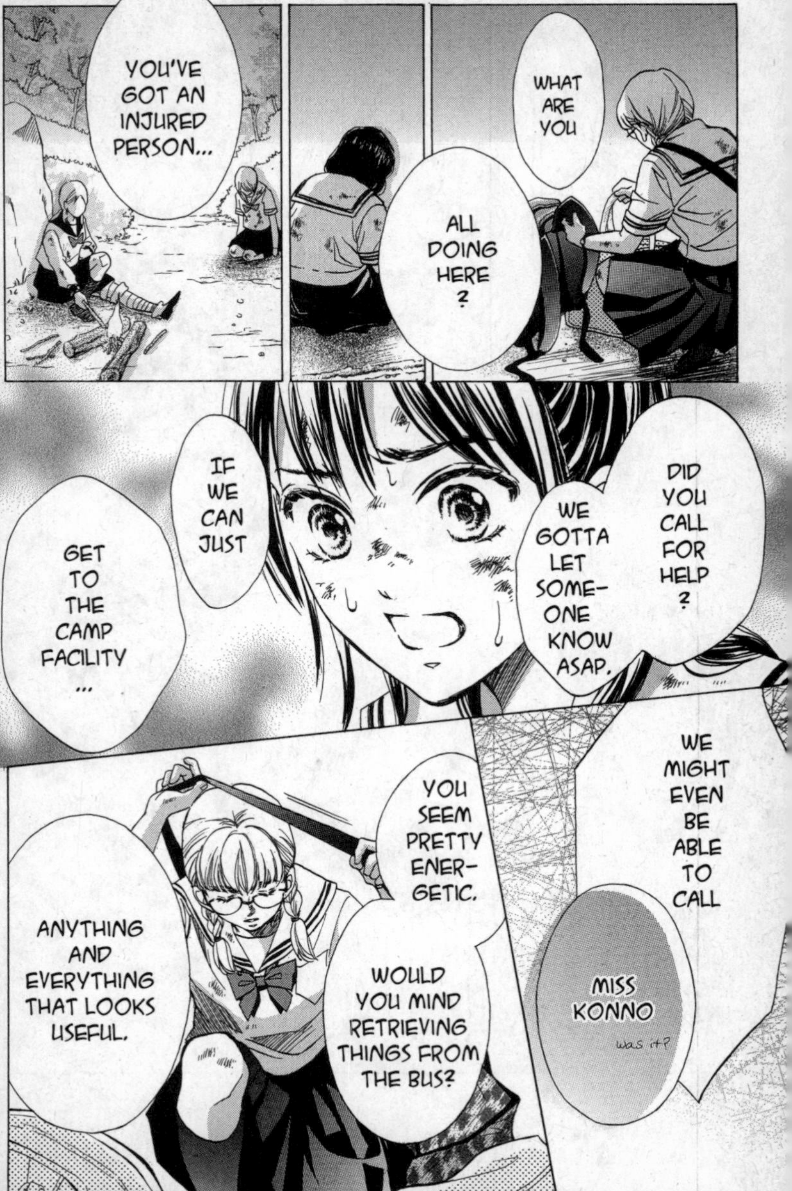
WHAT ARE YOU
ALL DOING HERE?
YOU'VE GOT AN INJURED PERSON...
DID YOU CALL FOR HELP?
WE GOTTA LET SOME-ONE KNOW ASAP.
IF WE CAN JUST
GET TO THE CAMP FACILITY ...
WE MIGHT EVEN BE ABLE TO CALL
MISS KONNO
was it?
YOU SEEM PRETTY ENER-GETIC.
WOULD YOU MIND RETRIEVING THINGS FROM THE BUS?
ANYTHING AND EVERYTHING THAT LOOKS USEFUL.

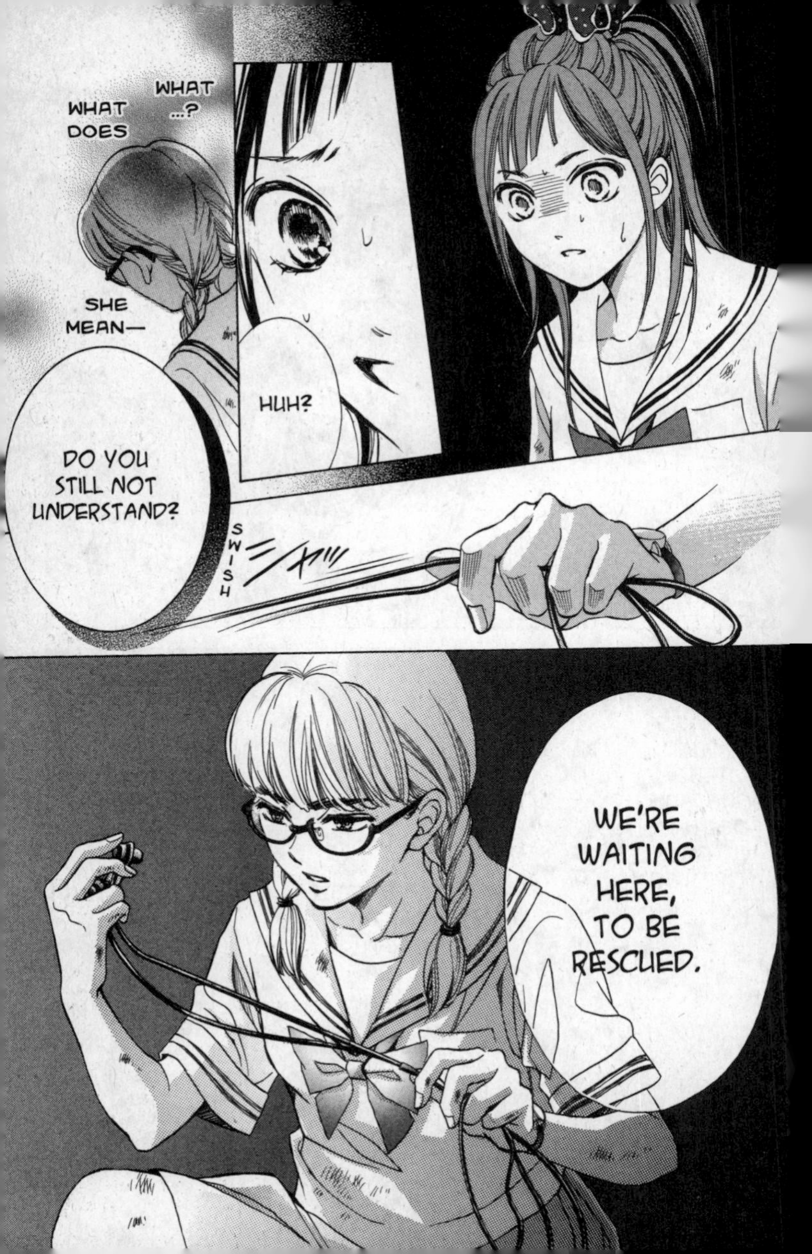
HUH?
WHAT ...?
WHAT DOES SHE MEAN—
DO YOU STILL NOT UNDERSTAND?
SWISH
WE'RE WAITING HERE, TO BE RESCUED.

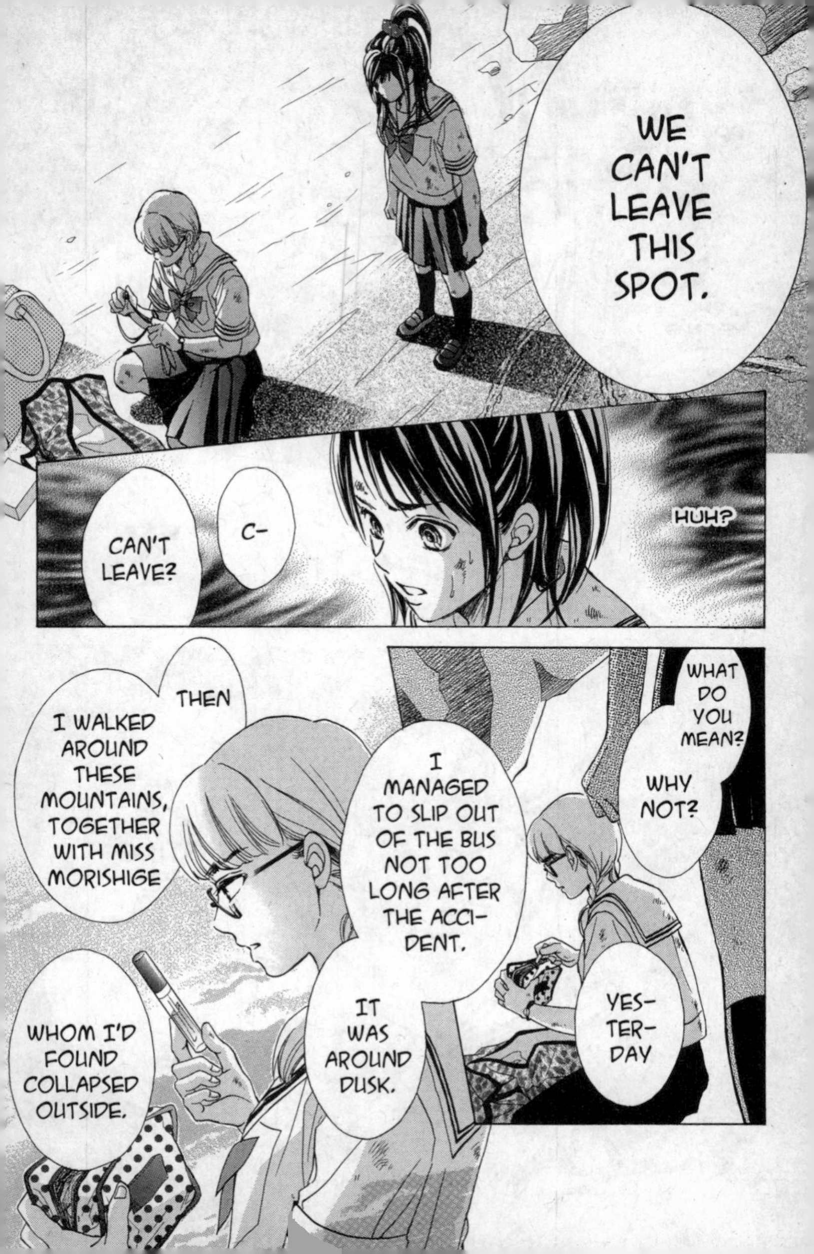
WE CAN'T LEAVE THIS SPOT.
HUH?
C-
CAN'T LEAVE?
WHAT DO YOU MEAN?
WHY NOT?
YES-TER-DAY
I MANAGED TO SLIP OUT OF THE BUS NOT TOO LONG AFTER THE ACCI-DENT.
IT WAS AROUND DUSK.
THEN I WALKED AROUND THESE MOUNTAINS, TOGETHER WITH MISS MORISHIGE
WHOM I'D FOUND COLLAPSED OUTSIDE.

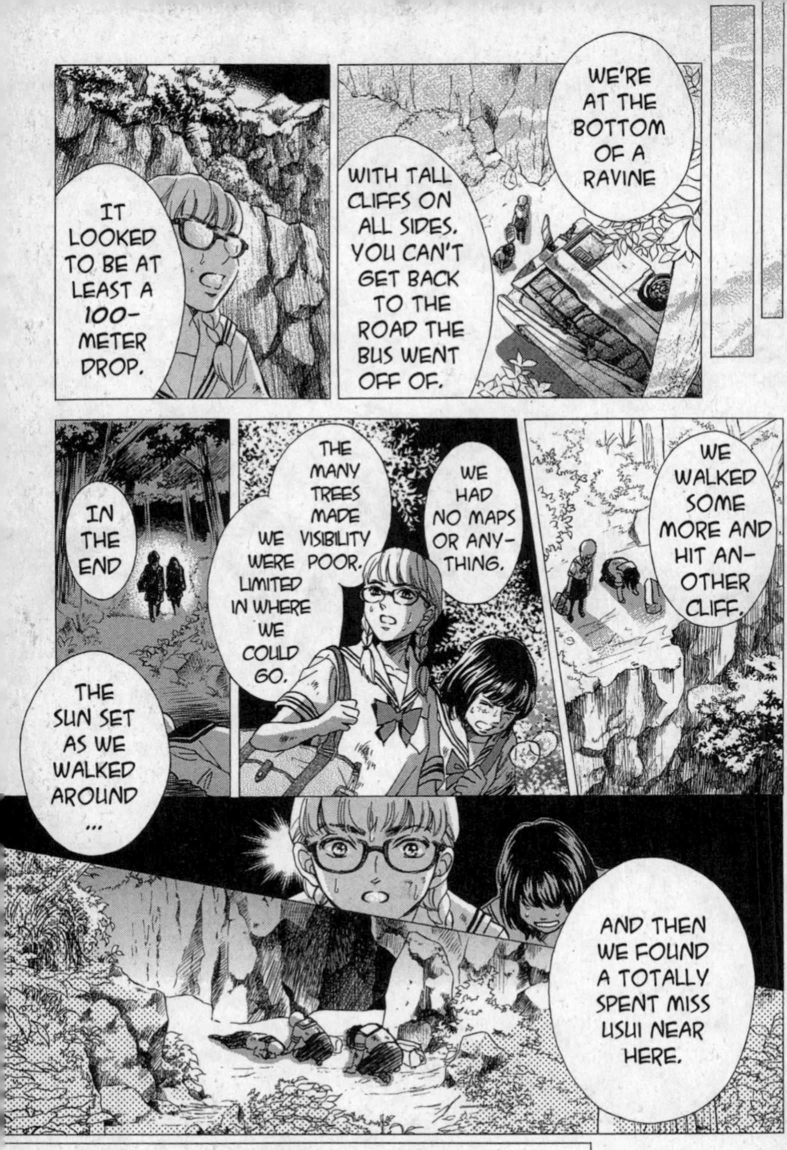
WE'RE AT THE BOTTOM OF A RAVINE
WITH TALL CLIFFS ON ALL SIDES. YOU CAN'T GET BACK TO THE ROAD THE BUS WENT OFF OF.
IT LOOKED TO BE AT LEAST A 100-METER DROP.
WE WALKED SOME MORE AND HIT ANOTHER CLIFF.
WE HAD NO MAPS OR ANYTHING.
THE MANY TREES MADE VISIBILITY POOR.
WE WERE LIMITED IN WHERE WE COULD GO.
IN THE END
THE SUN SET AS WE WALKED AROUND ...
AND THEN WE FOUND A TOTALLY SPENT MISS USUI NEAR HERE.

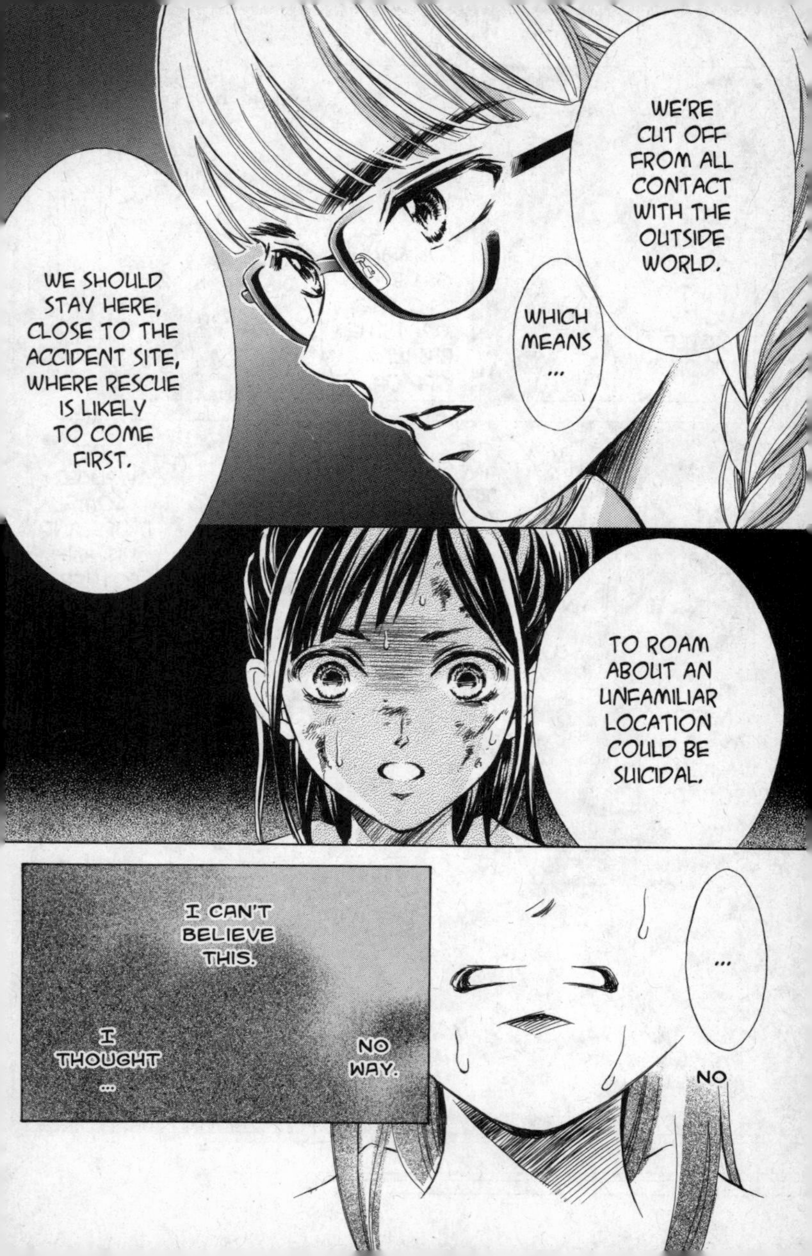
WE'RE CUT OFF FROM ALL CONTACT WITH THE OUTSIDE WORLD.
WHICH MEANS ...
WE SHOULD STAY HERE, CLOSE TO THE ACCIDENT SITE, WHERE RESCUE IS LIKELY TO COME FIRST.
TO ROAM ABOUT AN UNFAMILIAR LOCATION COULD BE SUICIDAL.
...
NO
I CAN'T BELIEVE THIS.
NO WAY.
I THOUGHT ...

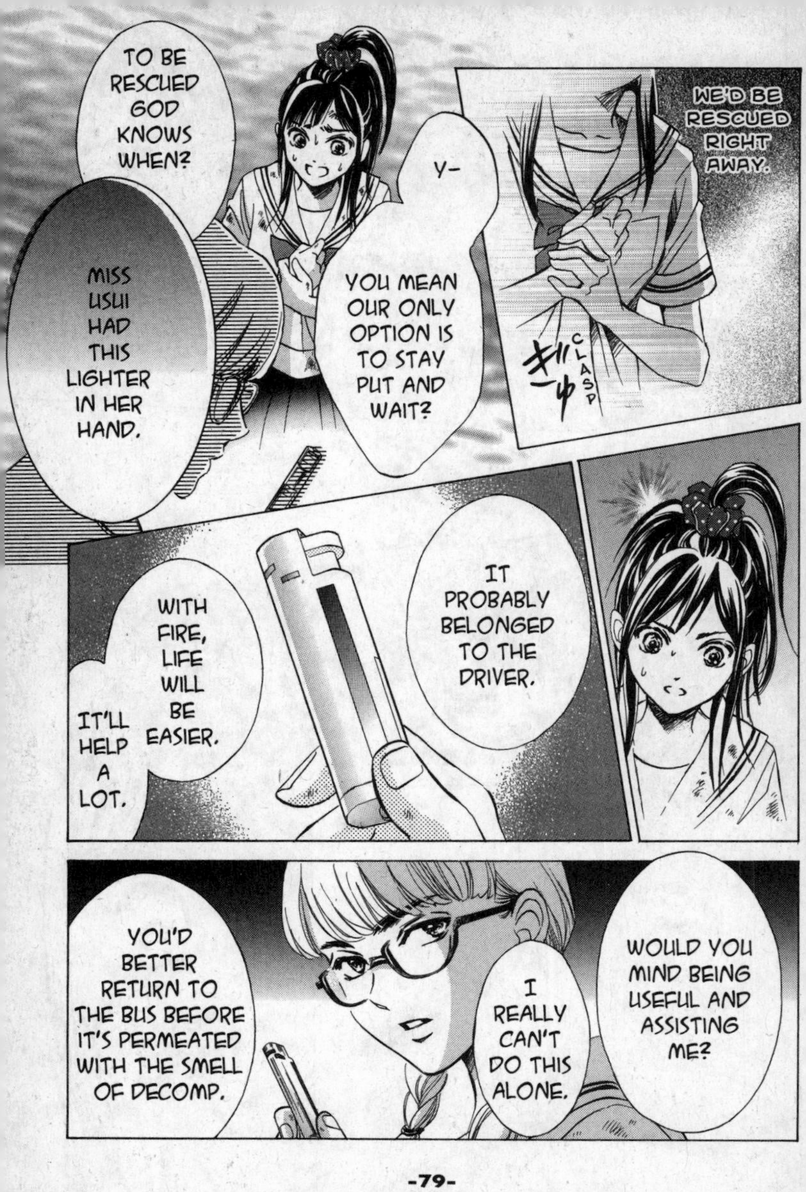
WE'D BE RESCUED RIGHT AWAY.
CLASP
Y-
YOU MEAN OUR ONLY OPTION IS TO STAY PUT AND WAIT?
TO BE RESCUED GOD KNOWS WHEN?
MISS USUI HAD THIS LIGHTER IN HER HAND.
IT PROBABLY BELONGED TO THE DRIVER.
WITH FIRE, LIFE WILL BE EASIER.
IT'LL HELP A LOT.
WOULD YOU MIND BEING USEFUL AND ASSISTING ME?
I REALLY CAN'T DO THIS ALONE.
YOU'D BETTER RETURN TO THE BUS BEFORE IT'S PERMEATED WITH THE SMELL OF DECOMP.

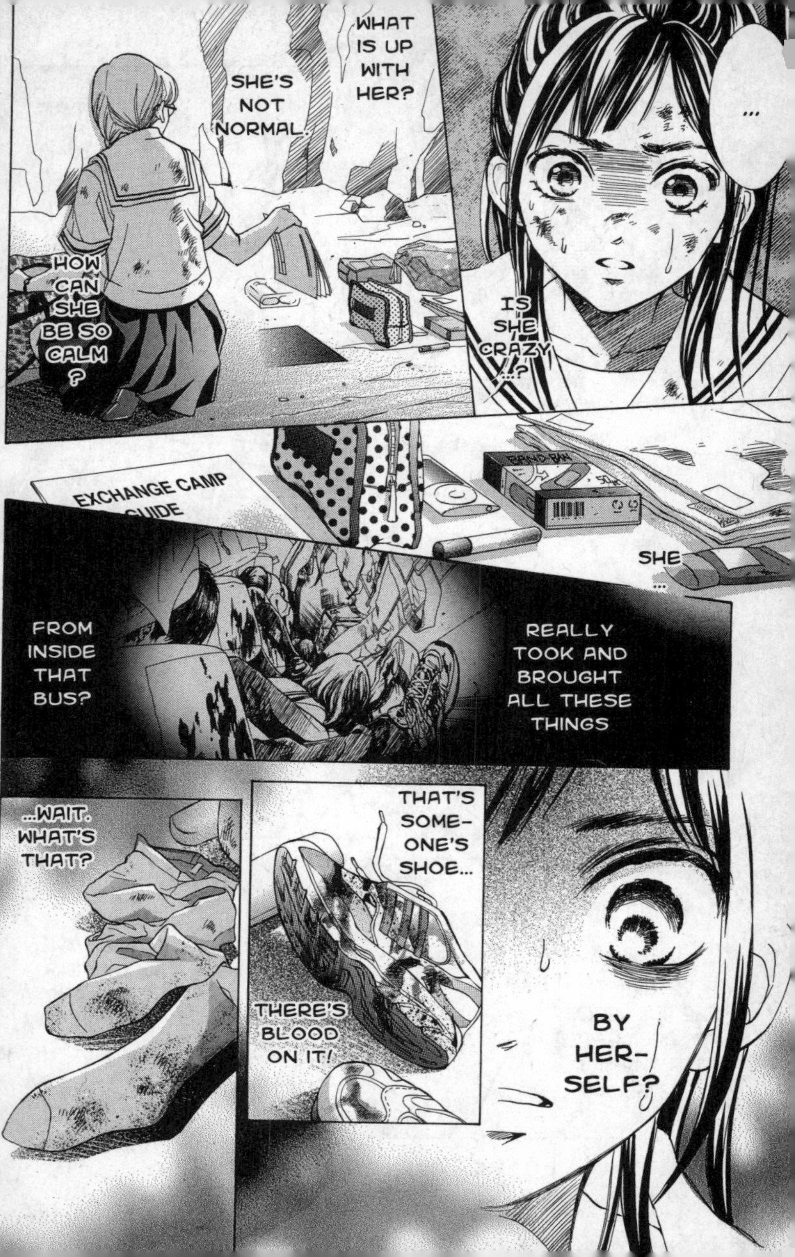
...
IS SHE CRAZY ...?
WHAT IS UP WITH HER?
SHE'S NOT NORMAL.
HOW CAN SHE BE SO CALM?
EXCHANGE CAMP
SHE ...
REALLY TOOK AND BROUGHT ALL THESE THINGS
FROM INSIDE THAT BUS?
BY HER-SELF?
THAT'S SOME-ONE'S SHOE...
THERE'S BLOOD ON IT!
...WAIT. WHAT'S THAT?

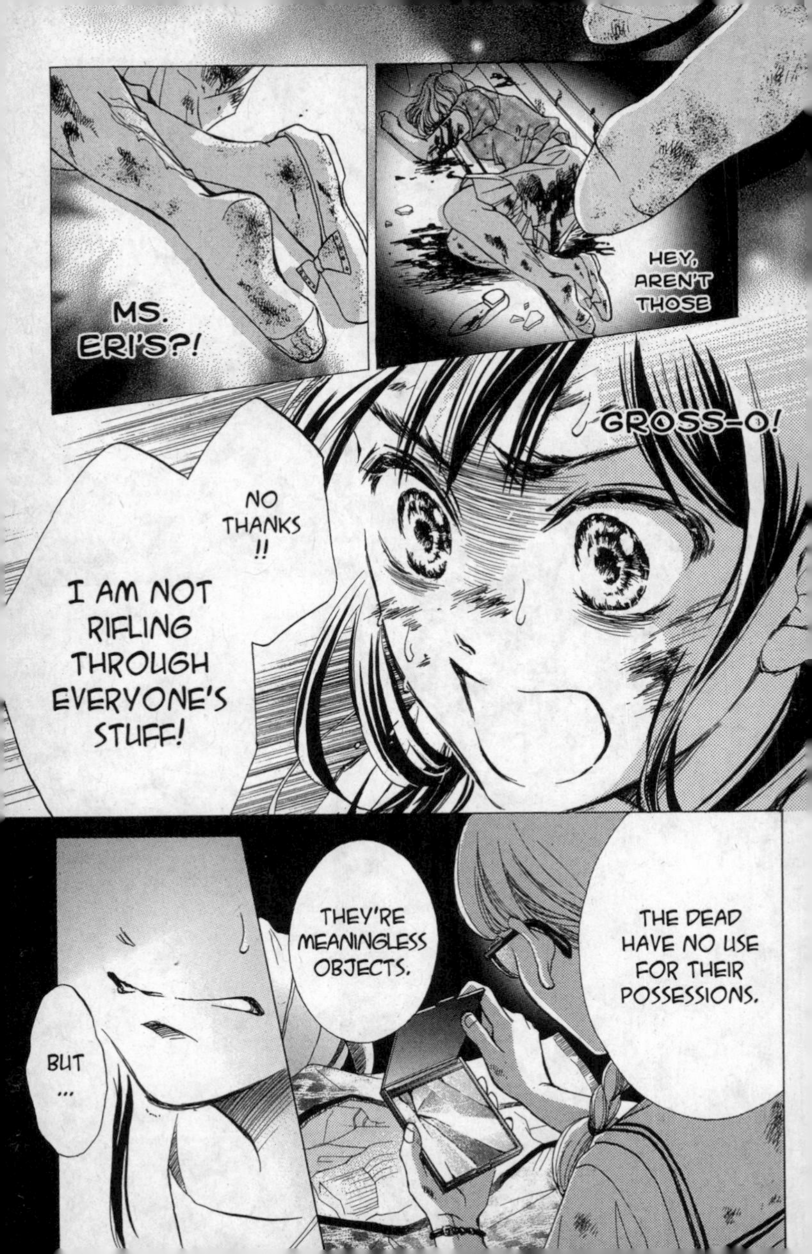
HEY, AREN'T THOSE
MS. ERI'S?!
GROSS-O!
NO THANKS !!
I AM NOT RIFLING THROUGH EVERYONE'S STUFF!
THE DEAD HAVE NO USE FOR THEIR POSSESSIONS.
THEY'RE MEANINGLESS OBJECTS.
BUT ...

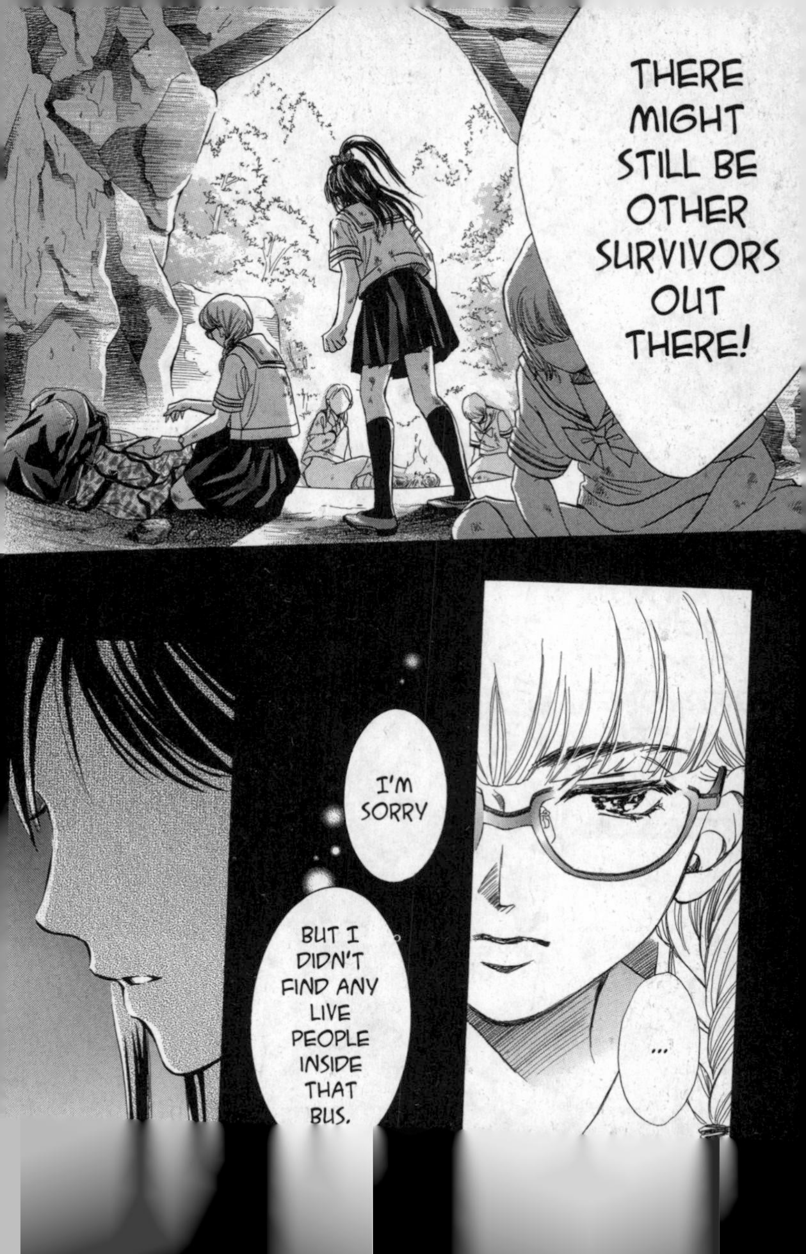
THERE MIGHT STILL BE OTHER SURVIVORS OUT THERE!
...
I'M SORRY
BUT I DIDN'T FIND ANY LIVE PEOPLE INSIDE THAT BUS.

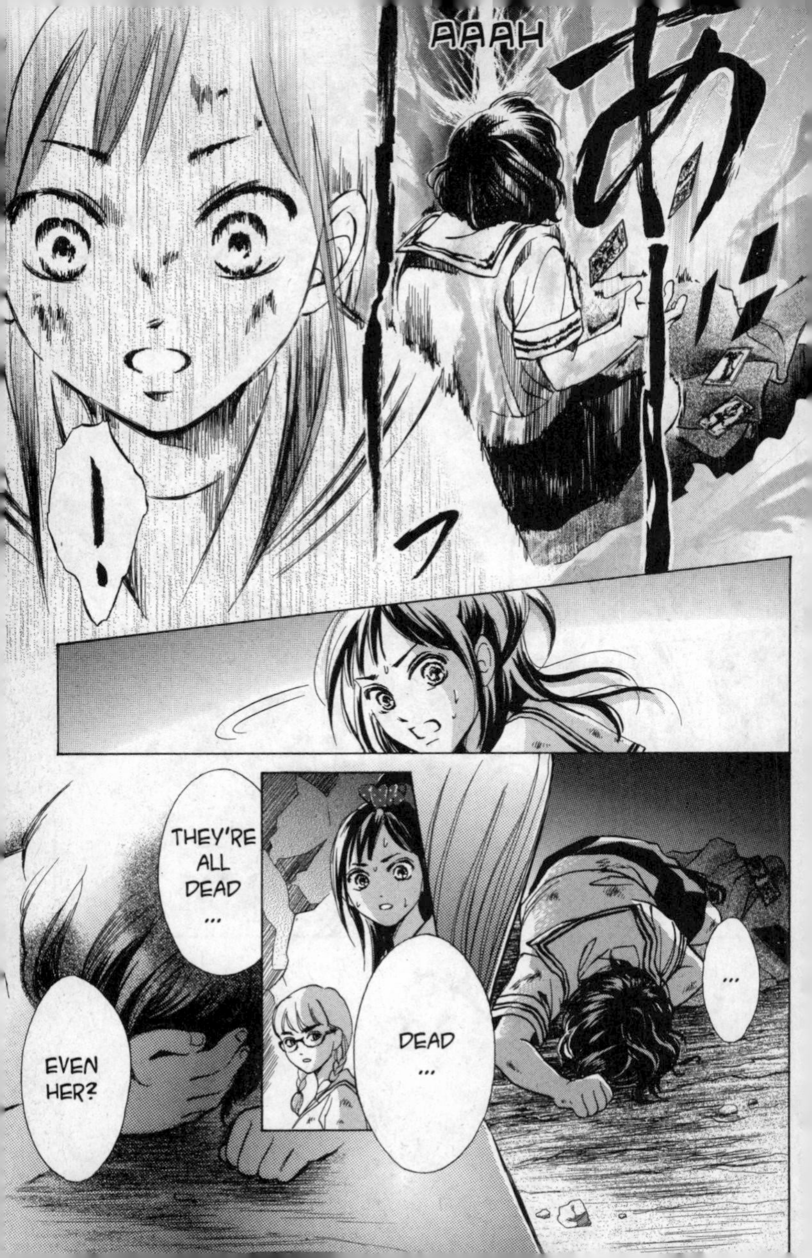
AAAH
あっ!!
!
THEY'RE ALL DEAD ...
...
DEAD ...
EVEN HER?

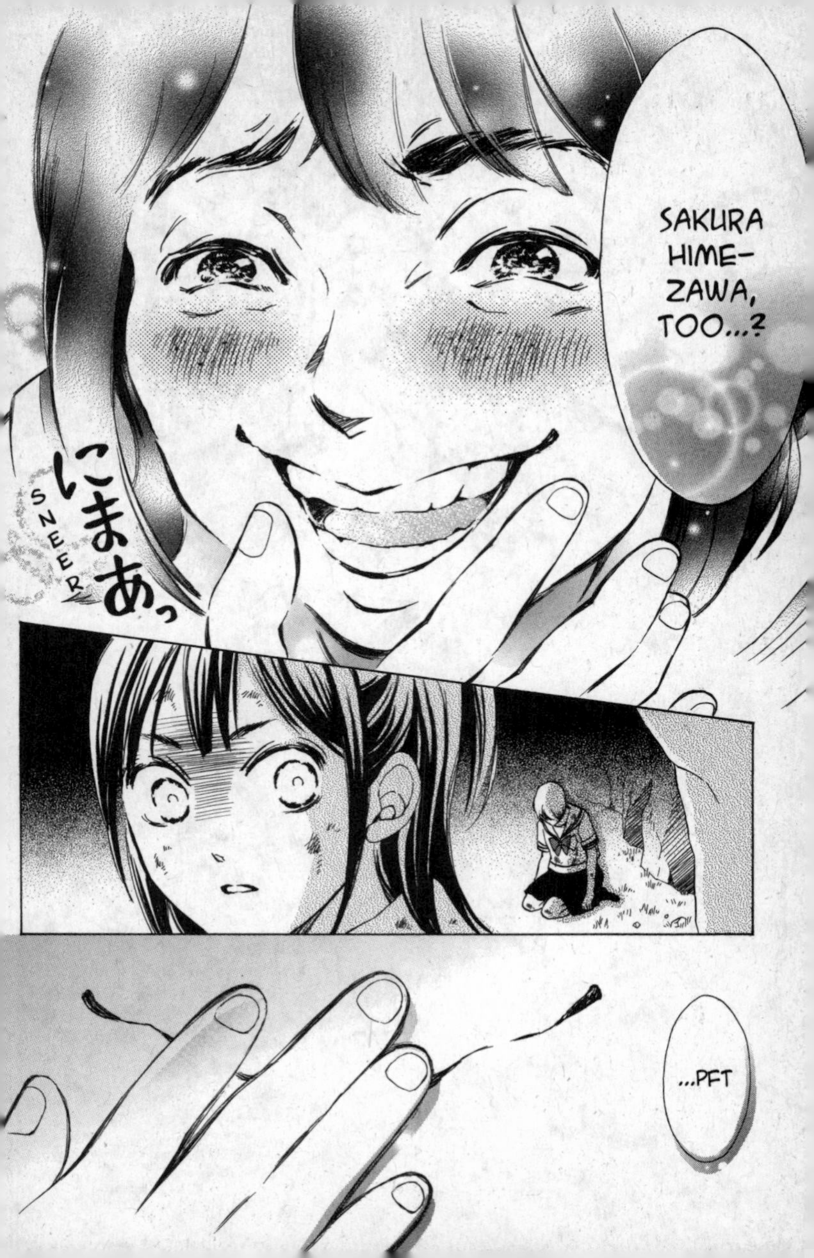
SAKURA HIME-ZAWA, TOO...?
にまあっ
SNEER
...PFT

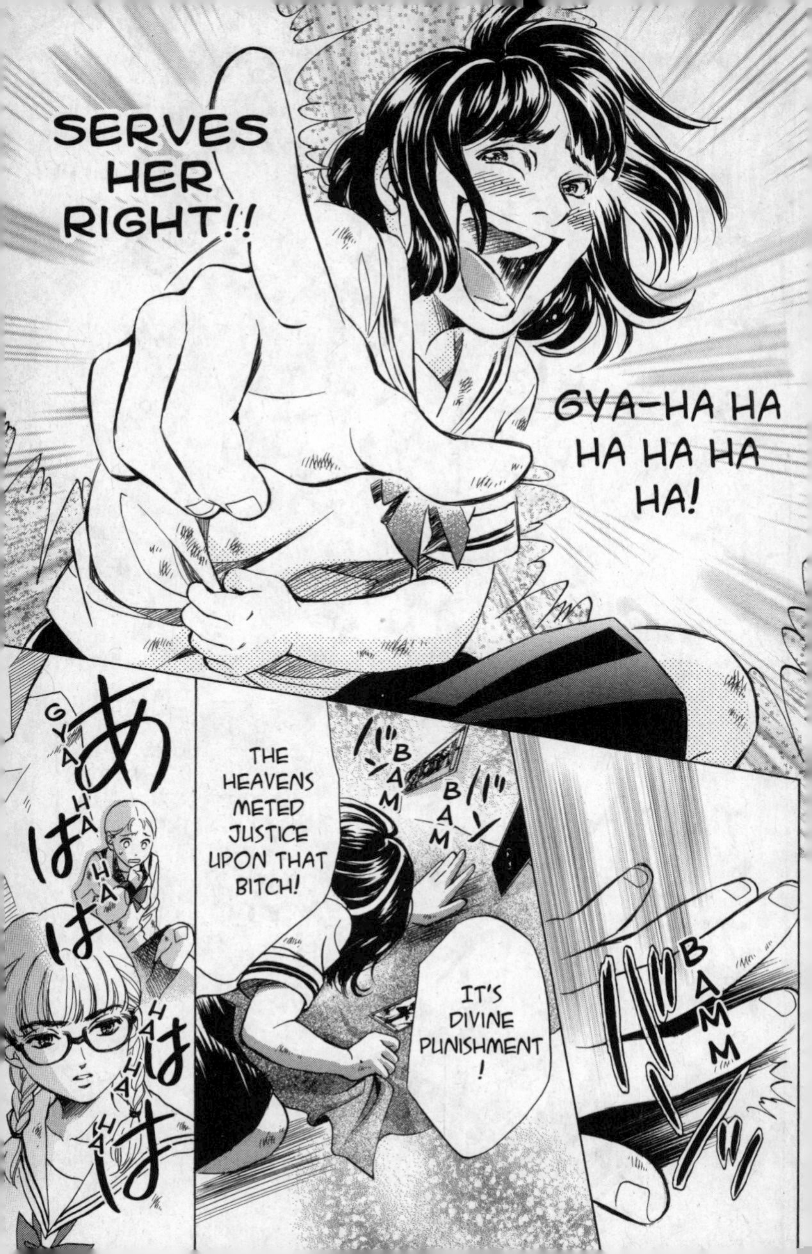
SERVES HER RIGHT!!
GYA-HA HA HA HA HA HA!
BAMM
BAM BAM
THE HEAVENS METED JUSTICE UPON THAT BITCH!
IT'S DIVINE PUNISHMENT!
あははは
GYA HA HA HA HA HA

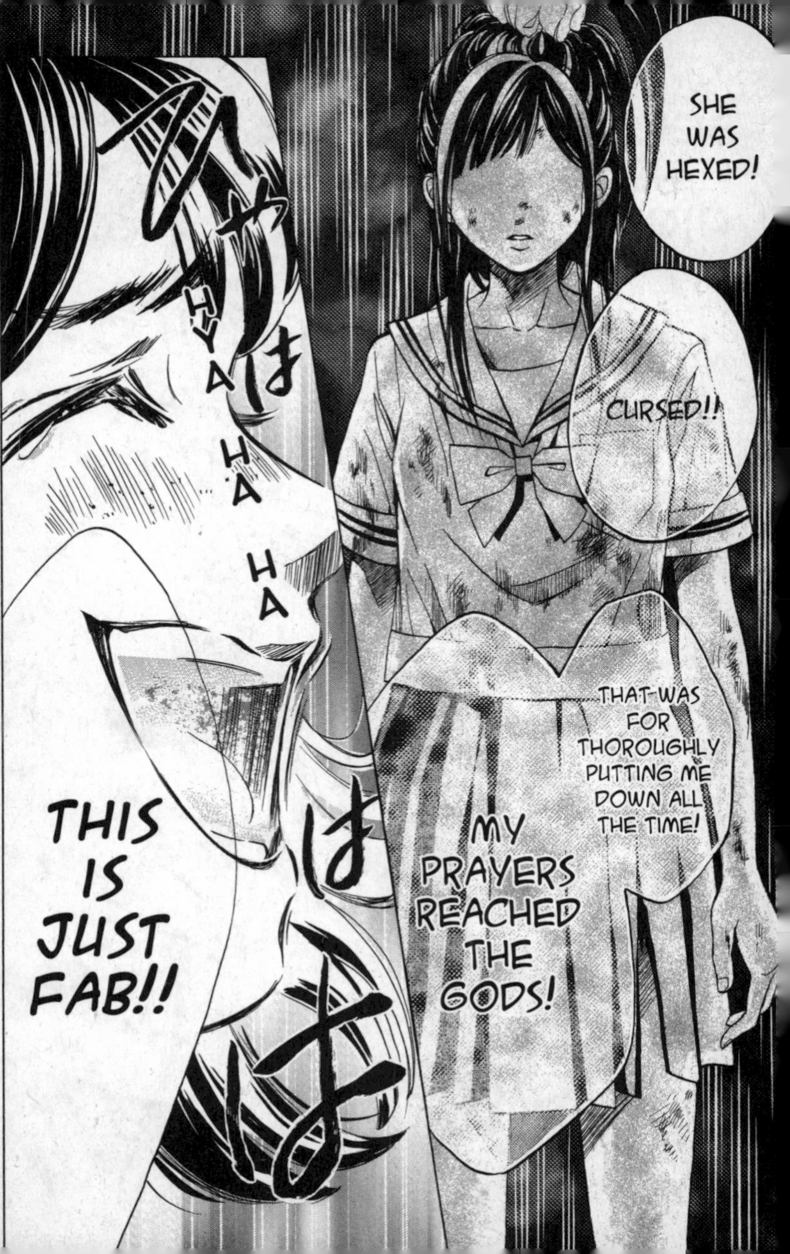
SHE WAS HEXED!
CURSED!!
THAT WAS FOR THOROUGHLY PUTTING ME DOWN ALL THE TIME!
MY PRAYERS REACHED THE GODS!
HYA HA HA HA
THIS IS JUST FAB!!

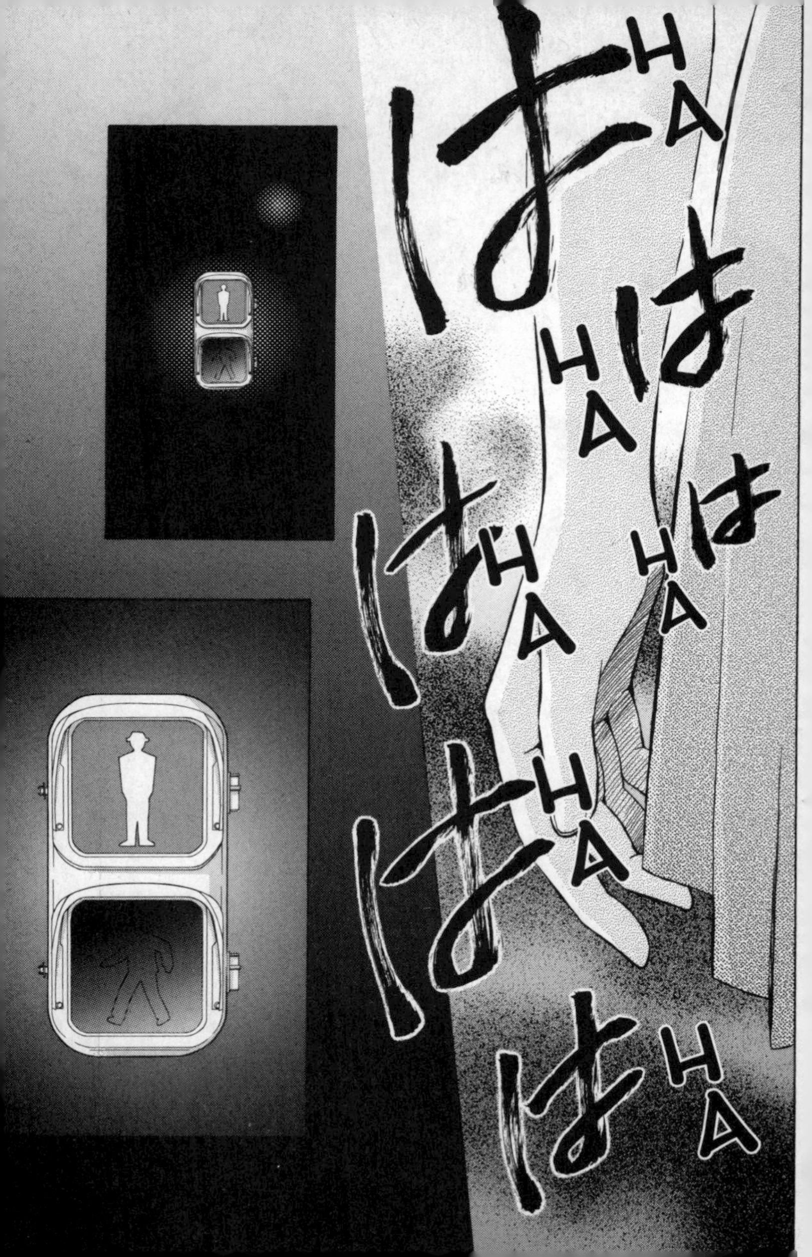
はHA
はHA
はHA
はHA
はHA
はHA

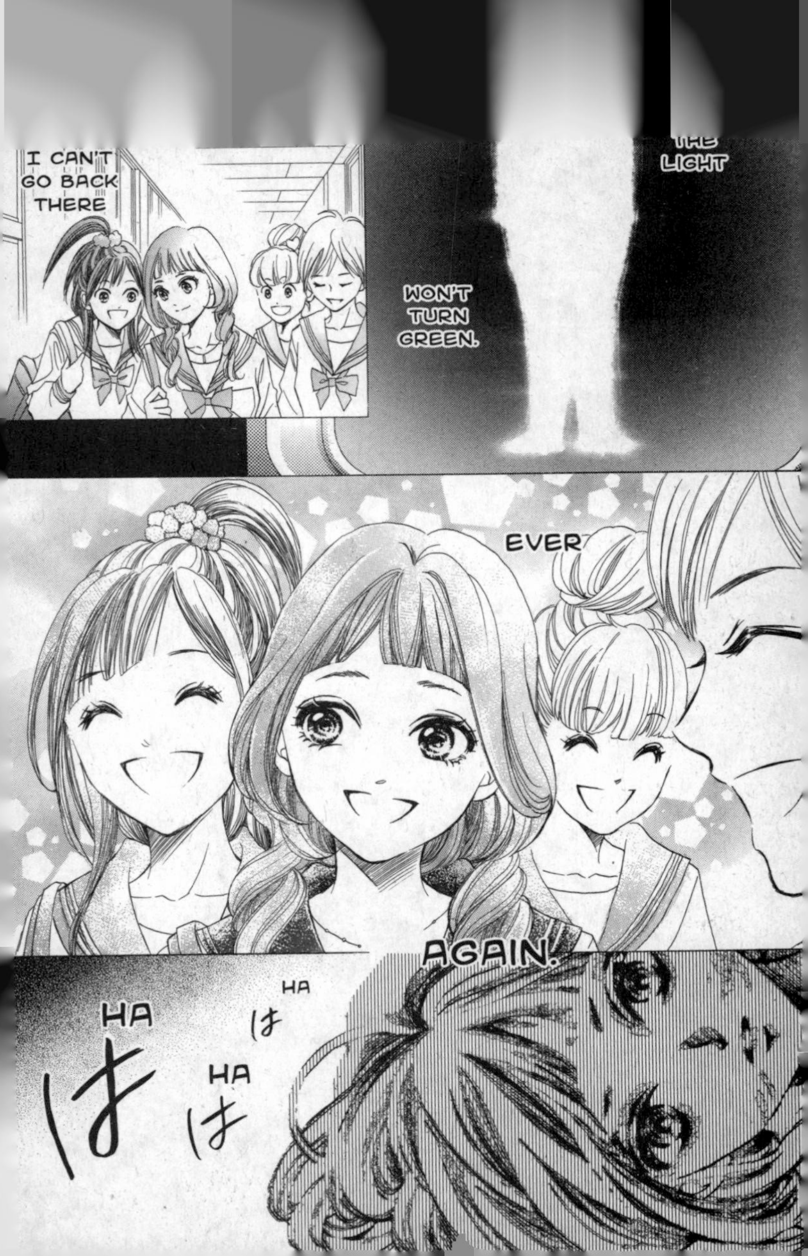
LIGHT
WON'T TURN GREEN.
I CAN'T GO BACK THERE
EVER
AGAIN.
HA
は
HA
は
HA
は

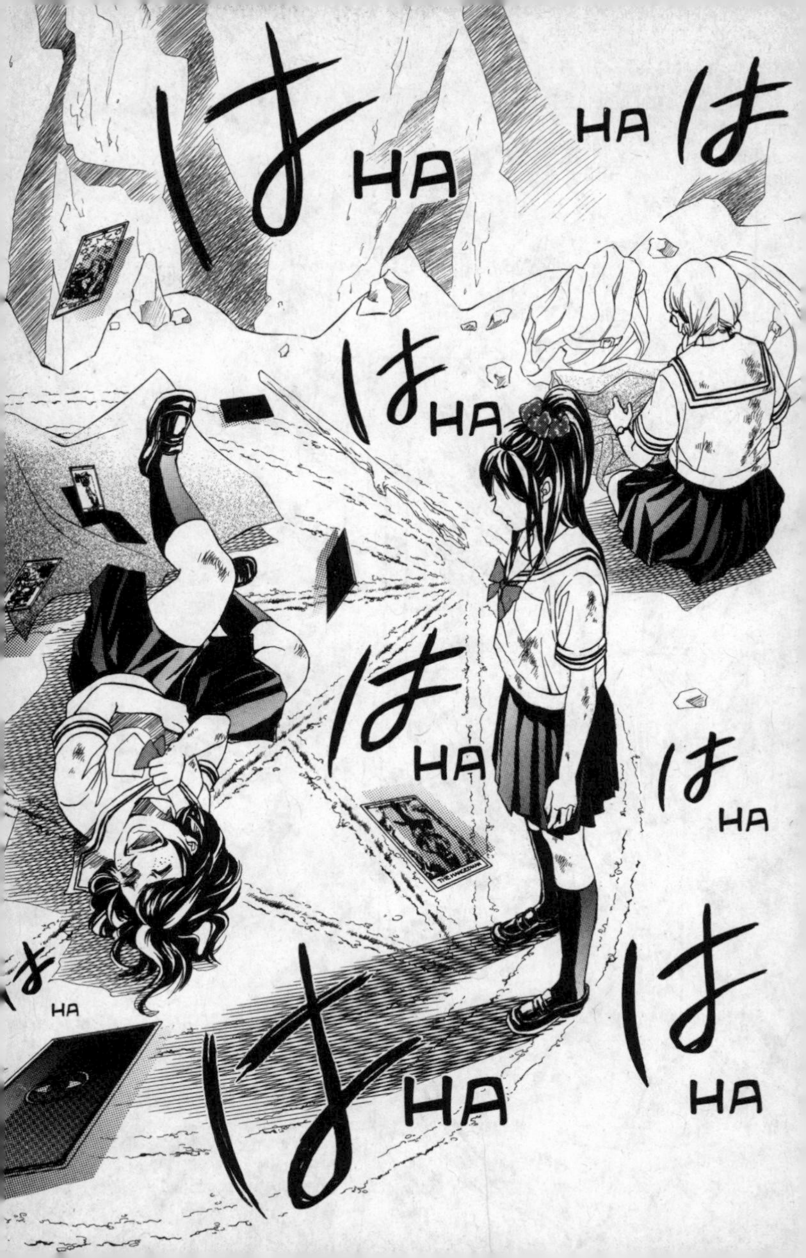
は HA
は HA
は HA
は HA
は HA
は HA
は HA
は HA

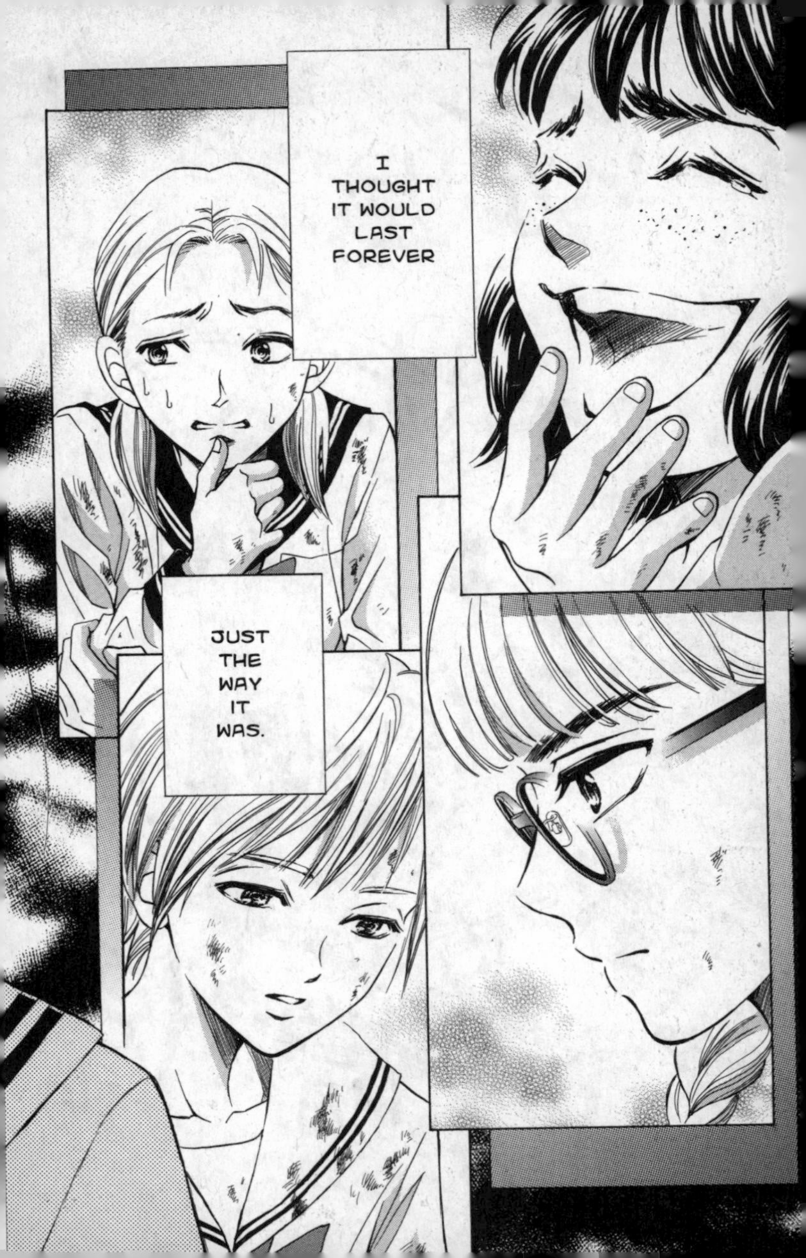
I THOUGHT IT WOULD LAST FOREVER
JUST THE WAY IT WAS.

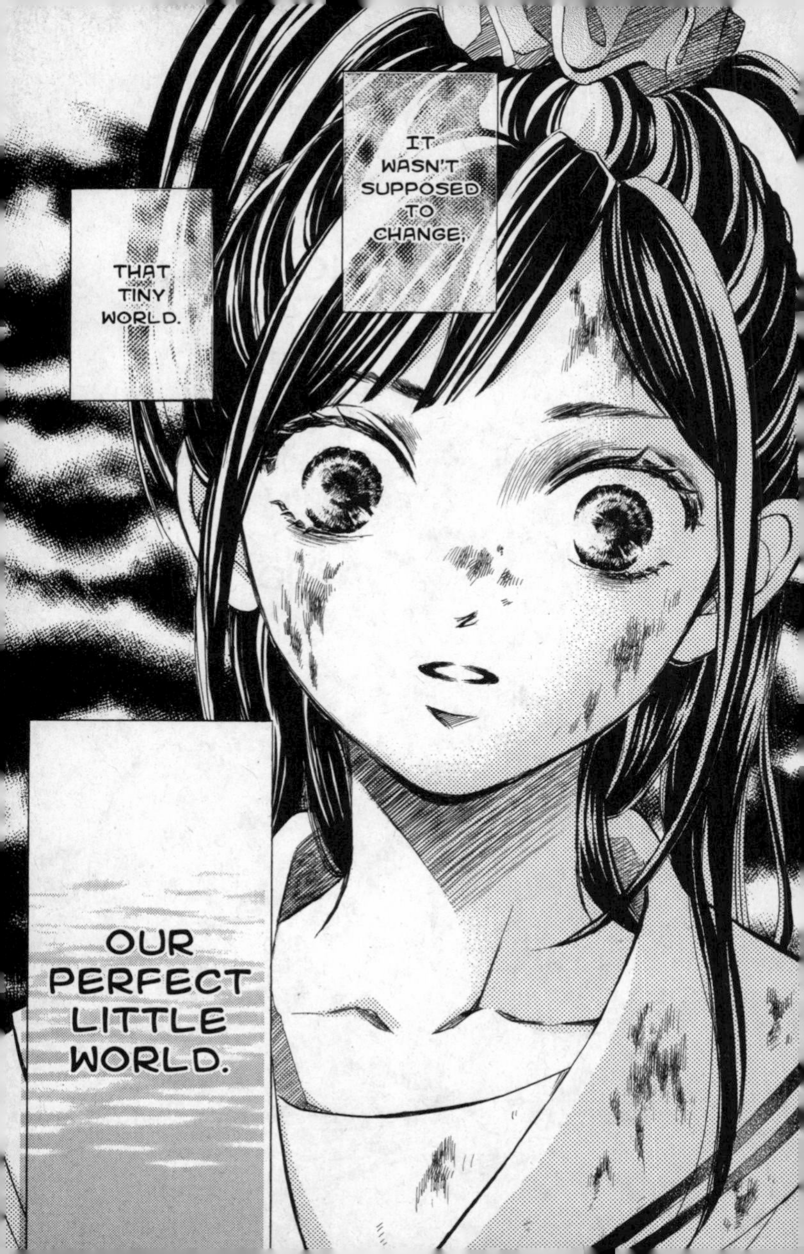
IT WASN'T SUPPOSED TO CHANGE,
THAT TINY WORLD.
OUR PERFECT LITTLE WORLD.

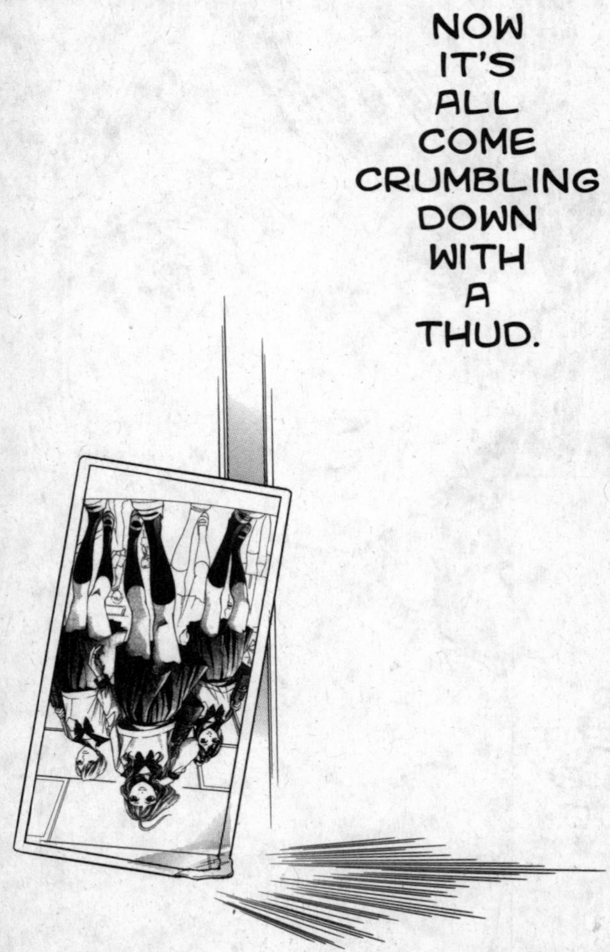
NOW IT'S ALL COME CRUMBLING DOWN WITH A THUD.

Scene.2 – The Strong vs. the Weak

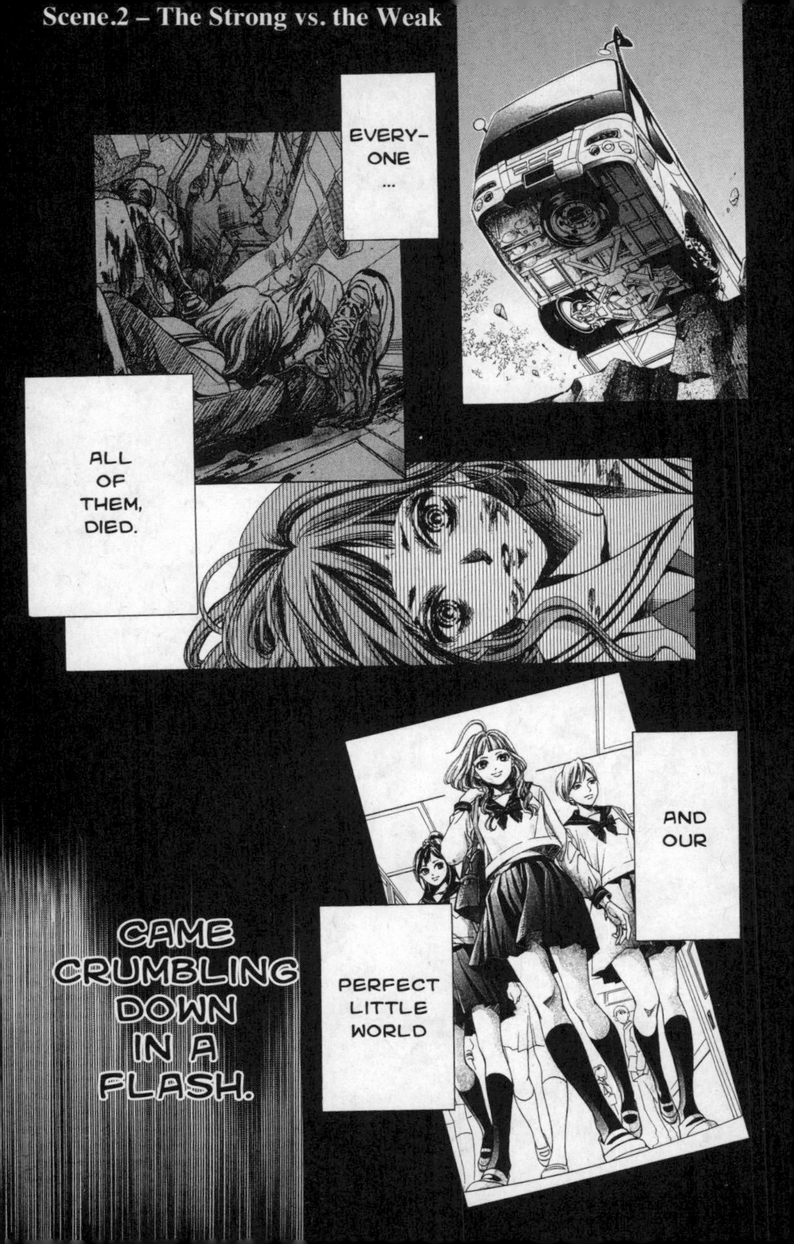
EVERY-ONE ...
ALL OF THEM, DIED.
AND OUR
PERFECT LITTLE WORLD
CAME CRUMBLING DOWN IN A FLASH.

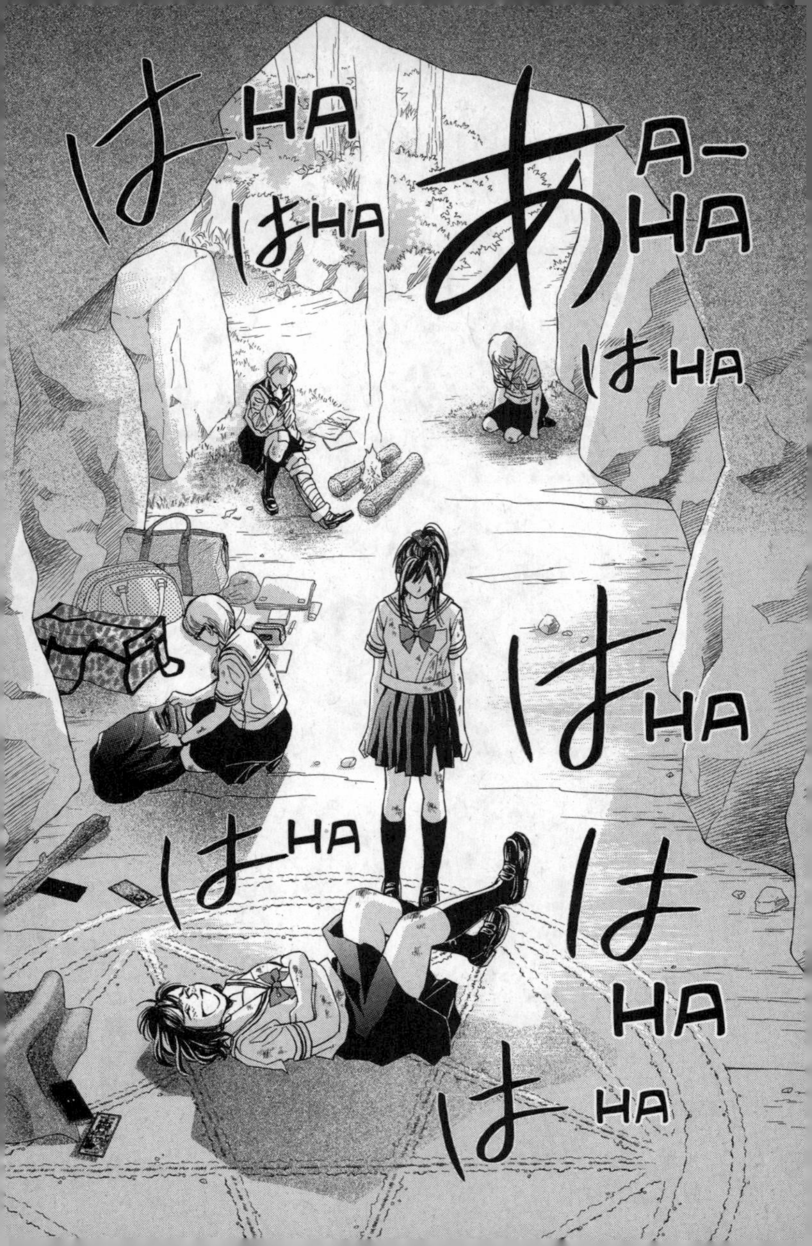

はHA
はHA
あA–HA
はHA
はHA
はHA
はHA
はHA

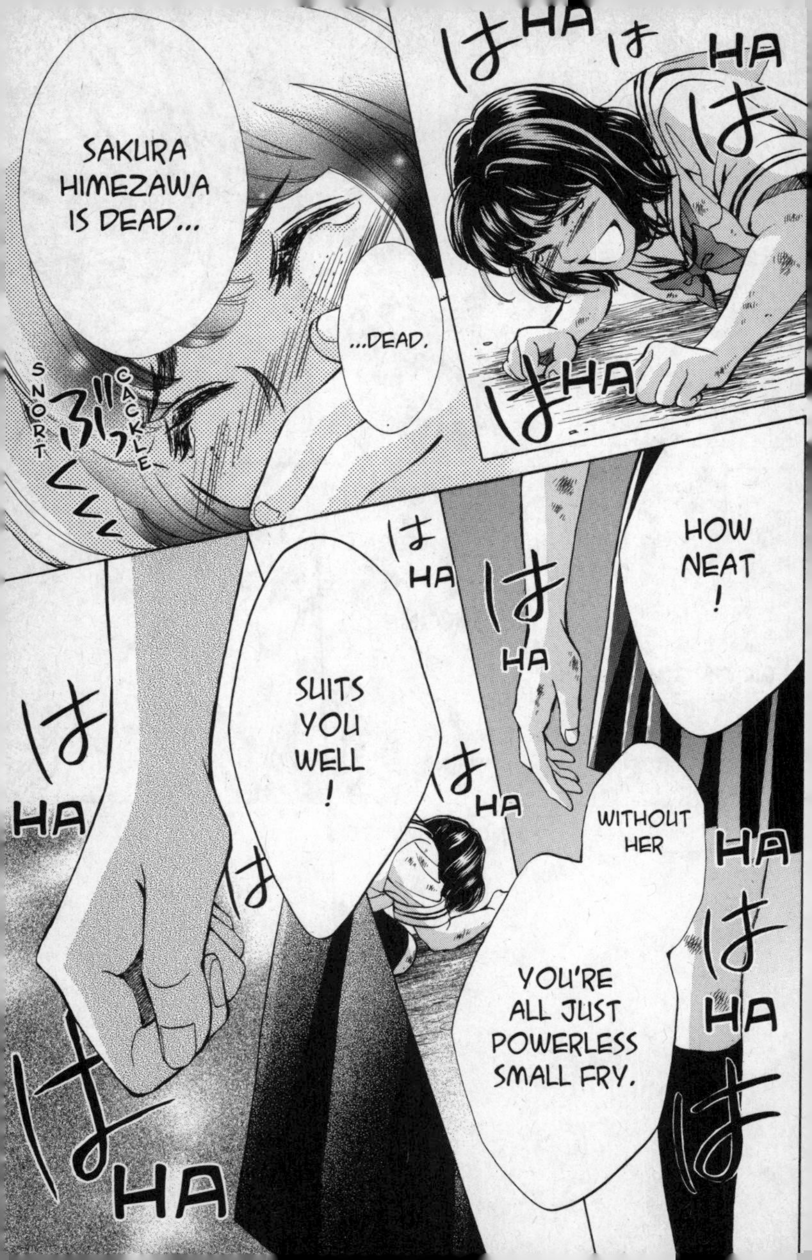
はHAはHA
は
はHA
SAKURA HIMEZAWA IS DEAD...
...DEAD.
SNORT ぶっ
CACKLE くくく
HOW NEAT!
はHA
はHA
はHA
WITHOUT HER
YOU'RE ALL JUST POWERLESS SMALL FRY.
HA は HA は
SUITS YOU WELL!
は
はHA
はHA

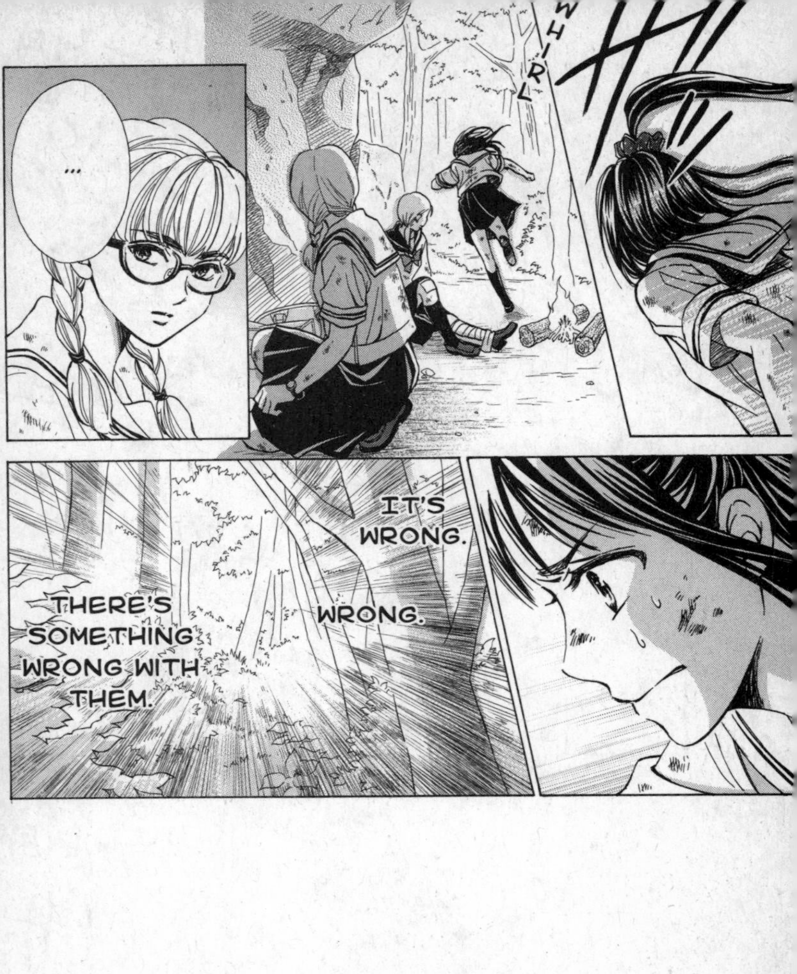
WHIRL
...
IT'S WRONG.
WRONG.
THERE'S SOMETHING WRONG WITH THEM.

LIMIT

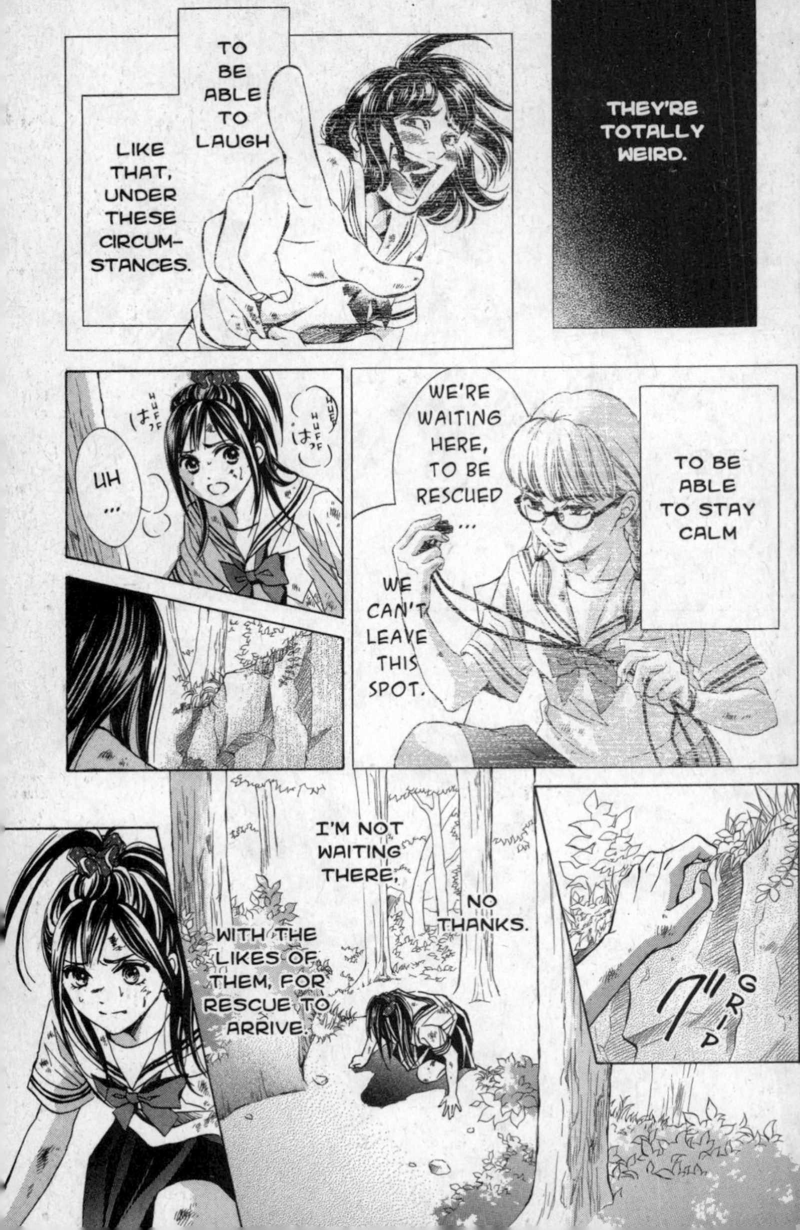
THEY'RE TOTALLY WEIRD.
TO BE ABLE TO LAUGH
LIKE THAT, UNDER THESE CIRCUMSTANCES.
TO BE ABLE TO STAY CALM
WE'RE WAITING HERE, TO BE RESCUED ...
WE CAN'T LEAVE THIS SPOT.
は HUFF
UH ...
は HUFF
グ GRIP
I'M NOT WAITING THERE,
NO THANKS.
WITH THE LIKES OF THEM, FOR RESCUE TO ARRIVE.

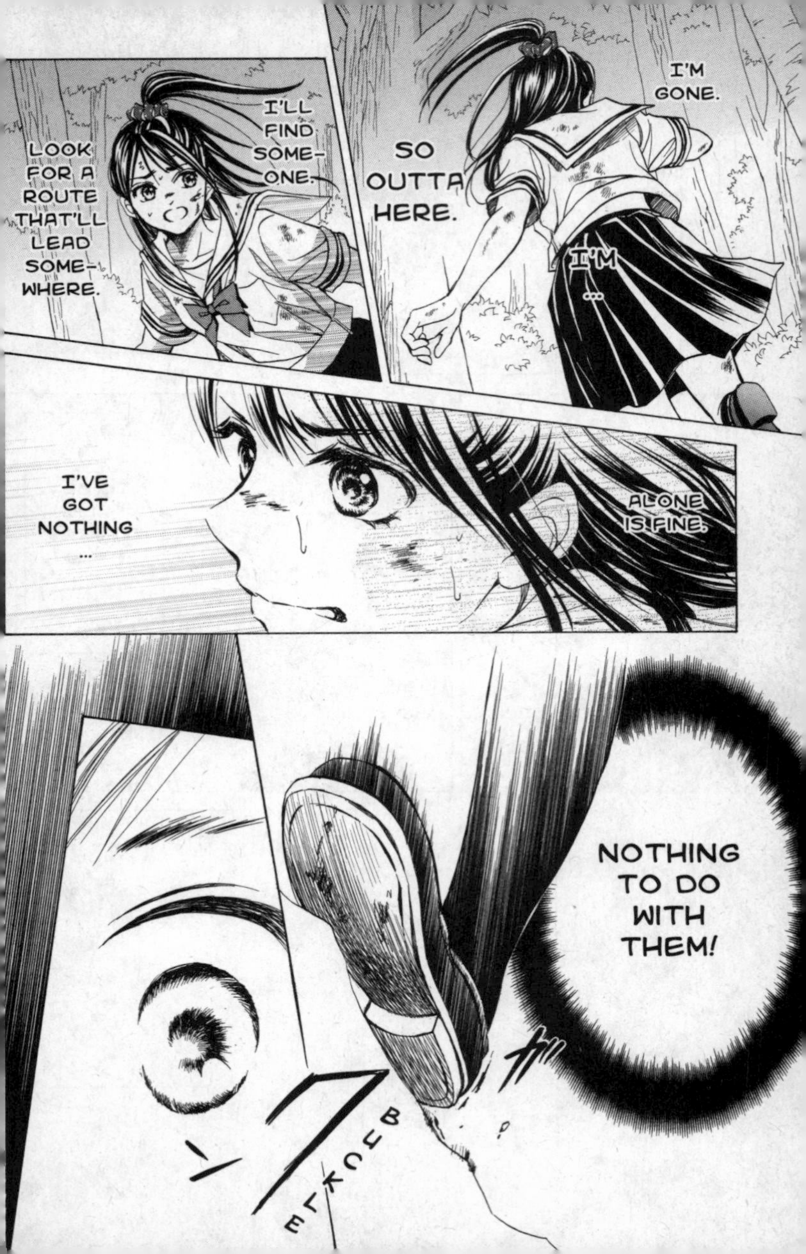
I'M GONE.
SO OUTTA HERE.
I'M ...
I'LL FIND SOME-ONE.
LOOK FOR A ROUTE THAT'LL LEAD SOME-WHERE.
ALONE IS FINE.
I'VE GOT NOTHING ...
NOTHING TO DO WITH THEM!
BUCKLE

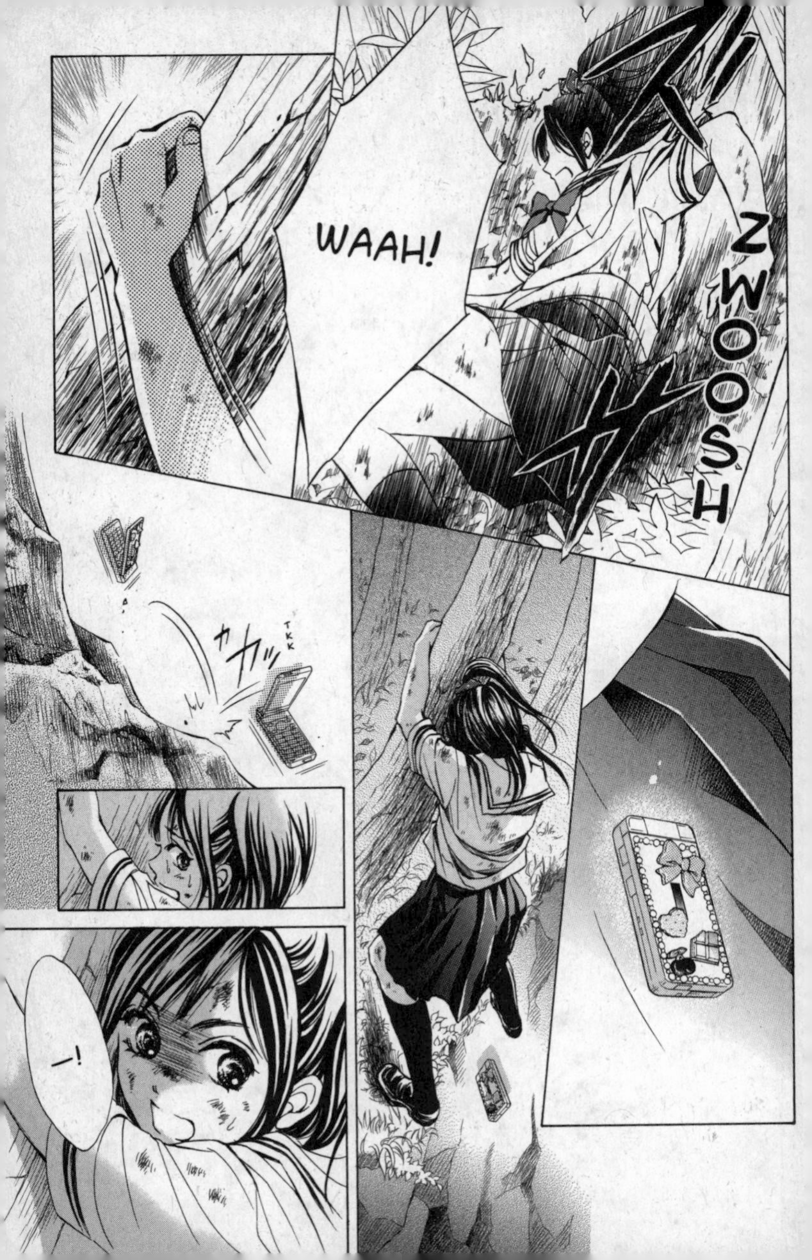
ZWOOSH
WAAH!
カカッ
TKK
—!

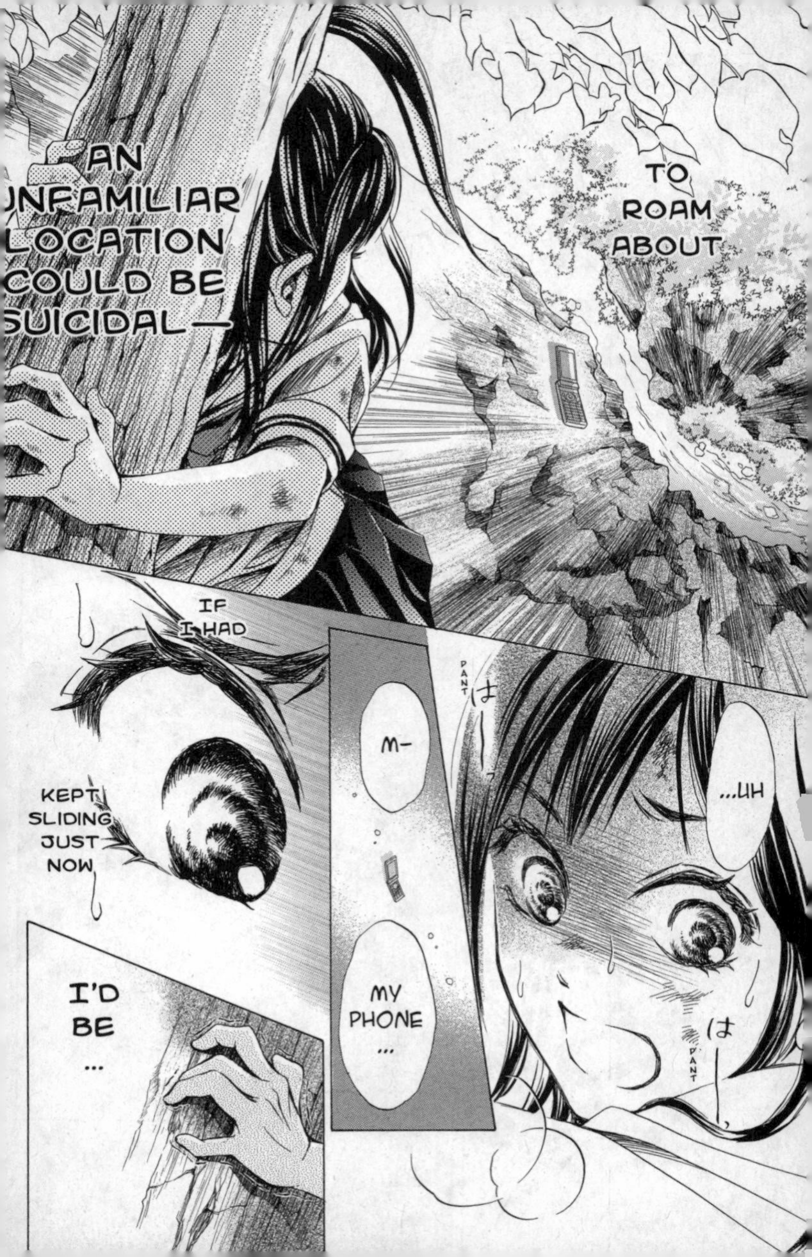
TO ROAM ABOUT
AN UNFAMILIAR LOCATION COULD BE SUICIDAL—
PANT
はー
...UH
は
PANT
M-
MY PHONE ...
IF I HAD
KEPT SLIDING JUST NOW
I'D BE ...

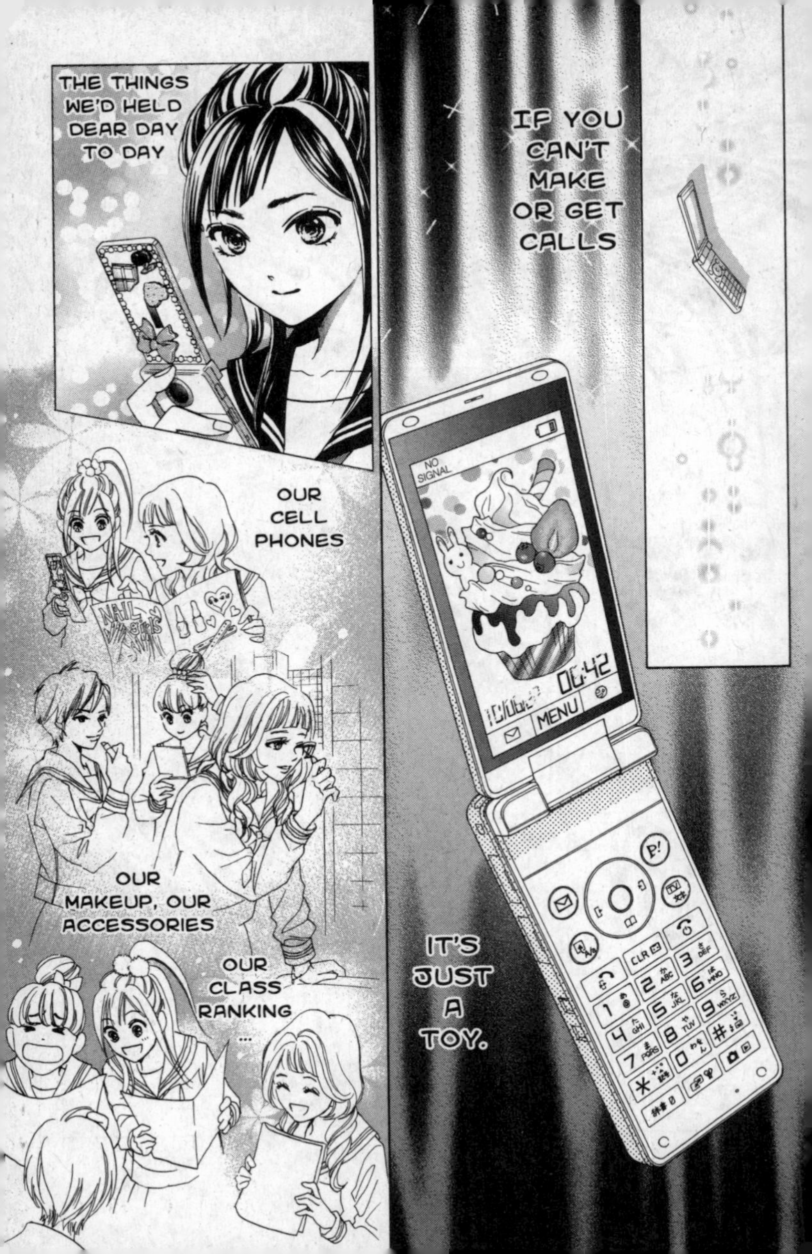
IF YOU CAN'T MAKE OR GET CALLS
NO SIGNAL
06:42
MENU
IT'S JUST A TOY.
THE THINGS WE'D HELD DEAR DAY TO DAY
OUR CELL PHONES
OUR MAKEUP, OUR ACCESSORIES
OUR CLASS RANKING ...

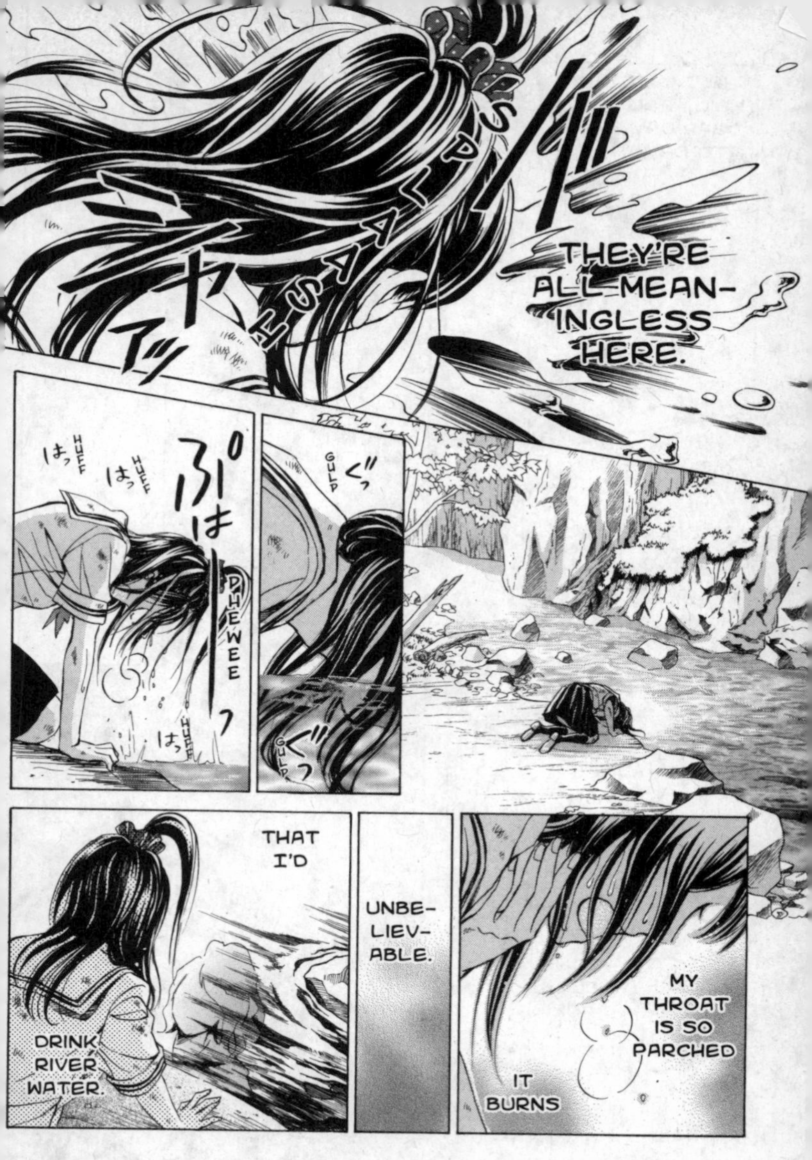
SPLASH
THEY'RE ALL MEAN-INGLESS HERE.
ぐっ GULP
ぐっ GULP
ぷはーっ PHEWEE
はっ HUFF
はっ HUFF
はっ HUFF
MY THROAT IS SO PARCHED
IT BURNS
UNBE-LIEV-ABLE.
THAT I'D
DRINK RIVER WATER.

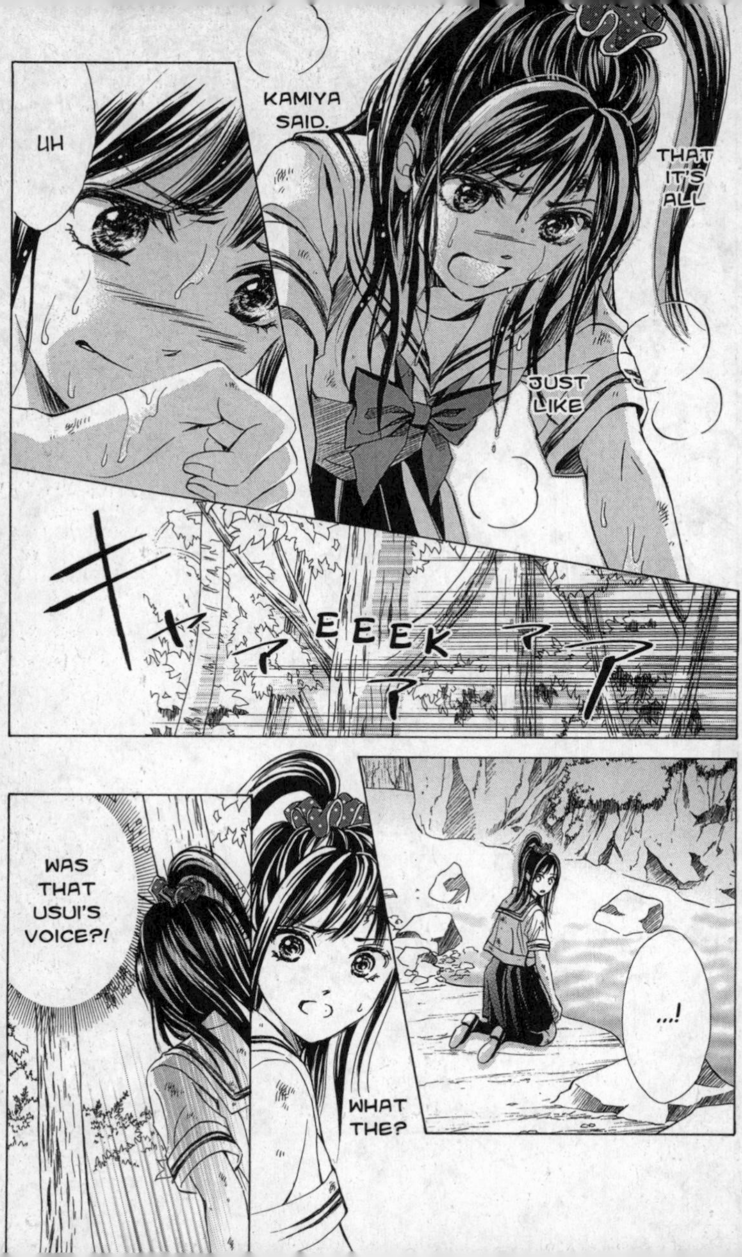
THAT IT'S ALL
JUST LIKE
KAMIYA SAID.
UH
キャアアア
EEEK
...!
WAS THAT USUI'S VOICE?!
WHAT THE?

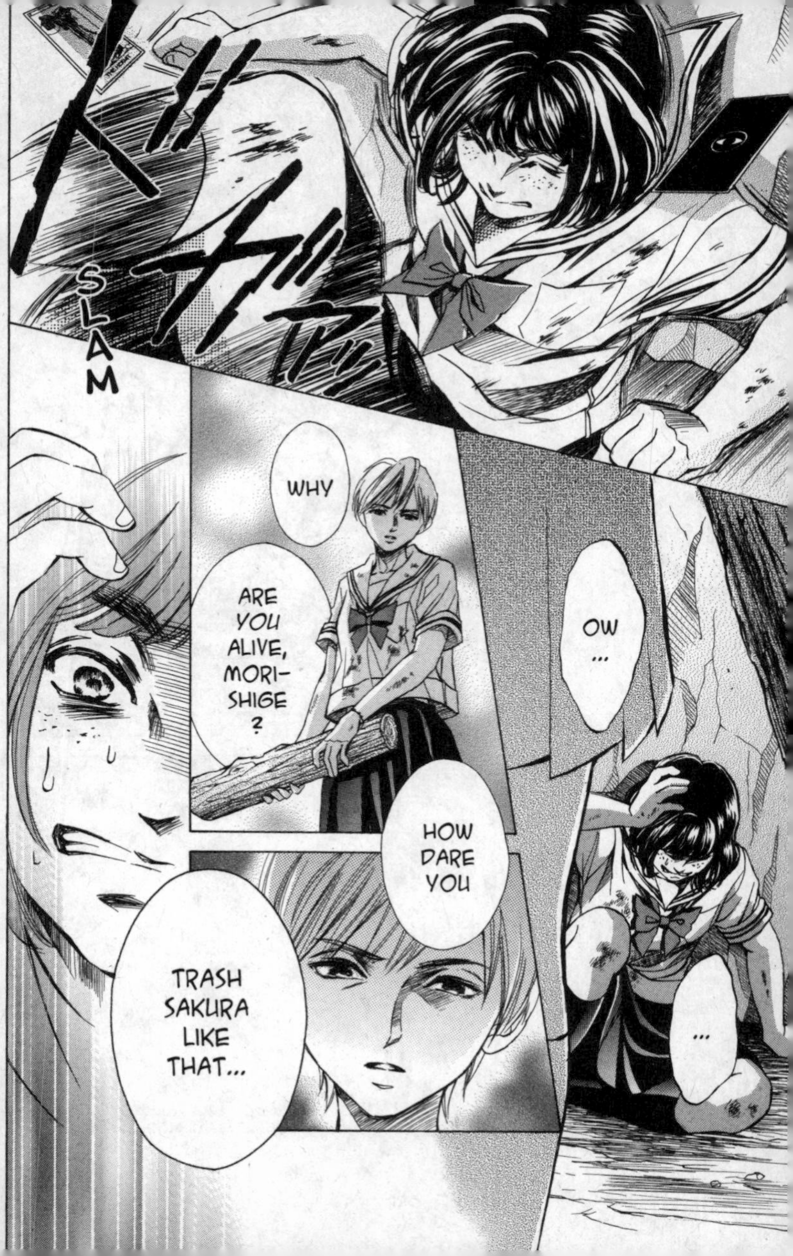
SLAM
OW ...
...
WHY
ARE YOU ALIVE, MORI-SHIGE?
HOW DARE YOU
TRASH SAKURA LIKE THAT...

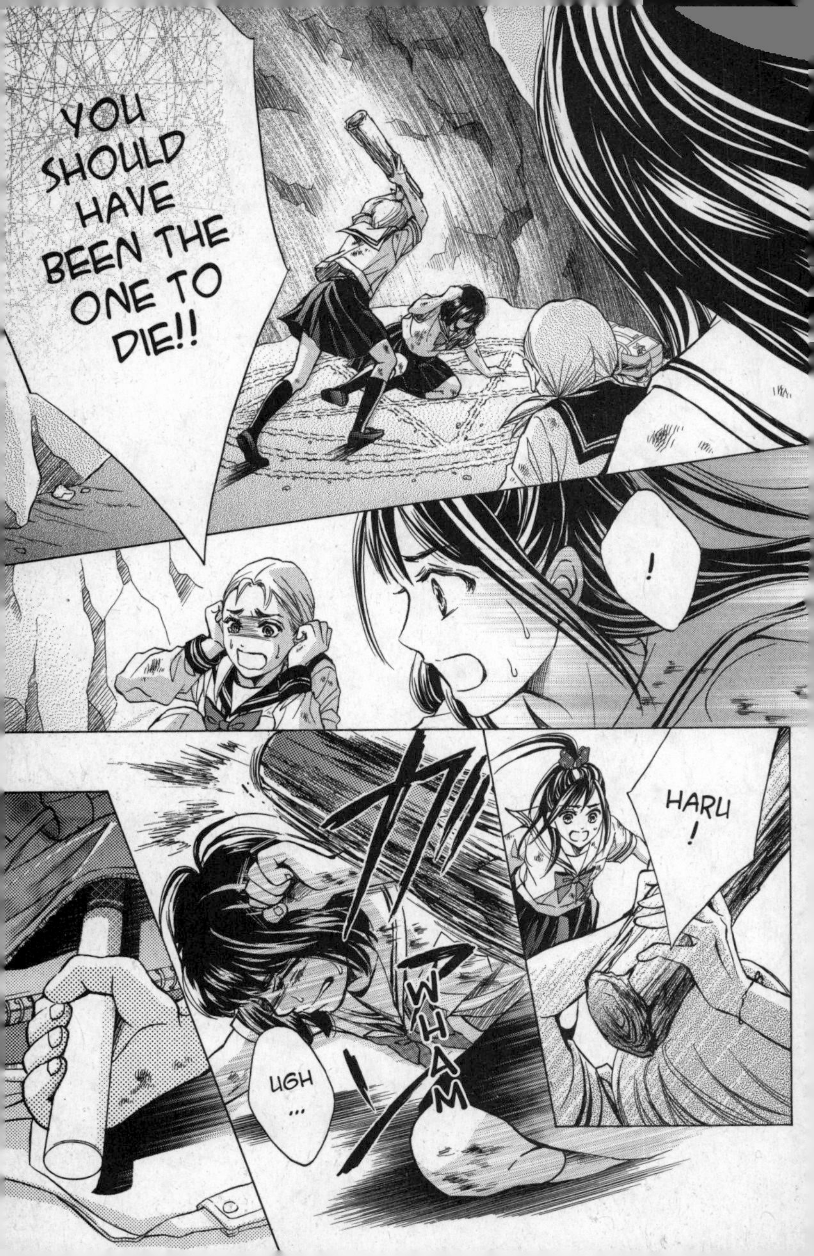
YOU SHOULD HAVE BEEN THE ONE TO DIE!!
!
HARU!
WHAM
UGH ...

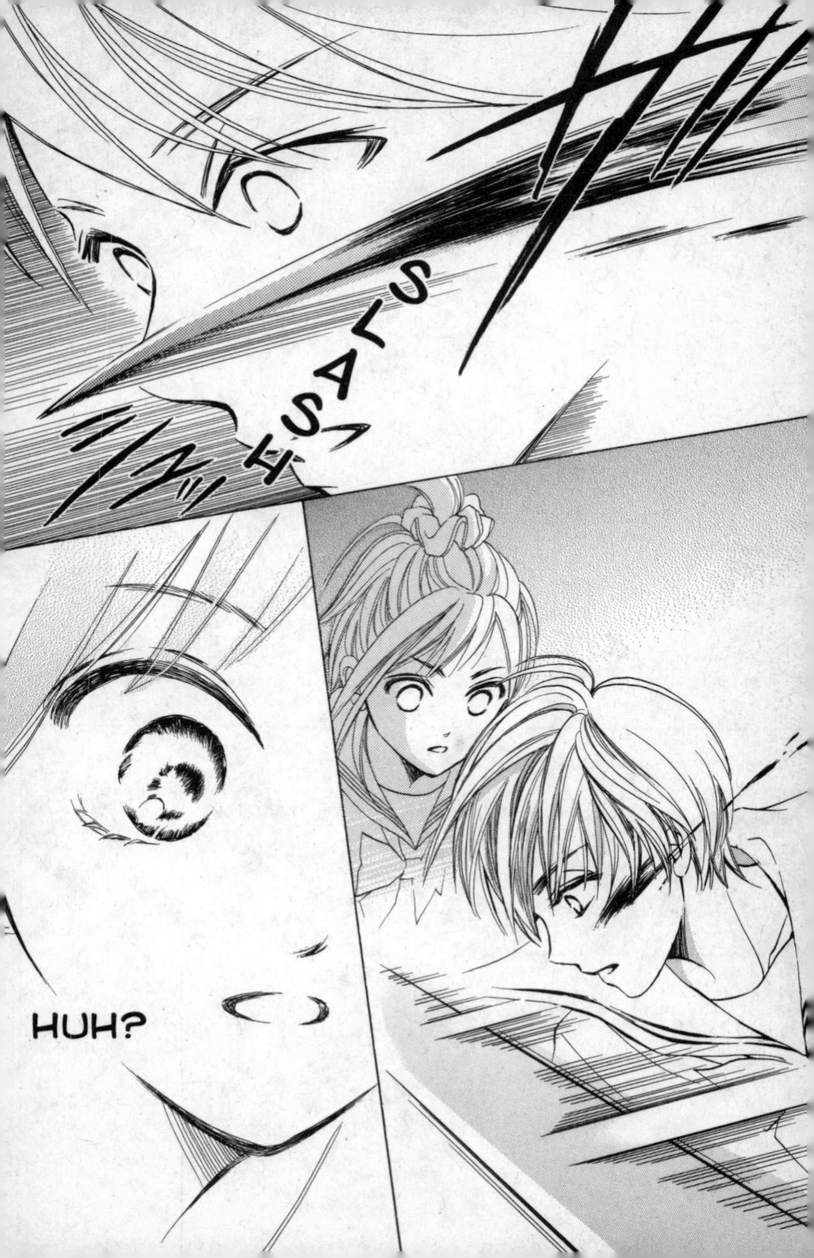
SLASH
HUH?

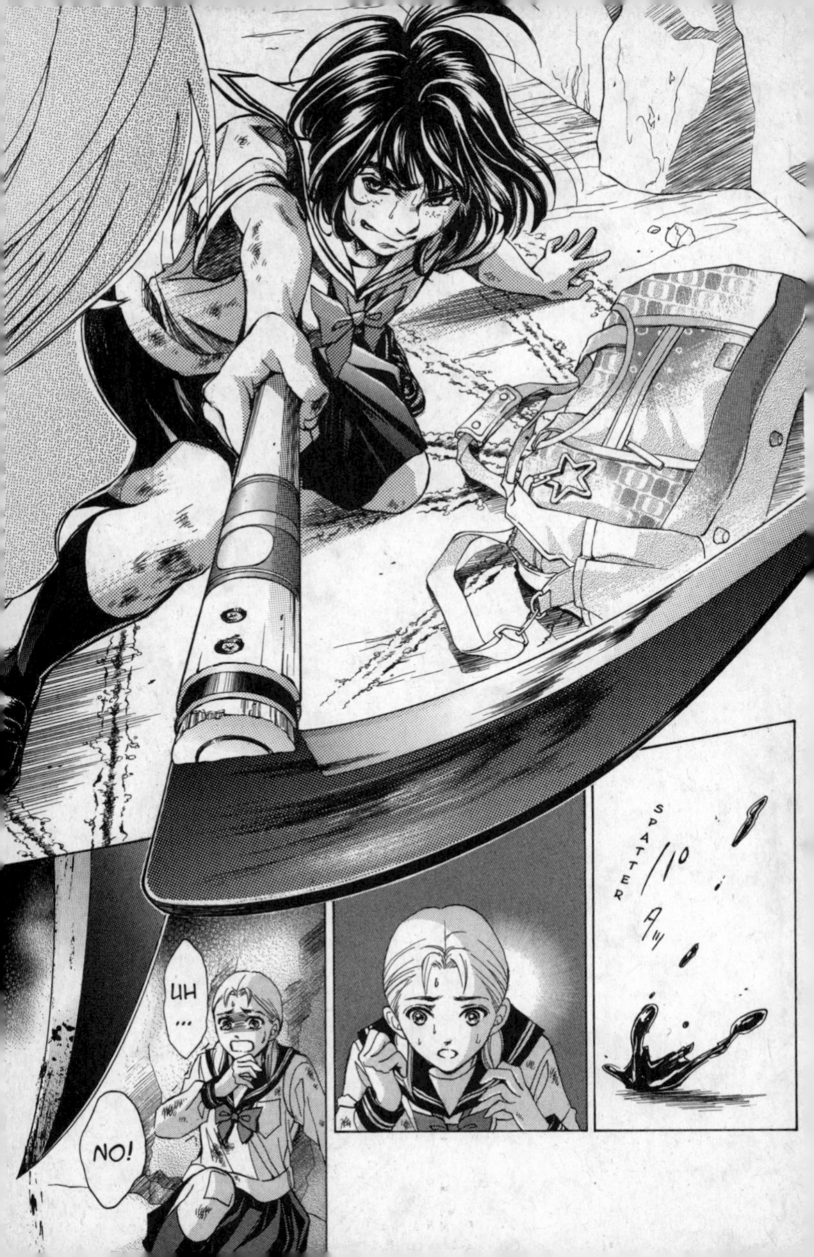
SPATTER
UH ...
NO!

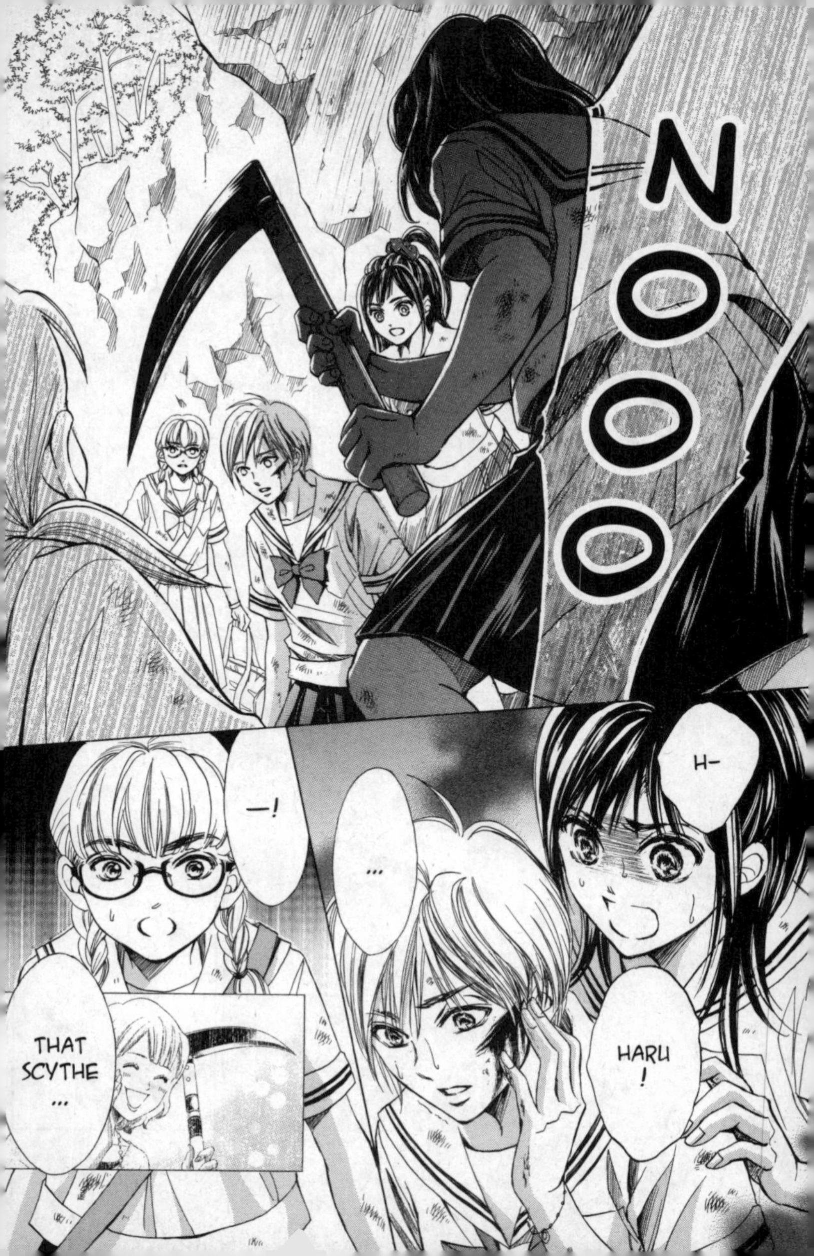
NOOOO
H-
...
HARU!
—!
THAT SCYTHE ...

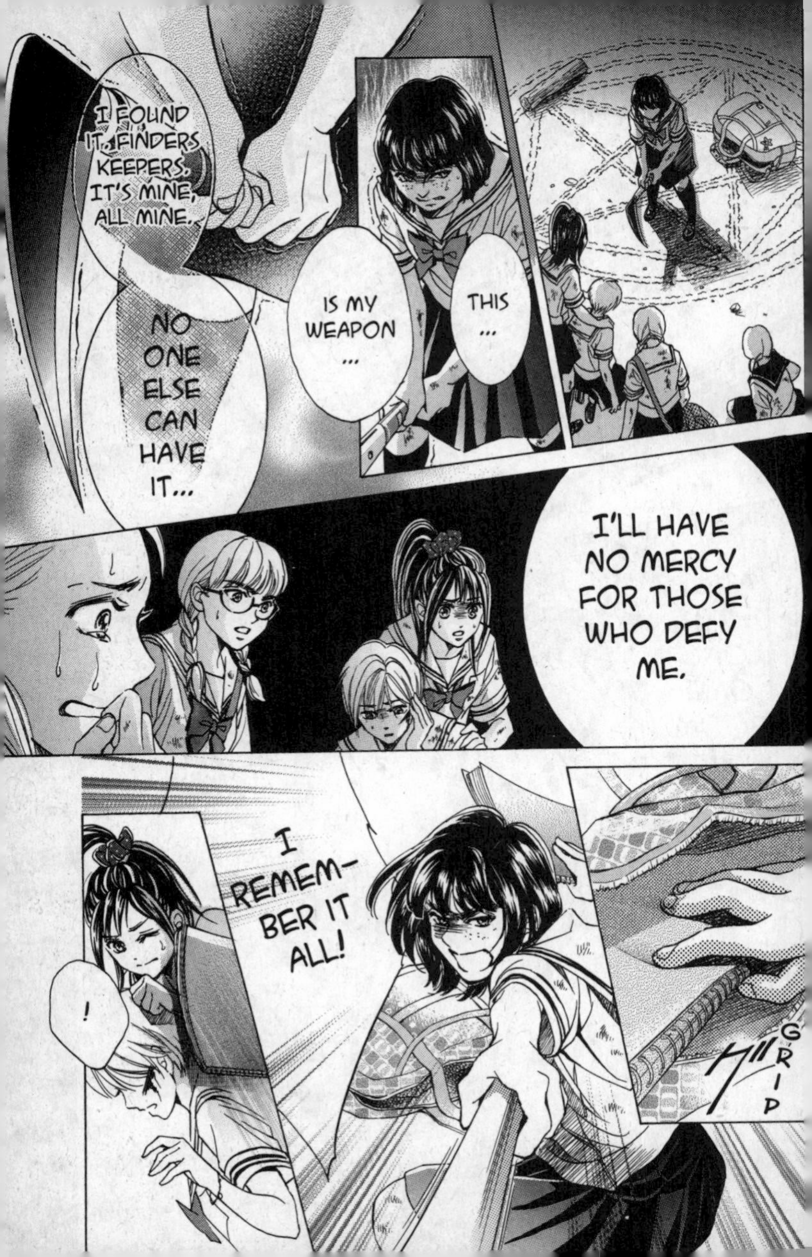
THIS ...
IS MY WEAPON ...
I FOUND IT. FINDERS KEEPERS. IT'S MINE, ALL MINE.
NO ONE ELSE CAN HAVE IT...
I'LL HAVE NO MERCY FOR THOSE WHO DEFY ME.
GRIP
I REMEMBER IT ALL!
!

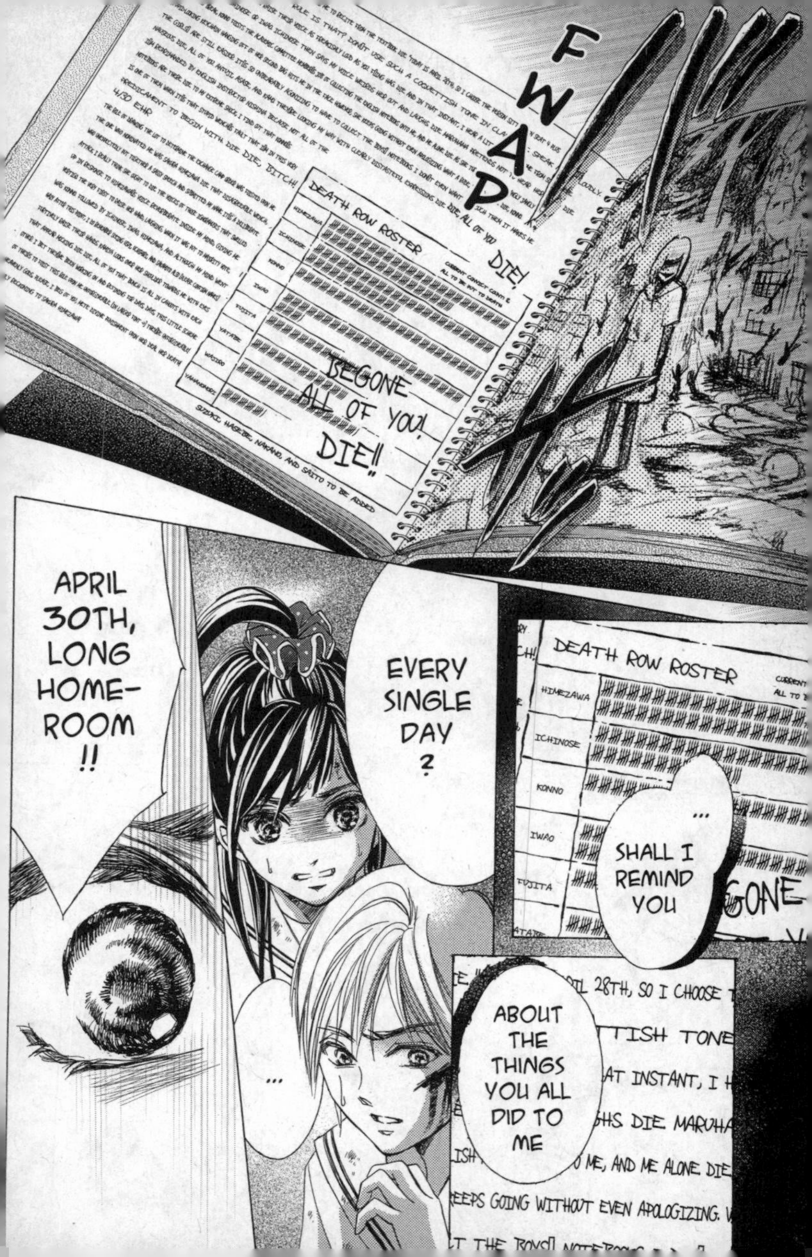
FWAP
DEATH ROW ROSTER
DIE!
BEGONE ALL OF YOU! DIE!!
SUZUKI, HAGETE, NAKANO, AND SAITO TO BE ADDED
DEATH ROW ROSTER
HIMEZAWA
ICHINOSE
KONNO
IWAO
FUJITA
... SHALL I REMIND YOU
ABOUT THE THINGS YOU ALL DID TO ME
EVERY SINGLE DAY?
...
APRIL 30TH, LONG HOME-ROOM!!

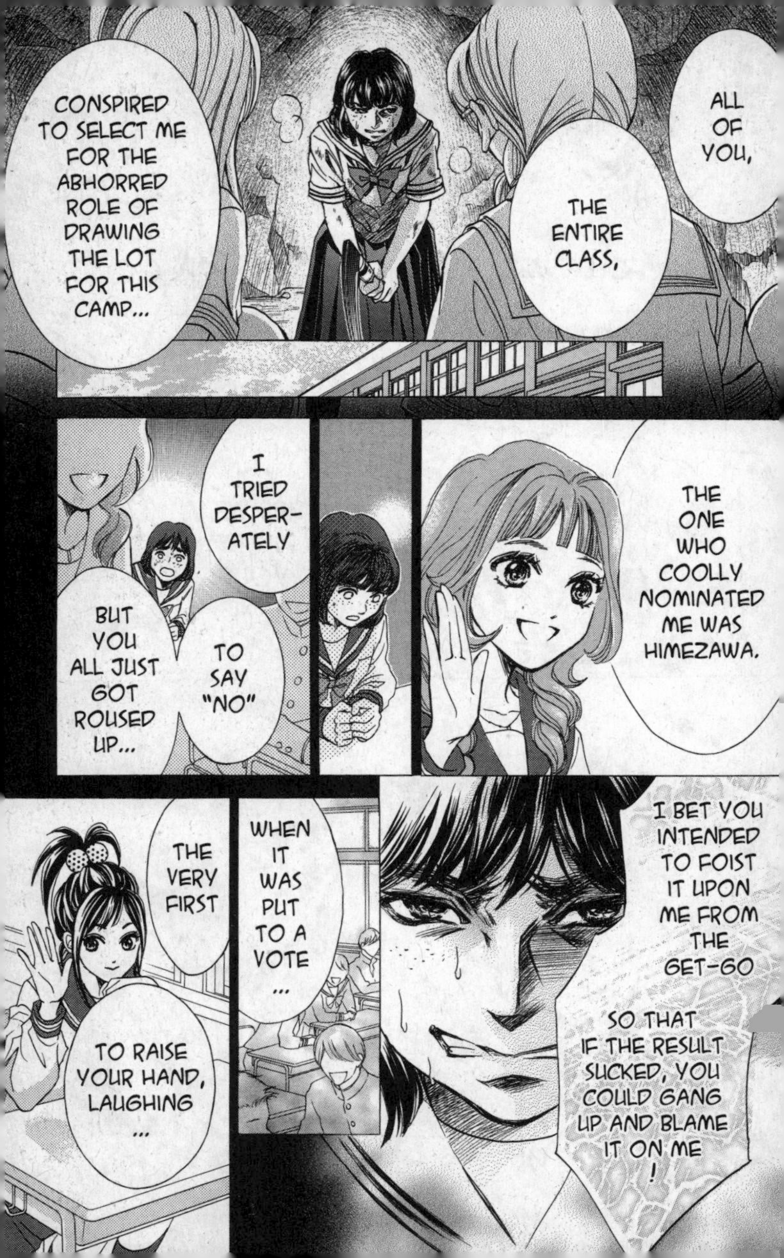
ALL OF YOU,
THE ENTIRE CLASS,
CONSPIRED TO SELECT ME FOR THE ABHORRED ROLE OF DRAWING THE LOT FOR THIS CAMP...
THE ONE WHO COOLLY NOMINATED ME WAS HIMEZAWA.
I TRIED DESPERATELY
TO SAY "NO"
BUT YOU ALL JUST GOT ROUSED UP...
I BET YOU INTENDED TO FOIST IT UPON ME FROM THE GET-GO
SO THAT IF THE RESULT SUCKED, YOU COULD GANG UP AND BLAME IT ON ME!
WHEN IT WAS PUT TO A VOTE ...
THE VERY FIRST
TO RAISE YOUR HAND, LAUGHING ...

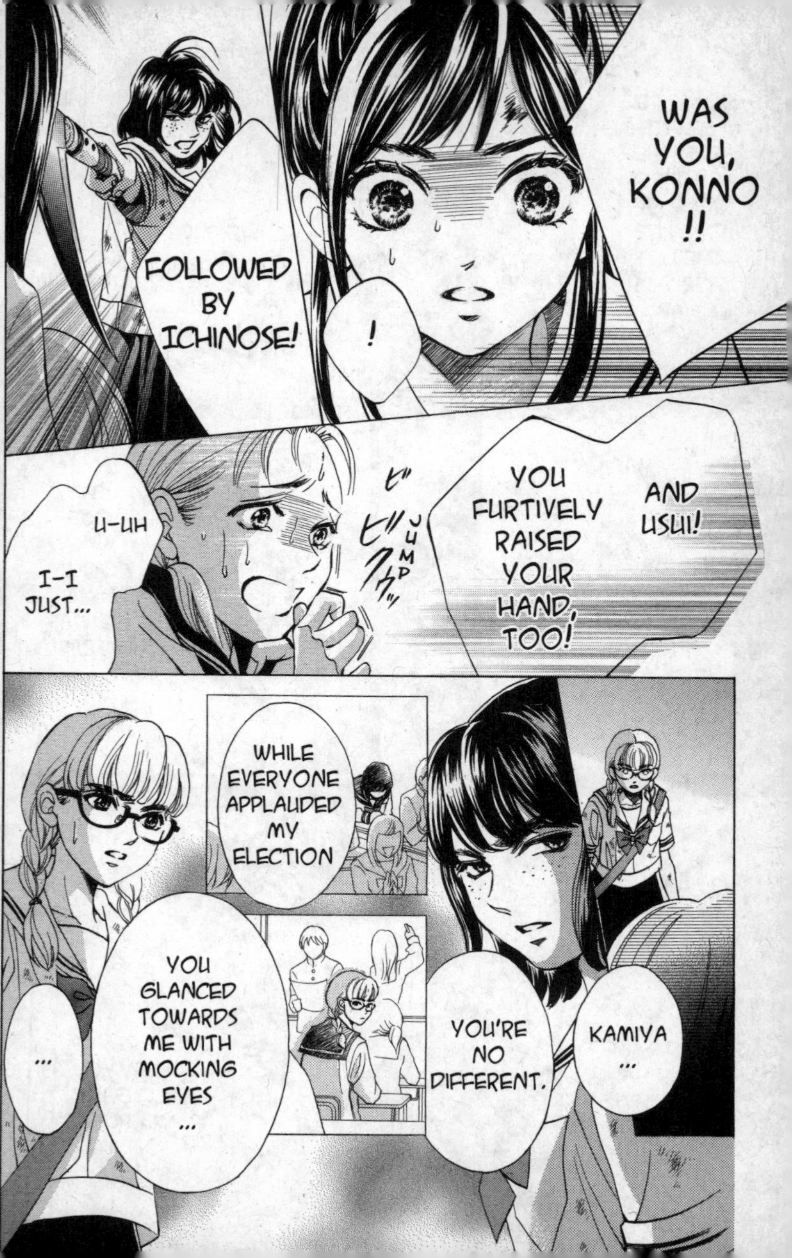
WAS YOU, KONNO!!
!
FOLLOWED BY ICHINOSE!
AND USUI!
YOU FURTIVELY RAISED YOUR HAND, TOO!
JUMP
U-UH
I-I JUST...
KAMIYA ...
YOU'RE NO DIFFERENT.
WHILE EVERYONE APPLAUDED MY ELECTION
YOU GLANCED TOWARDS ME WITH MOCKING EYES ...
...

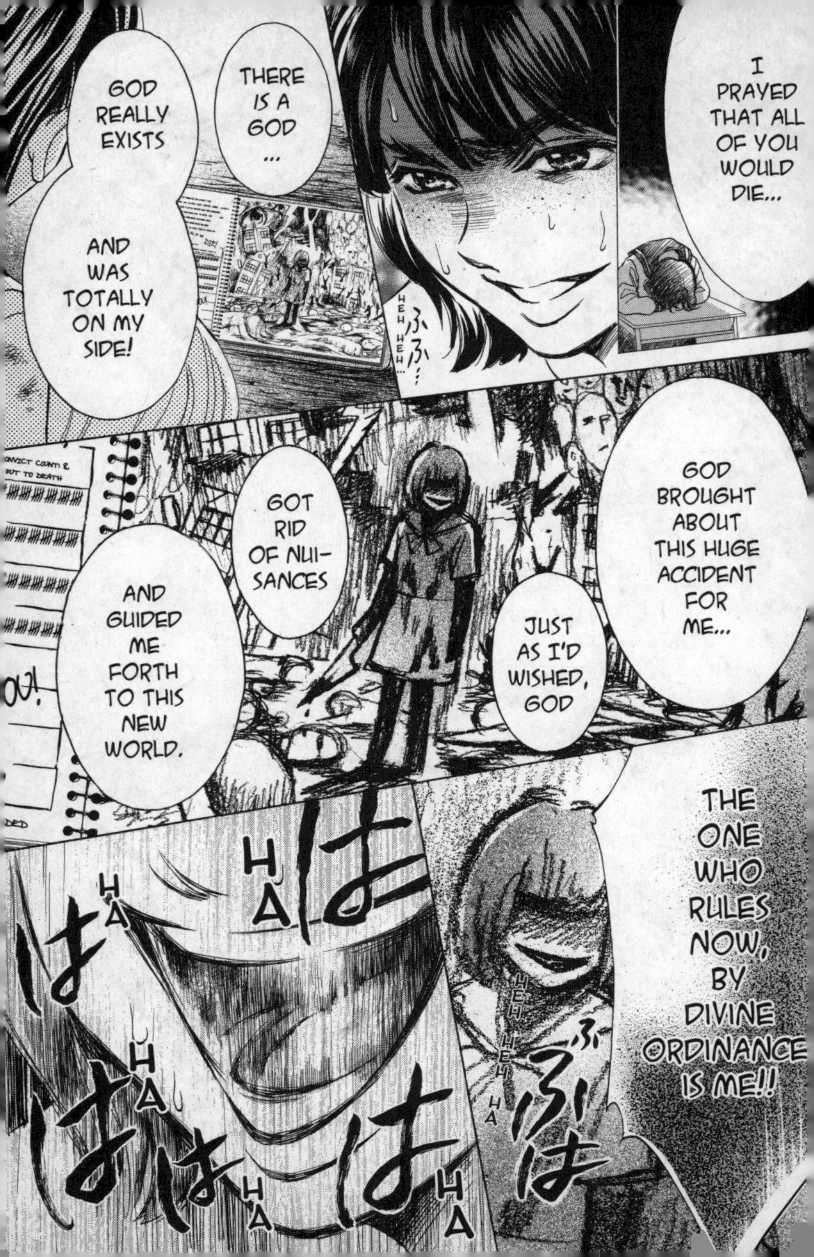
I PRAYED THAT ALL OF YOU WOULD DIE...
ふふ
HEH HEH HEH...
THERE IS A GOD ...
GOD REALLY EXISTS
AND WAS TOTALLY ON MY SIDE!
GOD BROUGHT ABOUT THIS HUGE ACCIDENT FOR ME...
JUST AS I'D WISHED, GOD
GOT RID OF NUI-SANCES
AND GUIDED ME FORTH TO THIS NEW WORLD.
THE ONE WHO RULES NOW, BY DIVINE ORDINANCE IS ME!!
ふふは
HEH HEH HEH HA
はははは
HA HA HA HA HA

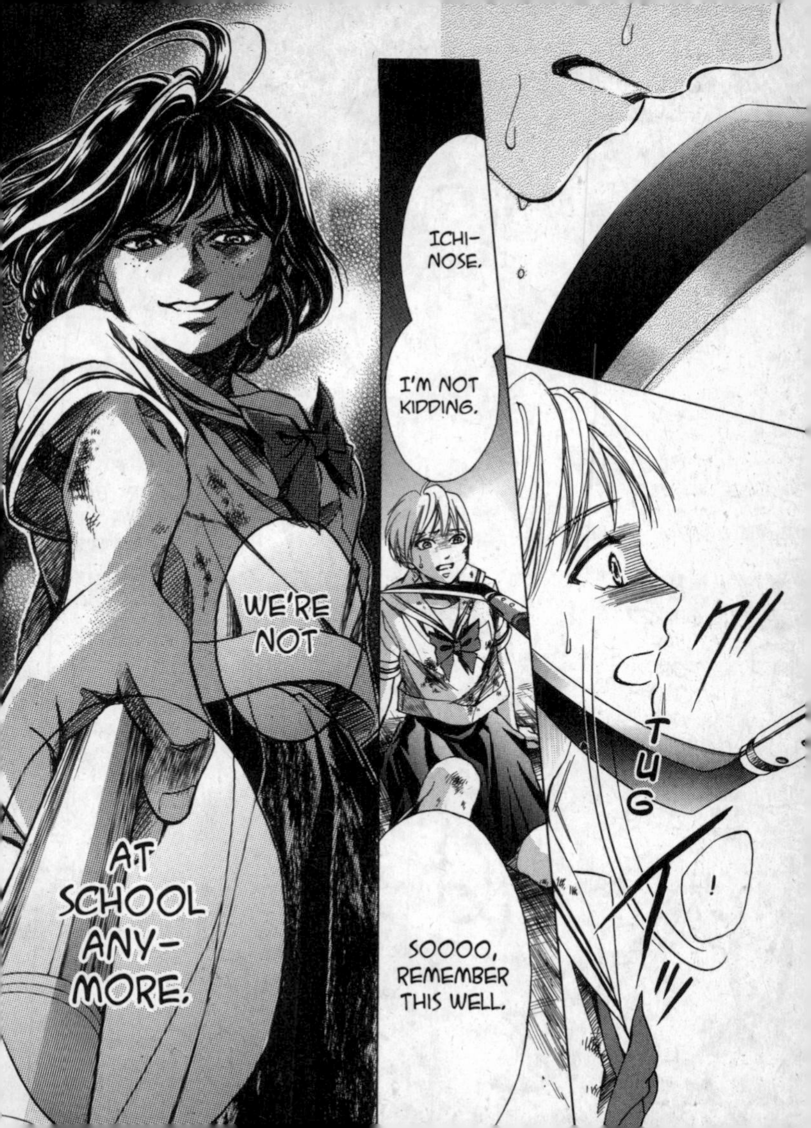
ICHI-NOSE.
I'M NOT KIDDING.
TUG
!
SOOOO, REMEMBER THIS WELL.
WE'RE NOT
AT SCHOOL ANY-MORE.

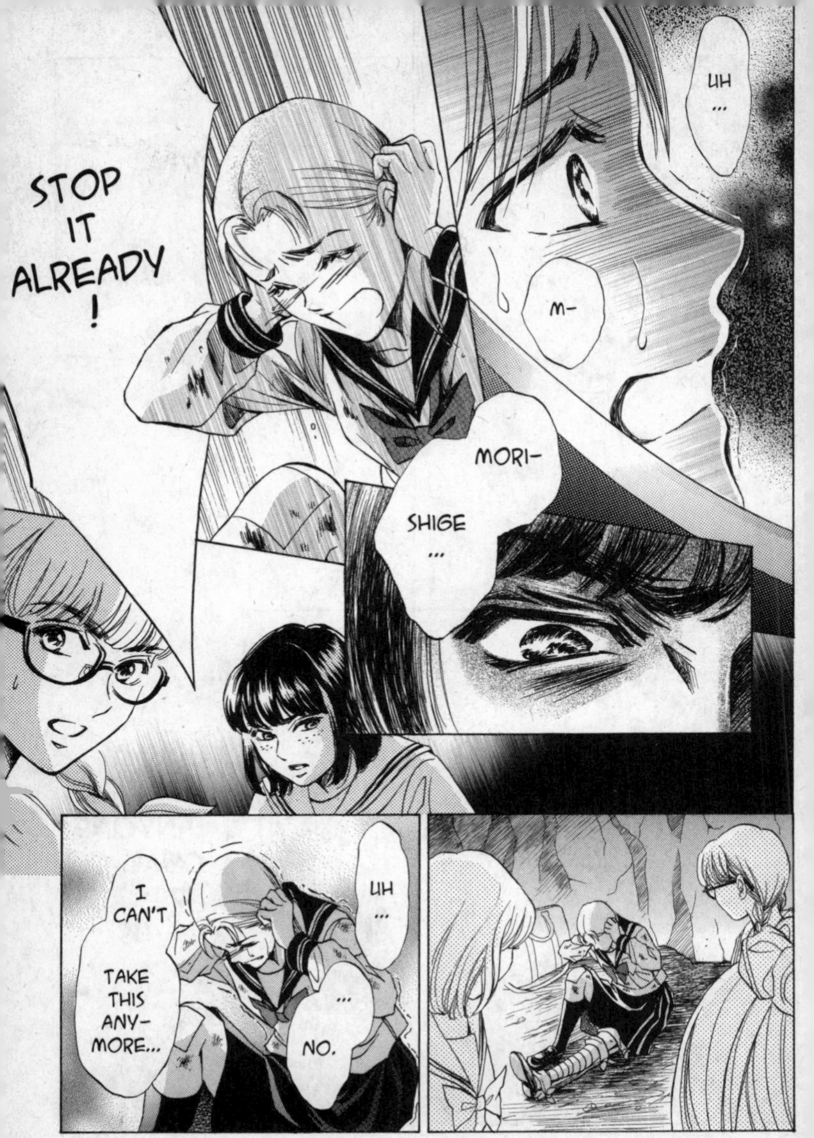
UH ...
M-
STOP IT ALREADY !
MORI- SHIGE ...
UH ...
... NO.
I CAN'T TAKE THIS ANY- MORE...

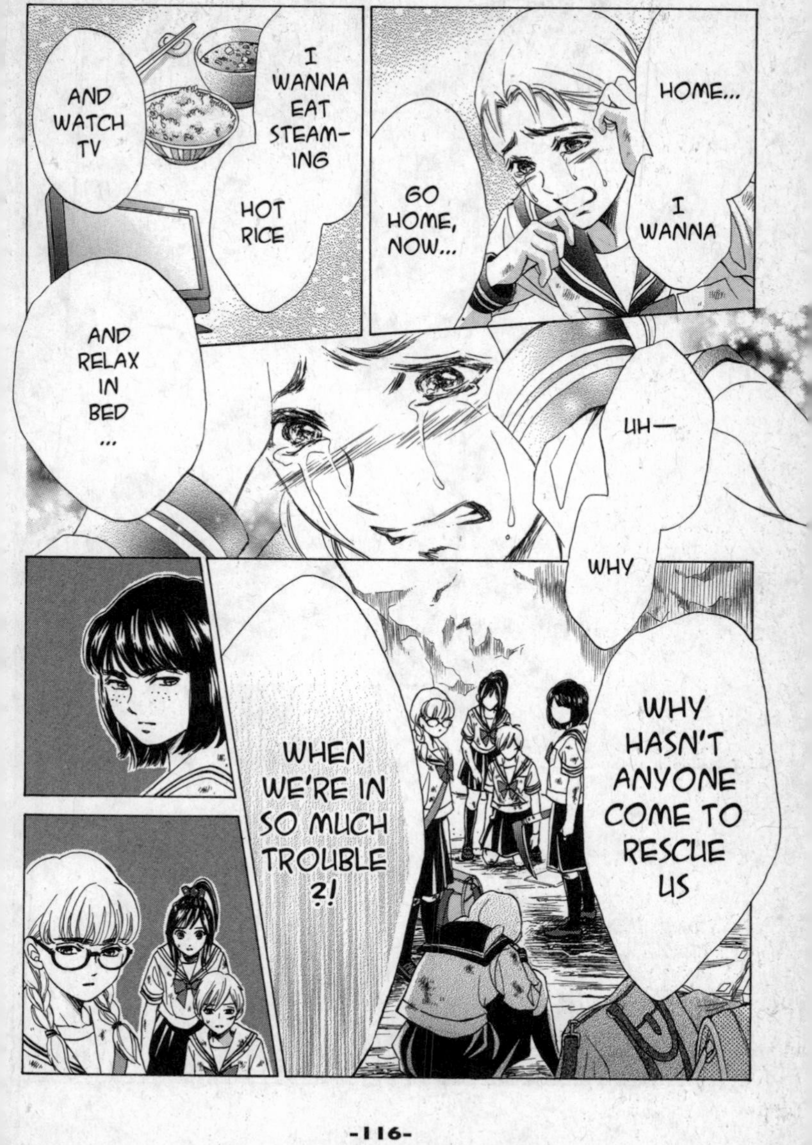
HOME...
I WANNA
GO HOME, NOW...
I WANNA EAT STEAMING
HOT RICE
AND WATCH TV
AND RELAX IN BED ...
UH—
WHY
WHY HASN'T ANYONE COME TO RESCUE US
WHEN WE'RE IN SO MUCH TROUBLE ?!

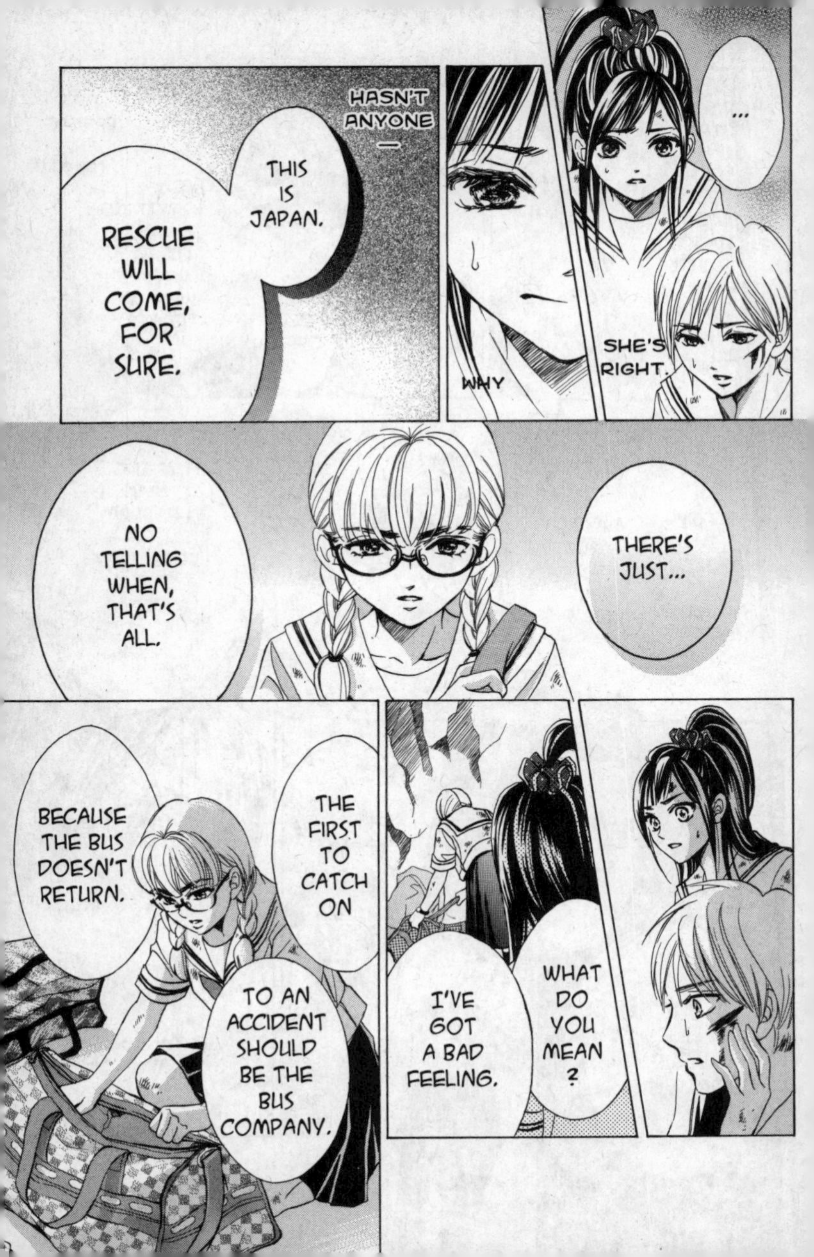
...
SHE'S RIGHT.
WHY
HASN'T ANYONE —
THIS IS JAPAN.
RESCUE WILL COME, FOR SURE.
THERE'S JUST...
NO TELLING WHEN, THAT'S ALL.
WHAT DO YOU MEAN ?
I'VE GOT A BAD FEELING.
THE FIRST TO CATCH ON
TO AN ACCIDENT SHOULD BE THE BUS COMPANY.
BECAUSE THE BUS DOESN'T RETURN.

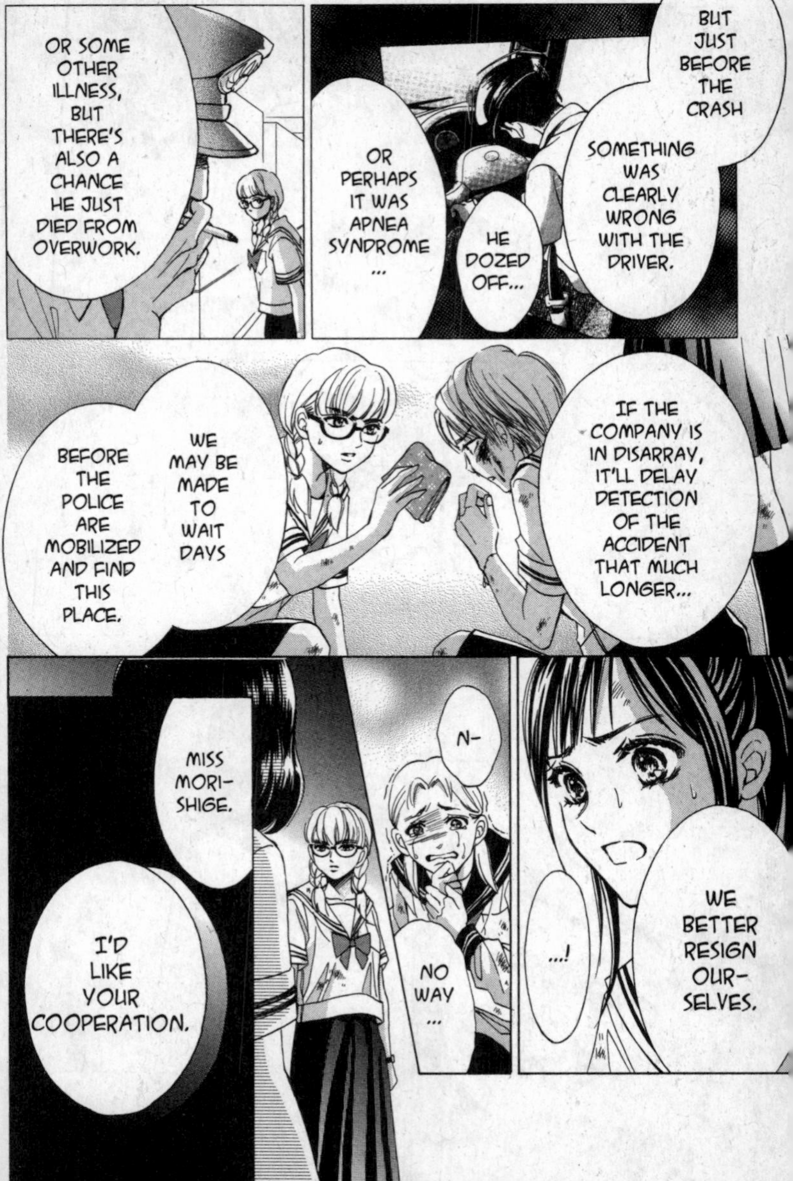
BUT JUST BEFORE THE CRASH
SOMETHING WAS CLEARLY WRONG WITH THE DRIVER.
HE DOZED OFF...
OR PERHAPS IT WAS APNEA SYNDROME ...
OR SOME OTHER ILLNESS, BUT THERE'S ALSO A CHANCE HE JUST DIED FROM OVERWORK.
IF THE COMPANY IS IN DISARRAY, IT'LL DELAY DETECTION OF THE ACCIDENT THAT MUCH LONGER...
WE MAY BE MADE TO WAIT DAYS
BEFORE THE POLICE ARE MOBILIZED AND FIND THIS PLACE.
WE BETTER RESIGN OUR-SELVES.
...!
N-
NO WAY ...
MISS MORI-SHIGE.
I'D LIKE YOUR COOPERATION.

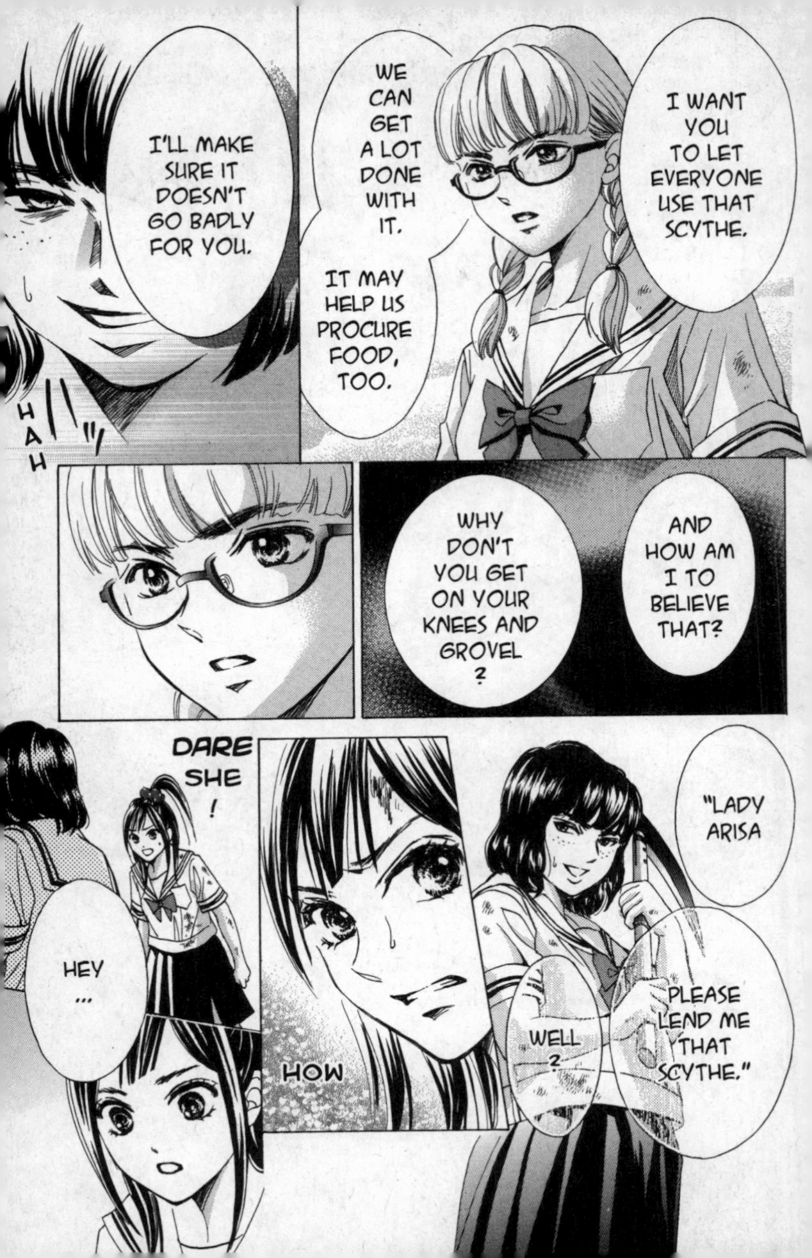
I WANT YOU TO LET EVERYONE USE THAT SCYTHE.
WE CAN GET A LOT DONE WITH IT.
IT MAY HELP US PROCURE FOOD, TOO.
I'LL MAKE SURE IT DOESN'T GO BADLY FOR YOU.
HAH
AND HOW AM I TO BELIEVE THAT?
WHY DON'T YOU GET ON YOUR KNEES AND GROVEL?
"LADY ARISA
PLEASE LEND ME THAT SCYTHE."
WELL?
HOW
DARE SHE!
HEY...

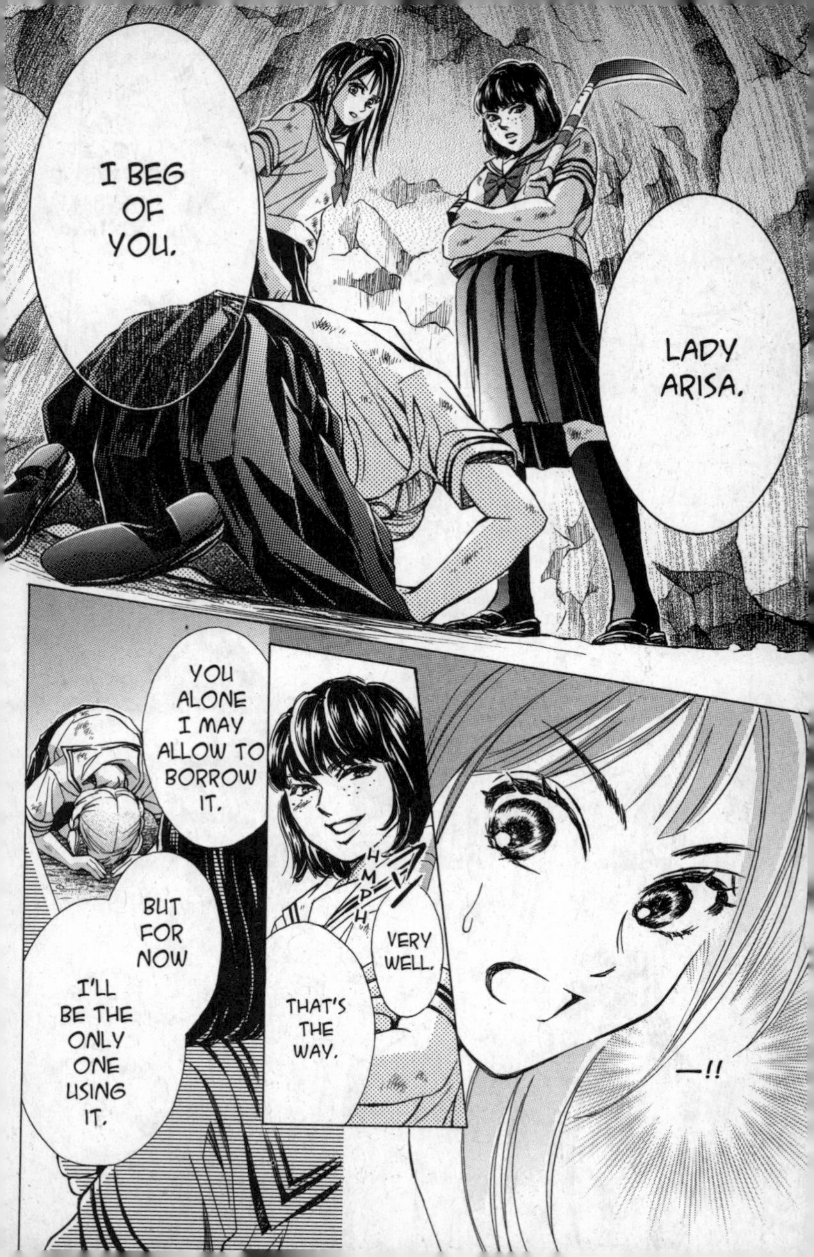
LADY ARISA.
I BEG OF YOU.
HMPH
VERY WELL.
THAT'S THE WAY.
YOU ALONE I MAY ALLOW TO BORROW IT.
BUT FOR NOW
I'LL BE THE ONLY ONE USING IT.
—!!

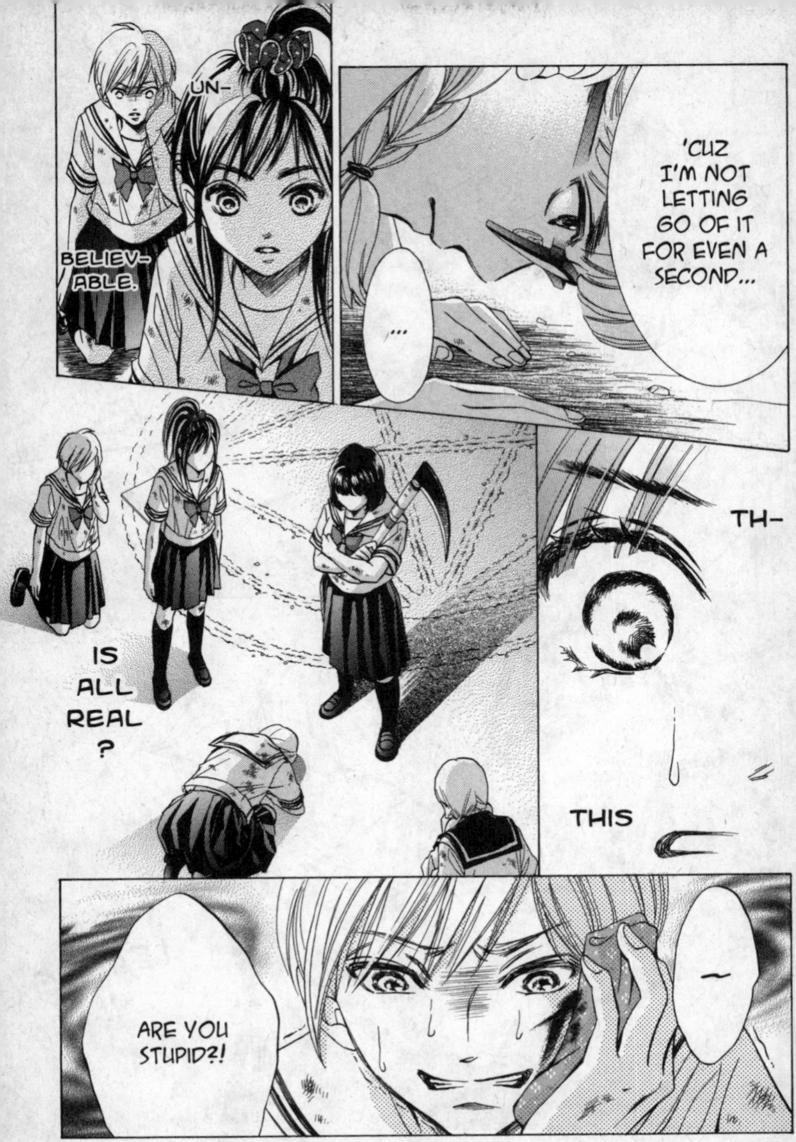
'CUZ I'M NOT LETTING GO OF IT FOR EVEN A SECOND...
...
UN-
BELIEV-ABLE.
TH-
THIS
IS ALL REAL ?
ARE YOU STUPID?!

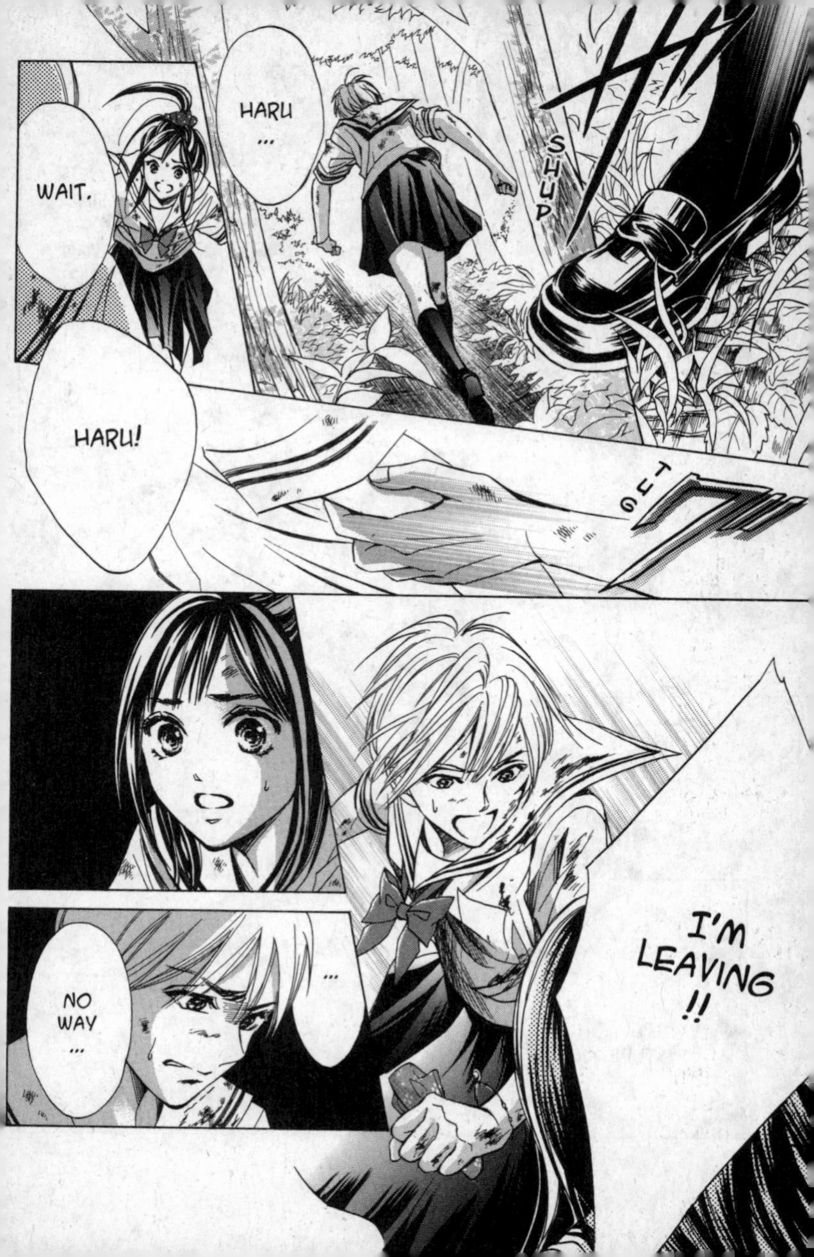

SHUP
HARU ...
WAIT.
HARU!
TUG
I'M LEAVING !!
...
NO WAY ...

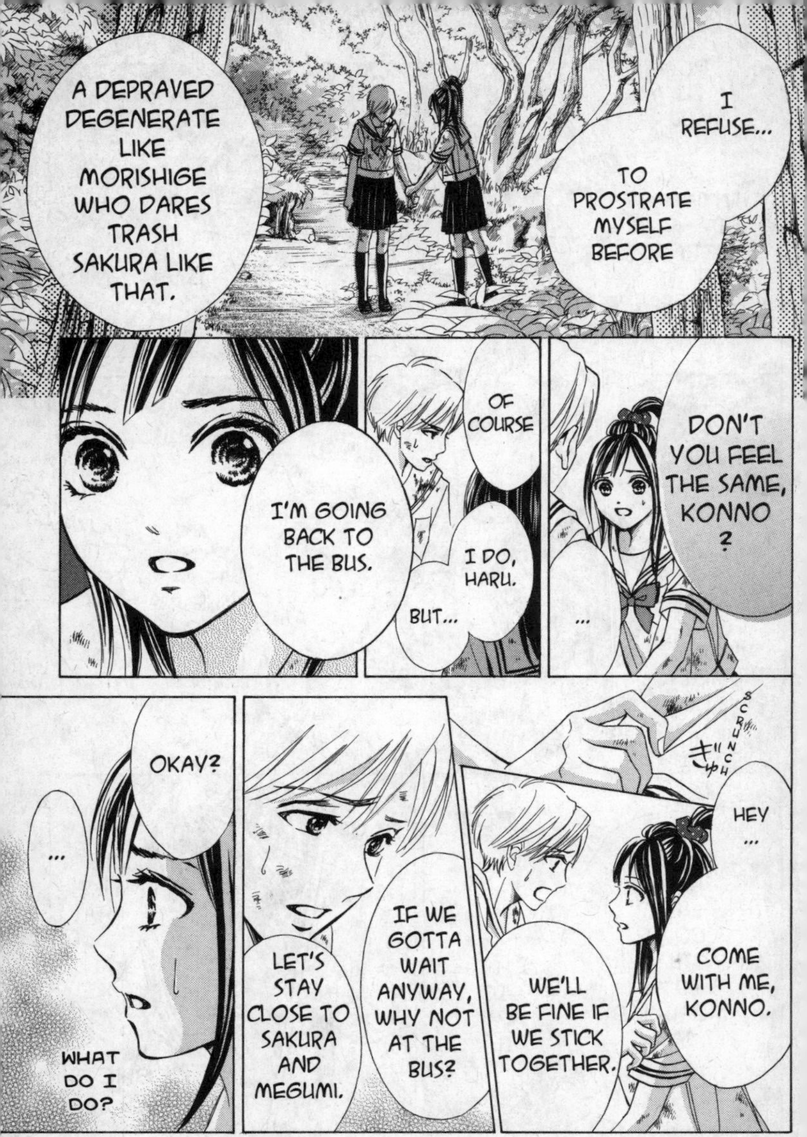
I REFUSE...
TO PROSTRATE MYSELF BEFORE
A DEPRAVED DEGENERATE LIKE MORISHIGE WHO DARES TRASH SAKURA LIKE THAT.
DON'T YOU FEEL THE SAME, KONNO?
...
OF COURSE
I DO, HARU.
BUT...
I'M GOING BACK TO THE BUS.
SCRUNCH
ぎゅ
HEY ...
COME WITH ME, KONNO.
WE'LL BE FINE IF WE STICK TOGETHER.
IF WE GOTTA WAIT ANYWAY, WHY NOT AT THE BUS?
LET'S STAY CLOSE TO SAKURA AND MEGUMI.
OKAY?
...
WHAT DO I DO?

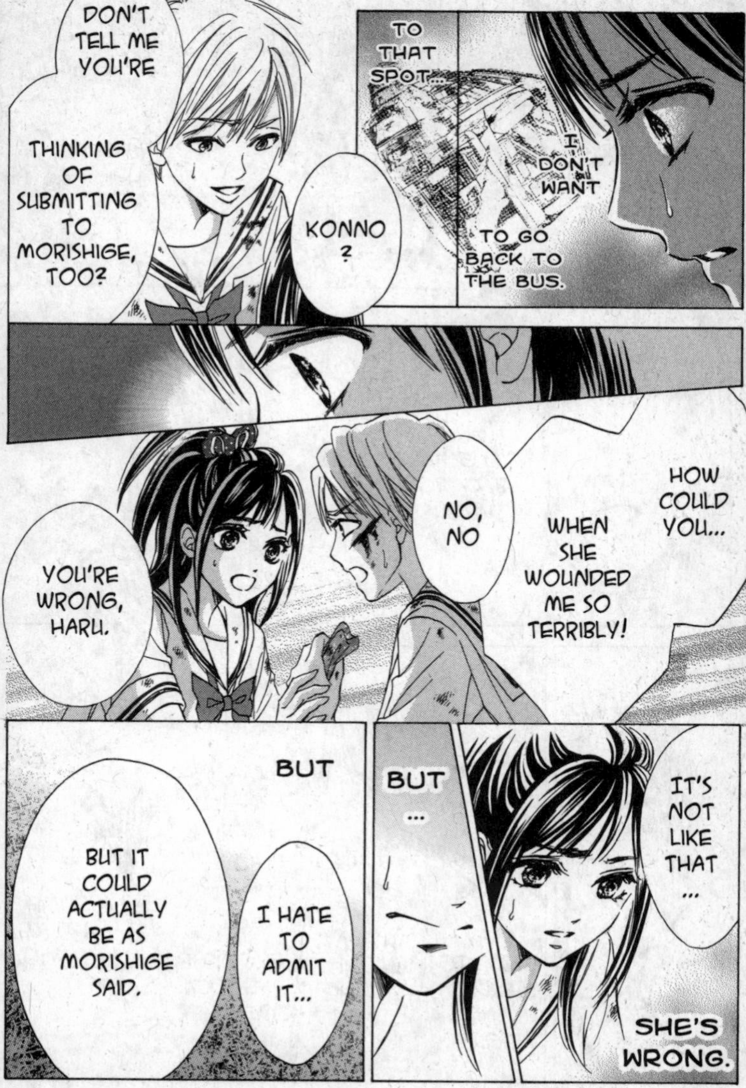
TO THAT SPOT...
I DON'T WANT
TO GO BACK TO THE BUS.
DON'T TELL ME YOU'RE
THINKING OF SUBMITTING TO MORISHIGE, TOO?
KONNO?
HOW COULD YOU...
WHEN SHE WOUNDED ME SO TERRIBLY!
NO, NO
YOU'RE WRONG, HARU.
IT'S NOT LIKE THAT...
SHE'S WRONG.
BUT...
BUT
I HATE TO ADMIT IT...
BUT IT COULD ACTUALLY BE AS MORISHIGE SAID.

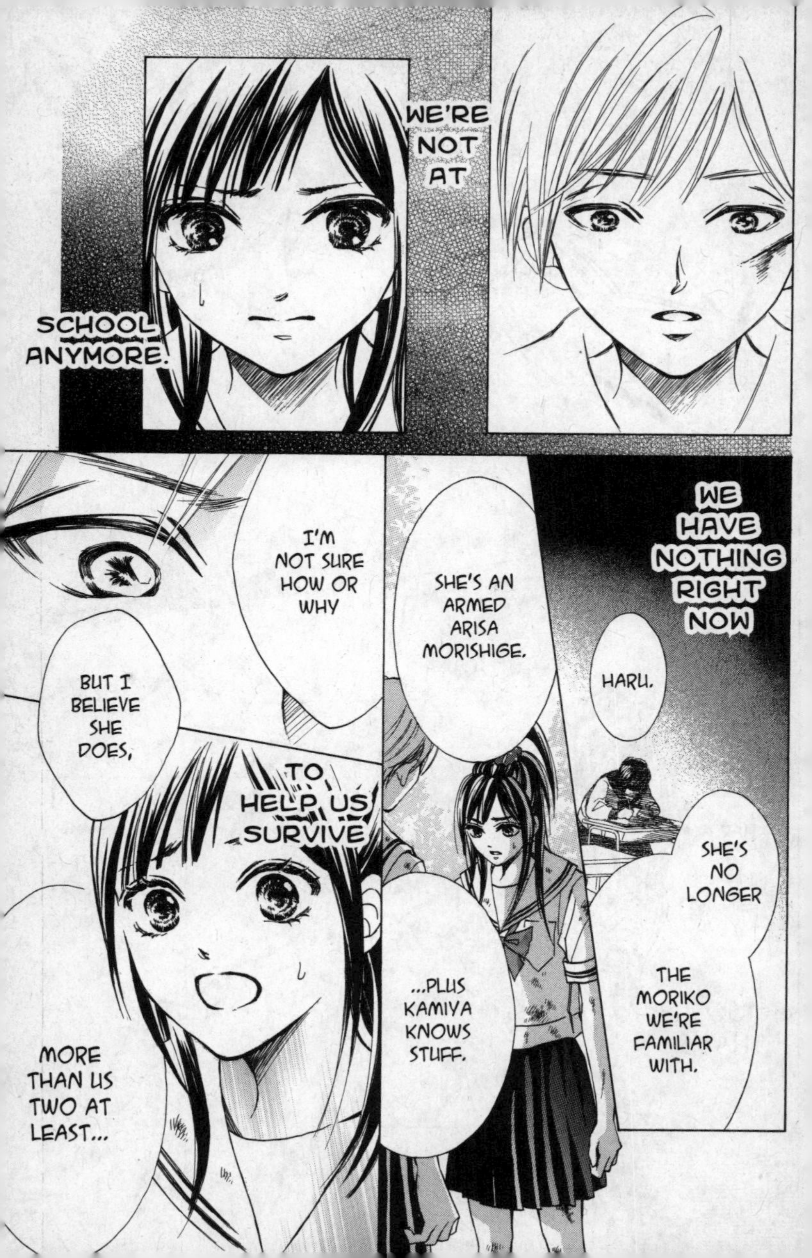
WE'RE NOT AT
SCHOOL ANYMORE.
WE HAVE NOTHING RIGHT NOW
HARU.
SHE'S AN ARMED ARISA MORISHIGE.
SHE'S NO LONGER
THE MORIKO WE'RE FAMILIAR WITH.
...PLUS KAMIYA KNOWS STUFF.
I'M NOT SURE HOW OR WHY
BUT I BELIEVE SHE DOES,
TO HELP US SURVIVE
MORE THAN US TWO AT LEAST...

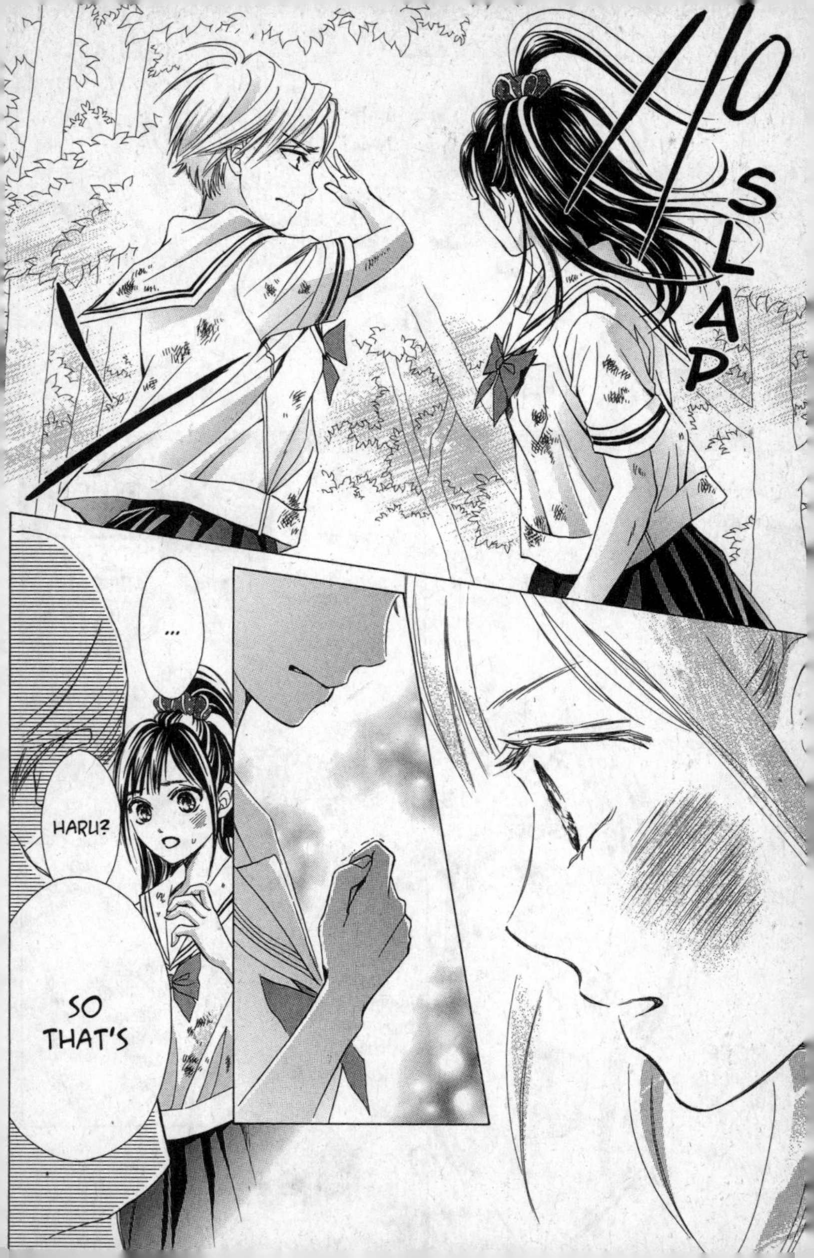
SLAP
...
HARU?
SO THAT'S

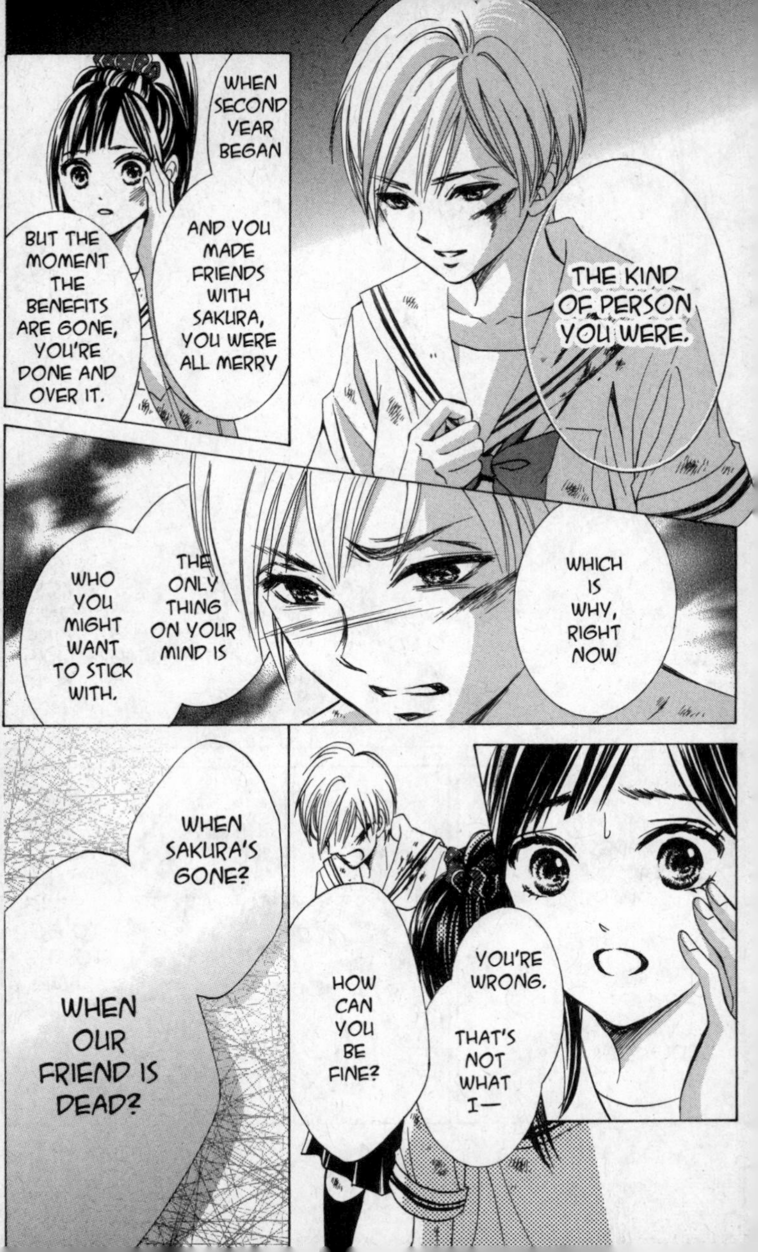
THE KIND OF PERSON YOU WERE.
WHEN SECOND YEAR BEGAN
AND YOU MADE FRIENDS WITH SAKURA, YOU WERE ALL MERRY
BUT THE MOMENT THE BENEFITS ARE GONE, YOU'RE DONE AND OVER IT.
WHICH IS WHY, RIGHT NOW
THE ONLY THING ON YOUR MIND IS
WHO YOU MIGHT WANT TO STICK WITH.
YOU'RE WRONG.
THAT'S NOT WHAT I—
HOW CAN YOU BE FINE?
WHEN SAKURA'S GONE?
WHEN OUR FRIEND IS DEAD?

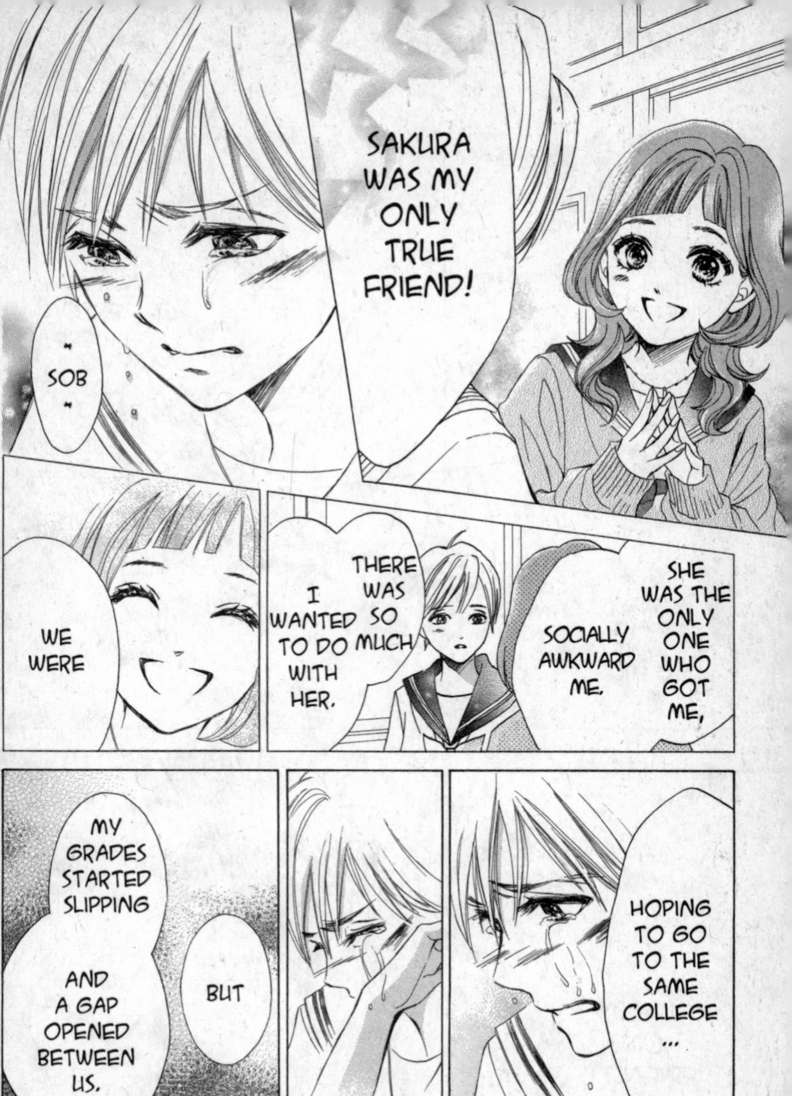
SAKURA WAS MY ONLY TRUE FRIEND!
SOB
SHE WAS THE ONLY ONE WHO GOT ME,
SOCIALLY AWKWARD ME.
THERE WAS SO MUCH
I WANTED TO DO WITH HER.
WE WERE
HOPING TO GO TO THE SAME COLLEGE ...
BUT
MY GRADES STARTED SLIPPING
AND A GAP OPENED BETWEEN US.

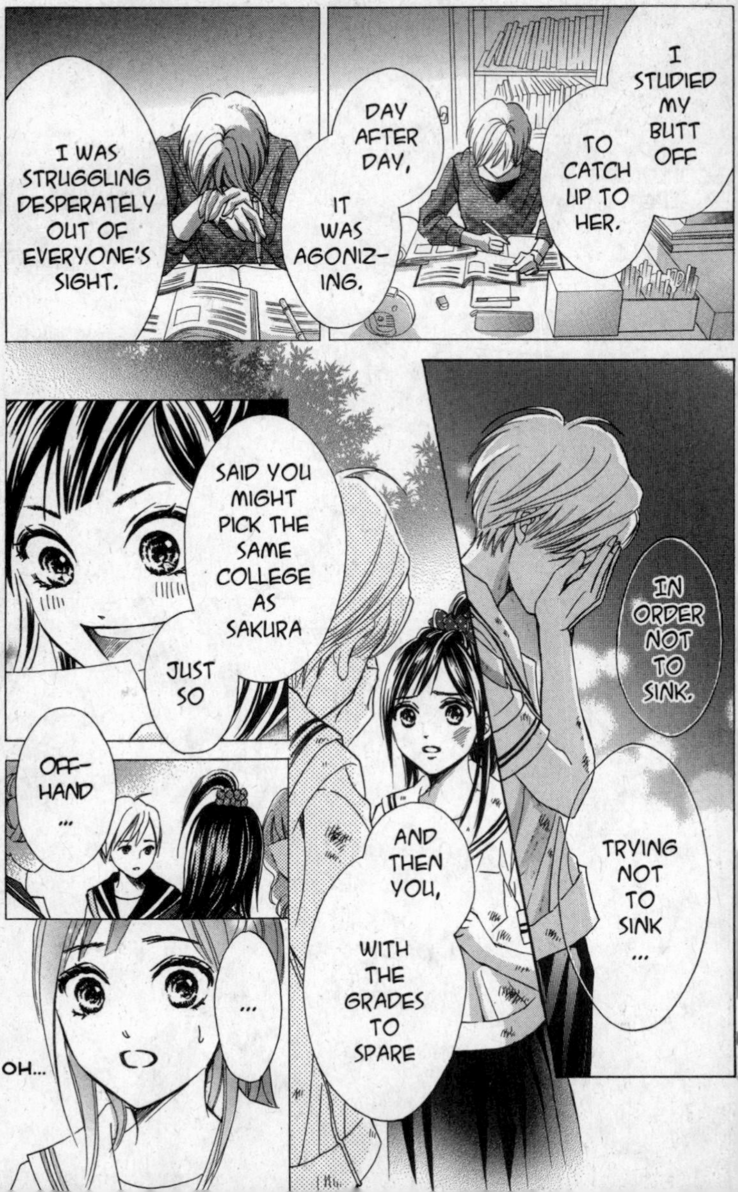
I STUDIED MY BUTT OFF
TO CATCH UP TO HER.
DAY AFTER DAY,
IT WAS AGONIZ-ING.
I WAS STRUGGLING DESPERATELY OUT OF EVERYONE'S SIGHT.
IN ORDER NOT TO SINK.
TRYING NOT TO SINK ...
AND THEN YOU,
WITH THE GRADES TO SPARE
SAID YOU MIGHT PICK THE SAME COLLEGE AS SAKURA
JUST SO
OFF-HAND ...
...
OH...

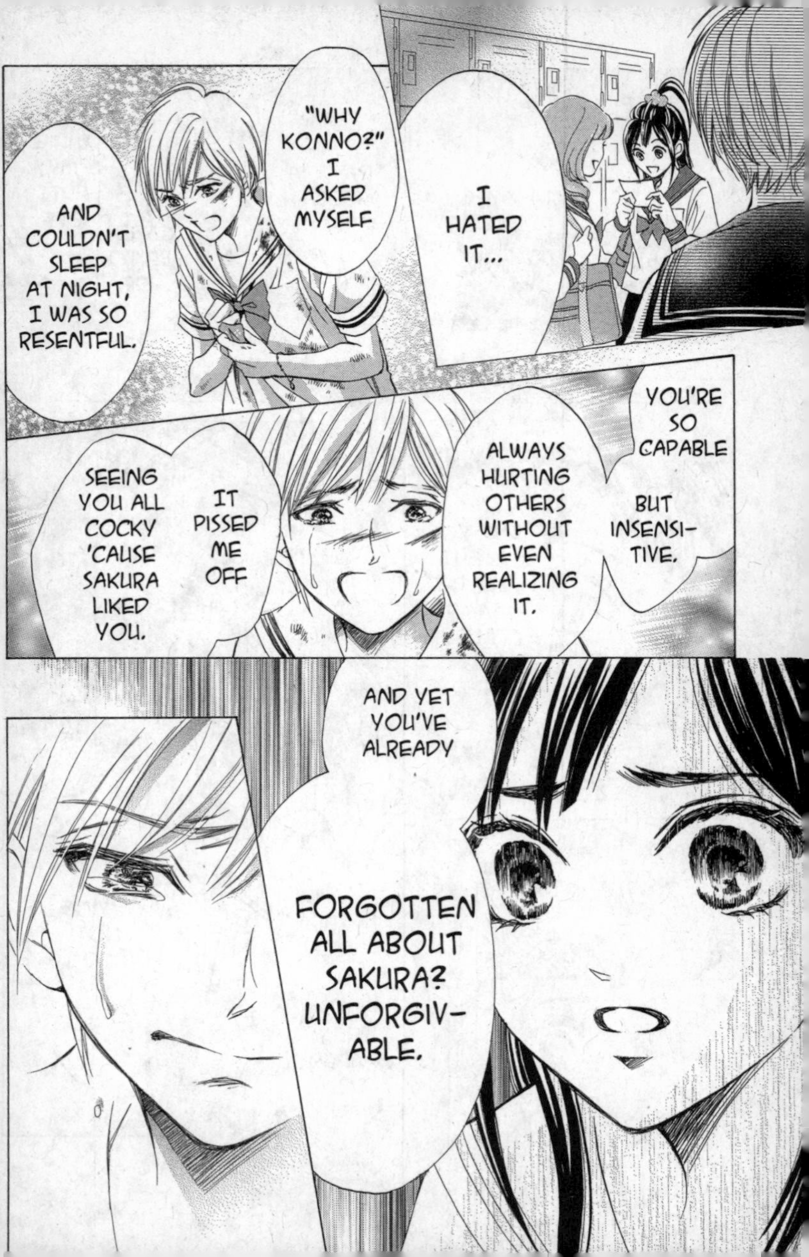
I HATED IT...
"WHY KONNO?" I ASKED MYSELF
AND COULDN'T SLEEP AT NIGHT, I WAS SO RESENTFUL.
YOU'RE SO CAPABLE
BUT INSENSITIVE.
ALWAYS HURTING OTHERS WITHOUT EVEN REALIZING IT.
IT PISSED ME OFF
SEEING YOU ALL COCKY 'CAUSE SAKURA LIKED YOU.
AND YET YOU'VE ALREADY
FORGOTTEN ALL ABOUT SAKURA? UNFORGIV-ABLE.

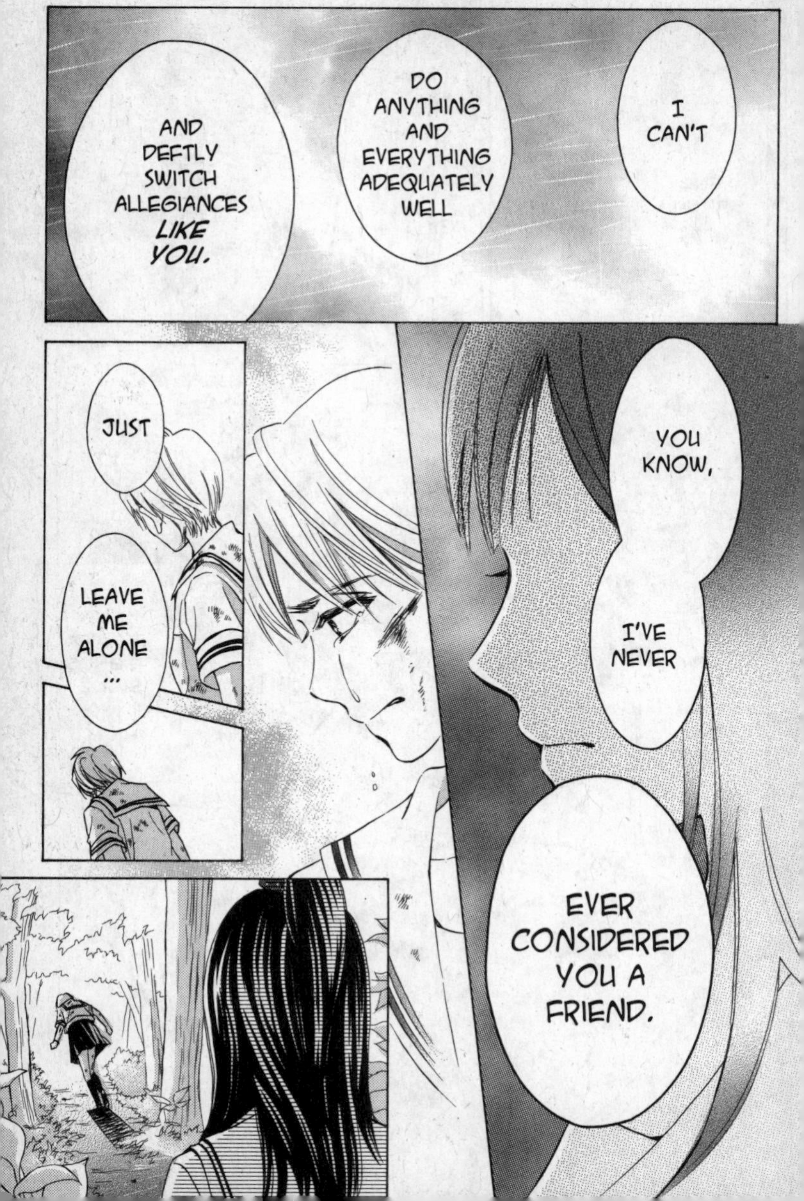
I CAN'T
DO ANYTHING AND EVERYTHING ADEQUATELY WELL
AND DEFTLY SWITCH ALLEGIANCES *LIKE YOU.*
YOU KNOW,
I'VE NEVER
EVER CONSIDERED YOU A FRIEND.
JUST
LEAVE ME ALONE ...

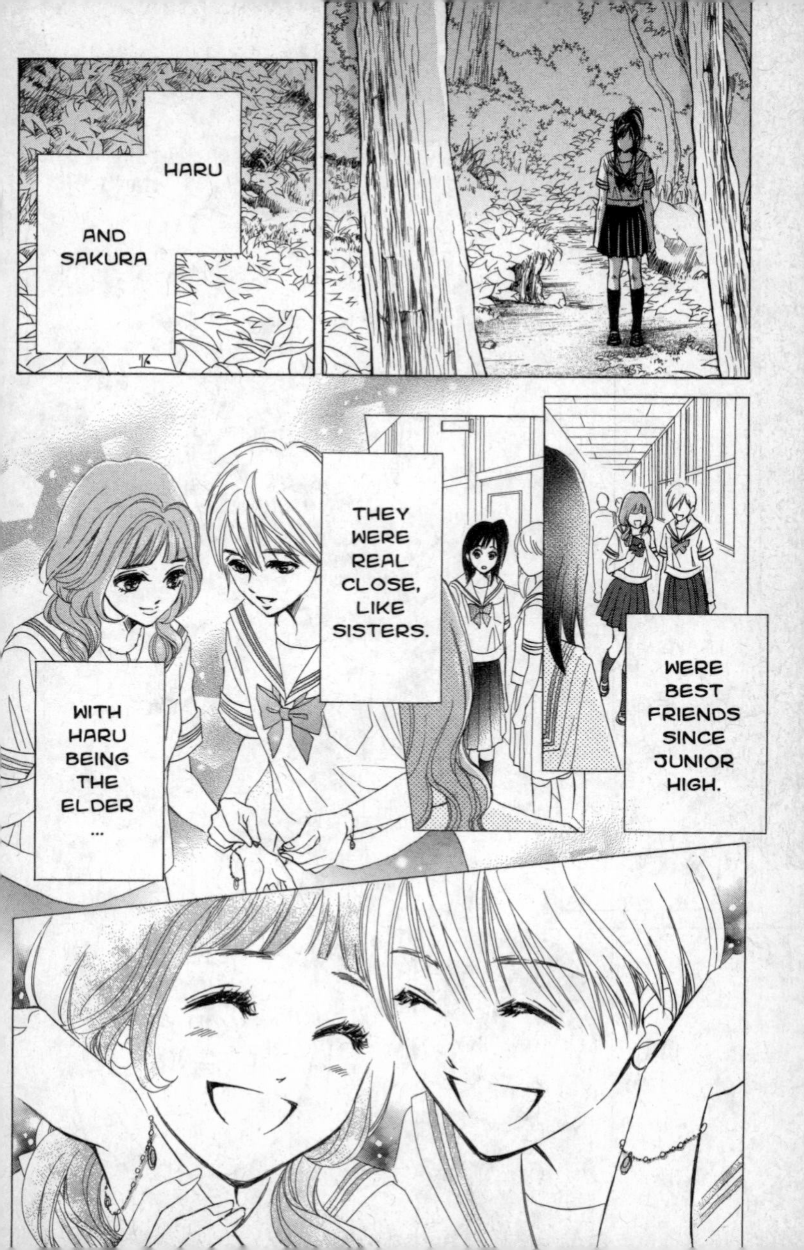
HARU
AND SAKURA
WERE BEST FRIENDS SINCE JUNIOR HIGH.
THEY WERE REAL CLOSE, LIKE SISTERS.
WITH HARU BEING THE ELDER ...

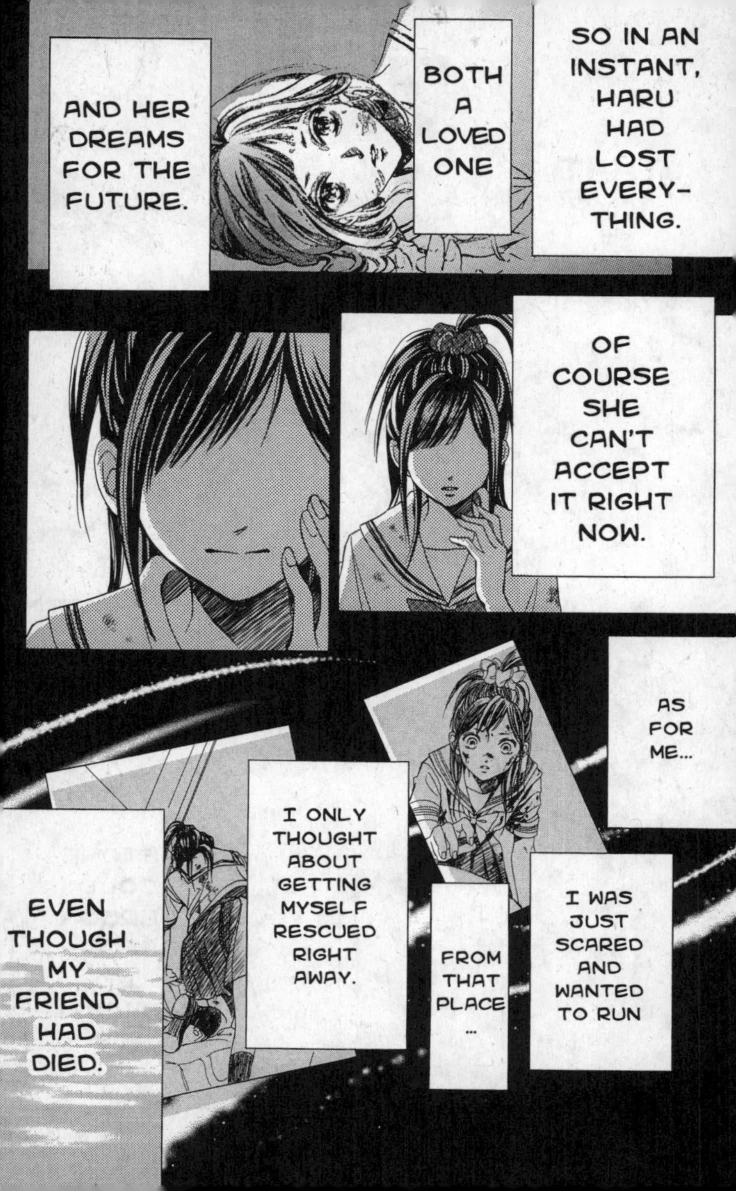
SO IN AN INSTANT, HARU HAD LOST EVERY-THING.
BOTH A LOVED ONE
AND HER DREAMS FOR THE FUTURE.
OF COURSE SHE CAN'T ACCEPT IT RIGHT NOW.
AS FOR ME...
I WAS JUST SCARED AND WANTED TO RUN
FROM THAT PLACE...
I ONLY THOUGHT ABOUT GETTING MYSELF RESCUED RIGHT AWAY.
EVEN THOUGH MY FRIEND HAD DIED.

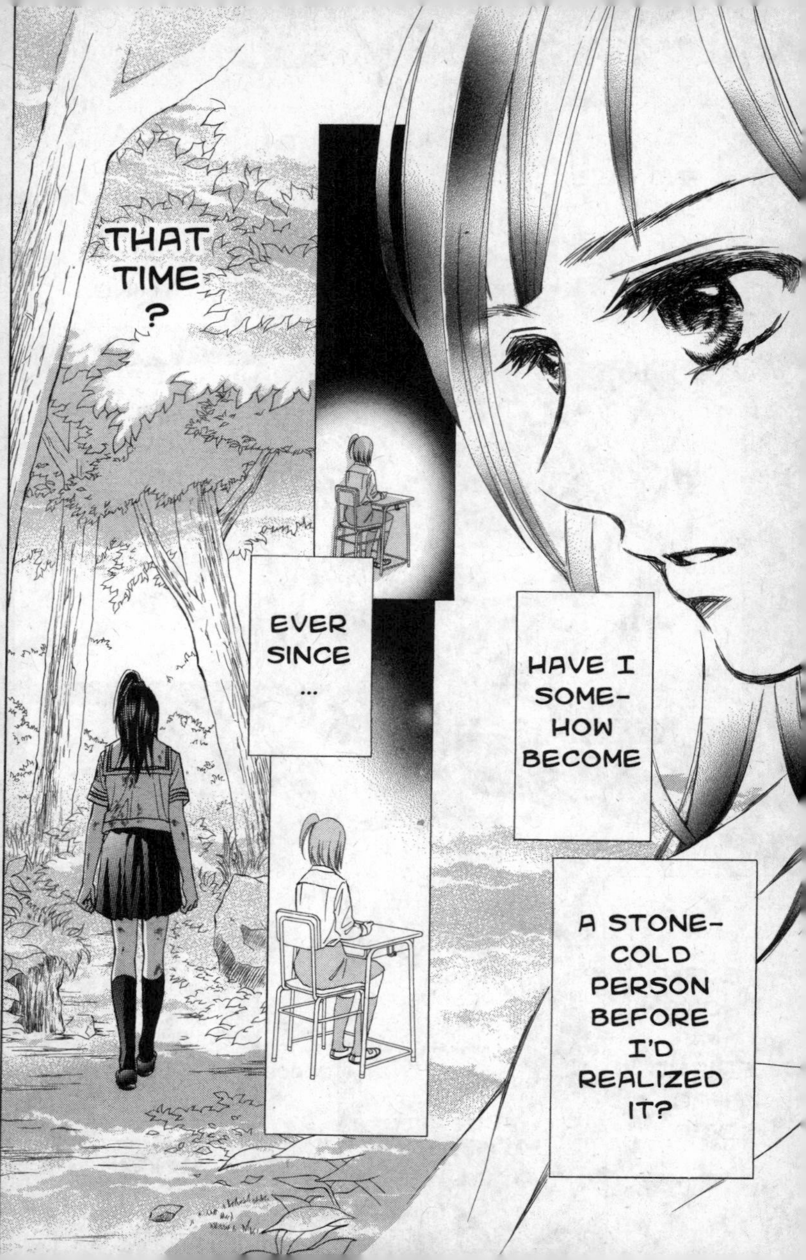
HAVE I SOME-HOW BECOME
A STONE-COLD PERSON BEFORE I'D REALIZED IT?
EVER SINCE ...
THAT TIME ?

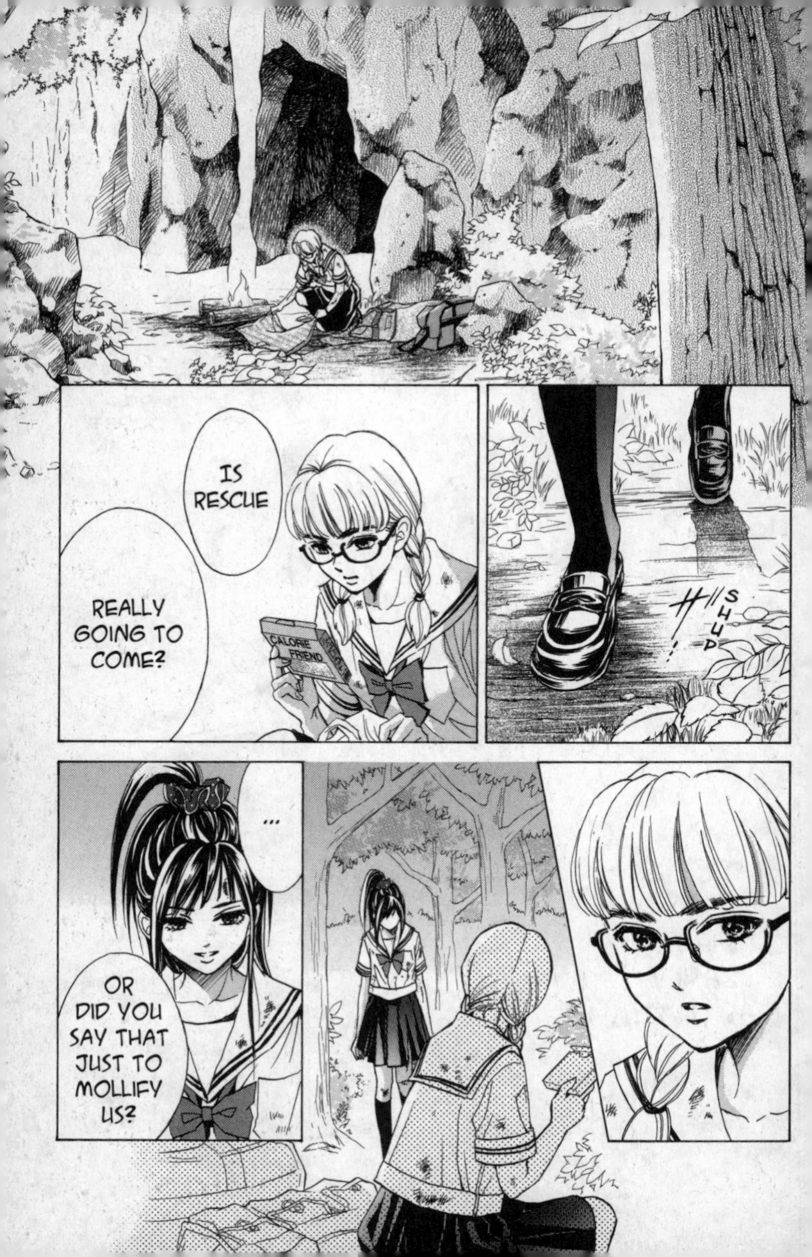
SHUD
IS RESCUE
REALLY GOING TO COME?
CALORIE FRIEND
...
OR DID YOU SAY THAT JUST TO MOLLIFY US?

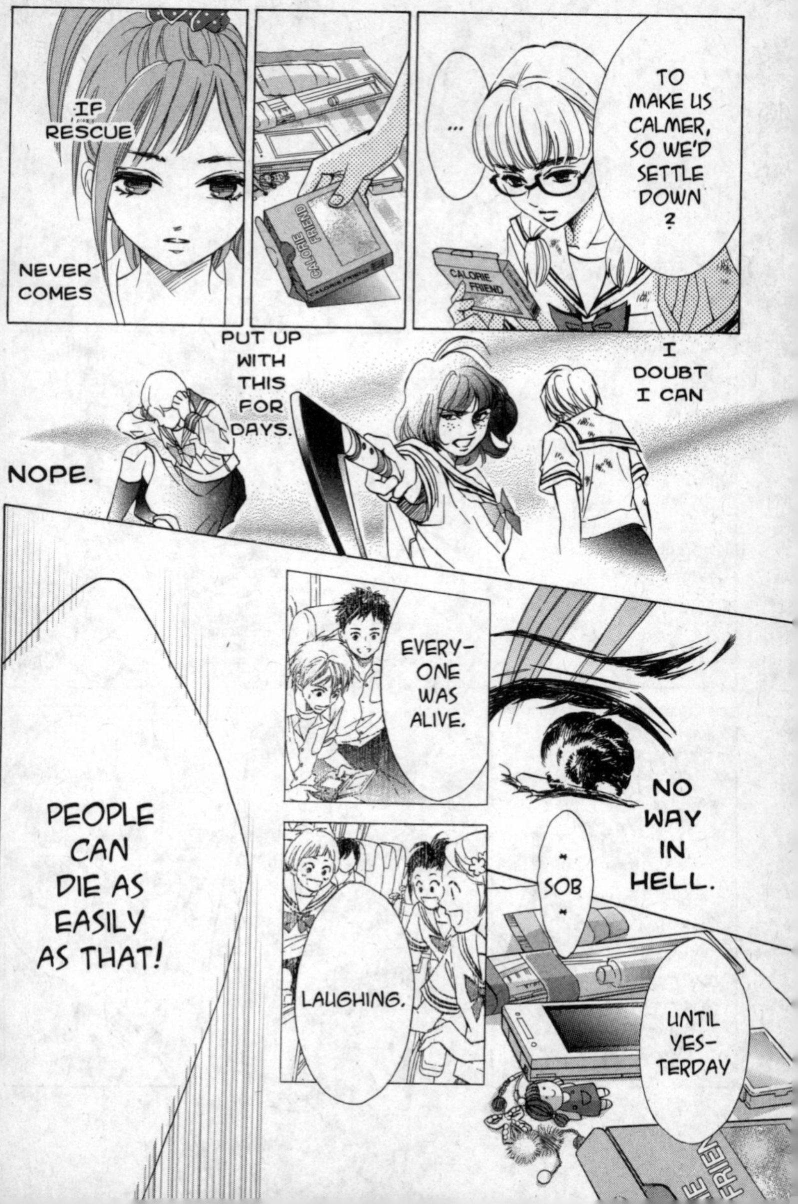
...
TO MAKE US CALMER, SO WE'D SETTLE DOWN?
CALORIE FRIEND
CALORIE FRIEND
IF RESCUE NEVER COMES
I DOUBT I CAN
PUT UP WITH THIS FOR DAYS.
NOPE.
NO WAY IN HELL.
SOB
UNTIL YESTERDAY
EVERY-ONE WAS ALIVE.
LAUGHING.
PEOPLE CAN DIE AS EASILY AS THAT!

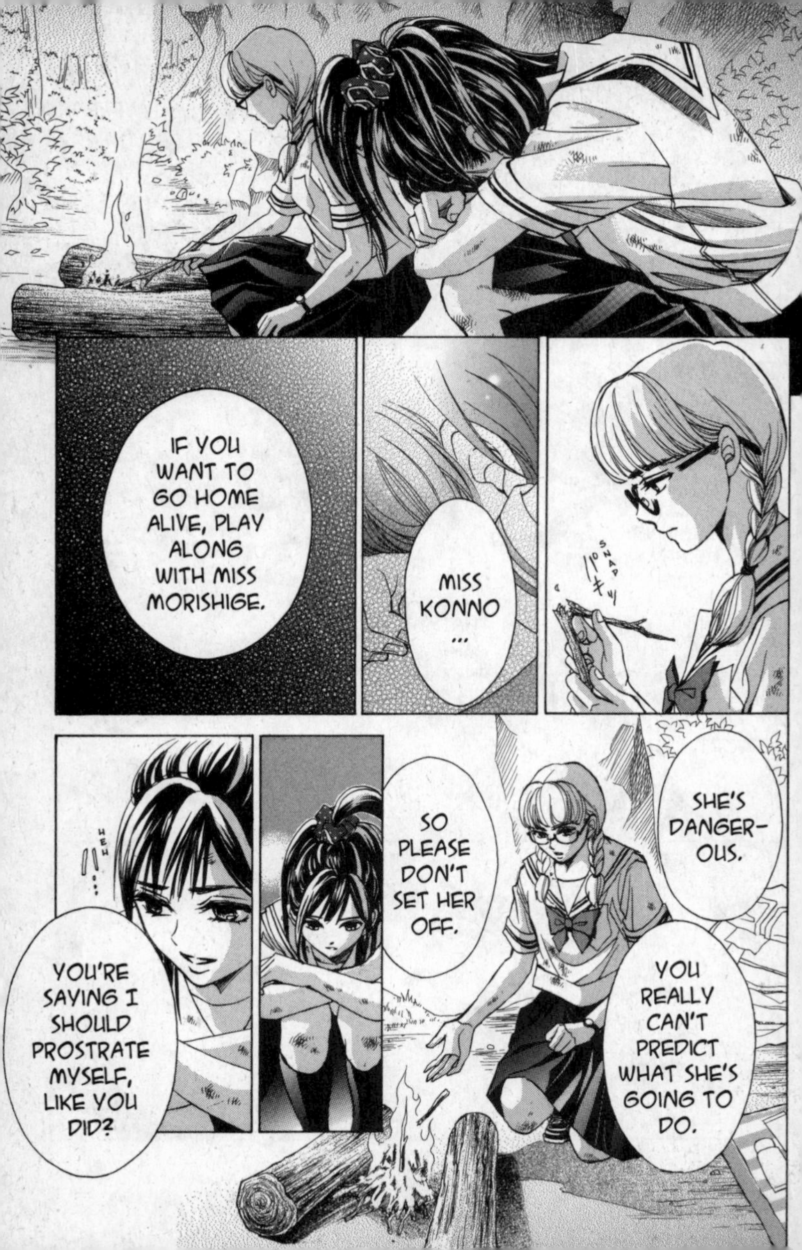
SNAP
MISS KONNO ...
IF YOU WANT TO GO HOME ALIVE, PLAY ALONG WITH MISS MORISHIGE.
SHE'S DANGER-OUS.
YOU REALLY CAN'T PREDICT WHAT SHE'S GOING TO DO.
SO PLEASE DON'T SET HER OFF.
HEH
YOU'RE SAYING I SHOULD PROSTRATE MYSELF, LIKE YOU DID?

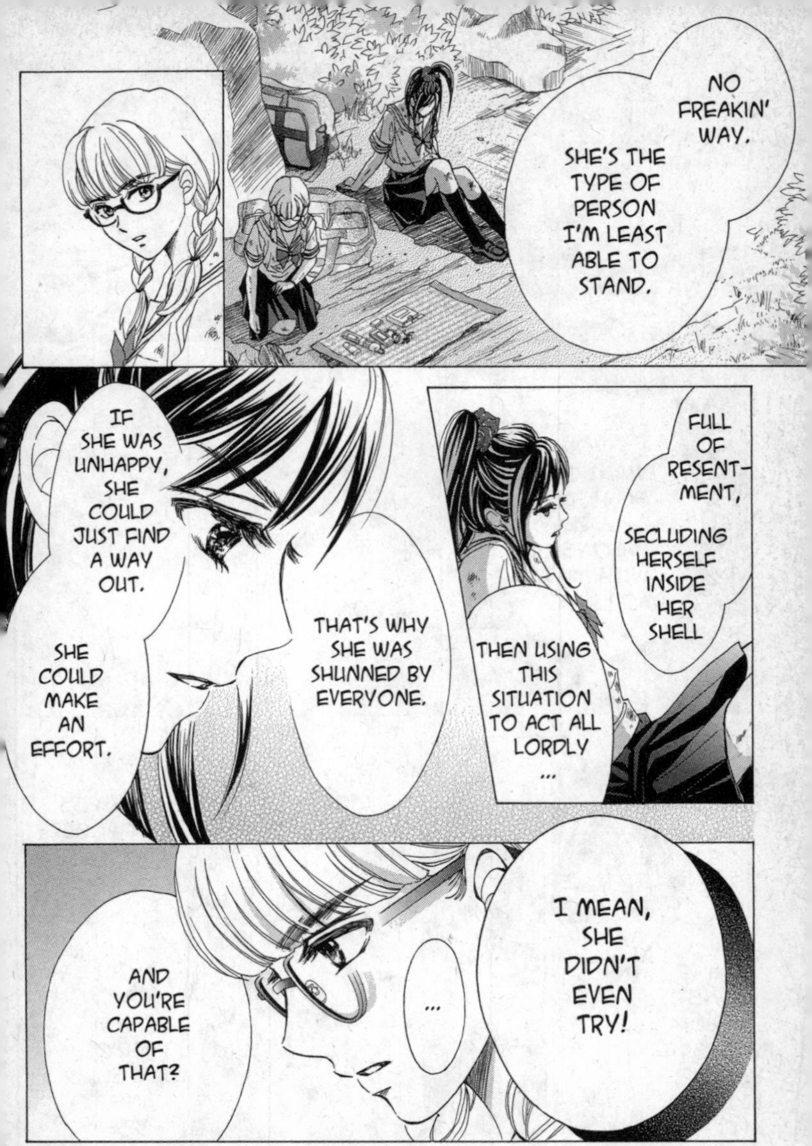
NO FREAKIN' WAY.
SHE'S THE TYPE OF PERSON I'M LEAST ABLE TO STAND.
FULL OF RESENT-MENT,
SECLUDING HERSELF INSIDE HER SHELL
THEN USING THIS SITUATION TO ACT ALL LORDLY ...
IF SHE WAS UNHAPPY, SHE COULD JUST FIND A WAY OUT.
SHE COULD MAKE AN EFFORT.
THAT'S WHY SHE WAS SHUNNED BY EVERYONE.
I MEAN, SHE DIDN'T EVEN TRY!
...
AND YOU'RE CAPABLE OF THAT?

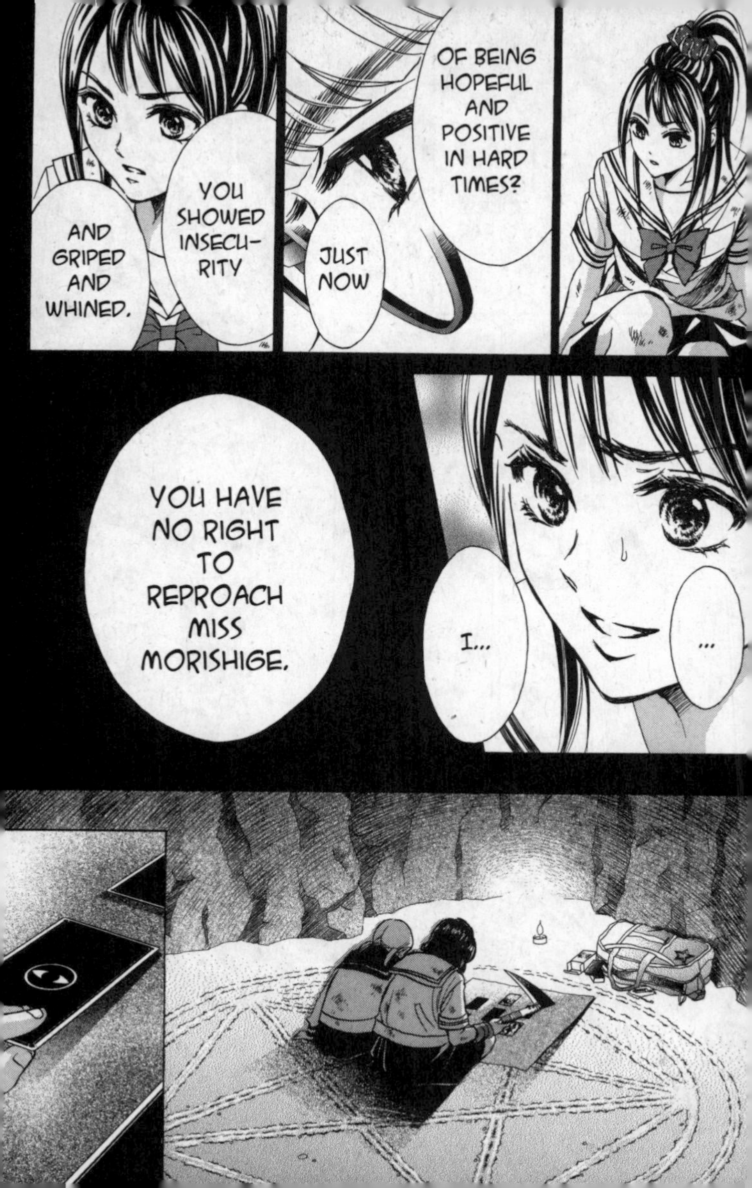
OF BEING HOPEFUL AND POSITIVE IN HARD TIMES?
JUST NOW
YOU SHOWED INSECU-RITY
AND GRIPED AND WHINED.
...
I...
YOU HAVE NO RIGHT TO REPROACH MISS MORISHIGE.

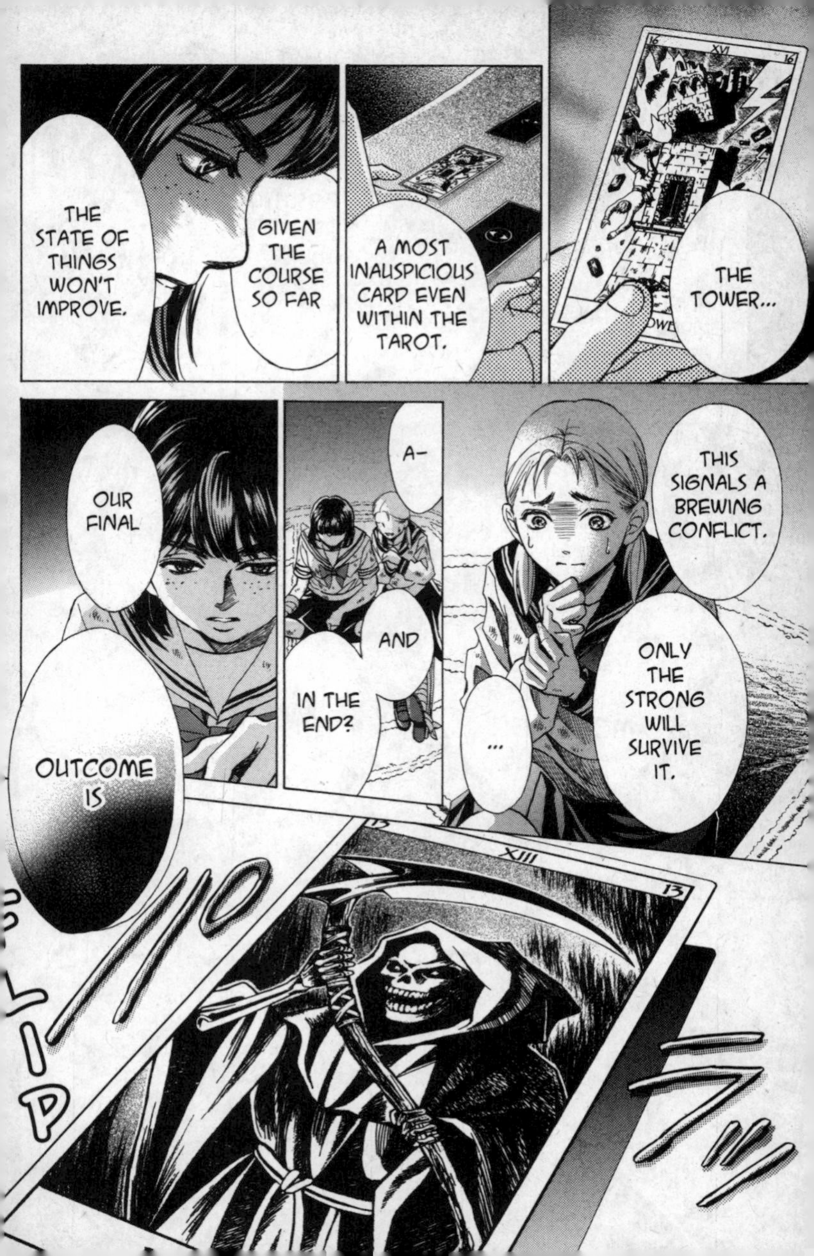

THE TOWER...
A MOST INAUSPICIOUS CARD EVEN WITHIN THE TAROT.
GIVEN THE COURSE SO FAR
THE STATE OF THINGS WON'T IMPROVE.
THIS SIGNALS A BREWING CONFLICT.
ONLY THE STRONG WILL SURVIVE IT.
...
A-
AND
IN THE END?
OUR FINAL
OUTCOME IS
SLIP

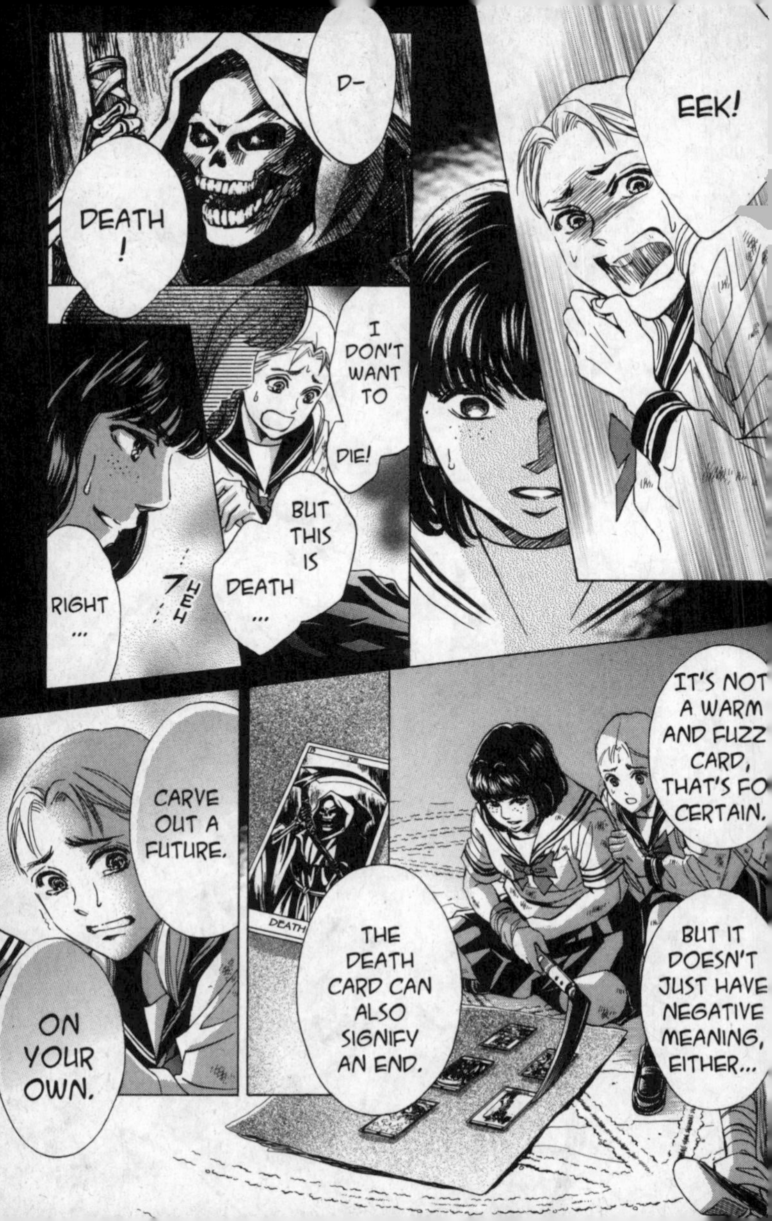
EEK!
D-
DEATH !
I DON'T WANT TO DIE!
BUT THIS IS DEATH ...
HEH
RIGHT ...
IT'S NOT A WARM AND FUZZ CARD, THAT'S FO CERTAIN.
BUT IT DOESN'T JUST HAVE NEGATIVE MEANING, EITHER...
DEATH
THE DEATH CARD CAN ALSO SIGNIFY AN END.
CARVE OUT A FUTURE.
ON YOUR OWN.

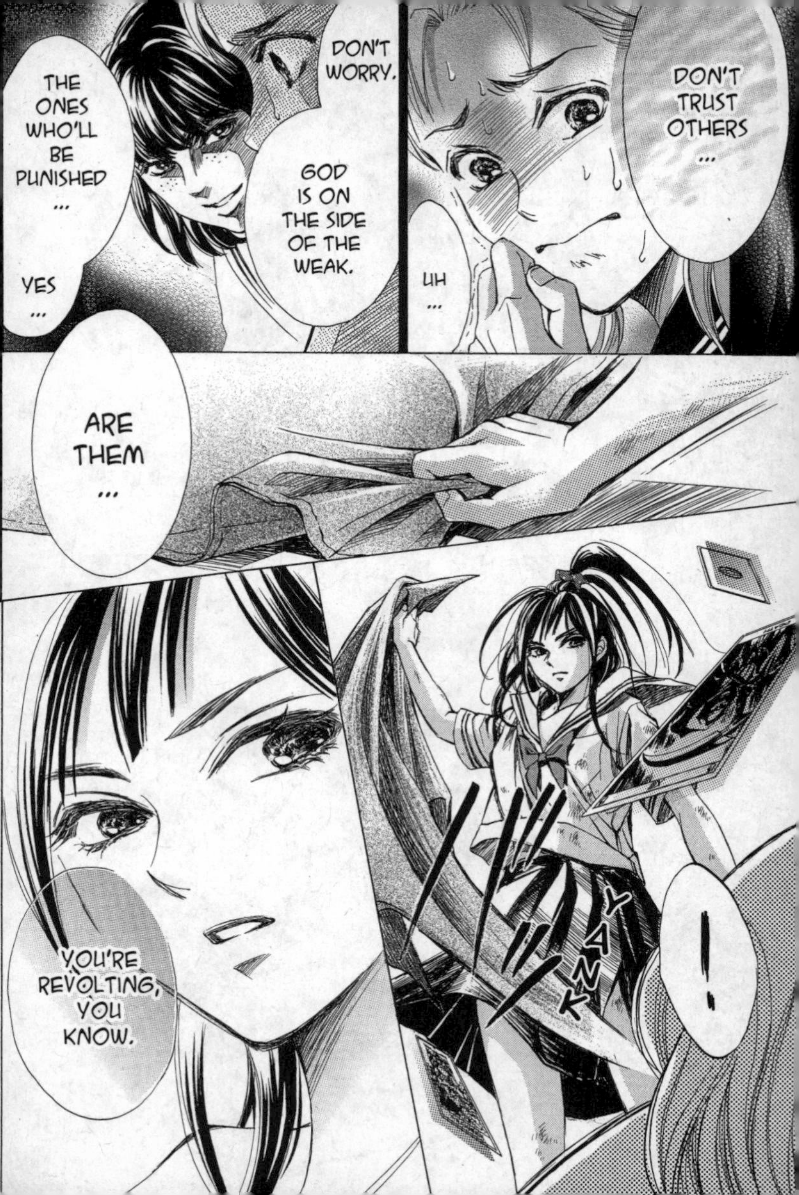
DON'T TRUST OTHERS ...
UH ...
DON'T WORRY.
GOD IS ON THE SIDE OF THE WEAK.
THE ONES WHO'LL BE PUNISHED ...
YES ...
ARE THEM ...
!
YANK
YOU'RE REVOLTING, YOU KNOW.

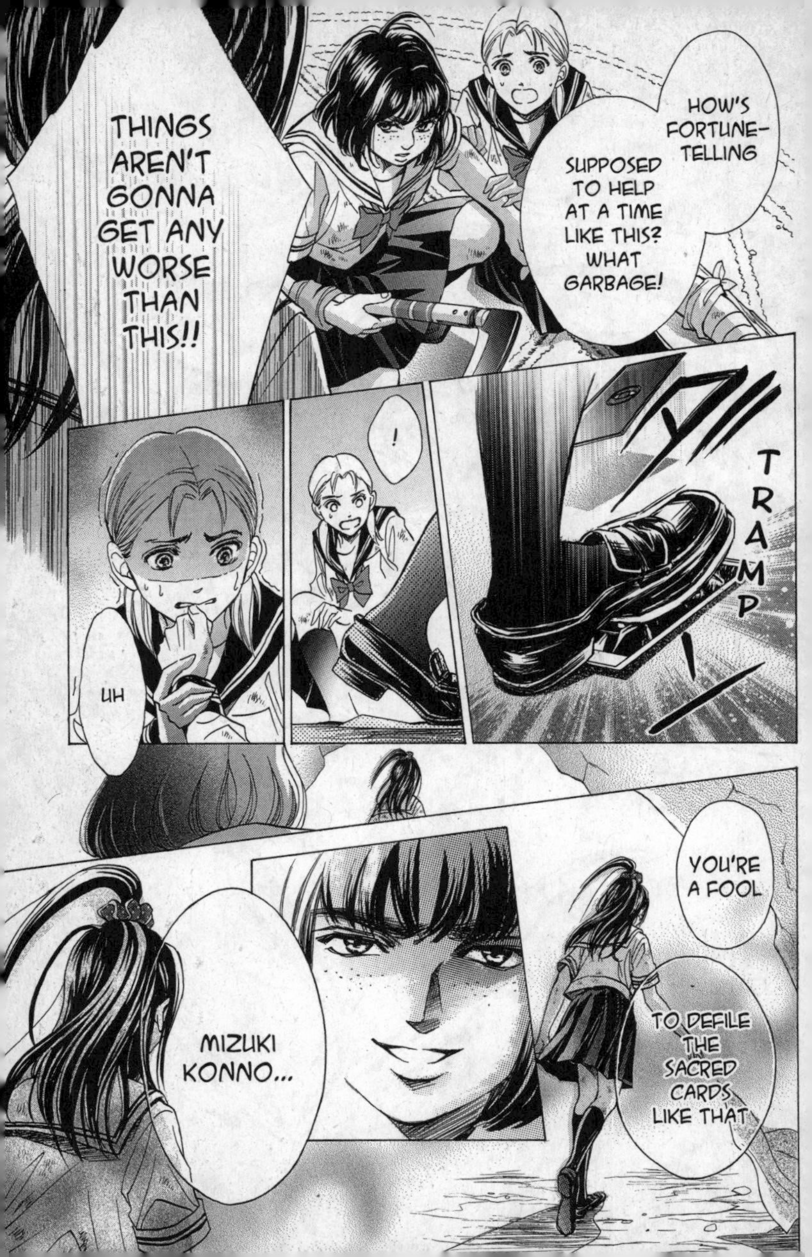
HOW'S FORTUNE-TELLING
SUPPOSED TO HELP AT A TIME LIKE THIS? WHAT GARBAGE!
THINGS AREN'T GONNA GET ANY WORSE THAN THIS!!
TRAMP
!
UH
YOU'RE A FOOL
TO DEFILE THE SACRED CARDS LIKE THAT
MIZUKI KONNO...

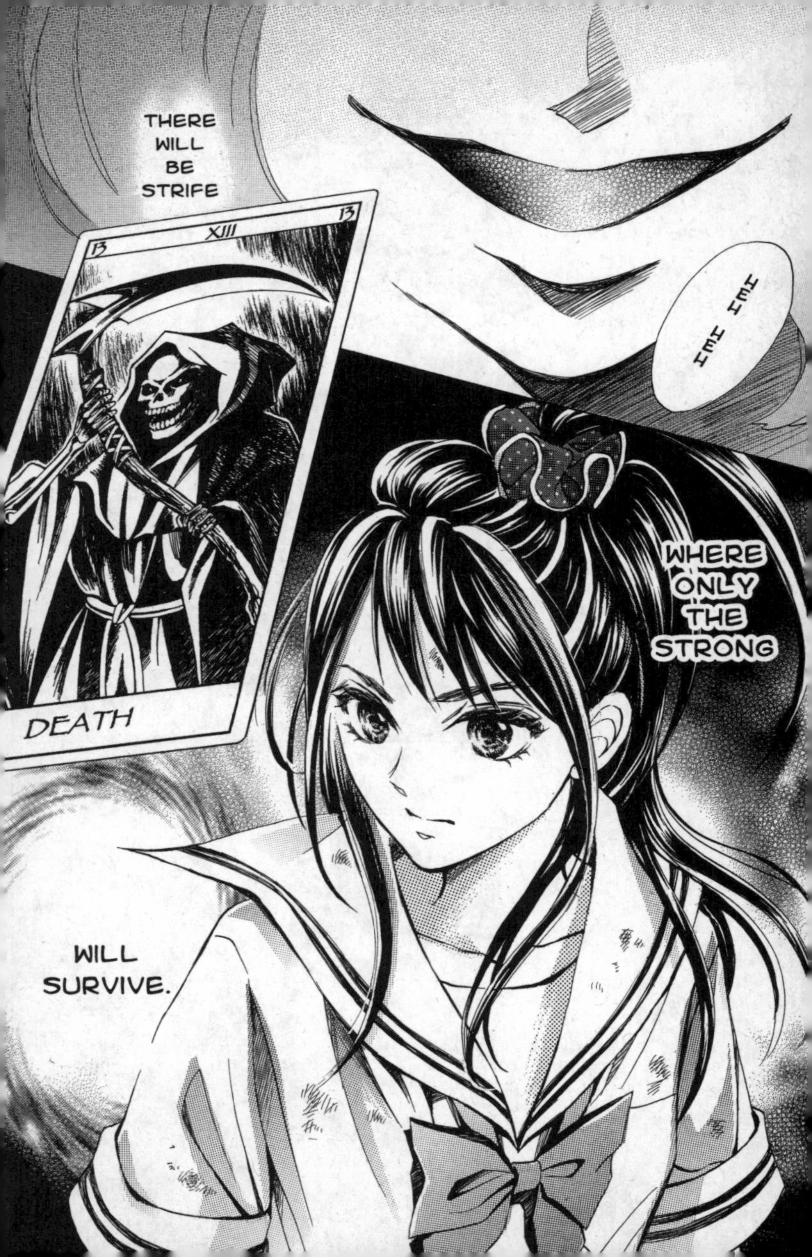
HEH HEH
THERE WILL BE STRIFE
13 XIII 13
DEATH
WHERE ONLY THE STRONG
WILL SURVIVE.

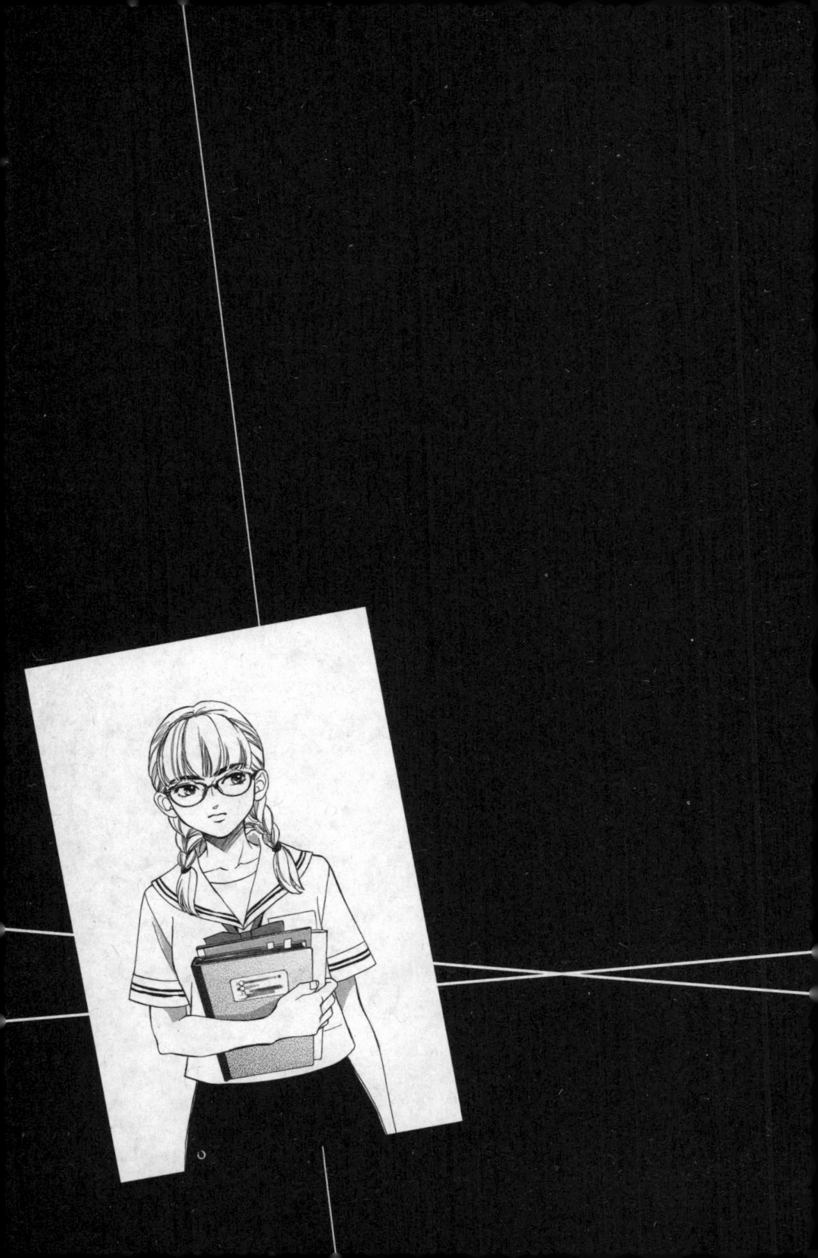

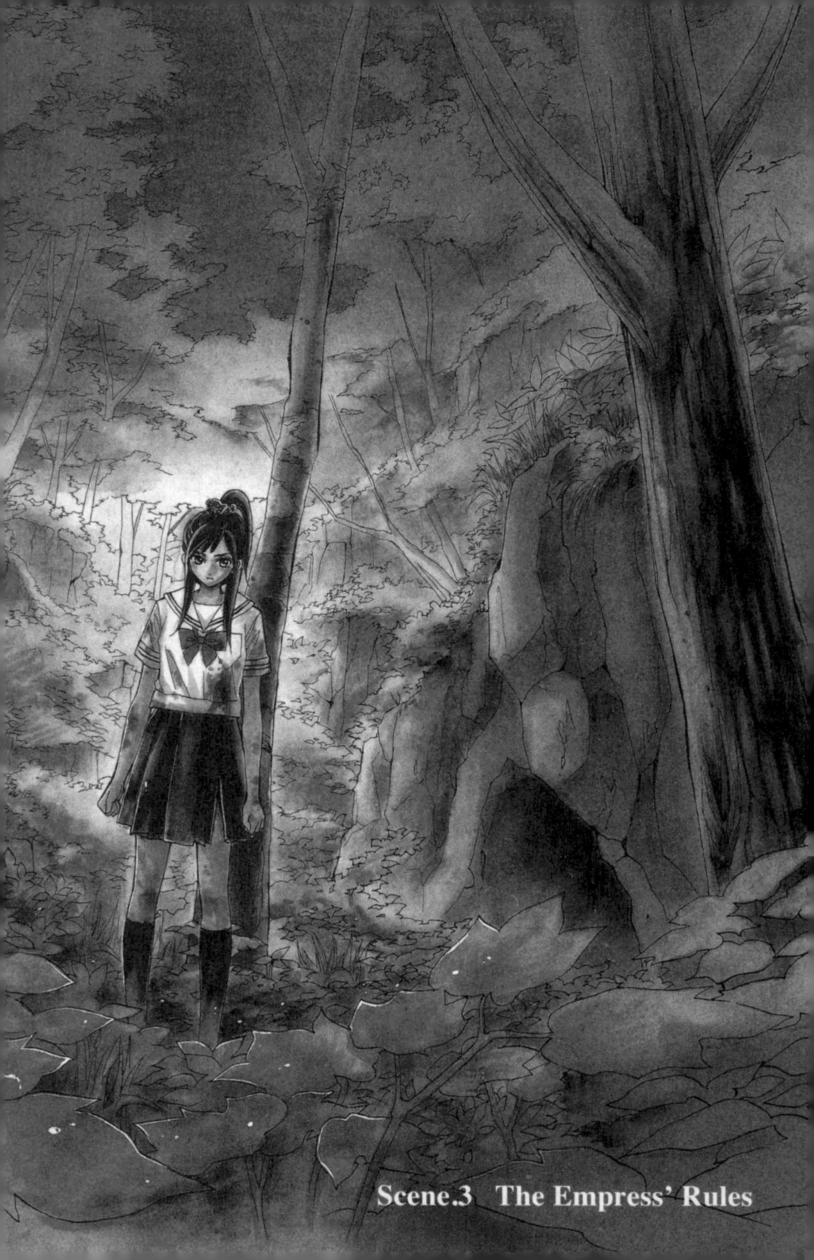

Scene.3 The Empress' Rules

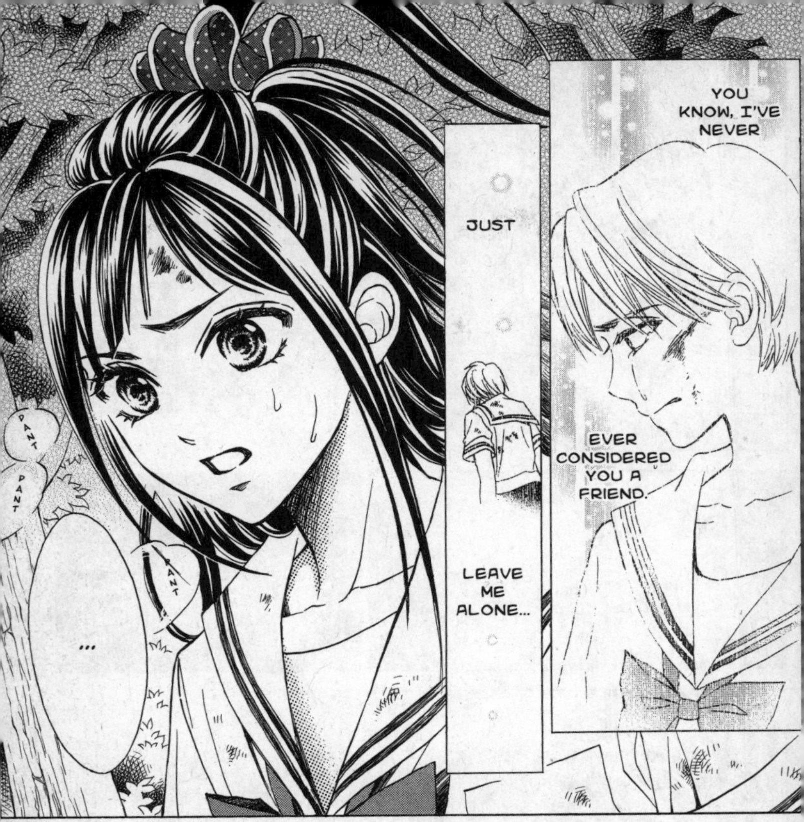
YOU KNOW, I'VE NEVER
EVER CONSIDERED YOU A FRIEND.
JUST
LEAVE ME ALONE...
PANT
PANT
PANT
...

LIMIT

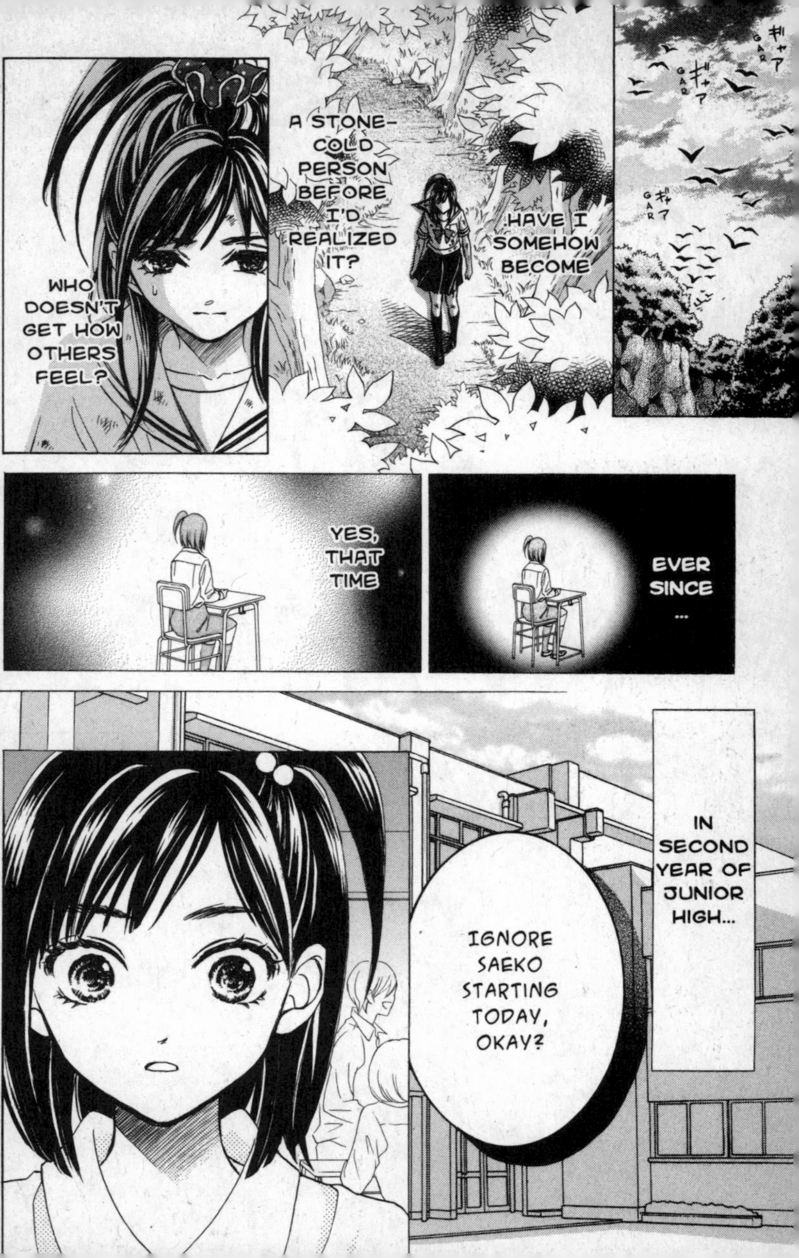
GAR ギャア
GAR ギャア
GAR ギャア
HAVE I SOMEHOW BECOME
A STONE-COLD PERSON BEFORE I'D REALIZED IT?
WHO DOESN'T GET HOW OTHERS FEEL?
EVER SINCE ...
YES, THAT TIME
IN SECOND YEAR OF JUNIOR HIGH...
IGNORE SAEKO STARTING TODAY, OKAY?

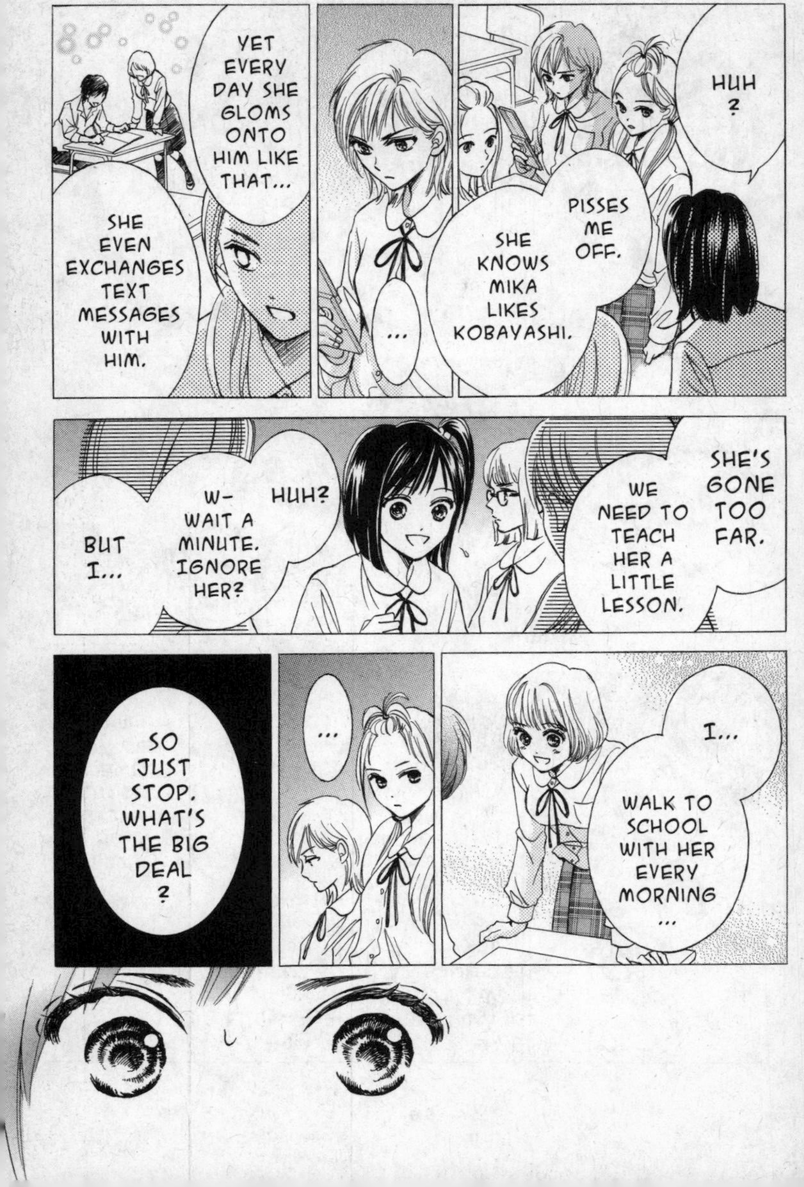
HUH ?
SHE KNOWS MIKA LIKES KOBAYASHI. PISSES ME OFF.
...
YET EVERY DAY SHE GLOMS ONTO HIM LIKE THAT...
SHE EVEN EXCHANGES TEXT MESSAGES WITH HIM.
SHE'S GONE TOO FAR.
WE NEED TO TEACH HER A LITTLE LESSON.
HUH?
W- WAIT A MINUTE. IGNORE HER?
BUT I...
I...
WALK TO SCHOOL WITH HER EVERY MORNING ...
...
SO JUST STOP. WHAT'S THE BIG DEAL ?
し

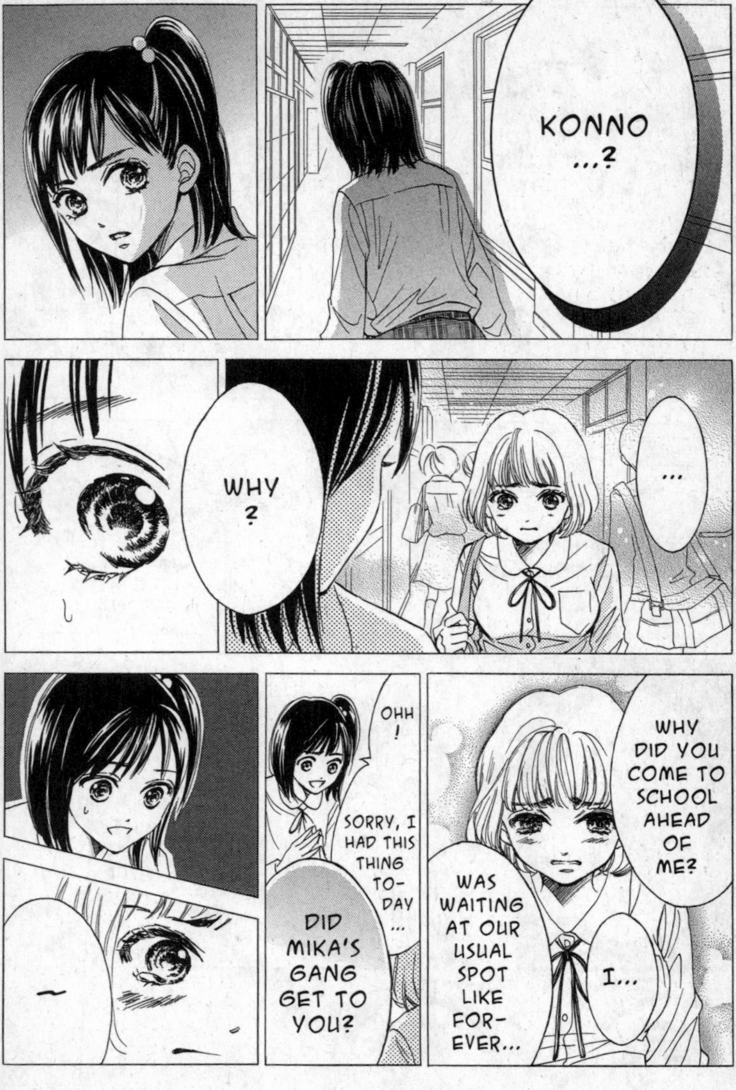
KONNO ...?
...
WHY ?
WHY DID YOU COME TO SCHOOL AHEAD OF ME?
I...
WAS WAITING AT OUR USUAL SPOT LIKE FOR-EVER...
OHH !
SORRY, I HAD THIS THING TO-DAY ...
DID MIKA'S GANG GET TO YOU?

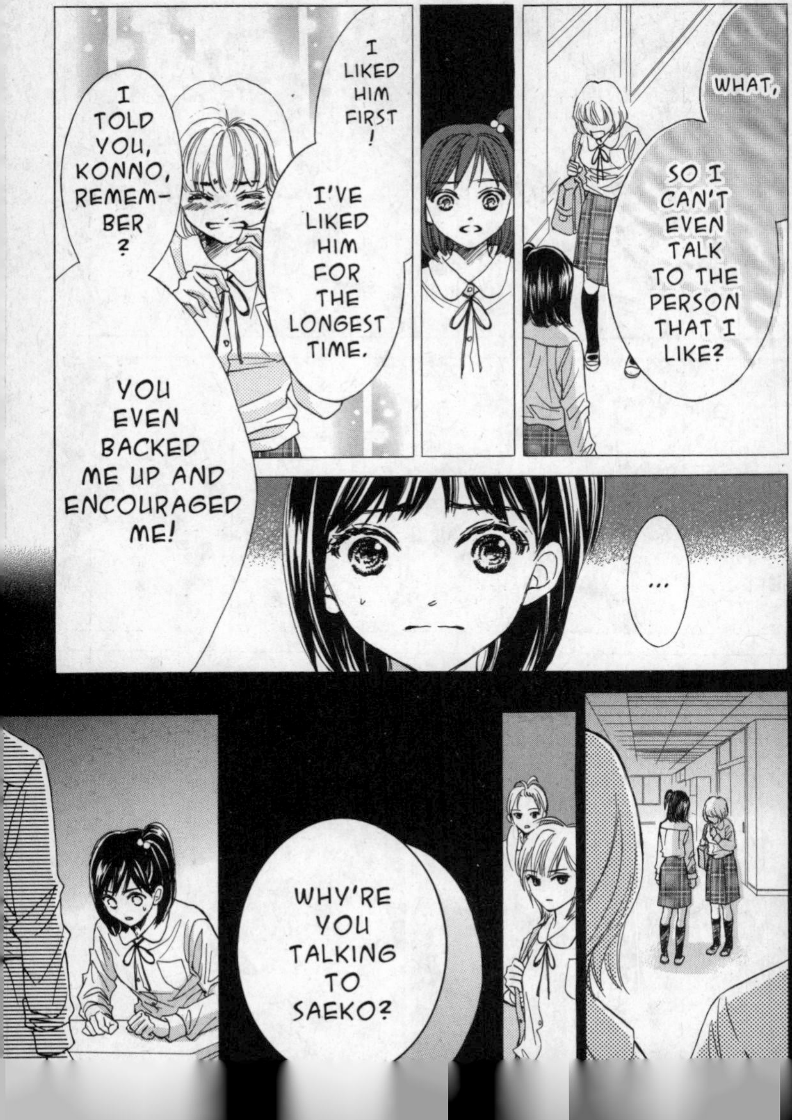
WHAT,
SO I CAN'T EVEN TALK TO THE PERSON THAT I LIKE?
...
I LIKED HIM FIRST!
I'VE LIKED HIM FOR THE LONGEST TIME.
I TOLD YOU, KONNO, REMEM-BER?
YOU EVEN BACKED ME UP AND ENCOURAGED ME!
WHY'RE YOU TALKING TO SAEKO?

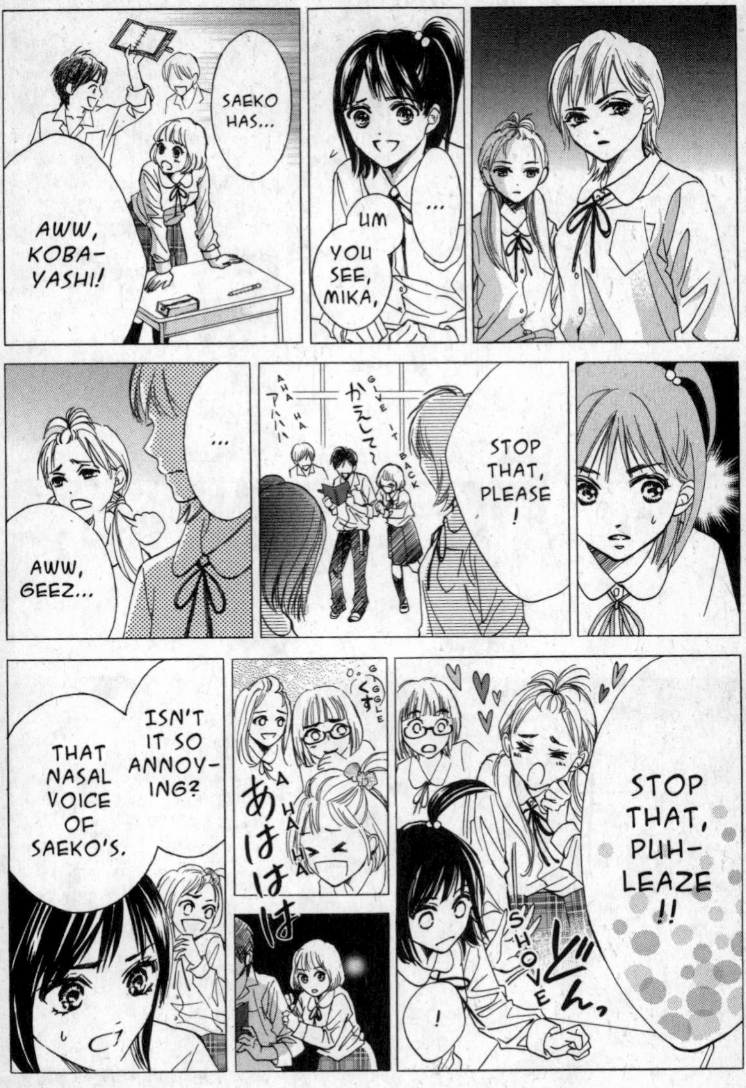
...
UM
YOU SEE, MIKA,
SAEKO HAS...
AWW, KOBA-YASHI!
STOP THAT, PLEASE!
かえして~
GIVE IT BACK
アハハ
AHA HA
...
AWW, GEEZ...
STOP THAT, PUH-LEAZE!!
どんっ
SHOVE
!
くす
GIGGLE
あははは
AHAHAHA
ISN'T IT SO ANNOY-ING?
THAT NASAL VOICE OF SAEKO'S.

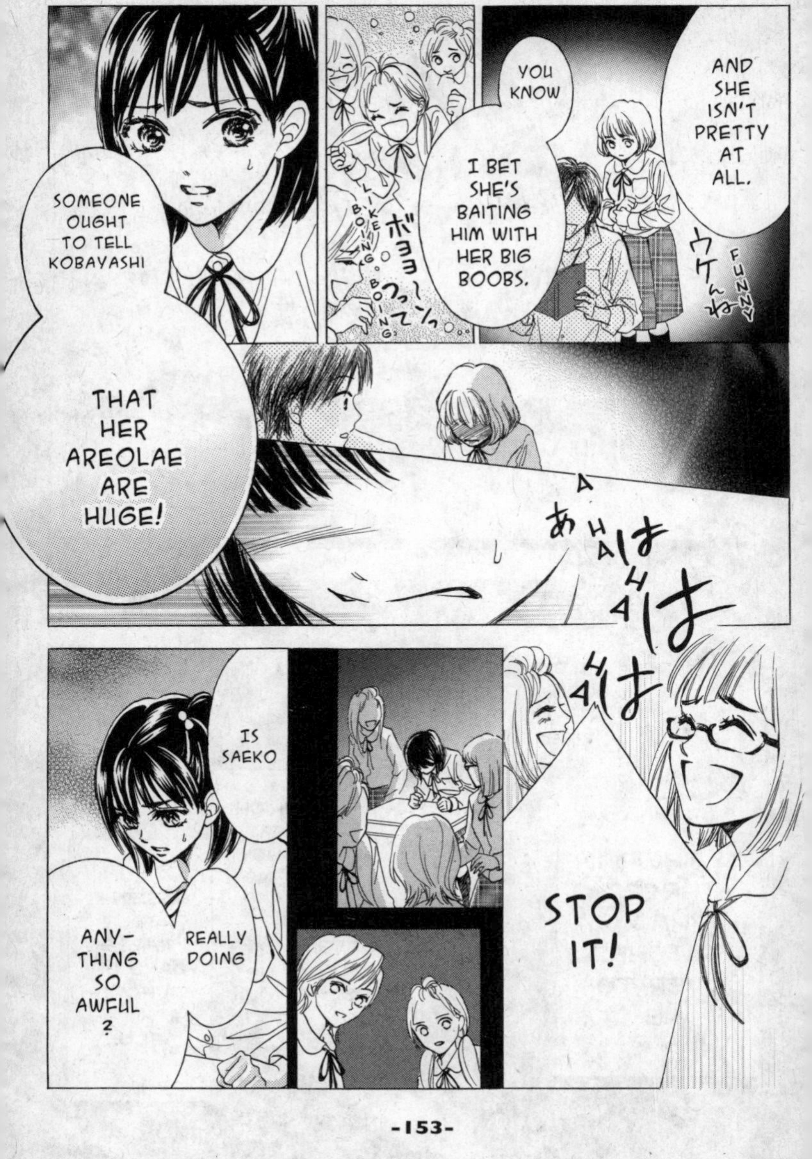
AND SHE ISN'T PRETTY AT ALL.
ウケんね
FUNNY
YOU KNOW
I BET SHE'S BAITING HIM WITH HER BIG BOOBS.
LIKE BOING BOING
SOMEONE OUGHT TO TELL KOBAYASHI
THAT HER AREOLAE ARE HUGE!
あはは
A HA HA
STOP IT!
IS SAEKO
REALLY DOING
ANYTHING SO AWFUL?

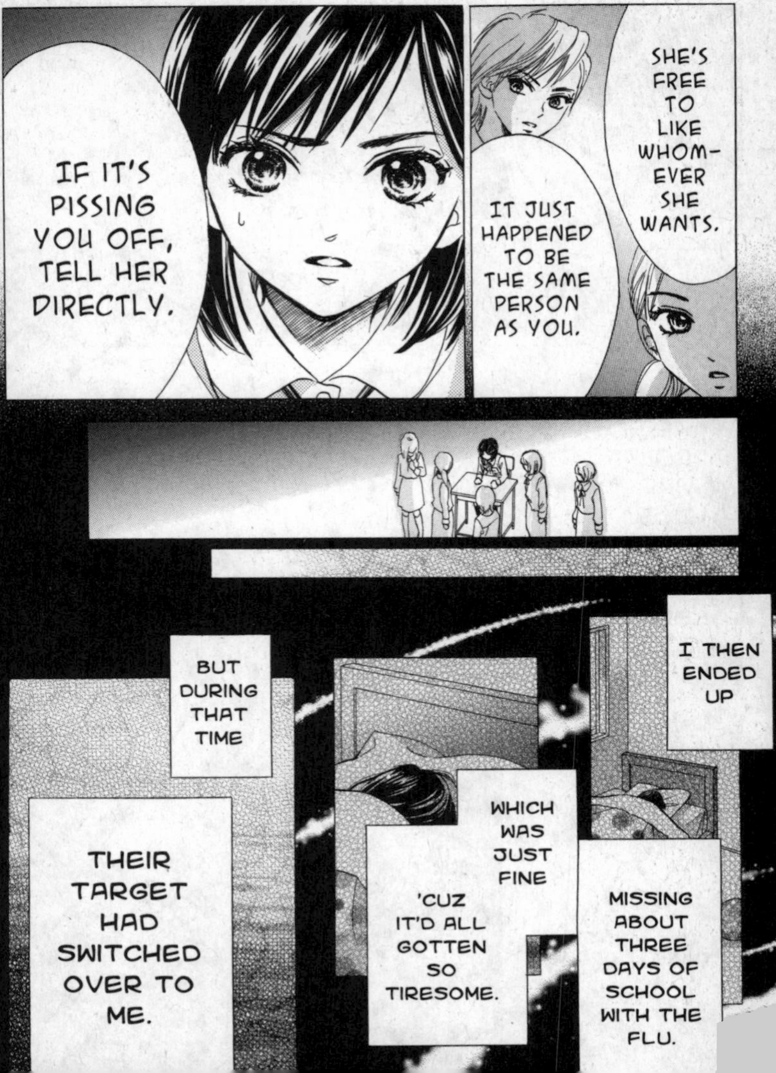
SHE'S FREE TO LIKE WHOM-EVER SHE WANTS.
IT JUST HAPPENED TO BE THE SAME PERSON AS YOU.
IF IT'S PISSING YOU OFF, TELL HER DIRECTLY.
I THEN ENDED UP
MISSING ABOUT THREE DAYS OF SCHOOL WITH THE FLU.
WHICH WAS JUST FINE
'CUZ IT'D ALL GOTTEN SO TIRESOME.
BUT DURING THAT TIME
THEIR TARGET HAD SWITCHED OVER TO ME.

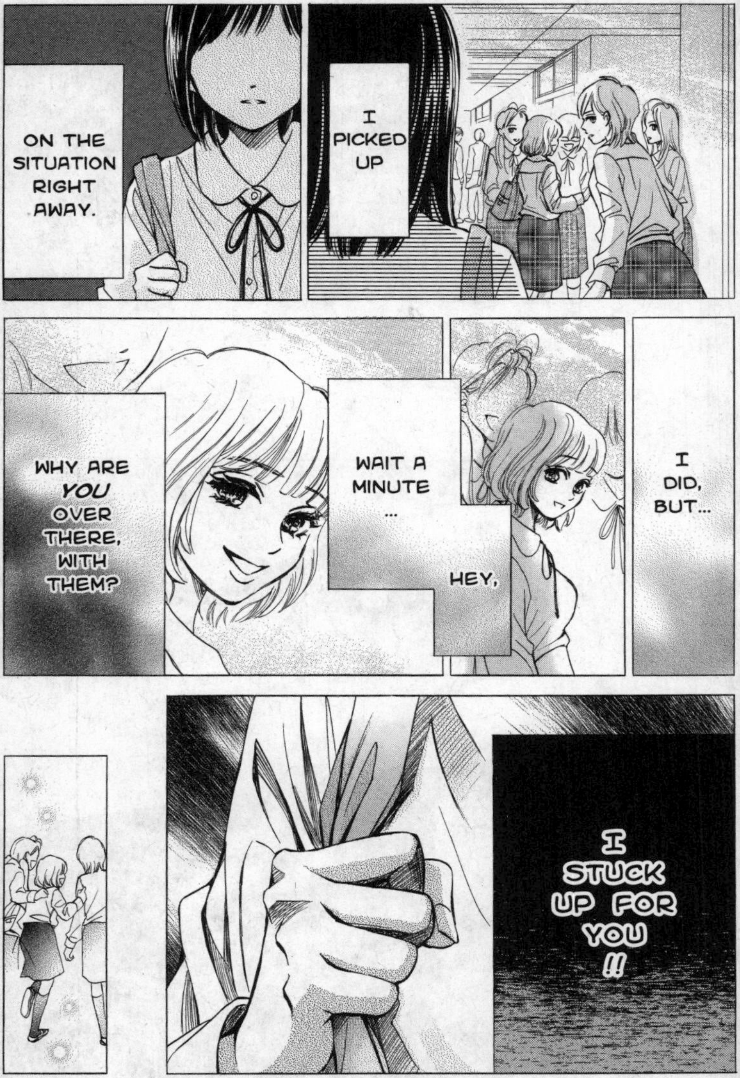
I PICKED UP
ON THE SITUATION RIGHT AWAY.
I DID, BUT...
HEY,
WAIT A MINUTE ...
WHY ARE *YOU* OVER THERE, WITH THEM?
I STUCK UP FOR YOU !!

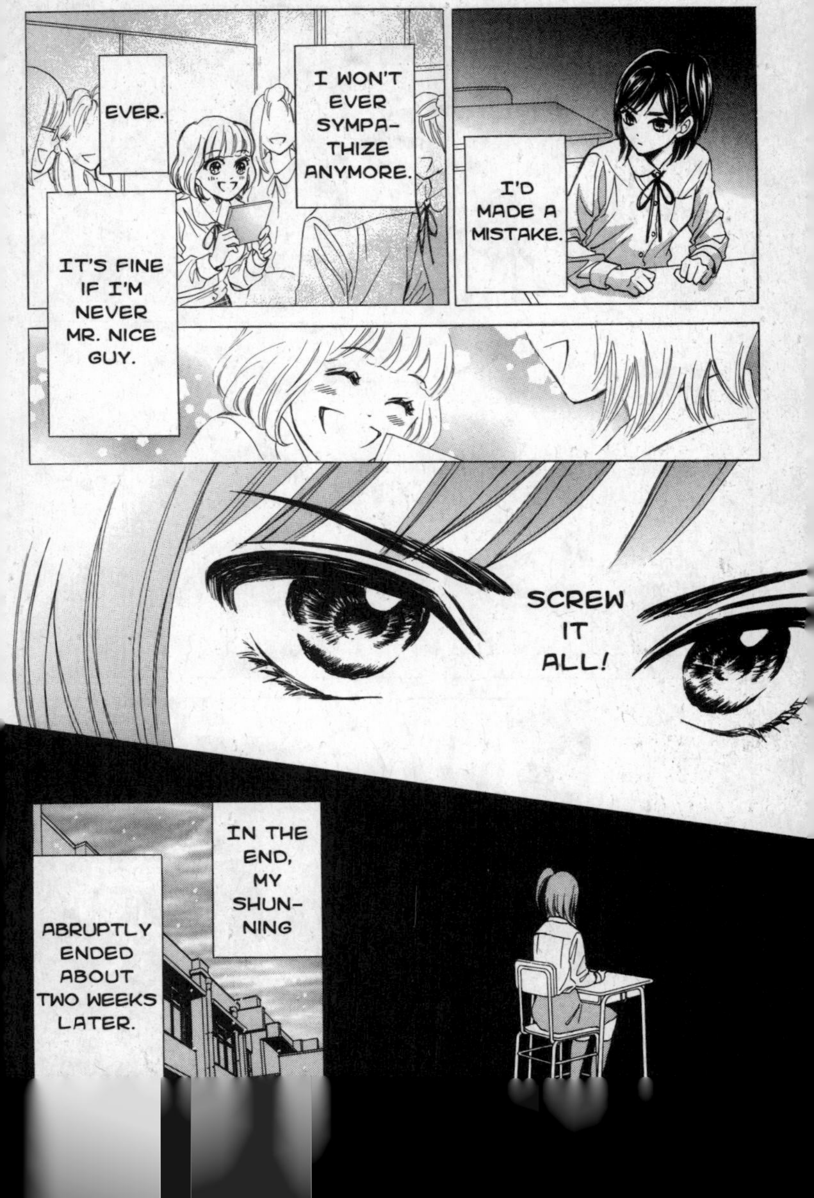
I'D MADE A MISTAKE.
I WON'T EVER SYMPA-THIZE ANYMORE.
EVER.
IT'S FINE IF I'M NEVER MR. NICE GUY.
SCREW IT ALL!
IN THE END, MY SHUN-NING
ABRUPTLY ENDED ABOUT TWO WEEKS LATER.

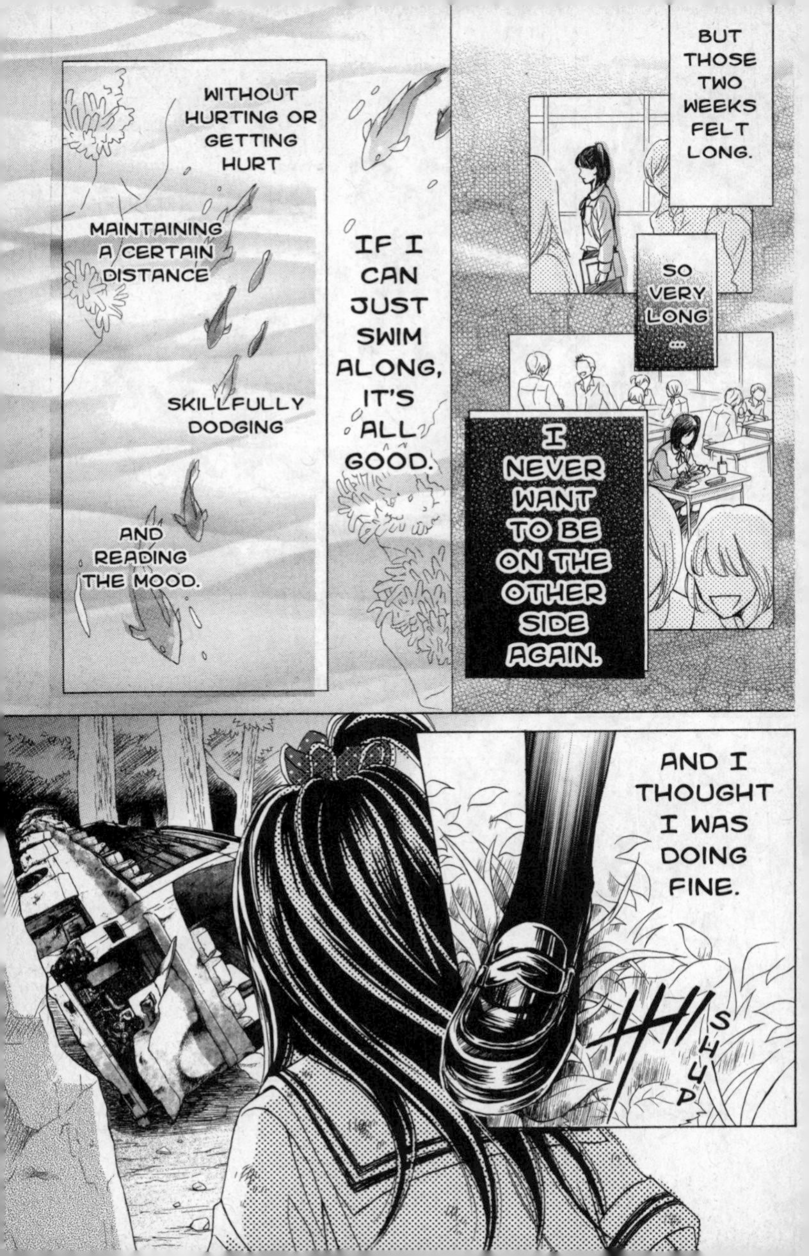

WITHOUT HURTING OR GETTING HURT
MAINTAINING A CERTAIN DISTANCE
SKILLFULLY DODGING
AND READING THE MOOD.
IF I CAN JUST SWIM ALONG, IT'S ALL GOOD.
BUT THOSE TWO WEEKS FELT LONG.
SO VERY LONG ...
I NEVER WANT TO BE ON THE OTHER SIDE AGAIN.
AND I THOUGHT I WAS DOING FINE.
SHUD

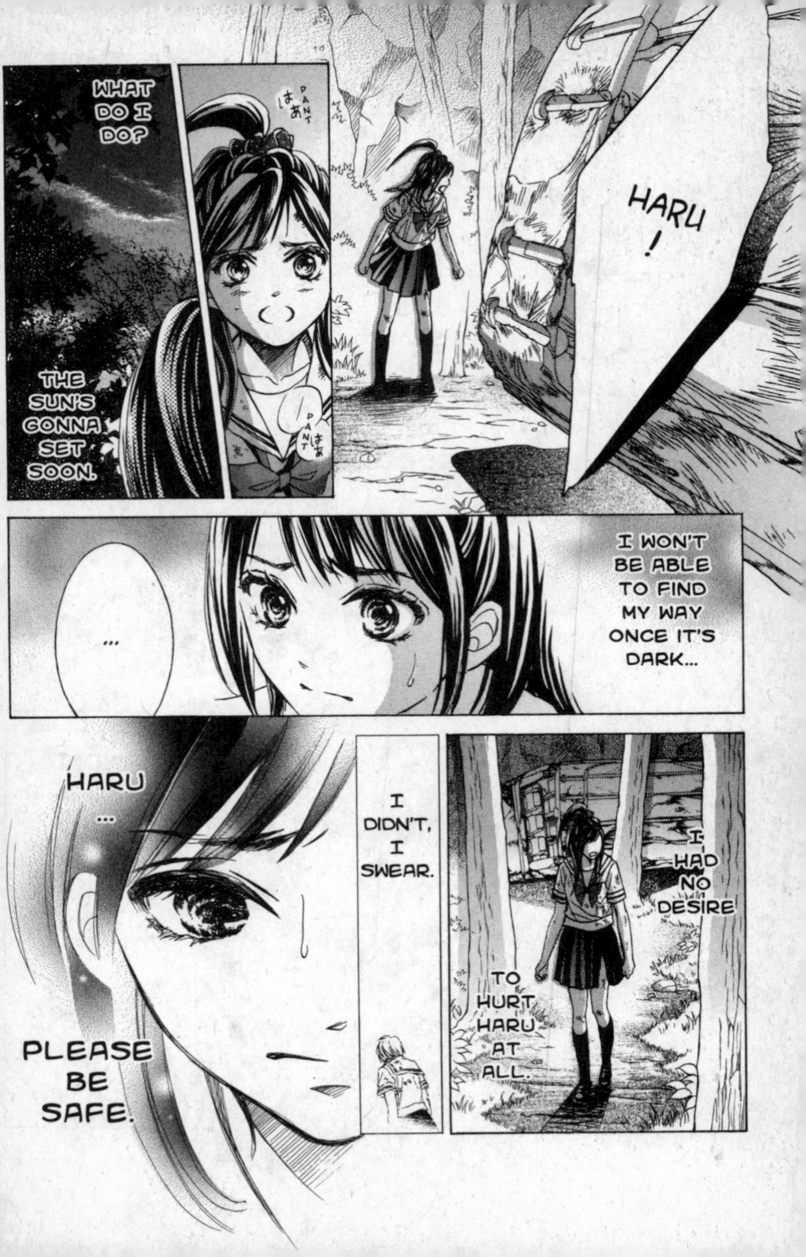
HARU!
はあ PANT
はあ PANT
WHAT DO I DO?
THE SUN'S GONNA SET SOON.
I WON'T BE ABLE TO FIND MY WAY ONCE IT'S DARK...
...
I HAD NO DESIRE
TO HURT HARU AT ALL.
I DIDN'T, I SWEAR.
HARU ...
PLEASE BE SAFE.

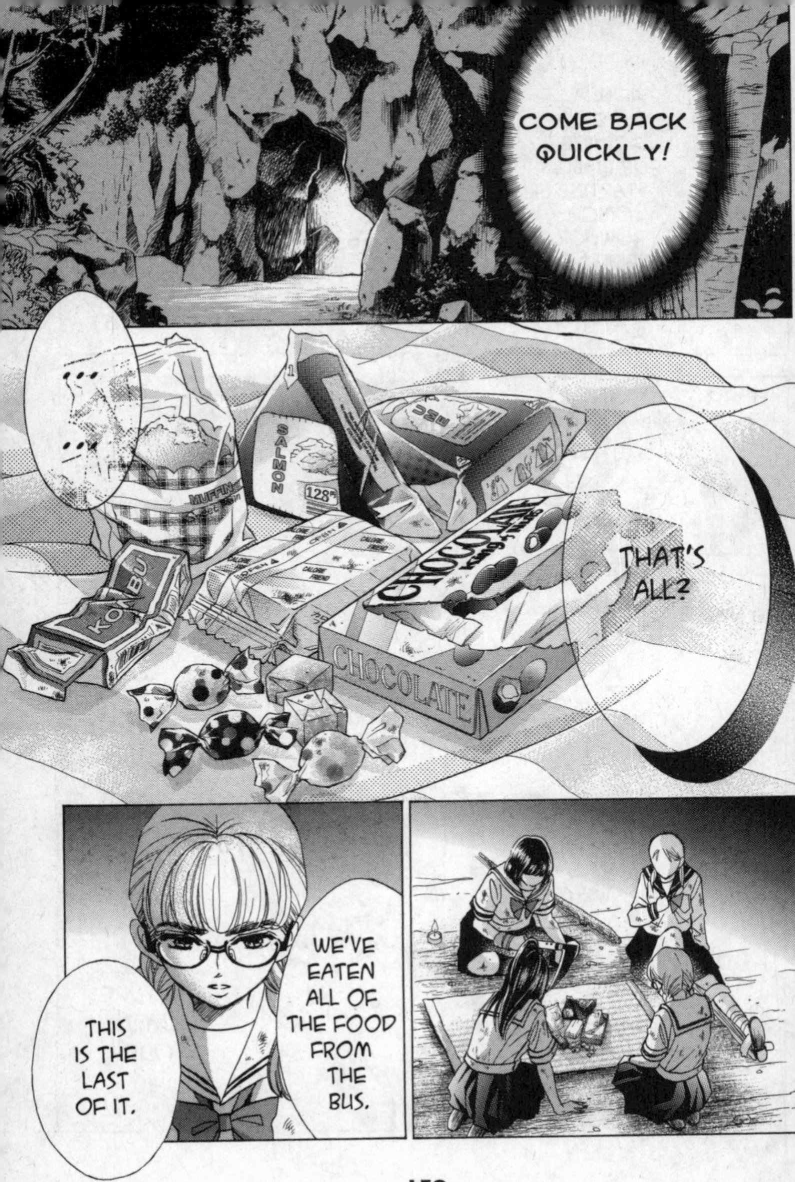
COME BACK QUICKLY!
THAT'S ALL?
....
SALMON
KONBU
CHOCOLATE
CALORIE FRIEND
CHOCOLATE
WE'VE EATEN ALL OF THE FOOD FROM THE BUS.
THIS IS THE LAST OF IT.

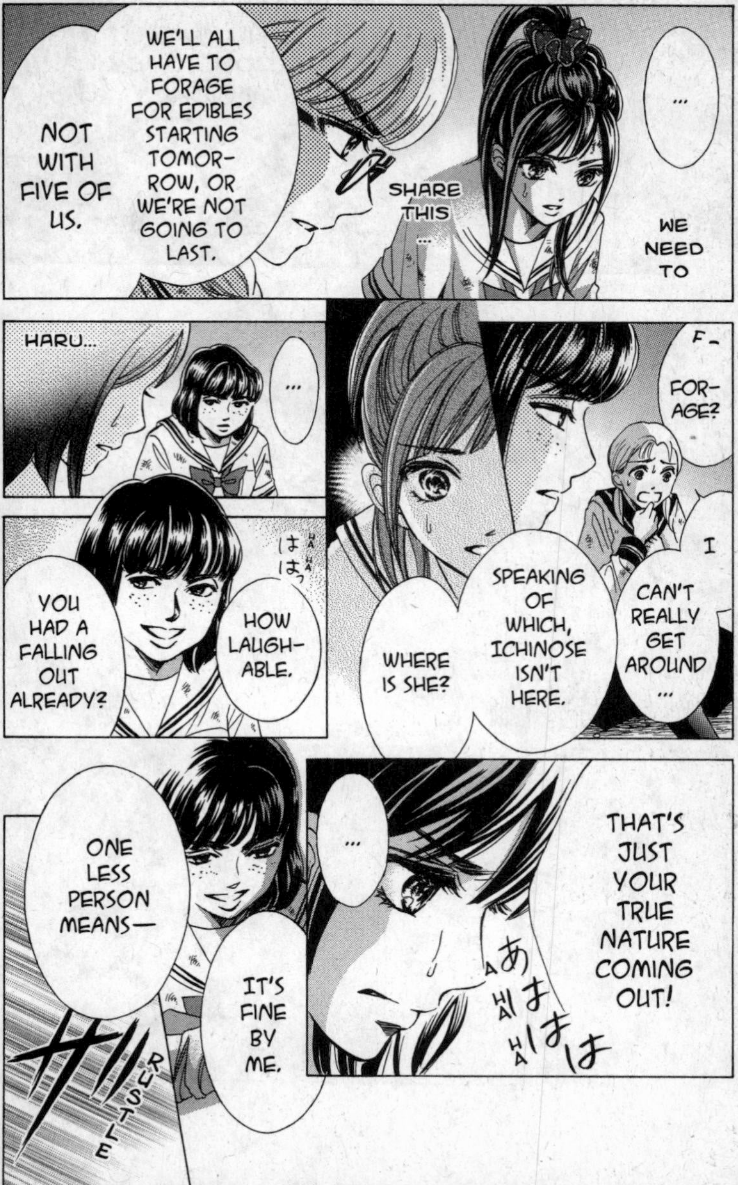
...
WE NEED TO
SHARE THIS ...
WE'LL ALL HAVE TO FORAGE FOR EDIBLES STARTING TOMORROW, OR WE'RE NOT GOING TO LAST.
NOT WITH FIVE OF US.
F- FOR-AGE?
I CAN'T REALLY GET AROUND ...
SPEAKING OF WHICH, ICHINOSE ISN'T HERE.
WHERE IS SHE?
...
HARU...
ははっ HA HA
HOW LAUGHABLE.
YOU HAD A FALLING OUT ALREADY?
THAT'S JUST YOUR TRUE NATURE COMING OUT!
あははは HA HA HA
...
IT'S FINE BY ME.
ONE LESS PERSON MEANS—
RUSTLE

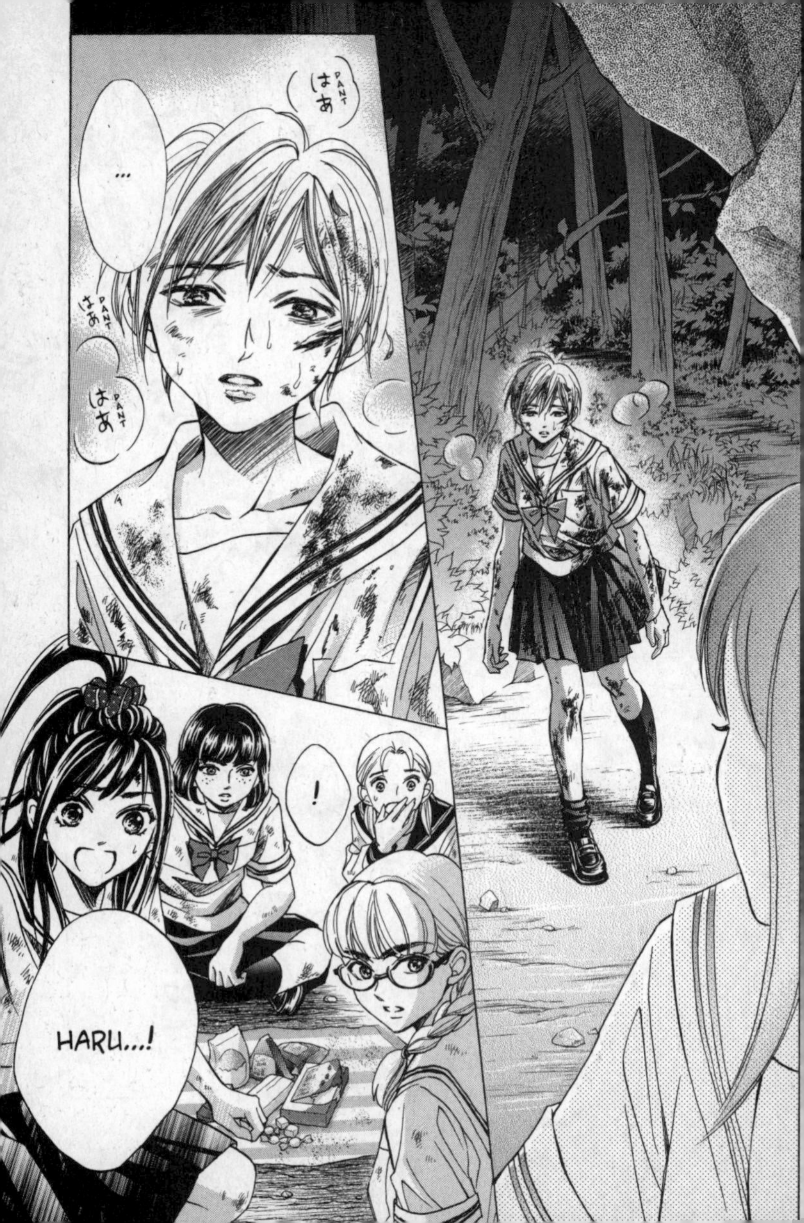
はあ PANT
...
はあ PANT
はあ PANT
!
HARU...!

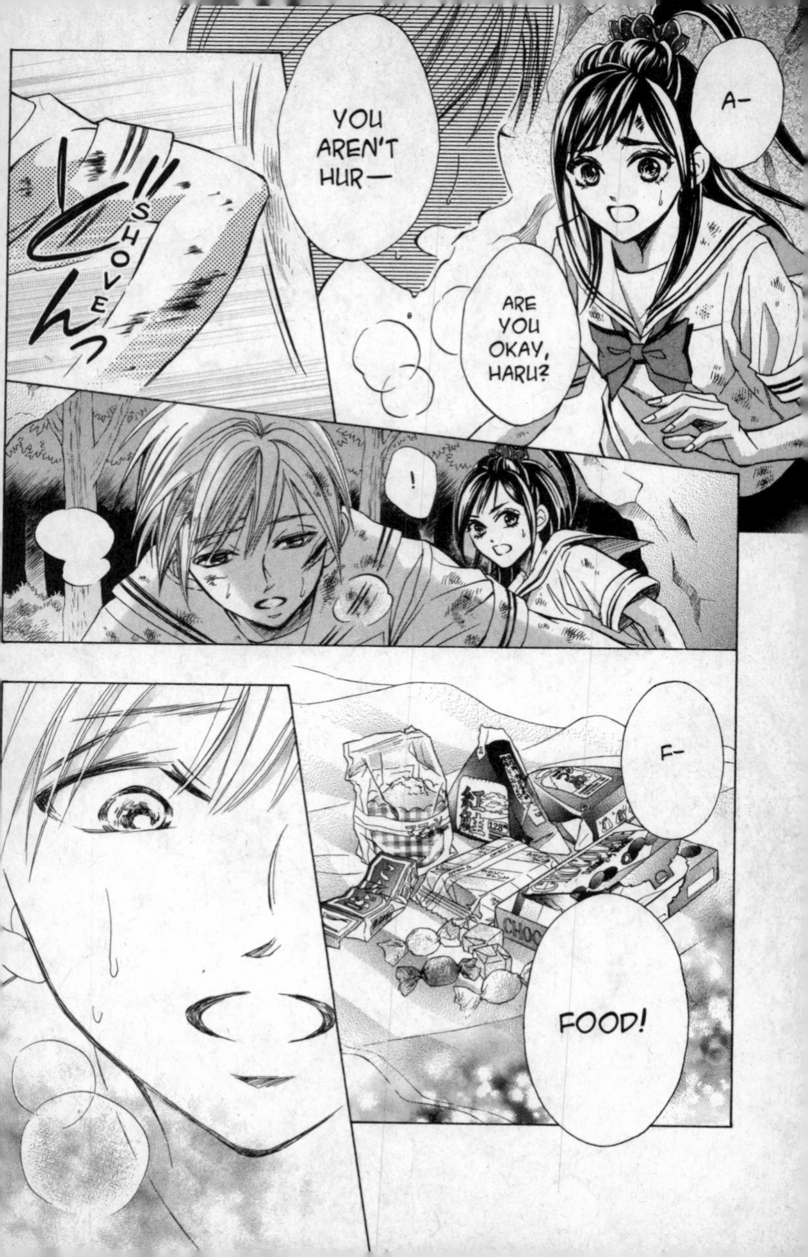
A-
ARE YOU OKAY, HARU?
YOU AREN'T HUR—
どんっ
SHOVE
!
F-
FOOD!

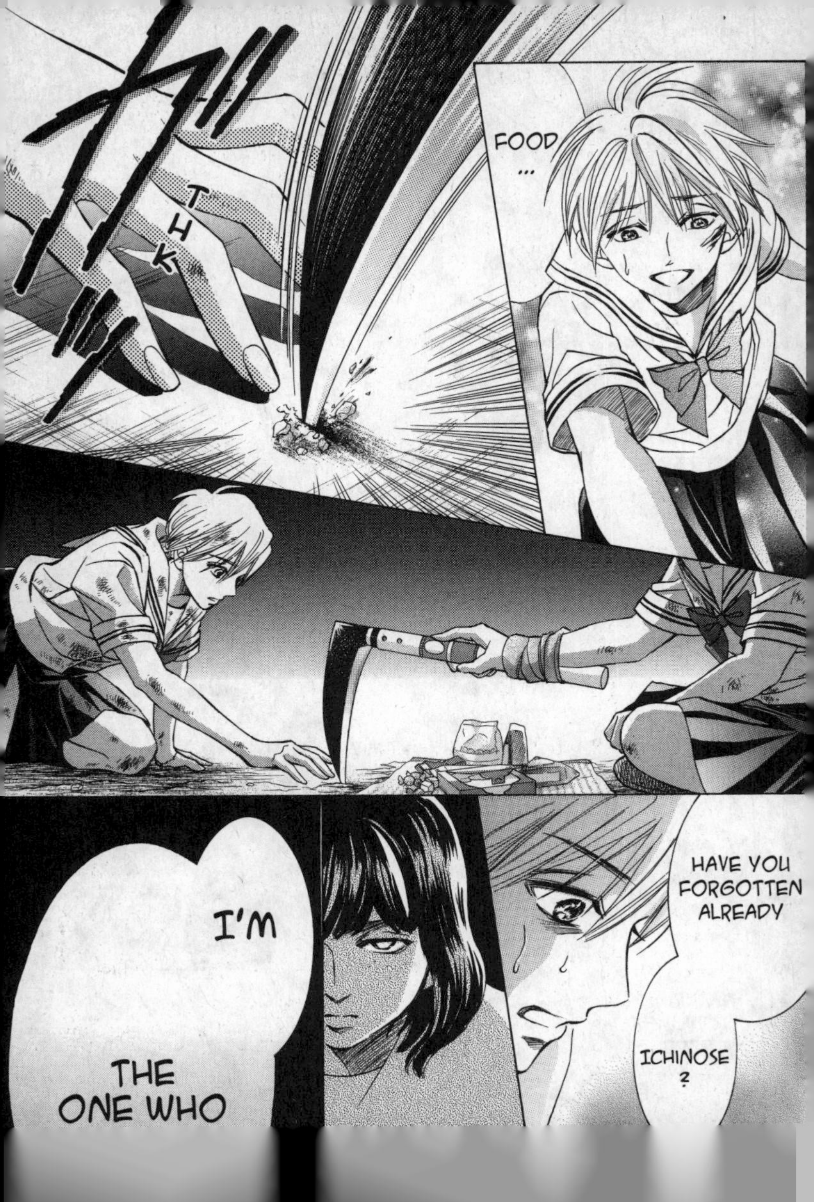
FOOD ...
THK
HAVE YOU FORGOTTEN ALREADY
ICHINOSE?
I'M
THE ONE WHO

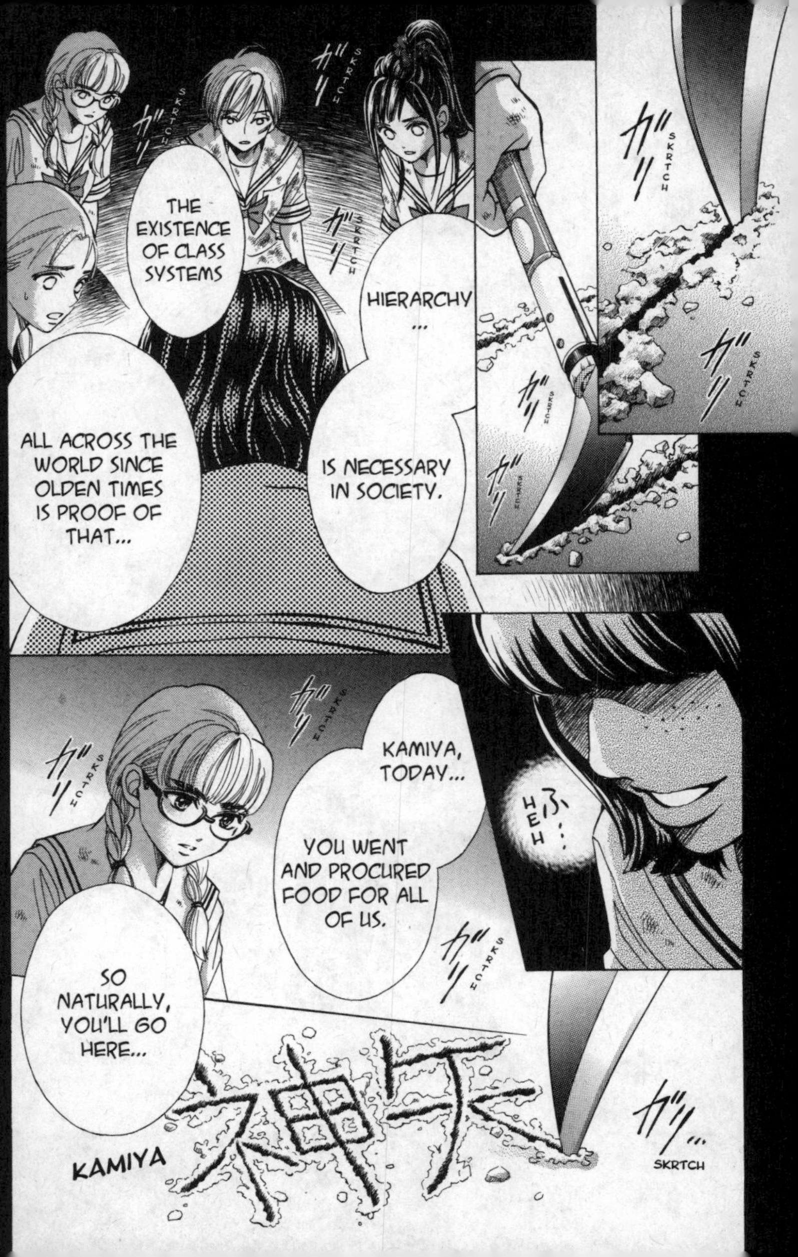
SKRTCH
SKRTCH
SKRTCH
SKRTCH
SKRTCH
SKRTCH
SKRTCH
HIERARCHY...
IS NECESSARY IN SOCIETY.
THE EXISTENCE OF CLASS SYSTEMS
ALL ACROSS THE WORLD SINCE OLDEN TIMES IS PROOF OF THAT...
ふ... HEH
KAMIYA, TODAY...
YOU WENT AND PROCURED FOOD FOR ALL OF US.
SKRTCH
SKRTCH
SKRTCH
SO NATURALLY, YOU'LL GO HERE...
KAMIYA
SKRTCH

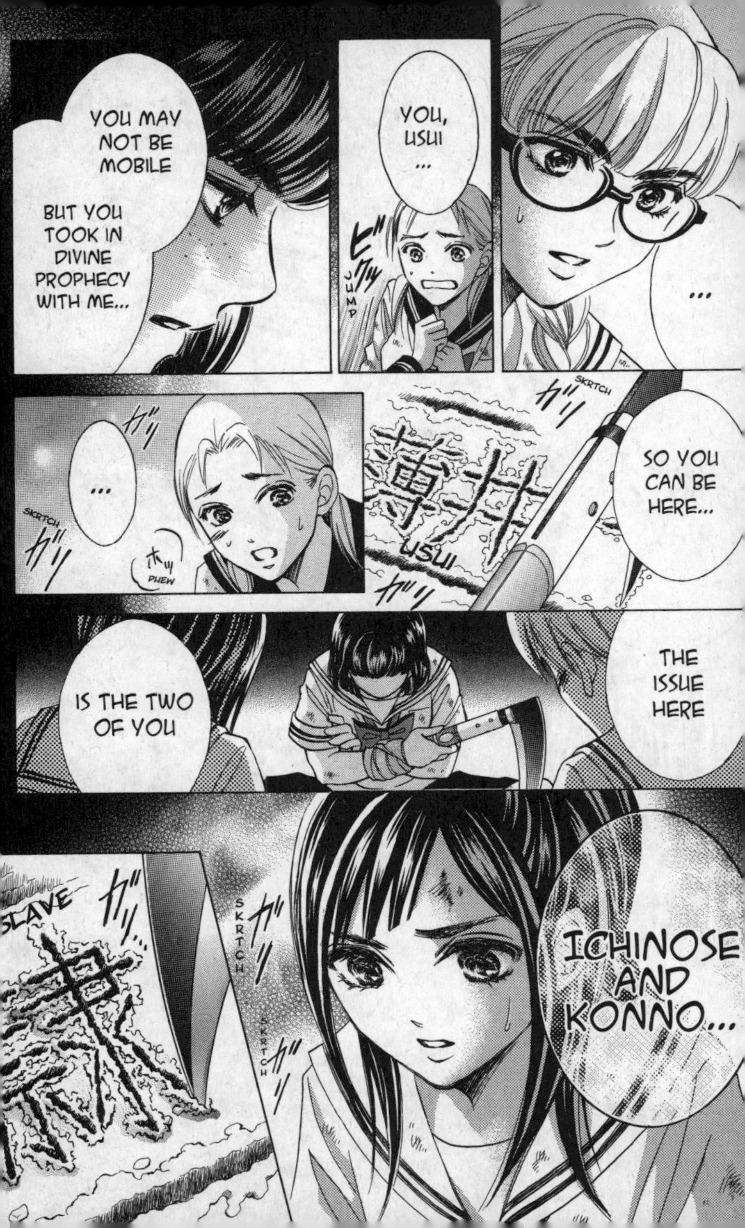
...
YOU, USUI ...
JUMP
YOU MAY NOT BE MOBILE
BUT YOU TOOK IN DIVINE PROPHECY WITH ME...
SKRTCH
SO YOU CAN BE HERE...
USUI
...
SKRTCH
PHEW
THE ISSUE HERE
IS THE TWO OF YOU
ICHINOSE AND KONNO...
SKRTCH
SKRTCH
SLAVE

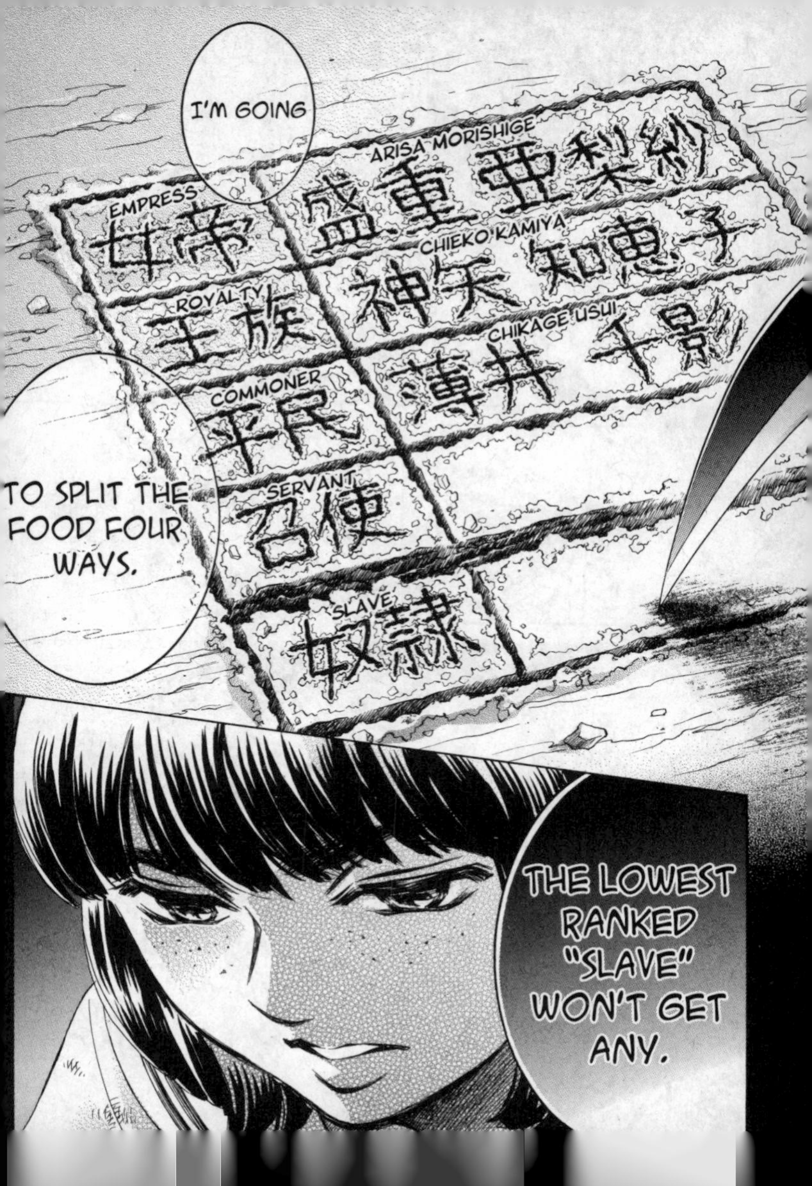
I'M GOING
TO SPLIT THE FOOD FOUR WAYS.
ARISA MORISHIGE
盛重亜梨紗
EMPRESS
女帝
CHIEKO KAMIYA
神矢知恵子
ROYALTY
王族
CHIKAGE USUI
薄井千影
COMMONER
平民
SERVANT
召使
SLAVE
奴隷
THE LOWEST RANKED "SLAVE" WON'T GET ANY.

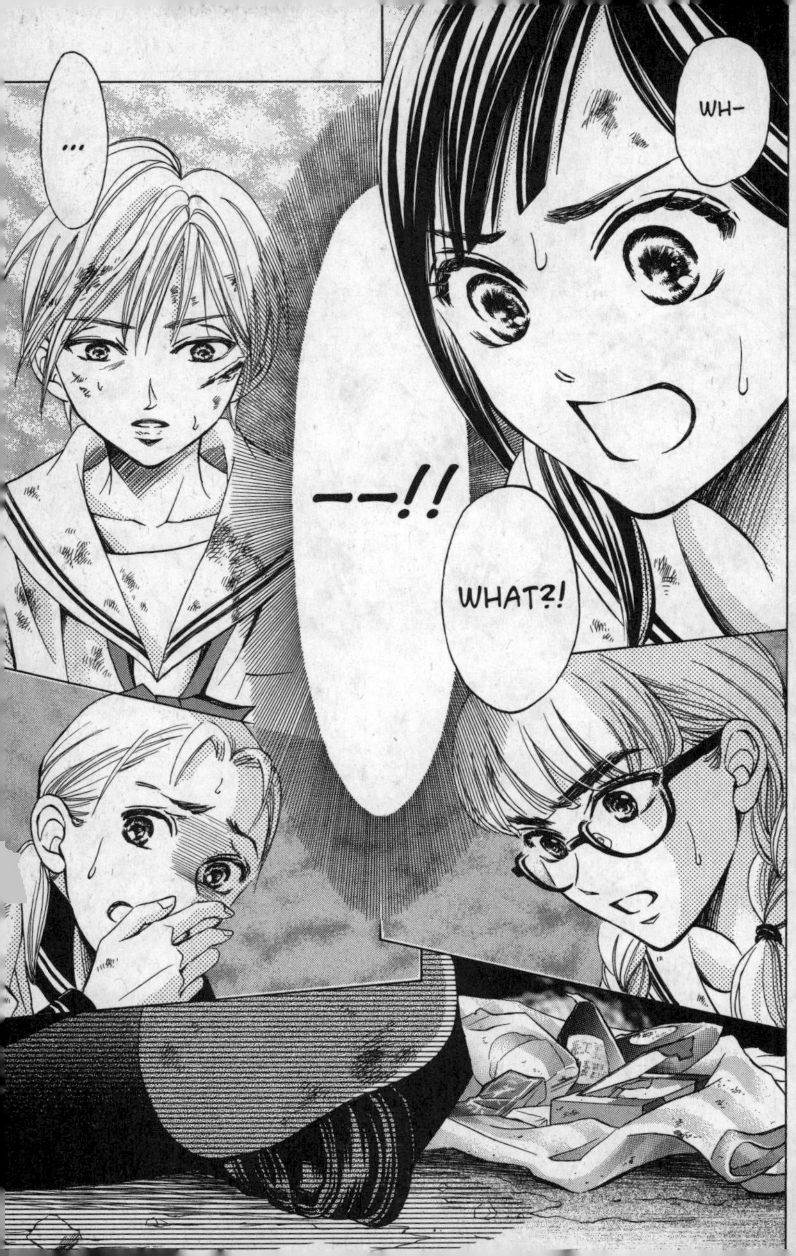

WH-
WHAT?!
...
——!!

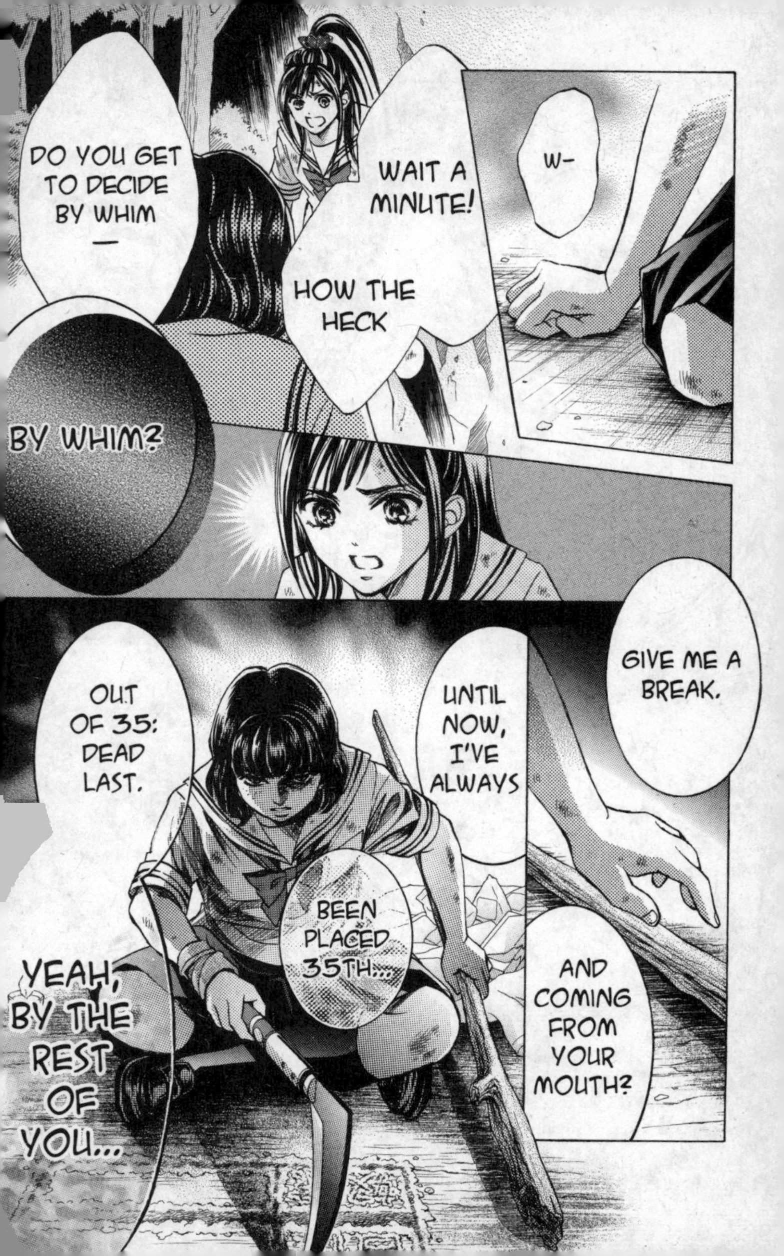
W-
WAIT A MINUTE!
HOW THE HECK
DO YOU GET TO DECIDE BY WHIM
—
BY WHIM?
GIVE ME A BREAK.
UNTIL NOW, I'VE ALWAYS
BEEN PLACED 35TH...
OUT OF 35: DEAD LAST.
YEAH, BY THE REST OF YOU...
AND COMING FROM YOUR MOUTH?

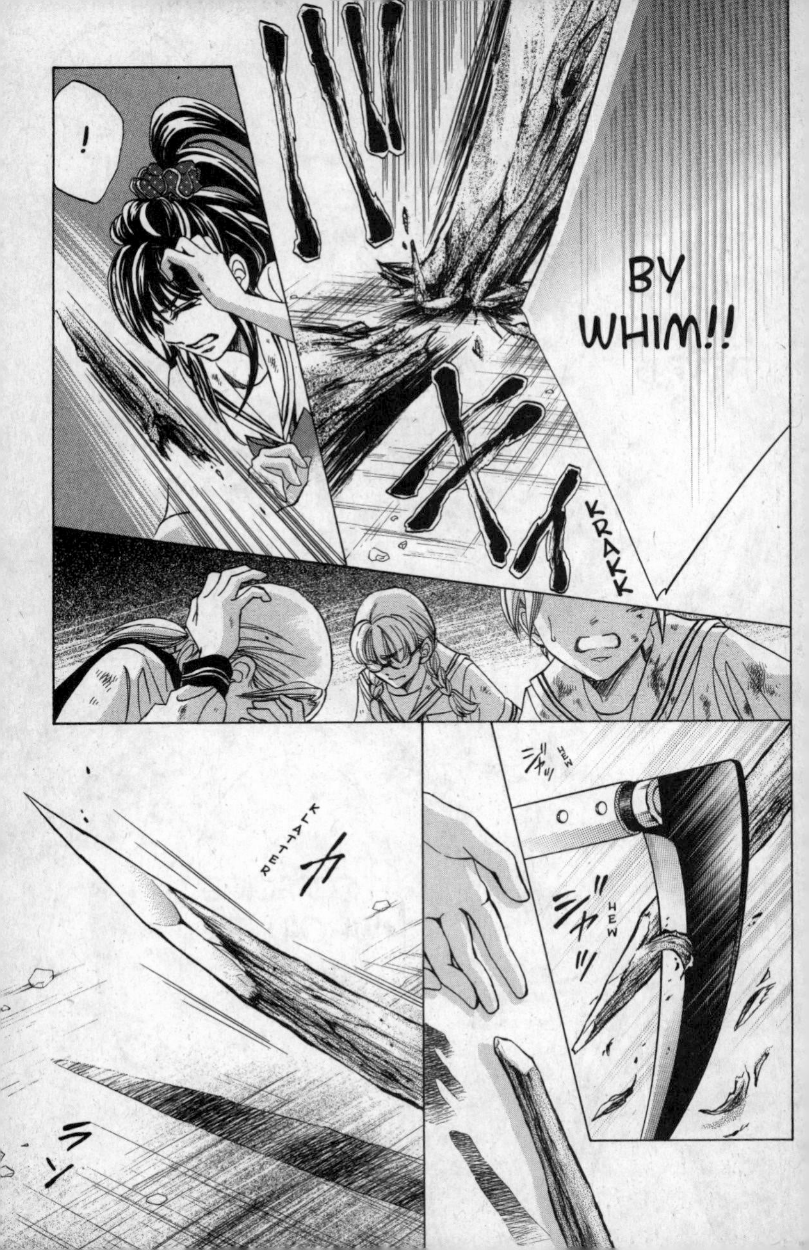
BY WHIM!!
KRAKK
!
HEW
HEW
KLATTER

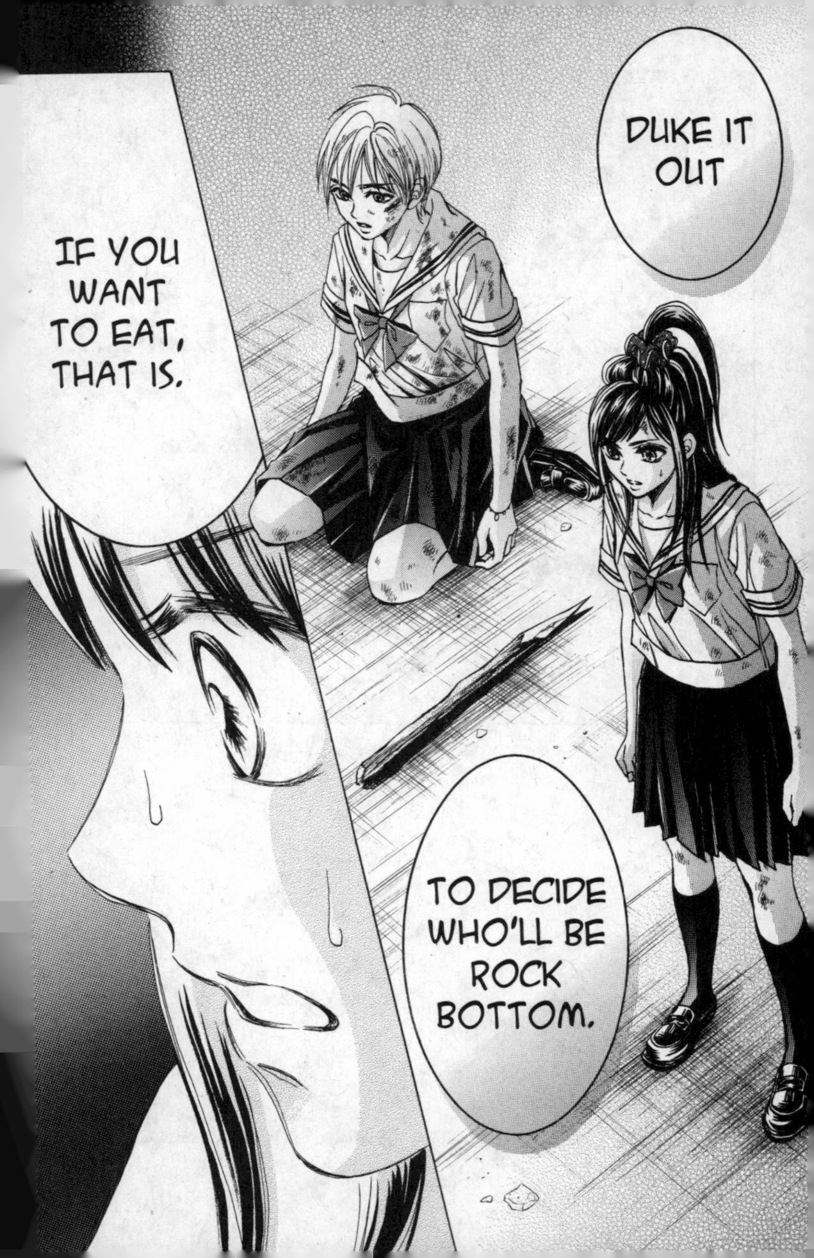
DUKE IT OUT
TO DECIDE WHO'LL BE ROCK BOTTOM.
IF YOU WANT TO EAT, THAT IS.

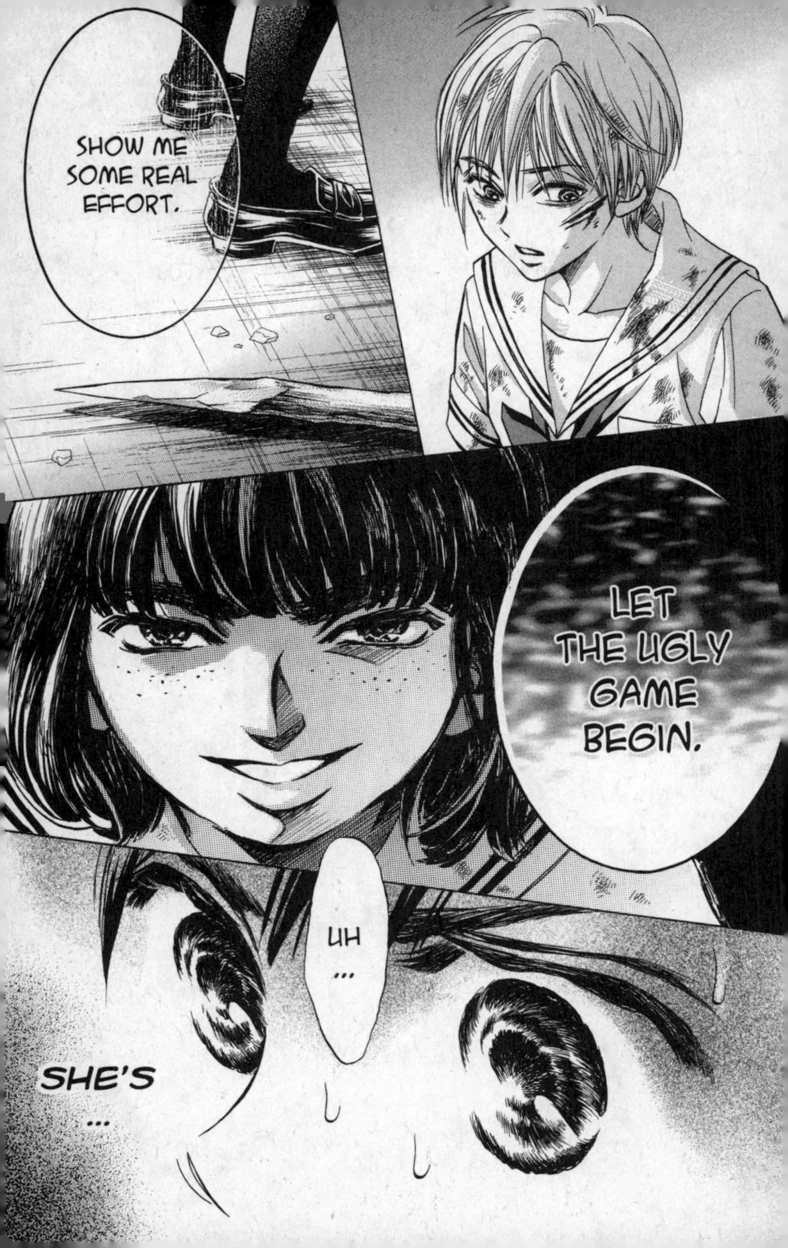
SHOW ME SOME REAL EFFORT.
LET THE UGLY GAME BEGIN.
UH ...
SHE'S ...

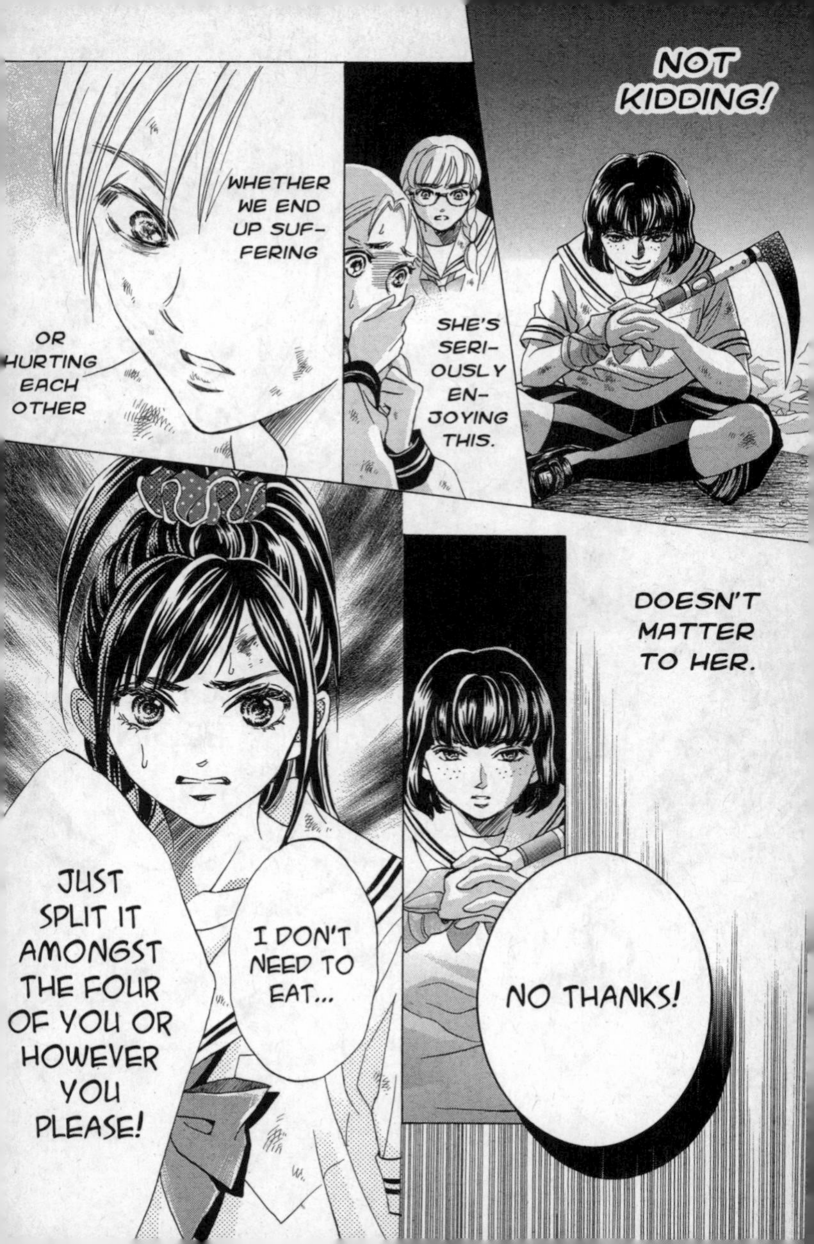

NOT KIDDING!
SHE'S SERIOUSLY ENJOYING THIS.
WHETHER WE END UP SUFFERING
OR HURTING EACH OTHER
DOESN'T MATTER TO HER.
NO THANKS!
I DON'T NEED TO EAT...
JUST SPLIT IT AMONGST THE FOUR OF YOU OR HOWEVER YOU PLEASE!

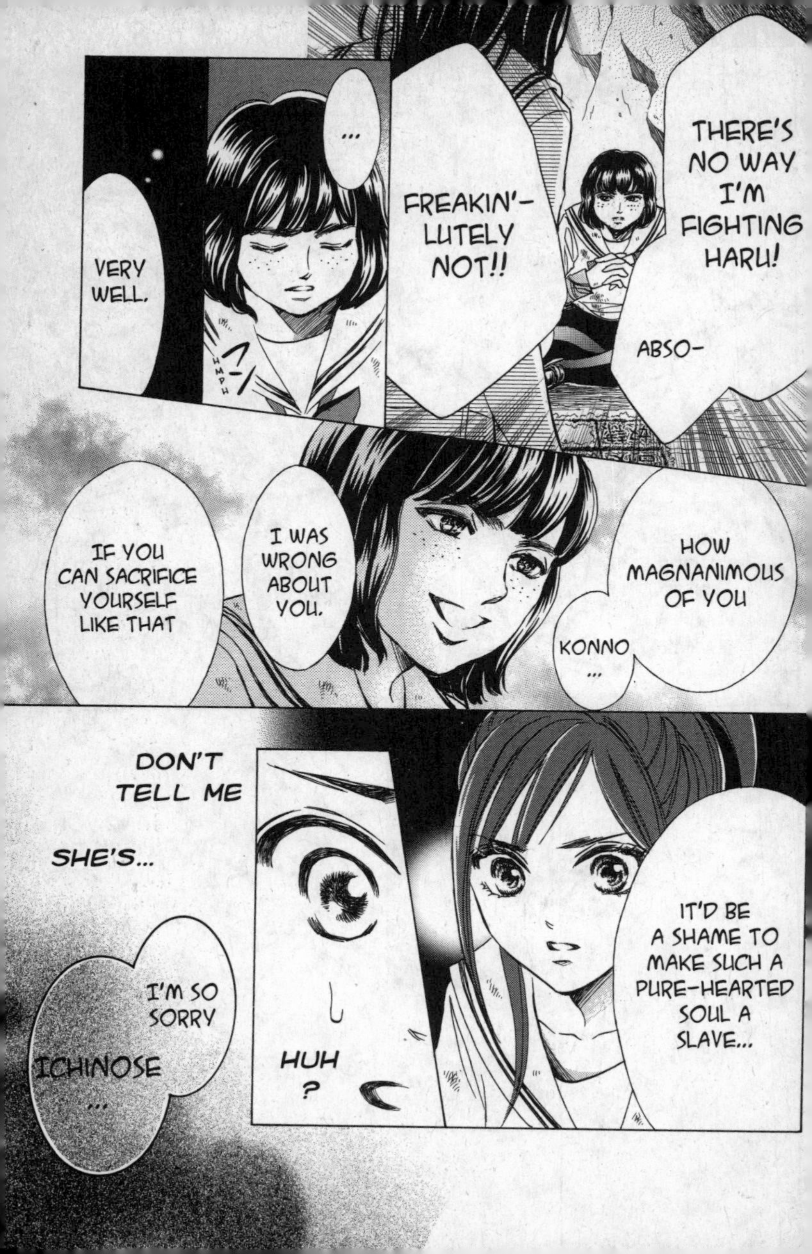
THERE'S NO WAY I'M FIGHTING HARU!
ABSO-
FREAKIN'-LUTELY NOT!!
...
VERY WELL.
HMPH
HOW MAGNANIMOUS OF YOU
KONNO ...
I WAS WRONG ABOUT YOU.
IF YOU CAN SACRIFICE YOURSELF LIKE THAT
IT'D BE A SHAME TO MAKE SUCH A PURE-HEARTED SOUL A SLAVE...
HUH?
DON'T TELL ME
SHE'S...
I'M SO SORRY
ICHINOSE ...

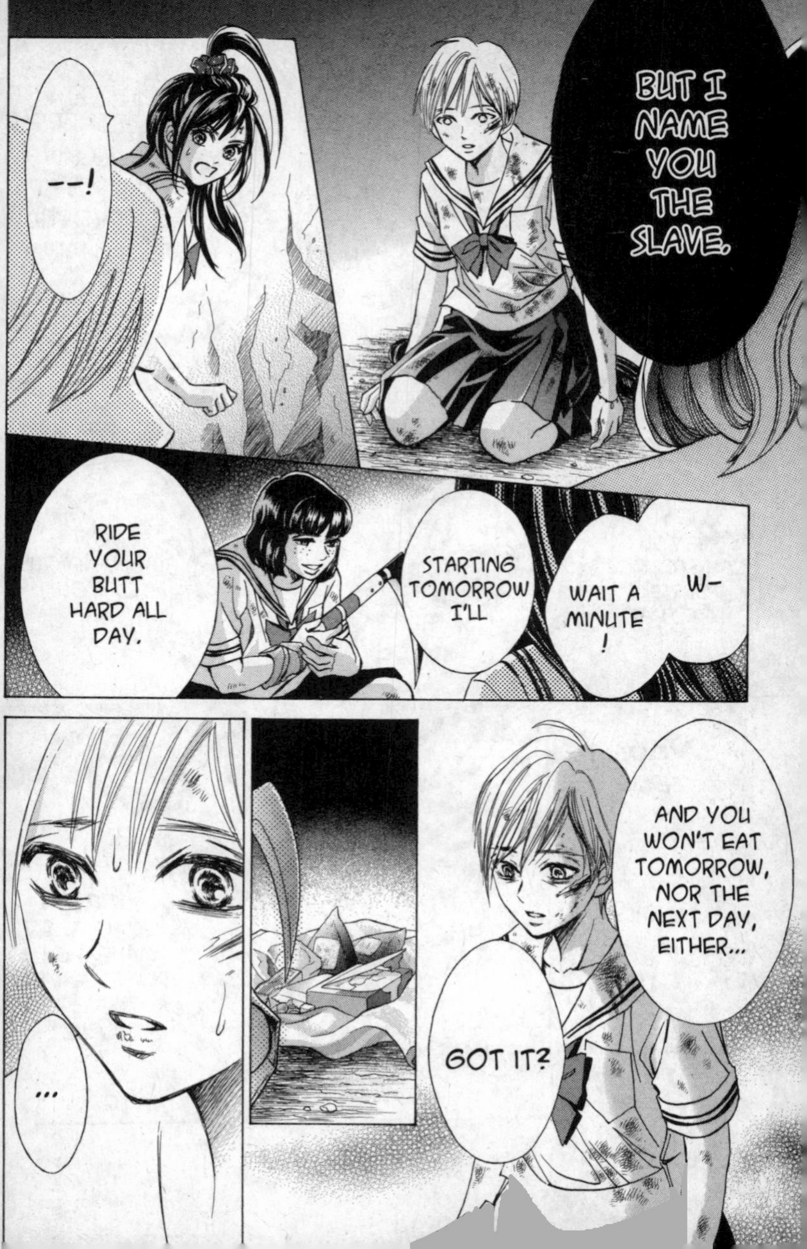
BUT I NAME YOU THE SLAVE.
--!
W-
WAIT A MINUTE!
STARTING TOMORROW I'LL
RIDE YOUR BUTT HARD ALL DAY.
AND YOU WON'T EAT TOMORROW, NOR THE NEXT DAY, EITHER...
GOT IT?
...

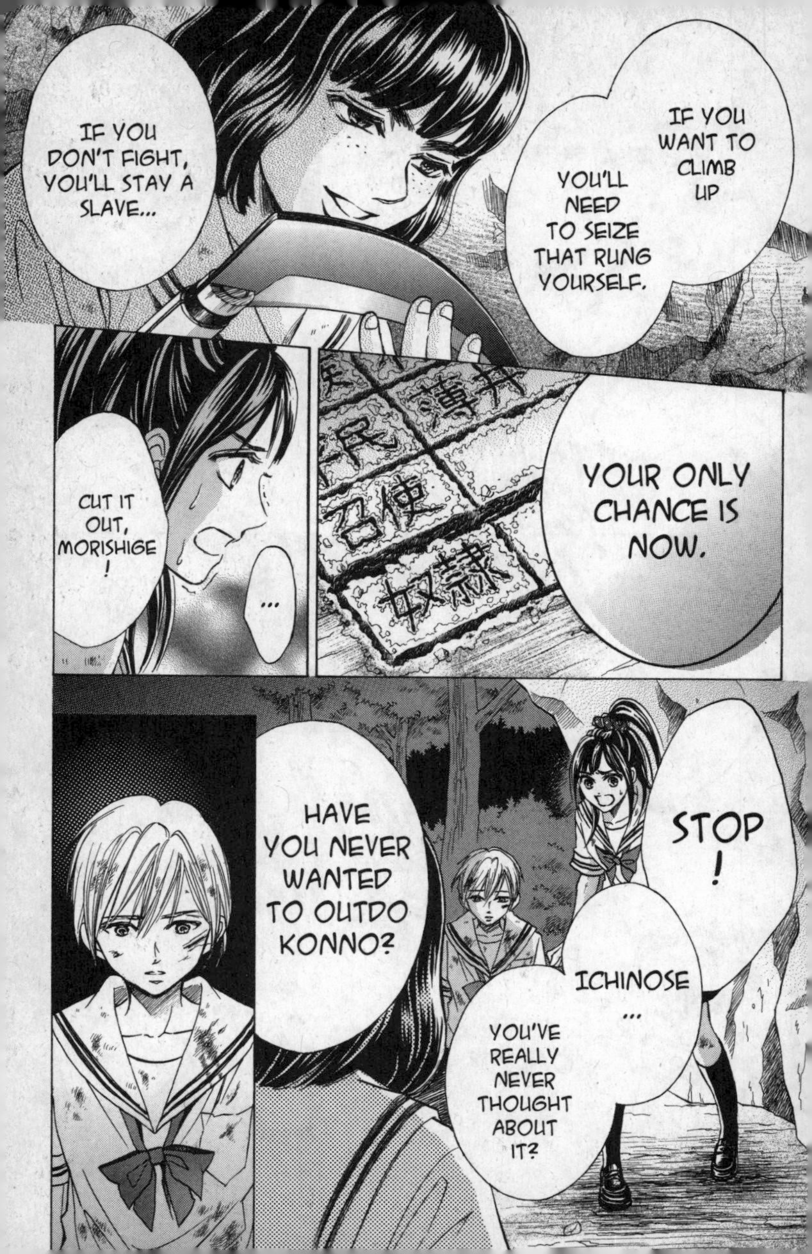
IF YOU WANT TO CLIMB UP
YOU'LL NEED TO SEIZE THAT RUNG YOURSELF.
IF YOU DON'T FIGHT, YOU'LL STAY A SLAVE...
YOUR ONLY CHANCE IS NOW.
CUT IT OUT, MORISHIGE!
...
STOP!
ICHINOSE...
YOU'VE REALLY NEVER THOUGHT ABOUT IT?
HAVE YOU NEVER WANTED TO OUTDO KONNO?

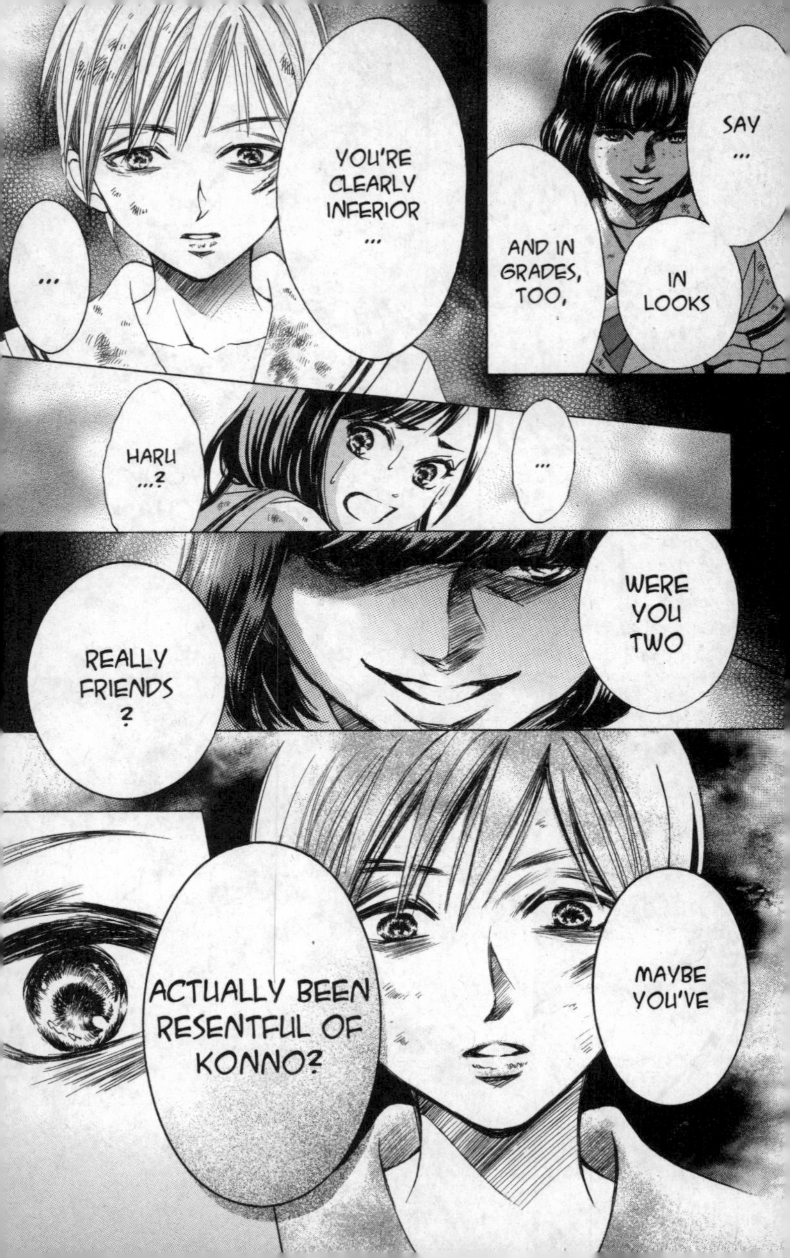
SAY ...
IN LOOKS
AND IN GRADES, TOO,
YOU'RE CLEARLY INFERIOR ...
...
...
HARU ...?
WERE YOU TWO
REALLY FRIENDS?
MAYBE YOU'VE
ACTUALLY BEEN RESENTFUL OF KONNO?

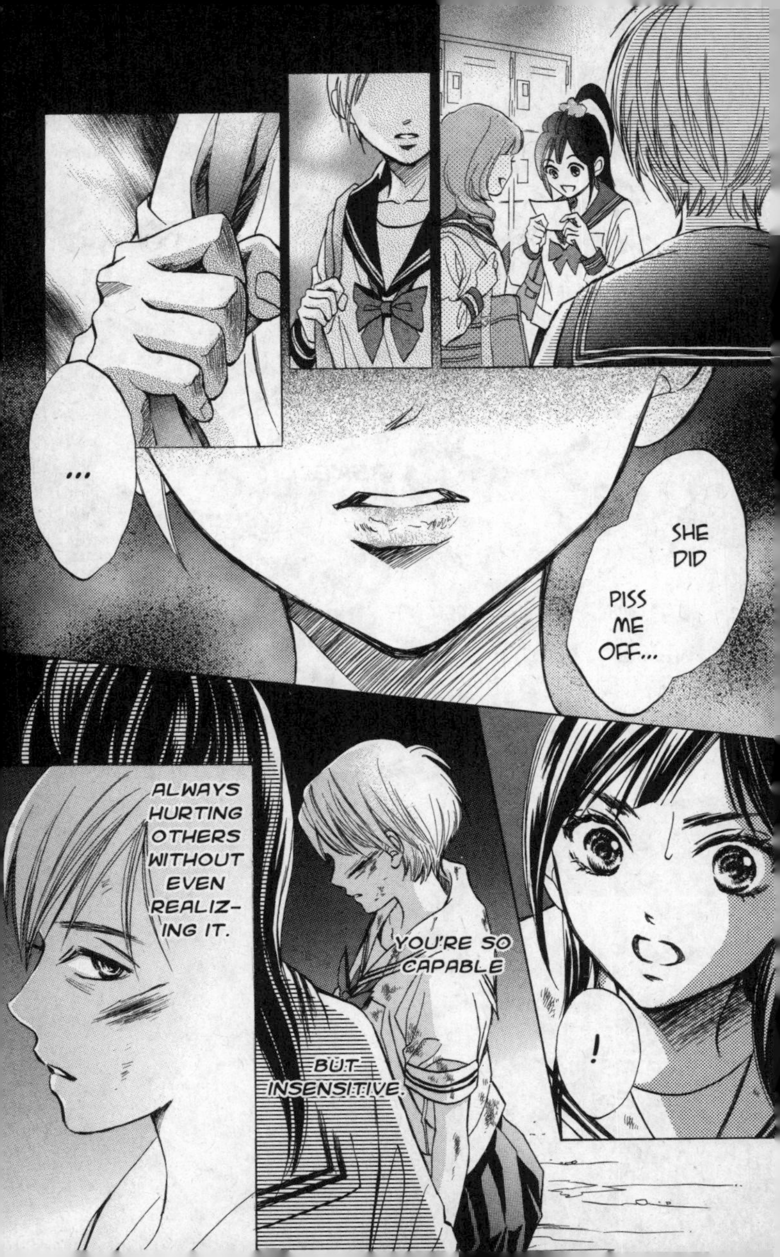
SHE DID PISS ME OFF...
...
!
YOU'RE SO CAPABLE
BUT INSENSITIVE.
ALWAYS HURTING OTHERS WITHOUT EVEN REALIZ-ING IT.

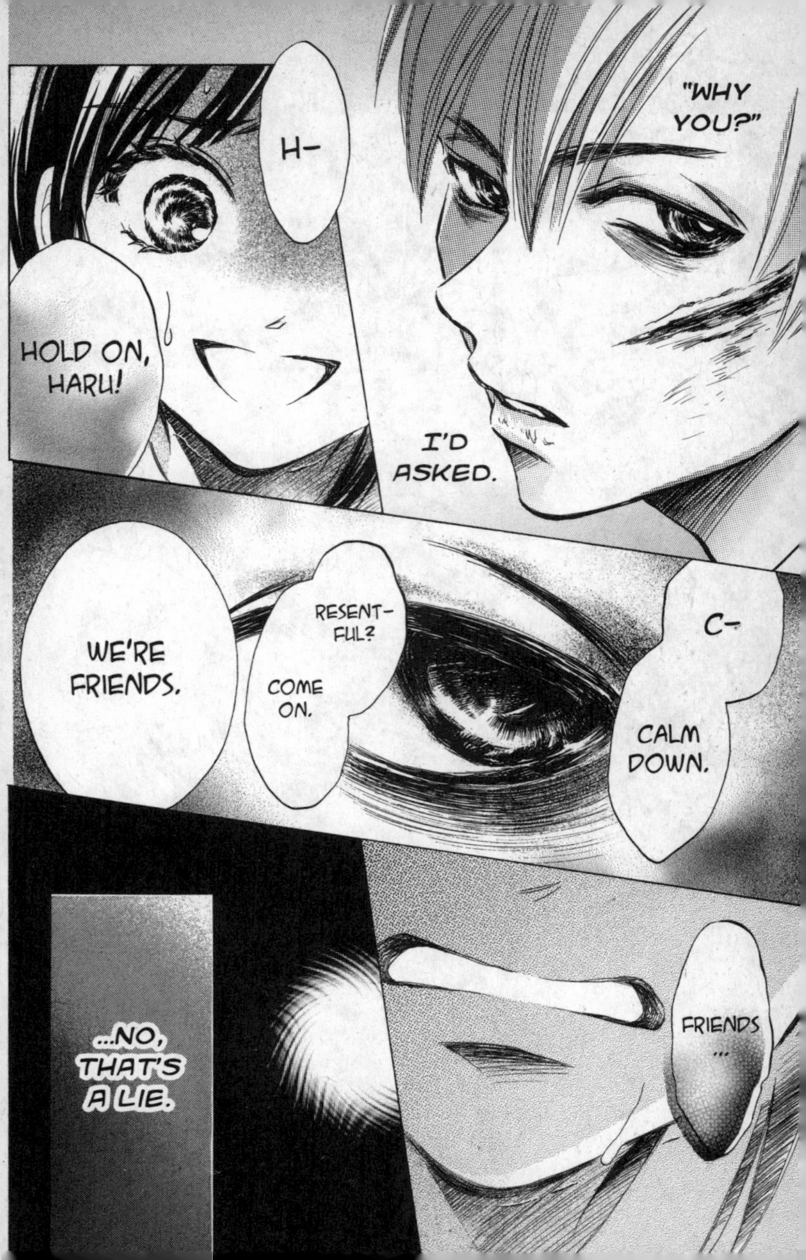
"WHY YOU?"
I'D ASKED.
H-
HOLD ON, HARU!
C-
CALM DOWN.
RESENT-FUL?
COME ON.
WE'RE FRIENDS.
FRIENDS...
...NO, THAT'S A LIE.

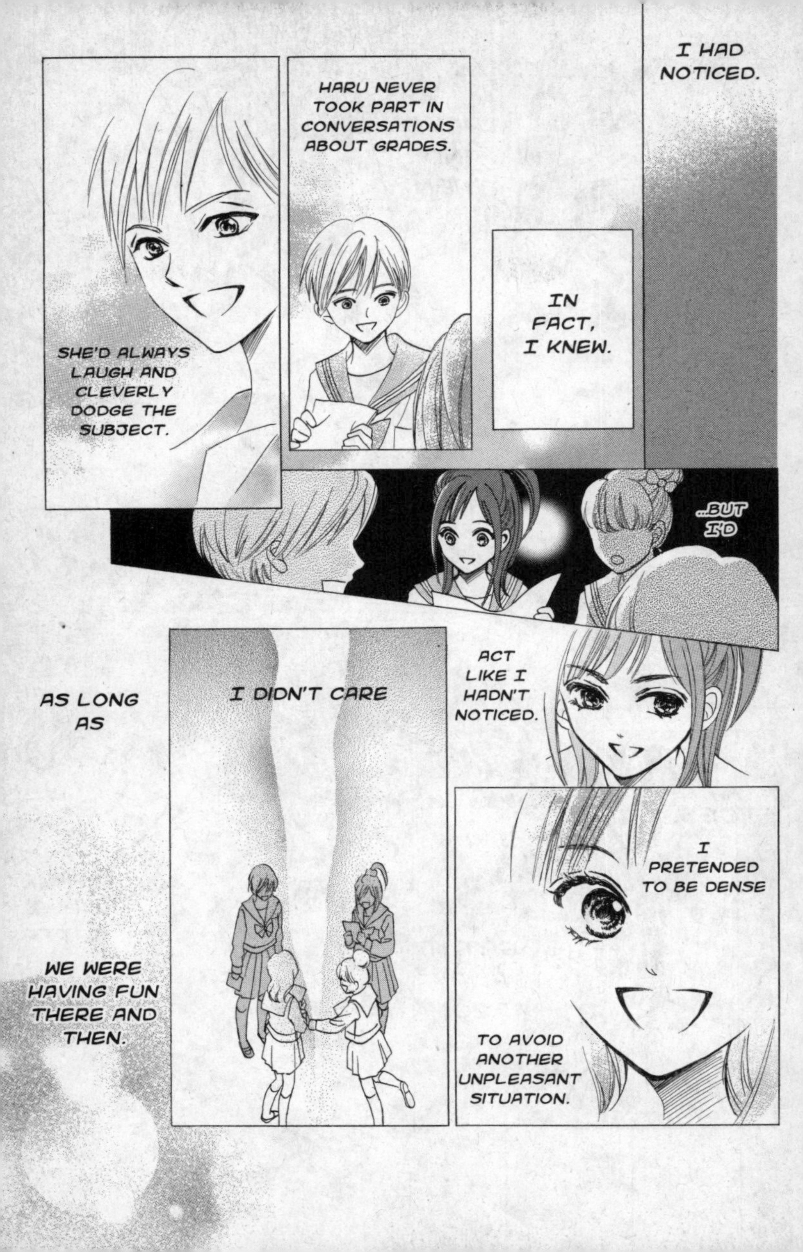
I HAD NOTICED.
IN FACT, I KNEW.
HARU NEVER TOOK PART IN CONVERSATIONS ABOUT GRADES.
SHE'D ALWAYS LAUGH AND CLEVERLY DODGE THE SUBJECT.
...BUT I'D
ACT LIKE I HADN'T NOTICED.
I PRETENDED TO BE DENSE
TO AVOID ANOTHER UNPLEASANT SITUATION.
I DIDN'T CARE
AS LONG AS
WE WERE HAVING FUN THERE AND THEN.

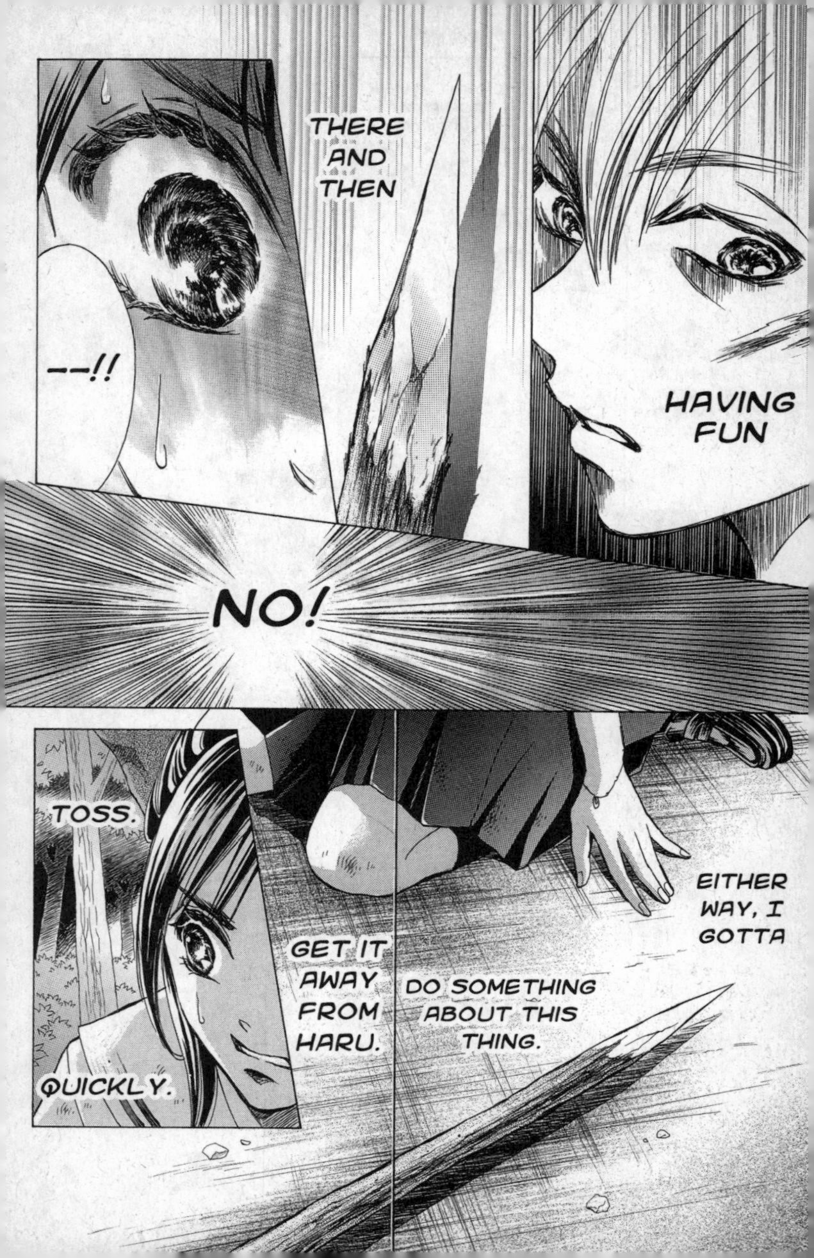
HAVING FUN
THERE AND THEN
--!!
NO!
EITHER WAY, I GOTTA
DO SOMETHING ABOUT THIS THING.
GET IT AWAY FROM HARU.
TOSS.
QUICKLY.

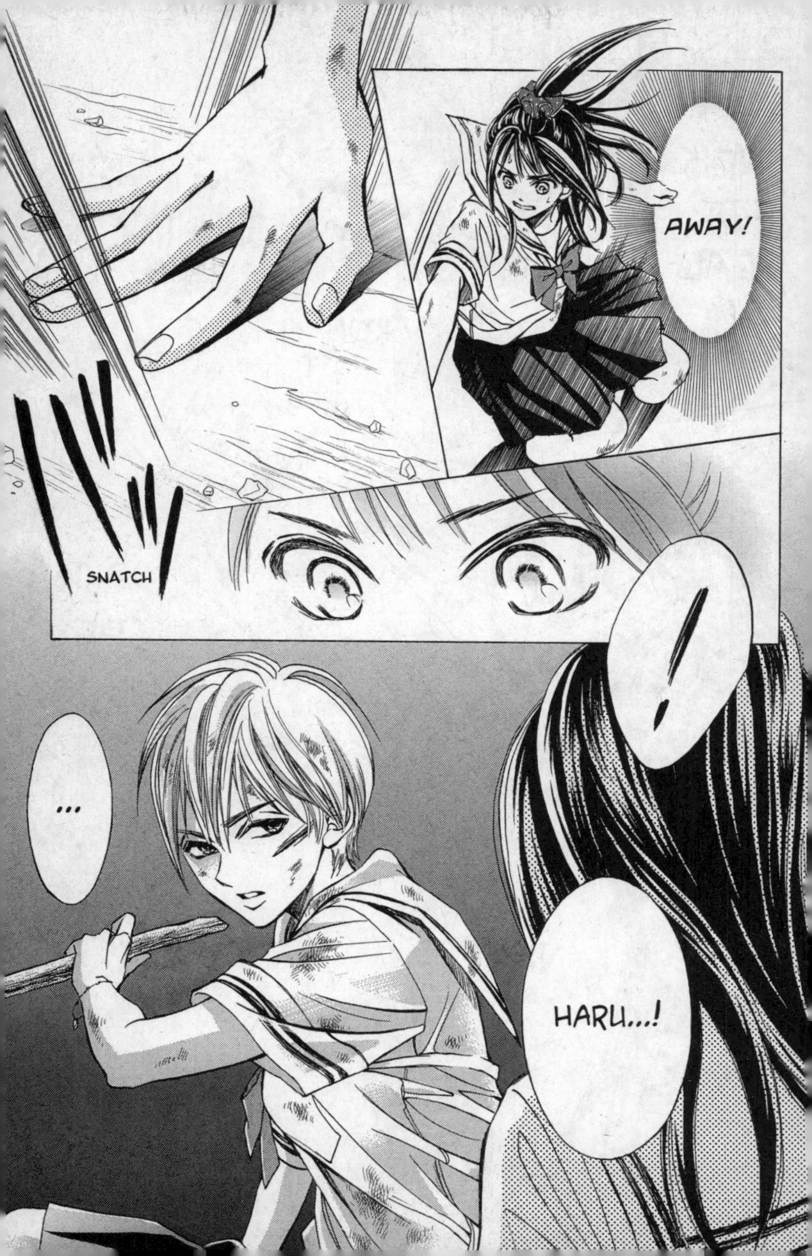
AWAY!
SNATCH
!
HARU...!
...

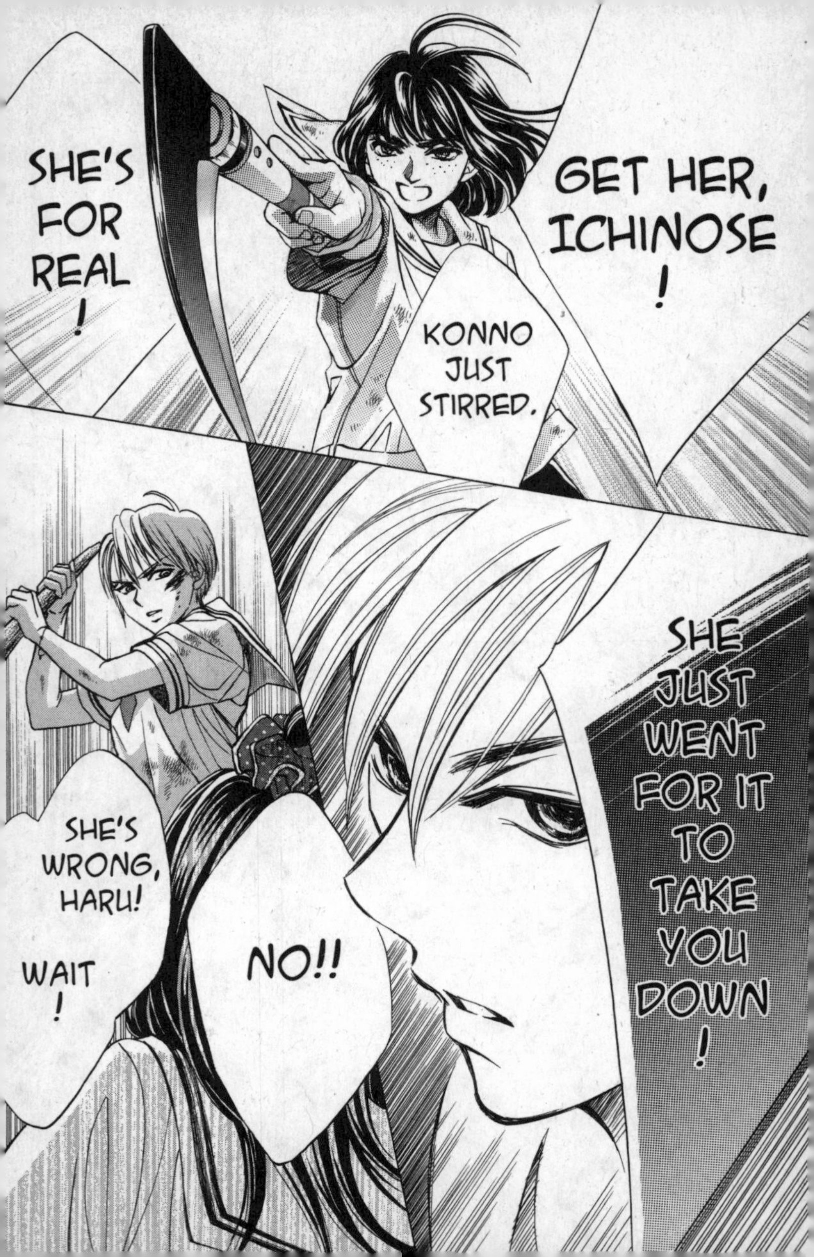
GET HER, ICHINOSE!
KONNO JUST STIRRED.
SHE'S FOR REAL!
SHE JUST WENT FOR IT TO TAKE YOU DOWN!
NO!!
SHE'S WRONG, HARU!
WAIT!

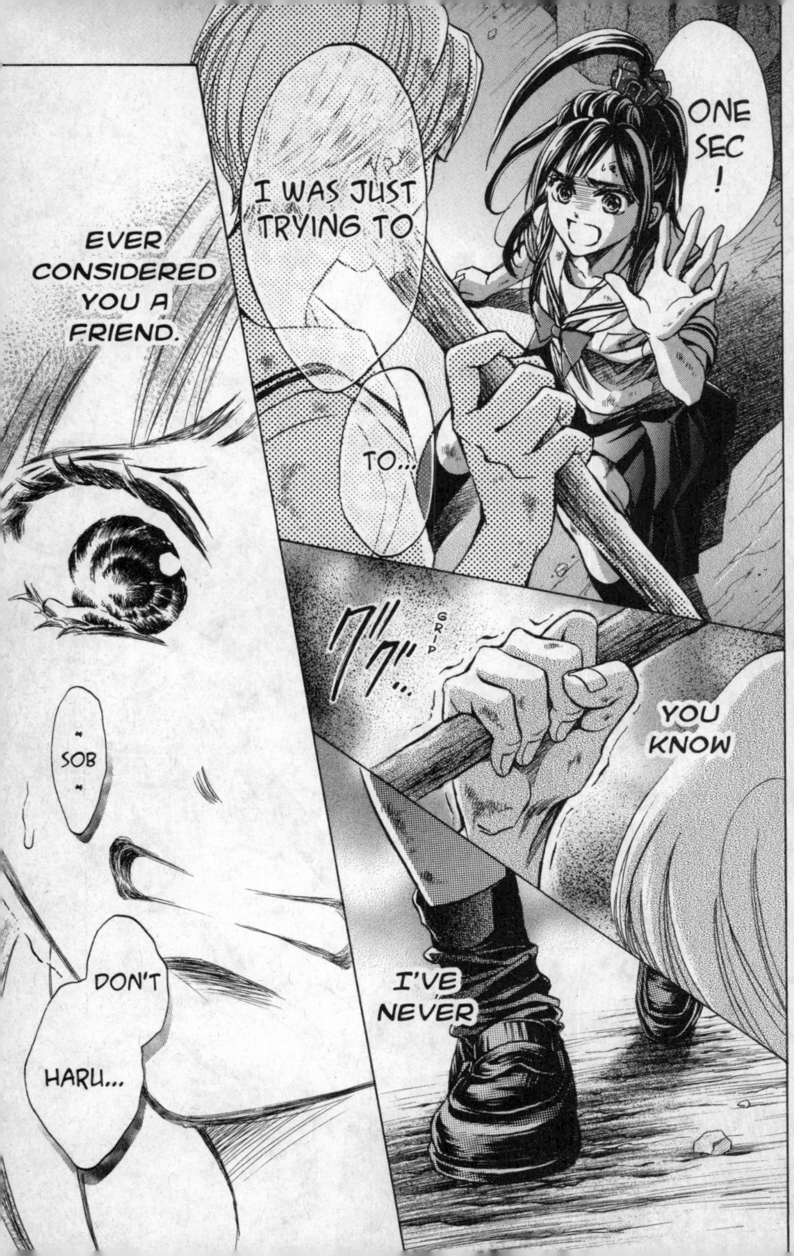
ONE SEC!
I WAS JUST TRYING TO
TO...
GRIP
YOU KNOW
I'VE NEVER
EVER CONSIDERED YOU A FRIEND.
SOB
DON'T
HARU...

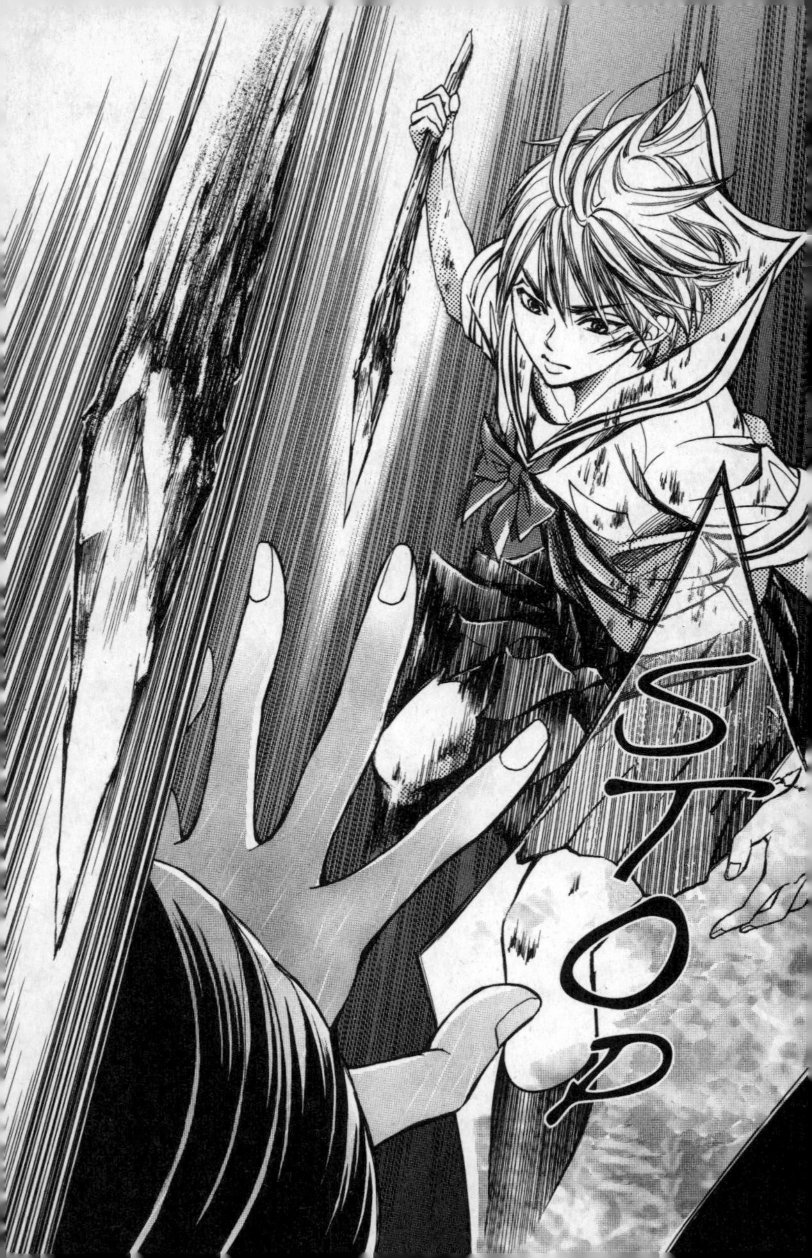
STOP

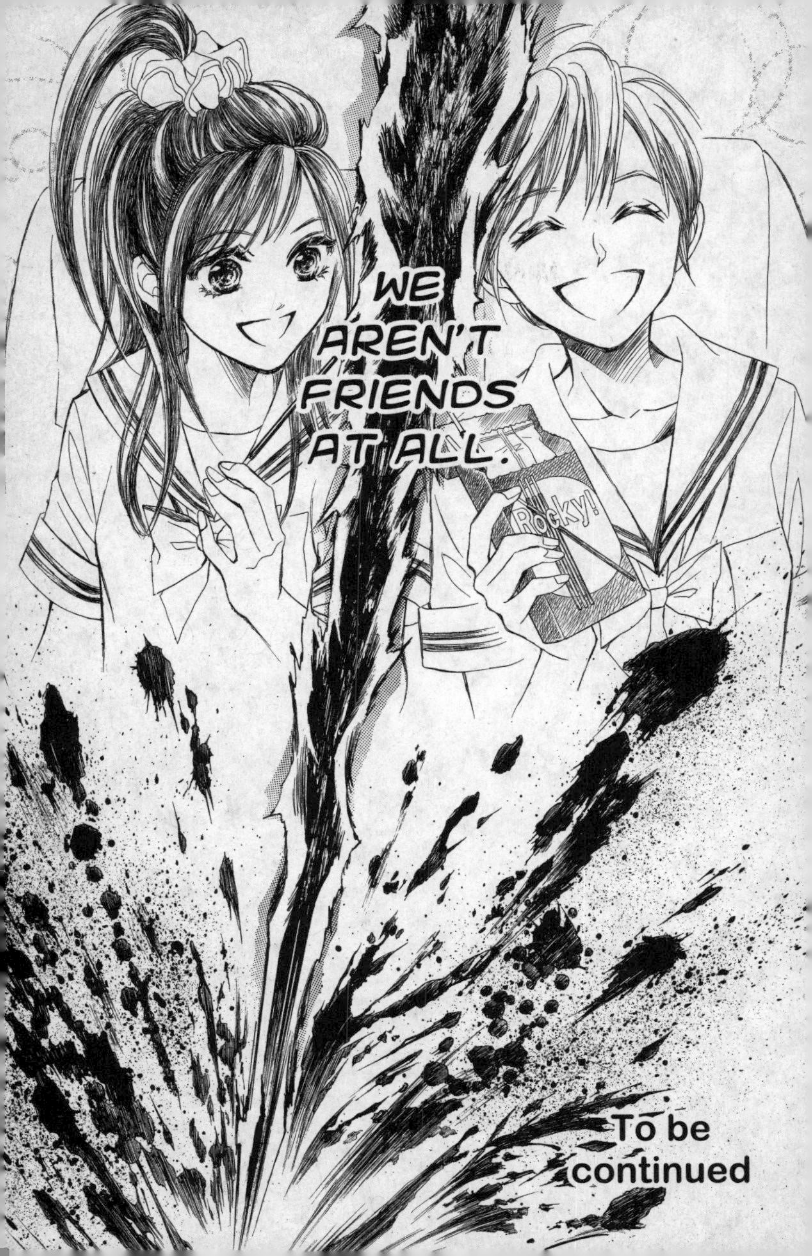
WE AREN'T FRIENDS AT ALL.
Rocky!
To be continued

MY WORKROOM.

~ Tools, etc., that I use a lot to draw manga ~

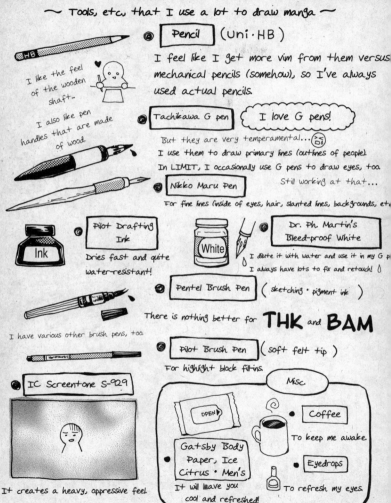

● **Pencil** (Uni · HB)

I feel like I get more vim from them versus mechanical pencils (somehow), so I've always used actual pencils.

I like the feel of the wooden shaft.

I also like pen handles that are made of wood.

● **Tachikawa G pen** I love G pens!

But they are very temperamental...

I use them to draw primary lines (outlines of people).

In LIMIT, I occasionally use G pens to draw eyes, too.

Still working at that...

● **Nikko Maru Pen**

For fine lines (inside of eyes, hair, slanted lines, backgrounds, et

Ink

● **Pilot Drafting Ink**

Dries fast and quite water-resistant!

White

● **Dr. Ph. Martin's Bleed-proof White**

I dilute it with water and use it in my G p

I always have lots to fix and retouch!

● **Pentel Brush Pen** (sketching · pigment ink)

There is nothing better for **THK** and **BAM**

I have various other brush pens, too.

● **Pilot Brush Pen** (soft felt tip)

For highlight block fill-ins.

● **IC Screentone S-929**

It creates a heavy, oppressive feel.

Misc.

OPEN

● **Gatsby Body Paper, Ice Citrus · Men's**

It will leave you cool and refreshed!

● **Coffee**

To keep me awake.

● **Eyedrops**

To refresh my eyes.

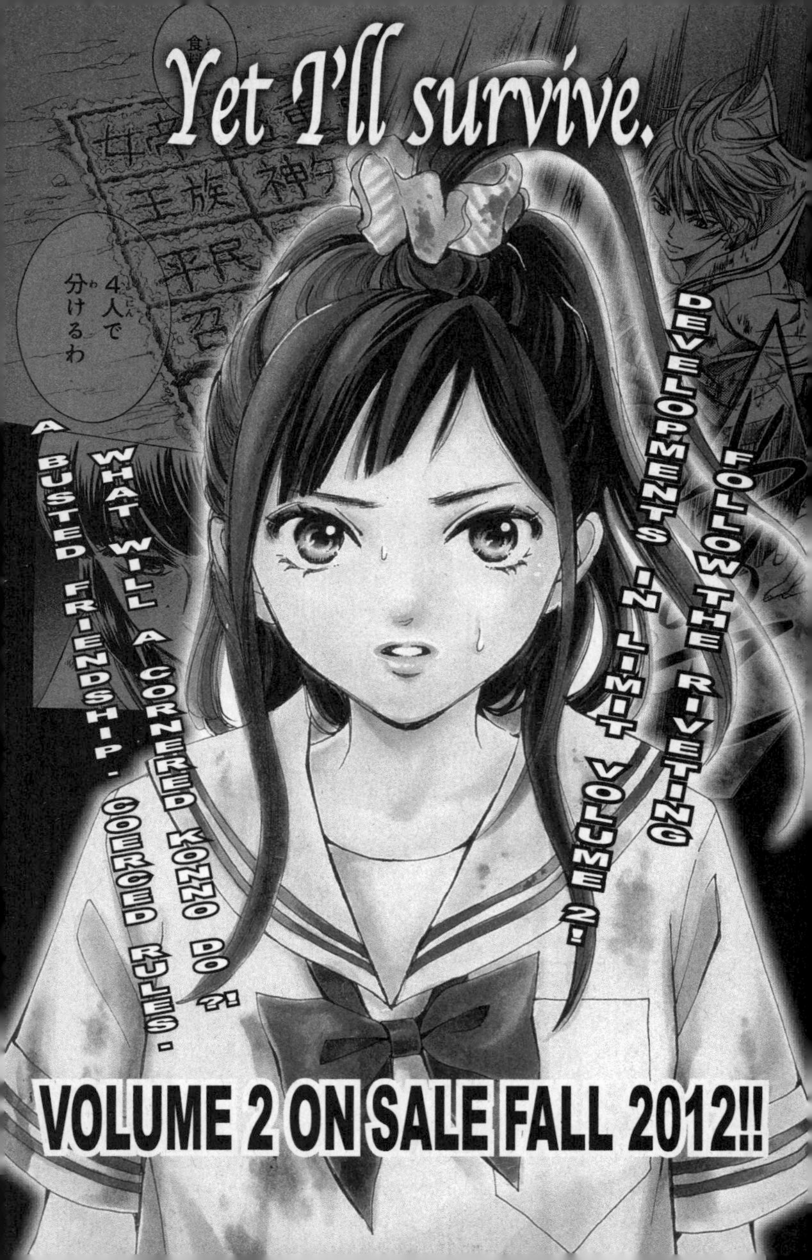
Yet I'll survive.
4人で分けるわ
FOLLOW THE RIVETING DEVELOPMENTS IN LIMIT VOLUME 2!
WHAT WILL A CORNERED KONNO DO?!
A BUSTED FRIENDSHIP. COERCED RULES.
VOLUME 2 ON SALE FALL 2012!!